William Marshall

Aarbert

a drama without stage or scenery

William Marshall

Aarbert
a drama without stage or scenery

ISBN/EAN: 9783744739290

Printed in Europe, USA, Canada, Australia, Japan

Cover: Foto ©Andreas Hilbeck / pixelio.de

More available books at **www.hansebooks.com**

A Drama

*WITHOUT STAGE OR SCENERY, WROUGHT OUT THROUGH
SONG IN MANY METRES, MOSTLY LYRIC*

BY

WILLIAM MARSHALL

NEW : AMSTERDAM : BOOK : COMPANY
156 : FIFTH : AVENUE : NEW : YORK : CITY

CONTENTS

CONTENTS

AARBERT.

PREFACE.

THE ARGUMENT OF THE POEM.

THE poem of ' Aarbert,' like Bunyan's prose allegory, describes a Christian pilgrim's progress from earthliness to heavenliness. But whilst in the allegory the pilgrim's feelings are expressed by the author in prose narrative and dialogue, they are in the poem expressed by the pilgrim himself in odes and hymns, and in the dialogues and soliloquies of verse. Again, whilst in the allegory the ' progress ' is from the pilgrim's quitting the ' city of destruction,' or worldly life, up to his reaching the river of death opposite to the gate of heaven, the progress in the poem is from his contented stay in that city up to his reaching the highway, on Christian ground, leading to that yet distant gate.

The poem is, in fact, a lyric drama, devoid of scenery—a drama through which the pilgrim, its hero, lays bare the state of his heart and mind during his long passage against every form of hindrance, on the part of his earthly affections, from worldliness to godliness; that is, during the process in him of what is commonly called heart-change and conversion.

The state of mind, the trials, and hindrances during

this heart-change are different in different men; and
the most that can be done by an author in making a
description of them general is to describe them as they
exist in one of the largest classes of men. The class
of which Aarbert is the representative is that of moral,
proud, self-righteous men; whilst he, as one of that
very large class, is a man singularly possessed of
everything which the world can give him to justify, as
it seems to him, his pride and self-righteousness. He
has a large estate, a good wife, loving children, robust
health, a powerful mind, a fine taste, and a quick conscience. Moreover, he is a man honourable, gentle,
loving, and by everyone who thoroughly knows him
beloved. His trials begin by his losing his estate,
then his reputation. His young brother, named Godard, who had been dependent on him, acts throughout the poem, so long as he lives, as his religious
guide. Godard is a clergyman, Evangelical, Protestant, and Puritan. Having an estate bequeathed to
him of half the worth of that which Aarbert has lost,
he gives him a very large share of it. Aarbert is
oppressed by the gift, and for the first time in his life
discovers pride as a sin in himself. He cannot rid
himself of the sin either by priestly help, or by outward ritualistic observances, or by good resolutions.
Godard sets before him the Gospel. Aarbert starts
very many of the objections commonly made to it by
unbelievers, and Godard answers the objections one
after another. Having weighed the answers, Aarbert
accepts the Gospel, but only with his mind. His
worldly heart still rejects it; and after a short flash of
joy, arising from false Christian peace and hope, he
sinks into wretched irresolution. Godard is sent
abroad for recovery of health, and Aarbert relapses
utterly into world-love. He now meets with worldly,

and even infidel, advisers, whose reasonings, however, he combats, and against whom, by help of Godard's letters, he holds his ground as at least an assenter to the Gospel's teaching. Godard returns to England and dies, leaving all his wealth to Aarbert; who soon afterwards himself becomes very ill, feels his sinfulness, is alarmed at his soul's danger, passes through an agony of self-conflict, and at last with his heart receives that teaching of the Gospel which hitherto his mind alone has taken in; gives himself wholly up to God through Christ, and gains peace. His wife, Milda, one of his own class, but more staid and lowly-minded, who has shared most of his experiences, follows him in self-surrender to God.

The crisis of change being past, the poem represents the utterance by the two pilgrims, and by their friend and adviser, Arnulph, of much Christian doctrine and sentiment; and it ends in leaving both of them entering upon a Christian life. It has in its course explained incidentally that the agony, gloom, irresolution, long self-conflict, and long delay, through which Aarbert passes are attributable exclusively to that worldliness, selfishness, or other faultiness which stubbornly rejects Christianity, and not to Christianity itself; and, moreover, that if a Christian is sad and slow during 'conversion,' it is because he is not hearty, thorough, and single-minded in seeking it.

THE MACHINERY OF THE POEM

is, as I have already said, somewhat dramatic. Its eight books have each many numbered divisions, all answering to scenes in a drama, but without representation of scenery, and all consisting of utterances by one or two or more persons. These utterances take the form of English blank verse, of classic hexameters, of elegiacs, of odes in Sapphic, Alcaic, Pindaric, and other metres, and very often of verse of a composite kind, unrecognised as standard. The chief speakers, besides Aarbert, are Milda, his wife; Godard, his brother; and an old friend to them both, named Arnulph.

THE READING OF CLASSIC METRES.

The metres of the poem being so often classic, with which most readers are unfamiliar, it may be as well that I should make some remarks on the reading of poetry generally. In music there is an accent at the beginning of every bar. If this accent, in reading the music, is not observed, the rhythm is unintelligible, and the notes are a mass of confusion. In all poetry the bar consists of the line, which, in the reading, should always be kept distinct. In some almost imperceptible way, whether by emphasizing an early accented syllable in the line, or whether by raising the voice very slightly more at the beginning than towards the end of the line, or whether by making a half-comma's pause at the end of the line, even if there is no stop there, or whether by all these three processes together, in some way or other, the line *in all poetry* should be by the reader kept so distinct that the swing of its melody may be in itself, in connection with that of the neighbouring lines; and all this management of the voice should go on utterly independently of the proper modulation of the voice required by the sense or by the accent within the line. The stops required by the sense should go on together with the almost imperceptible end line-stop, but not so as to mar the swing. That is to say, the stops required by the sense should be made in the course of the line; but the height of the voice during the stop should be kept suspended. The voice should not at a stop in the course of the line be lowered, and, after the stop is over, raised again with a fresh breathing.

In all this I have merely stated general rules for the right reading. of any poetry whatever. With, however, such general rules, much allowance must be left to the taste and skill of the reader for a discovery of the proper exceptions. Should my reader not understand my metres, I ask him to observe, without exaggerating, the general rules to which I have drawn his attention, and by them to read my lines, and especially those of my Sapphic and Pindaric odes, *as if they were prose*, without any attempt to bring them into something like the hop and jump, or hop and two jumps, or the reverse, which form what some people regard as the only rhythm proper to poetry. For, after all, the metres of poetry are more for the composer's help than for the reader's. They are merely means of making ordinary speech, or what is called prose, melodious. If, then, my reader, being a good prose-reader, ignore the metres altogether, and yet find the lines unmelodious, the fault will have been mine. I hope that he will not be able to prove it so. I implore him, if unskilled in the Greek metres, to read my adoption of them boldly as prose. By taking this advice, he will soon, I think, get into their swing as verse.

THE TONE OF THE POEM

is Protestant and Puritan. Its protest on behalf of the teaching of the Bible includes a loud and unflinching protest against every teaching, Ritualistic, Romish,

Antinomian, and infidel, which is in conflict with it. The Puritanism of ' Aarbert ' is, however, not more outspoken than is that of the Homilies and Articles of the Church of England. And if Roman Catholics may publish books, justifying all their many slaughters of Protestants during the Middle Ages, boasting their canonization of felons who, by the laws of this country, were justly hanged for high treason and conspiracy to murder, and recording the Council of Trent's bitter curses of Protestants and of all others who reject some Romish dogmas, my poem may surely be allowed to escape a charge of illiberality in its expressing its utmost disapproval of Popery or of any approach to it in language free from fear and withal free from uttering curses and threats of human violence.

THE LANGUAGE OF 'AARBERT.'

In my use of unfamiliar words in this poem, I have borne in mind that he who debases his country's language is guilty of a great crime; and I have taken care rather to restore than to debase my mother tongue. The strange words which I have used are thoroughly English; moreover, they are neither provincialisms nor Chaucerisms. I mean that they are not words used merely in one or other province of the country, nor are they words used throughout the country chiefly in the times of Chaucer and Wycliffe. They are words more than a thousand years old, used by all authors speaking the purest English at a time when the English tongue was at its best, when it was a tongue fuller, richer. stronger, and more capable of expansion—in short, in every way better, not only than the modern alloys of Latin, but than Latin itself.

I will justify every word which I have tried to restore, and I assert that the more my reader shall through my poem have learnt the words which I have used, by so much the more will he have increased his knowledge of English. Scott, Burns, and others have been allowed to make their beautiful Scotch dialect familiar to us in writings ten times more difficult to read than mine are, and whose difficulties consist very much of mere unfamiliar spellings of words. Literary quacks of all sorts have been allowed to load our dictionary with such utterly un-English words as ' Zoohygiantics,' ' Phthisozoics,' ' Geoponics,' ' Helminthology ' (see Roget's ' Thesaurus,' p. 374), and as ' aberuncate,' ' ablaqueation,' ' aculate,' ' adacted,' ' adunation,' ' adunque,' ' agnize,' ' amaritude,' ' amorist,' ' anfractuousness,' ' araneous,' and so on by the twenty thousand (see any dictionary); and I appeal to my reader's candour to say whether the hundred strange English words which appear in ' Aarbert ' are not more homely and intelligible than any of these twenty thousand far more strange and obsolete words. He need not fear that what I have done in recovering our classic words is a dangerous precedent. The power to bring any word into general acceptance is limited by at least the measure of the value of the word, the absence of a better, and the authority and publicity of the book in which the word appears. It is not in everybody's power to bring a word into use; nor is it in anybody's power to bring into lasting use an unfit word.

My attempt at the restoration of pure English must not be considered as a repetition of Spenser's, which utterly and deservedly broke down, as being silly, useless, and even mischievous. Mine is in everything the reverse of his. He used Anglo-Latinisms freely, but dressed all his uncouth words in obsolete forms. I have avoided Anglo-Latinisms in my poem—scarcely any will be found there—and I have dressed almost all my words, even those which are obsolete, in modern forms.

As to the question whether my writing in pure English this Evangelistic poem, full as it is of theological references, was wise, I can only say that I could not possibly have written it in Anglo-Latin. None of my words will long remain obsolete; and if, for a little while, they check my poem's religious usefulness, I am more than comforted in the feeling that, since the English language is so largely the means of spreading Christian lore, I, in so far as I help to make it worthy and capable of doing this, am furthering Christ's work on earth, to further which is the design of the poem.

I will now give a list of the obsolete words which I have used, justifying my use of each as I go, and merely premising that, whilst a few of them occur very frequently, most of them will be met with only twice or thrice in the whole poem.

'AARWORTH,' 'AAR,' 'AARBERT.'

Our fathers have in their books left to us four different words written as 'ar'—one of them unaccented, and the three others accented. The unaccented 'ar' has come down to us as 'ore.' Then, as if dropping an 'o,' they wrote 'ár' for what we have as 'oar.' As if dropping an 'e,' they wrote 'ár' for 'ær,' which we have in the word 'early'; and, as if dropping an 'a,' they wrote 'ár' for 'aar,' a word which we have quite lost, yet which exists in almost all the other Teutonic languages, and also in the Hebrew 'aur' and Latin 'aurum.' It means honour, glory. The Germans have it as 'ehre,' the Danes as 'aere,' the Dutch as 'eer,' the Swedes as 'ära,' the Icelanders as 'æra,' and the Frisians as 'ere.' 'Aar' is in Switzerland the name of a well-known river. 'Aarwordh' is honourable; and I have used 'Aarworth' as a noun meaning 'moral honour.' We have no other word to express this. 'Aarbert' is clearly Honour-bright. The acute accent's force in Old English words is a matter of debate. It sometimes merely guided the voice, as in distinguishing 'áras,' messengers, from 'arás,' arose.

'ANDGET'

means mental faculty or sense, such as that of sight. It is compounded of 'and,' the English form of $\dot{\alpha}\nu\tau\iota$, which we have in 'answer,' and of 'get,' which may come from the verb 'get' or from the noun 'gate,' and which gives much expression in either case. For instance, the 'andget' of hearing is that mental *oppositeness* to sound by which the mind *gets* the sound, or else is that *gate* which admits sound into the mind. The Anglo-Latin word 'sense' means many different things, and not one of them distinctly.

'ÆRIHT,'

which I modernize as 'æright,' is a grand word meaning justice. 'Æ,' which is a connection of the Greek $\dot{\alpha}\epsilon\iota$, is also a form of our 'ea,' a stream or river, from whose ever-flowing it gains a beautiful image of eternity; and this it embodies in its meaning of eternal law, such as the law of truth or mercy or righteousness, as opposed to 'lagu,' a 'laid' down or statute law having local or temporary force.

We have 'æ' in our 'aye of aye': and, when coupled with 'right,' it speaks clearly for itself as justice.

'ASTONDNES,'

a word which I prefer to keep in its original form, but which is 'outstandness,' is the English of the Anglo-

Latin word ' person,' as applied in the Athanasian doctrine of the Holy Trinity. The names of God in the Bible are two, Jehovah and Elohim. The former is in the singular number, and the latter in the plural. Now, the Bible says nothing more distinctly than that there is but one Jehovah. Therefore, whatever are the constituents of the Elohim, they are not three Jehovahs. What they are the Bible does not distinctly say. It speaks of the Word, and of the Wisdom, and of the Spirit, and of the Seven Spirits of Jehovah. It speaks also of the Son of God and of the Paraclete; but of the former distinctly only in His being the revealed or prerevealed Son of man also, as in the phrase, ' This day have I begotten Thee '; and of the latter distinctly only in His being the spiritual Advocate sent to man. In showing, therefore, as it distinctly does, Jesus both God and man, it distinctly shows Him, in so far as, apart from His manhood, He is God, to be one of the Elohim; but what and how such it does not distinctly show Him. Consequently, neither are all the constituents of the Elohim, nor are the precise conditions of any of them, nor are their precise relations to Jehovah, distinctly revealed to man. Nevertheless, it has been the delight of proud man distinctly to define these all-holy constituents, and their relations to each other, in figurative speech. Man begins by defining them as exactly three in number, although in four places in the Apocalypse we read of the Seven Spirits of God. Then the Greek, adopting the figure of a tripod of three legs united by one seat, calls them three ' hypostases,' or subsistences. The Roman, under figure of a dramatic mask, ' persona ' (from ' per-sonare,' to sound through)—literally, mouthpiece—calls them three ' Personas,' or dramatic characters. The Englishman of the present day, adopting the Roman figure, but misunderstanding the word 'persona,' calls them three Persons (Individuals); whilst the Englishman of King Alfred's times, adopting the figure of a tree, calls them three 'Astondneses' (Outstandingnesses), or Branches. Now, since we know little of our own being, and absolutely nothing of that of God, the last-named figure and name might be called the best, if any of them could be at all called good. The Latin 'persona,' a face or mouthpiece, is a word akin to the Greek 'prosōpon,' which appears in 2 Cor. i., ii., and which Conybeare and Howson there translate as 'tongue,' but which is, firstly, a face. 'Persona' appears in that most presumptuous compilation of a darkling age, the Athanasian Creed, so strangely beloved by Protestants; which, in so far as it adheres to the figure of a dramatic mask, is as purely monotheistic as any Deist could desire. It represents God as speaking through three masks, or faces, or mouthpieces, and as acting in three characters; and it takes much needless trouble in asserting that He, under each of these three faces, and in each of these three characters, is equal to Himself in each, and under each, of the other two. But the Word of God and the Holy Spirit, or Spirits of God, are more than faces, mouthpieces, and characters of God in the Bible. From 'persona's' having in the Anglo-Latin word 'person' slipped into meaning an individual being, the English acceptor of the Athanasian Creed escapes falling into Deism; but he falls into what is worse, Polytheism. He is led into supposing that God consists of three Individuals, all alike, all equal even to the Father's not having, in the Trinity, precedence or superiority over His Son in time, or power, or knowledge, or rank; each of which three Individuals is God; and yet that there are not three Gods, but one God.   And he calls this matter of his faith a mystery, mistaking even the word 'mystery,' which means, not an impenetrable secret, but a secret revealed only to the initiated.   Then as an impenetrable secret he believes it, just as he might believe that two and two were five, and yet were only four.   Neither is the Bible answerable for such a stumbling-block to faith in it, as is this self-contradiction; nor is our own word, 'Astondnes,' nor, to say soth, is the Athanasian Creed, guilty as it is of adding its own revelations to those of the Bible on a subject the most sacred which can be conceived, and on which that holy book has been studiously reserved.   The Anglo-Latin word 'person' alone is answerable for the stumbling-block to a reception of the doctrine of the Atonement made by the Lord Jesus, God and man, and to the doctrine of the work and office of the Holy Ghost, the Paraclete, in man.

'Aban'

means to command or proclaim.   It is a shorter and I think stronger word than 'command.'   It is from 'ban,' a prince, and as 'proclamation' we have it in our 'banns of marriage.'

'Alwielder,'

for thus I modernize 'alwalda,' means all-ruler, all-governor, which neither 'almighty' nor 'omnipotent' quite mean.   It is a fine word, as in the phrase, 'The Lord God alwielder reigneth.'

'Atfore'

is a word lost, and much wanted back.   It means, as 'coram' does, in front-and-in-presence-of; whilst 'before,' 'bye-fore,' which also should mean this, means usually merely 'in front of.'

'ANTWHETHER'

is from 'and,' the English form of $\dot{a}\nu\tau\acute{\iota}$, which we have in 'answer,' and from 'whether.' It means notwithstanding or in spite of. 'Antwhether rain' means against-whether-or-not-rain.

'BOD,' 'BEBOD,'

are the nouns of 'bid' 'bebid.' 'Bod' is a commandment, and 'bebod,' 'bye-bod,' is a gentle command or exhortation. Besides being short, they have the recommendation of being of the few that rhyme with 'God.'

THE PREFIXES 'BE' AND 'GE,' AS IN 'BEHEST,' 'GELEAVE.'

'Be' is the prefix to nearly 600 English words. But its precise force in them has yet to be learnt. The prefix seems, as a form of the word 'bye,' to give an encircling and reflexive force of 'from-self-around-to-self.' Thus 'hest' is command and behest (command-brought-around-from-self-to-self) is promise. The force of 'ge' is more evident. It is the motive force of 'go' and 'goad,' and also the collective force of 'gather,' that of the Latin 'con' (together with). Dr. Bosworth says of 'ge' that besides its collective action it makes neuter verbs active. Thus 'to laugh,' as 'to gelaugh,' becomes 'to laugh-at.' It also changes their literal meaning to one figurative; thus 'to hold,' as 'to gehold,' becomes 'to preserve'; and it withal changes substantives into verbs. But he adds that 'ge' seems often void of signification. It cannot have been so, and when English is more understood this sad confession will not be called for. Two thousand five hundred of our words are compounded with 'ge.' We still have 'ge' as 'y,' and sometimes as 'a,' as in 'yclad' and in 'aright,' and once at least most disastrously as 'be.' We have utterly lost the large and rich meaning of 'geleaf' by spelling and pronouncing it as 'belief.' 'Geleave' means what it says—altogether-leave. They who 'geleave' in Christ altogether-leave-themselves-and-theirs in Christ. They who 'geleave' Christ's words give-leave to Christ's words to be to them all that He means them to be, and to do all that He wills that they do, even to the ruling and guiding them. Thus, 'geleaf' is a word amounting to obedience. Good works are included in it, and by the word St. Paul's and St. James's descriptions of faith are harmonized. 'Geleaf' is an instance, of which there are not a few, of an English word's describing a subject or a process of thought so well by standing forth as its name that, without its name, it is difficult to understand fully itself. 'Faith,' which is no connection of the Latin 'fides,' but rather of our own 'feud,' meant originally fidelity. Still, being English and short, it may well pass as a word dumbly signifying 'geleaf.'

'BILWHIT.'

Here is a charming little word lost to us, meaning simple, innocent, and taken from the fact that the bills or beaks of young birds are white. 'God dwells in the castle of His onefoldness and bilwhitness.'

'TO BROOK,' A 'BRICK.'

Our ignorance of our language tells hardly against Old English. 'To brook' is in the dictionaries derived from 'brucan,' and is said to mean to bear, to endure and also to use. What connection has the former sense of the word with the latter? None. The fact is that 'to brook' (to bear, to endure) does not

come at all from ' brucan,' but is the verb of ' brycg,'
which in Dutch is ' brug,' a bridge, whilst ' brucan '
simply means to use, eat, enjoy, and profit.   We have
a word, little suspected as representing ' brucan,' in
' brick.'   A man whom we like we call ' a brick '—
that is, a useful man, an agreeable companion.   But
this ' brick ' has a different derivation from the ' brick '
of a house, which is derived from ' brecan,' to break,
or, rather, from ' brice,' a fragment.   Like the two
' brooks,' the two ' bricks ' are supposed to be the
same word.   But Old English is not so poor as to re-
quire its words to do double duty.

' BISN,' ' BYSEN,'

is example, model, a thing by which another thing is
seen.   An Englishman is enlightened by discovering
that an ' example ' is a thing ' exemptum.'

' BOOKHOARD '

is library.   But since we have ' library,' why should
we re-adopt ' bookhoard '?   Simply because the word
' lubbery ' would be to nineteen and a half millions out
of twenty millions of our people as good a name for a
collection of books as ' library ' is.   A language is
rich, not when it is full of many worthless words, but
when its every word is a sentence explaining itself.
How many Englishmen know that ' liber ' is book?
Not many more than they who know that it is Bac-
chus.   ' Bookhoard ' is as good a word as ' bookshelf,'
and why should we not have other words built like it,
such as ' clotheshoard,' ' applehoard,' ' earthenware-
hoard,' and ' seedhoard '?

' TO COSTEN,' ' TO FAND,' ' TO PROVE,'

equally mean to try, but to ' costen,' from ' cos,' a kiss,
means to try alluringly, seducingly, whilst ' to fand,'

from ' fan,' means to try siftingly, winnowingly.   Our
gain of the foreign word ' tempt ' has cost us the loss
of both ' costen ' and ' fand,' by standing for both of
which it stands indistinctly—nay, falsely.   For instance, God is said to have tempted Abraham, but
God, says an Apostle, never tempts.   The fact is that
He never seduces to evil, but He ' fands.'   His fan is
in his hand.   We retain ' costen ' in our ' cozen,'
which has the third or fourth meaning of it, namely,
to trick, and we have it also in our ' coster,' a noun not
to be despised.   A costermonger is an alluring merchant—that is, a merchant who allures buyers by a
display of his goods, especially by ticketing them.
Such a merchant is a costermonger, whether his goods
are on a wheelbarrow or in a palatial shop in Regent
Street, London.   ' Profian,' to prove, is to try tast-
ingly, experimentally, essayingly.   It is a thorough
Teutonic word, merely a sister of ' probo.'   It does
not mean, as probo in its participle sometimes means,
to demonstrate.

' Dree,' ' Thole,' ' Gethyld.'

Here are three precious jewels cast away.   ' To
thole ' is to suffer.   It is taken from the thowl or pin
on which an oar works in rowing.   A word more expressive of patient, and even groaning, suffering could
not be formed.   It gives ' tholemod,' patient; ' thol-
ing,' patience; and ' tholemodness,' patient-minded-
ness.   ' Dree,' from ' dreogan,' is compounded of ' do '
and ' rough,' and means to do roughly, toilsomely,
sufferingly.   It has the great value of the joint meanings of ' do ' and ' thole.'   For instance, whilst I either
' do ' or ' thole ' an injury, I ' dree ' a sorrow or a
labour.   Chaucer renders ' dreogan ' as ' drugge,' ' to
drugge and to draw.'   We still have this form of the

word in 'drudge,' patient action in labour; and 'trudge,' patient walking; whilst by a confusion of 'dreogan' and 'dragan' we talk of 'dragging out a weary life,' when we mean that we 'dree' it, work it out toilsomely. 'Gethyld,' suffering together with, is a noun compounded of 'ge' and a derivative of 'thole,' and means what 'compassion' ought to mean, and, till its meaning slipped, did mean, to Latin scholars.

'To Dwin'

is to vanish; we have it in 'dwindle,' to go to the vanishing-point.

'To Dow'

is to profit, avail, prosper, valere. It has a noun which might be modernized as 'dowth,' and which means prosperity, advantage, virtue, excellence. We have 'dow' as an adjective in 'doughty,' and as a noun in 'daughter,' profiter; and itself is said by us every day, misspelt, and in ignorance of its meaning. A gentleman, when he says, 'How do you do?' means, 'How do you "dow," or prosper?' But he thinks that he says, 'How do you act?' yet his conscience gives a pass to the venerable nonsense uttered by him. He looks down, however, on a workman who, in offering one out of a choice of tools to a fellow-workman, says, 'Will this do you?' meaning, 'Will this "dow" you, or be of use to you?' The truth is, that none of us are taught our own language.

'Edrise,' 'Edrist,'

for so I render 'ærise,' 'ærist,' mean rise again, resurrection, 'ed,' a contraction of 'eft,' after, answering in English composition to the Latin 're.'

'Edliken,' 'Rightliken,'

are my renderings of 'edlæcan,' 'rihtlæcan.' 'Læcan,' says Dr. Bosworth, is to sacrifice, to offer; but 'læcan' in composition, as it is in these two words, is, says he, to do, to perform, to make real. Why? I ask. I deny this utter change of meaning, and give my reasons. 'Lic,' a corpse, is a word which we have in 'lichgate,' 'Lichfield,' and 'like,' and which gets the meaning of 'like' from the fact that in the earliest ages men embalmed and kept the dead bodies of their ancestors as their likenesses. Having this meaning, 'lic' easily passed into being the root of 'læcan,' to offer in sacrifice; for in sacrifices the 'lic,' or dead body, was the representative or likeness of the sacrificer, which he offered to his god, whilst he took on himself the likeness of his god, even to oneness with him; and this reflex action of giving and taking runs through the derivatives of 'læcan.' For 'læcan,' to offer, which is to give up self to Deity in the likeness of a slain animal, is met by 'læccan,' to seize, which verb stands ready to express the taking of Deity in the likeness of life, health, and favour, whilst 'lician,' to like, which is to give a feeling of love, is met by 'liccian,' to lick, which is to take a feeling of love (in the instance of a cow). 'Læcan' thus being to offer in idea the likeness of a thing, and to take in idea the likeness to it of another thing, is, in fact, to liken; and since 'læcan' uncompounded means all this, why should 'læcan' in composition not retain this meaning? I say that it does so. To liken is not·to make real anything. It is not to make two things alike, but to offer the 'lic,' look or appearance, of one thing to another thing which can and will take it, so as to give the same appearance to the two, and this can be done in mere thought. Thus, to 'edliken' an act, is to give an 'eft' (after) representation of it—that is, to repeat it. To evenliken a chair is to imitate it, not necessarily by making another chair equal to, or even with, it, but by giving a just likeness of it, which may be done with paper and pencil. To 'nearliken' is to approach by giving or taking likeness of nearness. To reckon one who is in want of our aid as a neighbour is to 'nearliken' him, although he may be in Africa and we in Europe. And so to 'rightliken' is not necessarily to make a man right or righteous at the time. It is not to do, perform, or make real, any righteousness in him. It is to justify him, to make him like being righteous. We are justified by our faith, which gives a likeness of ourselves, as dead on the cross of Jesus, whilst taking Him as our representative or likeness there; so that God, accepting our likeness of death in the flesh, gives us the likeness of His heavenly life; but we are made righteous only if Christ's righteousness is done, performed, and made real in us, and if we indeed live in and by Christ.

'EDNEWED'

is what we have as 'renewed.' 'Niwe' is an English word found also in every Teutonic language, whilst 'ed' is an English prefix formed from 'eft,' after. Yet we have discarded our 'ed,' and, in sheer ignorance of its existence, have gone to Latin to beg 're,' in order to make up the mongrel word 'renew.' 'New' is not at all from 'novus.'

'EGWHERE,'

or 'eachwhere,' is the old and shorter form of 'everywhere.' We have also 'egwhence' and 'egwhither.' Why not recover them all? Am not I justified in using such short and much-wanted words? Is the

Radical dangerous when he does the true Conservative's part, when he uproots a weed and replants a valuable root?

' EMB '

is what we express by ' about.' But ' about ' is properly ' emb-out '—that is to say, it is outside-what-is-emb. ' Emb ' is the prefix to a host of words, but is in itself valuable, as being shorter than ' about,' which is put into its place, thus leaving its own important place unfilled.

' ALBION,' ' ERIN,' ' BRITAIN,' ' BRETRIC,'<br>' ENGELKIN.'

' Albion ' is the oldest name by which the Isle of England, Scotland, and Wales was known to Aristotle in 350 B. C., and to Polybius in 260 B. C.; Ireland having been known to them as ' Ierne ' or ' Erin,' and the two islands together as ' Britain.' So says Pliny, according to Haydn in his ' Dictionary of Dates,' under ' Britain.' Whilst Bosworth, in his ' Dictionary,' under ' Bryten,' says, on the authority of Bede and Orosius, that Britain (so called in their times) is an island that was formerly called ' Albion.' A writer in the ' Penny Cyclopædia,' quoting Armstrong's Gaelic dictionary and Grant's ' Thoughts on the Origin of the Gael,' corroborates all this, and adds that the word ' Albinn ' is still the only name by which the Gaels of Scotland designate that country, as meaning the ' White ' or ' Fair ' Island, ' Alb ' being the same root as that which we find in ' albus,' and ' inn ' signifying island.

Now, may I respectfully suggest that we should return to our old names—that this island should be called Albion; her sister, Erin; the two, Britain; a native of Britain, a Briton; the divisions of Britain as now—England, Scotland, Ireland, and Wales; the British Empire, Bretoric; a man of British lineage, a Bretman; our colonies, Bretland; a native of one of them, a Bretlander; our Sovereign, the Bretwalda; his Queen, the Bretwalden; their eldest son, the Bretwald-in'g (with the accent on the ing); his wife, the Bret-waldin'de (with the accent on the inde); the race of all English-speaking people, whether in the Empire or in the United States, or elsewhere, Engelkin; their homes collectively, Engelkina; and all this without discarding our truly English names of King ('cyn + Ing,' son of the people) and Queen (woman of the people)?—a long question! but will my readers accept it, as that of a Scop,[1] for consideration and improvement, if possible? And, in any case, may I hope that, should it meet the eye of her gracious Majesty the Queen, she would be pleased to consider the suggestions which I have presumed most dutifully to make?

'ERRANDER'

is messenger. 'Errand,' happily for us, has nothing to do with 'errare,' but comes from 'ær,' before, which we now use as 'ere.' Besides its being a talking word, it avoids the double hiss in 'messenger.'

'FARSPY'

is a word built by myself, and offered for 'telescope,' to which in its parts and in its whole it precisely answers. We might from 'far' get 'farwrite' and 'farwrit,' for telegraph and telegram.

'FOLK,' OR 'VOLK.'

This much-wanted word has dropped out of general use within the present century. It is largely com-

---

[1] Poet (shaper, ποιητής).

pounded, and might be so very much more largely. Pronounced with full expression of the '1' in it, it is a sweetly-sounding word. 'Folk' without the article means people in general, the public; but 'a folk,' 'the folk,' and 'folks' mean a nation, the nation or people, and nations. We have dropped the word unworthily. I use it in its low-German form as 'volk.'

'FREFRIEND'

is the noble English rendering of παράκλητος, paraclete or advocate. It is made up of 'Frea' the Lord, and 'friend,' so that it means the 'Lord-friend'; but 'frea' is a connection of the prefix 'fræ,' answering to the Latin 'præ,' and meaning very, exceedingly; and 'friend' is a connection of 'fera,' which we still have as 'fere,' a companion in the journey (fare) of life. So that in these connections 'Frefriend' means the Lord, the exceedingly great Friend and Companion in the journey of life; whilst 'frofer,' from 'freo,' a lady in authority, loving and freeing, and from 'fera,' companion in journey, expressly means comforter, consolation. 'Frofer-Ghost,' accordingly, is the term given in John xiv. 26 to the Holy Ghost. 'Comforter,' a term much endeared to us, means simply consoler, strengthener, encourager. Let us keep it, but not keep out 'Frefriend' and 'frofer.'

'FOROD'

is decrepit, but also experienced, prudent. It is from 'to fare,' or to go, which we have in 'welfare,' 'farewell,' and 'thoroughfare'; and it expresses the being in the condition of one who shows marks of having gone through the journey of life by one or other quality, as the effect of its length.

'FORTHY'

answers exactly to the question 'why?' Surely it is a better form of answering to it than the mongrel word 'because' is.

'FOSTER'

is food, and a 'foster-brother' is a food-brother. The difference between 'foster' as food and 'foster' as a mere dissyllable is that between an egg and an eggshell. I say that our language is impoverished by our not having in our knowledge the contents of its words.

'FULDO,' 'FULDONENESS,'

are 'satisfy,' 'satisfaction.' What is 'satis'? what is 'fy'? Few of us know; and what we know of 'faction' enters not into 'satisfaction.' The meaning of 'satisfy' might as well have been labelled on 'disappoint' as on itself.

'TO FULFRAME'

is to perfect. A child can understand this at sight. He must go to the dictionary to know fully what 'to perfect' is.

'GARSEA'

is English for 'ocean,' which we pronounce as 'oshun'; and which is made up of two Greek words signifying swiftly flowing, and thus telling us that it is a vast river flowing swiftly round the earth. 'Garsea' is a word which talks in English, and tells the truth. It is made of 'gar,' a thrusting weapon, which we have in the verb 'to gar' (to cause), in 'Edgar' and such names, and in 'German.' So that 'garsea' is a promontory sea, whose bed lies off angular points of land abutting on it, such points of land as Land's End, Cape Finisterre, Cape Race, Cape St. Roque, and

Cape Verde. These mark out the Atlantic. Could mind invent a more self-asserting name for that sea which we call an ocean?

'GEBURNING'

means burning up altogether, or consuming. The 'ge' here has not only the collective and completing force of 'con' in 'consuming'; but it also has its own energetic force of goading, so that 'geburning' is a far stronger word than 'consuming,' besides being a speaking and not hissing word.

'TO GEDEEM.'

'To deem' is to judge: 'to gedeem' is to gather together and drive doom or judgment to its conclusion—that is, to condemn. 'Deem' and 'doom' do not come from 'damno,' and have no connection with it. Their root is, I believe, 'dem,' which means hurt, damage, 'doom' having been in early times mostly punishment of wrong. Even the once common curse 'damn' comes not from 'damno,' but from 'to dam,' or stop; and therefore is it that that word is severer than the word 'to condemn,' although the Latin 'damno' is not so severe as 'condemno.'

'TO GEHEAR,' 'GEHEARSOME.'

'To hear' includes somewhat of to obey, in English no less than in Hebrew, Greek, and Latin, as is shown in our versions of the Bible, and also in the close connection of our 'to hear' and 'to hire.' But 'to gehear,' or hear-together-with, is our more definite term for such complete hearing as includes obedience or concession, or at least reception of idea. 'To gehear,' therefore, is distinctly to obey, and 'gehearsome' as distinctly is obedient.

'KIND,' 'GEKIND,' AND 'MANKIN.'

'Kind,' spelt as 'cind' originally (for 'c' is no more 's' than 's' is 'c' in true English; and as for 'k' it is unknown there), is from 'cennan,' to beget, and means a kind or a nature; whilst 'gekind' means nature altogether or nature itself. We have its adjective in the phrase of our liturgy, 'the kindly (natural) fruits of the earth.' In this its own meaning we have lost it by putting the Anglo-Latin 'nature,' which we pronounce as 'neitchur,' in its place. We still, however, keep it in its second, third, and fourth meanings, of sort, species, and manner. Then, having displaced it from its first meaning of 'natura,' or nature itself, we use it as an adjective, meaning benevolent, loving; and thence we make up another noun than itself, 'kindness,' which in reality is natureness; and then we transform the adjective 'kindly' into an adverb meaning lovingly; and lastly, to complete the ruin of the word, we put it into the place of 'kin,' and say 'mankind' instead of 'mankin.' Now, 'kin' is a precious word meaning race. It is also a valuable noun-ending, as in 'fishkin,' 'birdkin,' 'angelkin,' 'mankin,' 'catkin,' but we hardly ever use it so. Our 'neitchur' has displaced 'kind,' and 'kind' has displaced 'kin.' Can we, could we, ever bring right and order out of this muddle? Yes, by means of the double sound of our 'i.' Leaving 'kind,' pronounced falsely and diphthongally as 'kaind,' to mean benevolent, we can bring back the use of 'kind,' rightly pronounced 'keend,' or else 'kinnd,' as nature. It will then remain merely for the printer to correct 'mankind' into 'mankin.' The accent properly is on 'man,' and not on 'kin,' and we should have placed it there had we known in how many other words than 'mankin' kin is an affix.

Even Tom Moore, writing ' mankind,' throws the accent on the ' man.'

' GELATHE '

is the English *proper* rendering of ' ecclesia,' although I admit that ' circ ' was the usual one. If ' church ' comes from ' circ,' a circular building, or even if it comes from κυριακον, the Lord's house, then we have no other than ' gelathe ' for ' ecclesia.' ' Basilica ' can no more stand for itself and ' ecclesia ' than ' harness ' can stand for itself and ' horse.' A house can no more stand for itself and its household than a suit of clothes can stand for itself and the man who usually wears it. Our use of ' church ' as a stone building, and also as the assembly which worships God in it, has led to much misunderstanding of Holy Writ, and to much misteaching of its doctrine. ' Lathe ' is familiar to us as the name of the apparatus used by the turner. It is the noun of ' lathian,' to invite, which is a derivative of ' to lead '; and it aptly describes the machinery by which the work of the treadle is invited and led to the work of the turner's knife. We are familiar with the word ' lathe,' but have utterly lost ' gelathe.' David in Psalm xxii. 22 says, ' I will declare Thy name unto my brethren. In the midst of the gelathung will I praise Thee.' In this verse in the old English Bible ' gelathe ' stands for congregation, or ecclesia, the gathering of Israelites who were led out from the nations to be God's people. As a representative of ' ecclesia,' the word ' gelathe ' will well stand a comparison with it. For whilst an ecclesia means an assembly invited by calling, ' gelathe ' means an assembly invited by leading, and so describes the work of God in the invitation better than the Greek word does. ' Gelathe ' might, at the speaker's convenience, be shortened to ' glathe '; and then, surely, as a phrase, the ' Glathe of England ' would be quite as euphonious as the ' Tshurtsh of England.'

'GHOST,' 'SOUL,' 'SPIRIT,' 'SHINLAC,' 'GLYDERING.'

Apparitions in Old English are called ' shinlacs ' (shining corpses), ' shinhiws ' (shining forms), and ' glyderings.' We get our notion of ghost or spirit, and of soul, from our Bible's rendering of two Greek words. ' Ghost ' is the English, and ' spirit ' is the Anglo-Latin, rendering of the Bible's $\pi\nu\varepsilon\tilde{\upsilon}\mu\alpha$; and ' soul ' is the English, and ' anima ' is the Latin, rendering of $\psi\upsilon\chi\acute{\eta}$. Both of these Greek nouns signify breath. The former comes from $\pi\nu\acute{\varepsilon}\omega$, and the latter from $\psi\upsilon\chi\omega$; and both these verbs mean ' I breathe '— the former as an angel does, and the latter as does an animal. St. Paul says: ' The word of God is quick, piercing, even to the dividing asunder of soul ($\psi\upsilon\chi\acute{\eta}$) and spirit ($\pi\nu\varepsilon\tilde{\upsilon}\mu\alpha$).' Again he says: ' It '—the body— ' is sown a soulish ($\psi\upsilon\chi\iota\kappa\acute{o}\nu$) body; it is raised a spiritual,' or ghostly ($\pi\nu\varepsilon\upsilon\mu\alpha\tau\iota\kappa\acute{o}\nu$), ' body. There is a soulish body, and there is a spiritual, ghostly body. The first Adam became a living soul; the last Adam became a quickening ghost. Howbeit, that is not first which is ghostly, but that which is soulish.' These texts are enough to prove that the word ' soul ' is not convertible with the words ' ghost ' and ' spirit.' But the Bible elsewhere shows that soul is more allied to flesh than to them. In Jas. iii. 15 the wisdom which is from beneath is said to be earthly, soulish, devilish. Here ' soulish ' ($\psi\upsilon\chi\iota\kappa\eta$) is included between ' earthly ' and ' devilish.' Again, St. Paul tells the Corinthians that the soulish ($\psi\upsilon\chi\iota\kappa\acute{o}\varsigma$) man receiveth not the things of the Spirit of God, and he cannot know them, for they are spiritually discerned. Such being man's

soul, how is it distinguished from man's life? Thus:
The soul is the immaterial part of the man, as an
earthly being or animal; the life, on the other hand, is
his quality of being. A tree has life, but not a soul; a
horse has life and has a soul, but not a ghost. A man
has all the three; whilst a Christian is a man who has,
in addition to these three, a portion of God's Holy
Ghost, which he gains by new birth from God, and to
which his own ghost is married; so that he becomes
thenceforth a ghostly man, having a soul subject to
him, instead of being what, till newly born, he had
been, a soulish man, having a ghost abiding in sub-
jection to him. The mind appears to me to be a third
constituent, apart from man's soul and his ghost, but
ministering to both, especially to that one which at
the time is the ruler. Worldly death may be said to
be the yielding up of the soul, or of the ghost, or of the
abstract life. Apparitions are not ghosts, and those
who call them so are simply betraying idiotic silliness
and ignorance. Apparitions are seen in a tall hat, a
dress or frock coat, trousers, and boots, or in a bonnet,
a silk gown, a shawl, and high-heeled shoes. These
are parts of the apparitions, and they are not ghostly
things.

It being, then, clear that the word ' soul ' is no more
than the word ' flesh ' convertible with the words
' ghost ' and ' spirit,' it only remains for me to show
that, besides being the English rendering, ' ghost ' is a
better rendering than ' spirit ' is of the Greek $\pi\nu\epsilon\tilde{\upsilon}\mu\alpha$.
Against the use of the word ' spirit ' it may be justly
argued that the connection in sound between ' spiritual ' and ' spirituous ' is unpleasantly close. As, for
instance, in the text: ' Be not drunk with wine, but be
filled with the Spirit.' The misuse of the Anglo-Latin
word ' spirit,' as derived from ' spiritus,' to express

alcohol, brandy, and whisky, is degrading it more than
the misuse of the word ' ghost ' to express apparition
has degraded ' ghost.'   But what is far more important is that that same misuse of the word in its English form makes it the source of false teaching.   From
our connecting the word ' spirit ' with things like gin
and rum, we have drifted into having an underlying
notion that it means a distilled volatile fluid or essence,
and that God is the Father of such essences.   But
' spiritus ' comes from ' spiro,' ' ghost ' from ' geisten,'
and $\pi\nu\epsilon\tilde{\nu}\mu\alpha$ from $\pi\nu\acute{\epsilon}\omega$. All these three verbs mean
' I breathe,' ' I blow '; and all their three nouns mean
breath and wind.   Dr. Bosworth says that ' ghost '
means, first, breath, blowing; second, a ghostly being,
such as an angel; and third, a guest.   Thus, ' ghost '
includes ' gust ' and ' guest '—the heavenly Gust,
' which bloweth where it listeth,' and the heavenly
Guest, ' who is sent to abide with us for ever '; whilst
' Ghost ' itself is that which God is, who is the ' Father
of ghosts.'   Oh, what a richness, what a fulness of all
the meaning which was wanted for ghost!   What does
the Anglo-Latin ' spirit ' mean?   Essence, exhalation,
distilled wine, and courage!   The terror of stirring, as
I am trying to do, a question of much of the English,
so called, of the day, which is really a more dead and
inanimate language to an ordinary Englishman than
Latin is to a Latin scholar who possesses its roots and
knows the contents of its words, and the utter and unworthy despair of ever recovering English, as a living
language, are strikingly shown in the persistence with
which even our latest translators of the Bible have
rendered $\psi\nu\chi\iota\kappa\acute{o}s$, soulish, as if it were $\phi\nu\sigma\iota\kappa\acute{o}s$, natural, thereby darkening the meaning of that important
word ' soul,' and some of the most important parts of
Holy Writ.

' Hælend,' ' Hael,' ' Haelth.'

' Hælend,' which expresses both healer, haler, hauler, and holder, is in English the title of Him whom we call Saviour, by an Anglo-Latin corruption of a French corruption of ' salvator,' which is a corrupt Latin word coined by the Christian Fathers as a translation of σωτήρ, which Greek word expresses only half of what ' Hælend ' does, and nothing at all of healing. ' Saviour' is a word now so endeared to us by countless associations, in the writings of our fathers, with sweet thoughts as to forbid any attempt to supplant it. I make no such attempt. I merely hope by recovery, for the use of those who desire it, of a word larger, truer, and fuller, to supplement its expression of what Jesus was, and what even the Greek word σωτήρ so imperfectly expresses that He was. The superiority of ' Hælend ' to ' Saviour ' is shown by the important fact that, whilst ' Saviour,' ' save,' ' safety,' and ' safe,' are connected with not one single other word in our language, ' Hælend ' is connected with the verbs ' to heal,' ' to help,' ' to hallow,' ' to hale,' ' to haul,' ' to hold,' and ' to held,' or preserve; with the nouns, ' æl,' oil, which is its root; ' haletta,' a hero: and ' hyld,' fidelity; and with the adjectives ' halig,' holy, and ' hæl,' whole. So that the Lord Jesus, as the ' Hælend,' is the Healer, the Helper, the Hallower, the Haler, or Rescuer, the Holder, the Helder, or Preserver, the Anointed One, the Haletta, or Hero, full of ' hyld,' or fidelity, the ' Halig,' or Holy One, the ' Hæl,' or whole of all things, and the ' Ealle ' or all in all. The bearings of ' halig ' and ' hæl ' alone on the word ' Hælend ' are a sermon of twenty pages, and the bearings on it of all the words named by me would be a large volume. ' Hælend ' means, as I have said, both heal and save;

but in my use of the word I leave its present forms of 'heal,' 'healer,' and 'health,' to their present significations; whilst for its significations of save, saviour, and salvation I go back to its old forms of 'hæl,' 'hælend,' and 'hælth,' merely resolving the 'æ' in the instances of the noun hælth and the verb hæl, into 'ae,' to be pronounced, as is the 'very' of 'every,' either as a monosyllable or as a diphthong at convenience.   The Anglo-Latin 'save,' in being disconnected with 'heal,' 'hallow,' 'hold,' 'whole,' misleads in most important doctrine, for Jesus does not deliver from death except by 'haling' from unhealth, by 'hallowing,' and by 'holding' as whole.

'HAFTLING'

is prisoner.   It is compounded of 'have' and 'ling.' 'Ling' comes from 'linian,' to lie down, and denotes the permanent state of a man, as in 'darling,' 'hireling,' 'fatling.'   'Ling' may be compounded to any extent.

'HEADSWIM'

speaks for itself.   It is, of course, vertigo.   How strange that I should explain it by this utter barbarism!

'HISELF.'

'Self' is the pronoun 'ipse.'   We use 'self' chiefly as a noun.   But let us at least use it grammatically. 'Himself' is right if in the accusative case, because 'self' is then a pronoun.   'Myself' is always right, because 'self' is then a noun.   'Herself' and 'itself' also are always right, because in either of them 'self' may be either a noun or a pronoun.   But 'he himself' and 'they themselves' are sheer nonsense.   'Self,' in each of them being in the nominative, should be treated as a noun, and should be compounded as 'hiself' and 'theirselves.' 'Self' should also at need be allowed, like 'ipse,' to stand alone; thus, 'I self' and 'Henry self,' rather than 'I myself,' 'Henry hiself.'

'HOPELEAST.'

Our fathers condensed 'lesnes,' or what we call 'less-ness,' as 'least'; and so 'hopelessness' was 'hope-least.' The 'less' here is from 'leas,' void, which we have in 'leasing,' falsehood, and not from 'læs,' the comparative of 'little.'

'HLINN.'

We much want a word for a musical note. Here it is, one of our own old words. We could not have a better. The 'h' gives it force, and the double 'n' gives it ring. It is a connection of 'hlist,' which we mutilate into 'list,' to listen, thus clashing it against 'list,' to desire, and 'list,' a stripe.

'HUNDICE.'

Why not? We have 'twice,' 'thrice,' why not 'for-rice,' 'fivice,' 'sixice,' 'sevenice,' 'eightice,' 'ninice,' 'tenice,' 'elevice,' 'twelvice,' 'thirteese,' etc., 'twenice,' 'twenonce,' 'twentwice,' 'twenthrice,' 'twenforrice,' etc., a 'hundice,' etc.? These words would be clear enough if we were accustomed to them, and they would spare to us much wasted breath and ink. I write them as an instance of how much may be done in but one small thing to improve our language.

'LARNED.'

When a poor old woman talks of 'learning' another to do a thing, we listen with a curled lip or a smile. We had much better reserve our scorn for its fitter objects—ourselves. We know no more than she does how a man can be learned without somebody's having learnt him, which person will then have the learning entirely on his side. The fact is that in English there are two distinct words: 'læran,' to teach, whence our 'lore'; and 'leornian,' to learn. The old woman was right, except that she should have pronounced 'learned' as 'larened.' I have written it 'larned,' and am content that she should 'larn' her children what they can rightly learn from her. It is dangerous to despise the English of the poor, who are the truest professors of it.

'LAWLEAP'

is modelled by me on 'æhlip.' 'Æ' has been already described as a fixed eternal law. 'Law' is from 'lagu,' a laid-down or statute law: but since the use of 'æ' has been dropped by us, and its sound is uncertain, I have written 'lawleap' instead of 'æleap.' I have very reluctantly dropped the 'h' in 'hlip.' For our fathers' leap was a 'hleap,' which makes its utterer wish at once to jump over a chair. 'Lawleap' means overleaping the law, but 'trespass' expresses merely overpassing, whilst it is a longer word with two hisses in it.

'LECH,' 'LECDOM,' 'LECCRAFT,' 'LECDRINK,' 'TO LEHHEN.'

What disgusting or mean sounds we have adopted in order to force our speech from its proper guttural character, which would have been its clearness, its strength, and charm! We have an instance of these in 'leech,' which we pronounce as 'leetsh,' and which thus debased we rightly give to be the name of a slimy worm. 'Lece,' rendered by the Germans as 'lech,'

and by the Frisians as 'leck,' is one of the oldest
words spoken by man. We have it in Danish, Rus-
sian, Irish, and even in our Indian 'lac.' What have
we instead of it? Physician, doctor, practitioner, and
surgeon. Now, a 'medical man,' who is not ashamed
to be called a naturalist, a teacher, a habitual doer,
and a handycraftsman, need not be ashamed to be
called a 'lech' or a 'leck,' but let him sturdily refuse
to be called a 'leetsh.' 'Leccraft' is the healing art.
'Lecdom,' a medical doom, is a prescription. 'Lecdrink' is a potion. 'Lecsalve' is an outward appli-
cation; and 'lehhen' pronounced gutturally (why not?)
might stand for to practise medicine. 'Lech' is capable of endless composition.

'LIGRAFT,' OR 'LIGWRIT,' OR 'LIGHTSWRIT.'

I offer one of these for photography. They give to
'ligrave,' to 'ligwrite,' and, as an abstract term,
'ligwrith.'

'LIHHOME,'

for so I render 'lichome,' in order to prevent its abuse
in pronunciation into 'litsh-home,' is the whole fleshly
man, consisting of his head, his limbs, and his body, if
the man is alive, for then these parts of him are the
home of his soul; but if the man is dead, the three
parts are those of his tenantless 'lic,' or flesh. Now,
no word could more aptly than 'lihhome' describe
what 'lihhome' is, and no word could more aptly than
'body' describe that part of the man which answers
to the German 'bottich,' a cask, to our own 'bottle'
and 'butt,' and which, like these, is derived from 'bot,'
a round swelling. But we have trodden 'lichome'
into the mire of Anglo-Latinism, so that its existence
is unknown, and then have perverted 'body' into
meaning the whole fleshly man, head, limbs, and body;

whilst we have borrowed 'trunk' from Latin to express the body itself. Finally, we crow over this borrowing as an enriching of our poor native tongue. Poor it is, for we have thrown its wealth away.

'LISS'

is a very old word akin to 'loose,' and it means forgiveness in its widest sense of absolution. It also means favour, grace, gratia.

'LYDEN'

is language. It is a connection of 'hlyd,' sound, and we have a form of it in 'loud.' 'Language' is our Anglo-Latin form of the Latin 'lingua,' or tongue. In ignorance of the many English renderings of 'lingua,' we have made our word 'tongue' do, as 'lingua' does, double duty, namely, as that which is uttered, and also as the instrument of the utterance. We might as well call a ball a bat, and then talk of striking a bat with a bat. 'Lyden' is at least as fair a word as language.

'LIST'

is the English for science. 'Listas læran,' to teach sciences, says Cædmon. 'List' is akin to 'listen.' It is a rich and modest word, full of talk to the purpose. What of that doubly hissing Anglo-Latin word 'science,' with its diphthongal 'i'? Knowledge! There is mockery in the term, as applied to that which is really inquiry in the dark, and in which knowledge is most uncertain, and ever shifting—that which is thirsting for new facts, although they destroy all past knowledge.

'LIDH.'

This word, spelt now as 'lithe,' and pronounced now with a diphthongal 'i,' means mild, gentle, ten-

der. I use it, and respectfully suggest its use, in its
original form, the ' i ' being that of ' lid,' for that sound
which is the opposite of ' loud.' Such a word is much
wanted in music. We have nothing for it but low,
soft, small, and still, which are adjectives applied to
height, touch, size, and motion, and which have not
that oppositeness in form and sound to ' loud ' which
' lidh ' would have.

' LORDHYLD.'

' Hyld ' is an old and beautiful word, a connection
of ' hold,' and meaning affection, favour, fidelity.
' Lordhyld ' is affectionate fidelity to one's lord, as, for
instance, to the Lord Jesus, loyalty being merely
obedience to law.

' LUNG-AIL.'

' Ail ' is the modern form of ' adl,' or what we describe by the mongrel word ' disease,' which at best
means uneasiness. An addled is an ' ailing ' egg, or
an egg made to ' ail '; and ' lung-ail ' is what we call
pulmonary disease. But we have contracted 'ail'
into ill, and ' ailness ' into illness. Then, without regard or knowledge of this, we have contracted ' evil '
into ill and illness, so that now a very sick person is
a very wicked one, and all illness is wickedness. ' Ill,'
as an adverb opposed to the adverb ' well,' is fitly contracted from ' evil ' (worse, worst), which is opposed to
' good ' (better, best). The fault is in the contraction
of ' ail ' into ill; but all our words have been left to
drift whither ever they liked. The reader will observe
that in ' adl ' the semivowel ' l ' stands in no need in
English of a vowel's support; so in ' apl,' ' emn,'
' edhm,' and many other words.

' MOYSES.'

'Mo-ushe' is the Coptic form of the great Hebrew legislator's name. It means 'drawn out of the water.' The Hebrew gives the name as 'Mô-sheh'; the Septuagint, as 'Mo-uses'; the Vulgate as 'Mo-yses'; and the Anglo-Latin, as usual in the most paltry form, as 'Moses.' I have in my poem adopted the form given in the Vulgate.

'MAN,' 'MAAN,' 'WER.'

Neither Greek nor Latin has a word so worthy to express 'Deity' as English has, for 'Gód' is the sum of all that is good. This is well known; but it is not so well known that our language faithfully and meekly describes 'mán' as, in reference to God, equally the sum of all that is 'maan' or *mean*. The accents on 'Gód' and 'mán' here denote the omission in the former of an *o*, and in the latter of an *a*. Since God, in reference to all, is always and only the good Being, we rightly drop the accent on His name, but we as rightly drop the accent on man when we speak of him not in immediate reference to God. Unaccented 'man' answers precisely to $\mathring{\alpha}\nu\vartheta\rho\omega\pi o\varsigma$ (anthrōpos) and to 'homo'; and, like them, means merely a human being. It therefore, like them, is of the common gender, and expresses woman as well as man. Then as in Greek $\mathring{\alpha}\nu\vartheta\rho\omega\pi o\varsigma$ is opposed to $\mathring{\alpha}\nu\acute{\eta}\rho$, and as in Latin 'homo' is opposed to 'vir,' so in English 'man' is opposed to 'wer.' $\mathring{A}\nu\acute{\eta}\rho$, 'vir,' and 'wer' equally mean a male human being—a husband, a soldier, and a man of high qualities. Then, as 'vir' gives 'virile,' 'virility,' and 'virtue,' so 'wer' gives 'werlike,' 'werhood,' and 'worth.' From 'wer' we also get 'war,' 'baron,' and 'world' ('wer-old').

For 'world,' or 'woruld,' as the Scotch rightly pronounce the word, means 'ævum,' an age; and 'world without end' means duration without end, not, as some suppose, earth without end. 'Maan' or 'mean' is man in a bad sense of the word 'man'; but even as 'middling' mean is no connection of 'medius,' it merely signifies 'short of excellence.'

'MAGEN' AND 'MAGENTHRYM.'

Our nouns 'might' and 'main' equally come from the verb 'may,' but whilst 'might' signifies ability, and political or other authority, potentia; 'main,' which should be written 'mayn,' if not 'magen,' signifies the means of these, such as helps, weapons, military or other external forces, and personal strength, robur. 'Thrym,' allied to the Latin 'turma,' but not derived from it, means, like it, a troop, a throng; but it has a second meaning of military escort, majesty, magnificence, and glory. The compounds of 'thrym,' and also of 'magen,' are grand words applied to monarchs and especially to God, such as 'thrymfast,' secure in glory; 'thrymful,' full of glory; 'thymwaldend,' ruling in glory; 'magenrof,' roofed with means, or immensely powerful; and 'magenthrym,' majesty in full court surrounded by its armies. The old English version of Matt. xxiv. 30, namely, 'Coming in the clouds of heaven with power and great glory,' is 'Coming in the clouds of heaven with much magen and magenthrym'; that is to say, coming with all means of might, and with majesty in full court surrounded by its armies.

'MITHWIST'

is the form in which I have reluctantly modernized 'midwist,' which means conscience, and is compounded of ' mid,' which used to stand for the Latin ' cum,' and of ' wist,' knowledge, which is the noun of ' to wiss,' whence ' I wist not ' and ' wise.' One of the very very few Anglo-Latin words which I envy is ' conscience.' Its exact English equivalent, ' mid-wist,' is lost to us from our having lost the right use of that precious preposition ' mid,' which the Germans have as ' mit.' Through early carelessness the Gothic ' mith ' meaning ' cum,' became misspelt as ' with '; and so ' with ' has sunk into meaning two exactly contrary things, namely ' cum ' and ' contra.' Therefore, for composition, ' with ' as ' contra ' and ' mid ' as ' cum ' are equally lost to us. We can build with neither prefix; and the precious compounds of ' with ' as ' contra ' and of ' mid ' as ' cum ' have fallen to the ground. We have indeed ' withhold ' as hold against, ' within ' or against the inside, ' without ' as against the outside, ' withsay ' as contradict, ' notwithstand-ing ' as not standing against, ' speak with ' as speak in answer, and ' fight with ' as fight against; but we won-der how these words and phrases can mean what they do. ' Midwife,' or accompanying woman (in labour), is the only instance, I believe, of the many compounds of ' mid ' which we retain. ' Mid ' as ' cum ' would not be beyond recovery if we chose to pronounce our vowels properly. Then ' mid ' would be, what we now call ' meed '; and ' meed ' would be ' mêêd '; and what we now call ' mid ' would be, what it used to be, ' midd.' If we did not choose to do all this we might take the Gothic ' mith ' instead of ' with,' where ' with ' is now perverted into meaning ' cum.' Either of these plans would affect only the speaker, the writer, and the printer. It would not affect at all our literature; and the gain of a clear and distinct English ' cum ' and ' contra ' would be very great.

'Nim.' 'Nimthe,' 'Nith.'

'To nim' is to seize. We have it in Corporal Nym, or Corporal Thief; and nimble is the word's diminutive. 'Nimthe' is take-away-that, or except that. 'Nith' is my own contraction of 'nimthe,' in order to replace 'save' when it stands for 'except.' Both 'except' and 'save' hiss, which neither 'nimthe' nor 'nith' does. English is said to be a hissing language. It is not so. Anglo-Latin is. Even our endings in 'ness' are in English 'nes,' with a soft *s*. An English *c* never hisses; nor is an English *g* ever *j:* whilst the plurals in English are formed by 'en.'

'Neat.'

'Ne-weet,' not to know, is the English term for any animals who 'nyton hwæt hi send,' do not know what they are; and accordingly the old translation of Gen. iii. 1 was, 'The serpent was more cunning than all the other neats'—'Thonne calle the othre nytenu.' In Greek what our fathers called 'neats' are properly called alōga zōa, reasonless animals. In Anglo-Latin they are brute-beasts. But the meanings of these two words have slipped, that of 'brute' into being cruel and that of 'beast' into being filthy. So the poor animals might have well complained of being described by them. In our modern translation of Genesis they are called cattle, from the Latin 'capitalis,' of 'caput.' But the word 'cattle' again has slipped. It originally meant chattels or personal goods (our chief or head goods). It now means domestic animals. But amongst these are certainly not included birds, snakes, and centipedes. Now, is it not worth while that we should recover our own little speaking word 'neat,' which in one syllable tells what two Greek words tell in five syllables, and what Anglo-Latin words cannot tell at all? I shall be triumphantly answered that we have the word 'neat' in daily use. Yes, as black cattle, which, as I have said, is not a definition of birds and fishes.

' Prest.'

Heaven and hell alone will tell all the mischief which has been done to men's souls by the double meaning of our word 'priest.' In the Old English Bible 'presbyter' was rendered by 'preost,' and 'sacerdos' or 'hiereus' by 'sacerd.' Now, neither has 'preost' the 'uteros' of 'presbuteros,' nor has the latter the 'o' of 'preost.' 'Preost' seems to have been a form of 'prafost,' and to have been, as such, accommodated to the expression of 'presbuteros '; for this reason, that 'prafost' or 'prafast' signified exactly what a 'presbyter' was in the ancient Church. namely, a president or rector. If 'priest' represents 'preost,' it does so badly in form; for it has an 'i,' which 'preost' has not, and it has not an 'o,' which 'preost' has; and it represents it utterly falsely in meaning, for it means both elder and sacrificer, both 'presbuteros' and 'hiereus' or 'sacerdos,' whilst 'preost,' as I have said before, did not do this. Accordingly, neither in form nor in meaning does 'priest' represent either 'preost' or 'presbuteros '; I therefore submit that we Protestants had better resign it altogether as the term for 'sacrificer,' and take in its stead, as the more proper term for 'presbuteros,' and the only fair modern form of 'preost,' 'prest,' which is the term used by Wycliffe for 'preost.' 'Prest' gives 'prestly' and 'presthood.'

' Rath '

is the positive of ' rather,' and means readily, quickly, heartily. It gives ' rathest,' a word well worth recovery.

' Rightliken '

is the form in which I have ventured to modernize the very important word ' rihtlæcan.' This old verb, as I have shown under the heading of ' edliken,' means to give the likeness of right or righteousness, and thus to ' justify,' as distinguished from ' to make righteous.' Mr. Conybeare, in one of his notes on the Epistle to the Romans, writes as follows: ' The first wish of a translator of St. Paul's epistles would be to retain the same English root in all the words employed as translations of the various derivatives of 1, δίκαιος; viz., 2, δικαιοσυνη; 3, δικαιοῦν; 4, δικαίωμα; 5, δικαίωσις; 6, δικαίως; and 7, δικαιοκρισία; but this is impossible, because no English root, of the same meaning, has these derivatives.' I presume to deny the impossibility. Taking ' right ' as the English root answering to the Greek root δίκη, I give the derivatives of ' right ' as they answer to the derivatives of δίκη, beginning with δίκαιος itself. And I number each set of English equivalents by the number which I have affixed to each Greek derivative in Mr. Conybeare's list, thus: 1, right, rightful, rightlike, rightwise (righteous), right-willed, rightfast, rightdomful, rightdomfast, æright, and upright; 2, rightness, rightfulness, rightlikeness, rightwisness, rightwillness, rightfastness, ærightness, rightdomfulness, downrightness, and uprightness; 3, to rightliken, to gerightwise, to aright, to berighten; 4, a right, an arightedh, a rightlekenth (see on page 55 my proposed method of making nouns out of past participles); 5, an arighting, a rightlikening, a gerihtwising, a right; 6, rightly, rightlikely, righteously, rightfastly, right-willedly, rightfully, and uprightly; 7, rightdoom, and ærightdom. Here is no poverty of language on the English side. The poverty is rather on the side of the Greek. English root-words lend themselves readily to composition, and our stock of English words might easily be made treble that which our fathers have left to us. On Rom. v. 15 Mr. Conybeare writes: 'So likewise the fruit of one acquittal (a being justified)($\delta\iota\varkappa\alpha\iota\acute{\omega}\mu\alpha\tau\circ\varsigma$) shall bring justification (a justifying),$\delta\iota\varkappa\alpha\acute{\iota}\omega\sigma\iota\nu$,the source of life;' whereas, adopting his form of the Greek passage, it might in English have been rendered thus: 'The fruit of one rightlikenedh or rightlikenth shall bring rightlikening (the source) of life.'

'To Mune'

is a connection of 'mind,' and means to meditate. When a person is meditating abstractedly at an unfit time and place, we say that he is mooning. We then rightly pronounce the word 'muning,' but in our ignorance of our language we use the word with an idea of the moon.

'Smilt,' 'Smiltness.'

'Mild' and 'smilt' are adjectives formed from the verb to melt, but whilst 'mild' expresses tenderness and gentleness of mind, 'smilt' describes the calmness and uncloudiness of weather. We, in our ignorance of 'smilt,' make 'mild' stand as itself and it, thus losing the distinctness of both the adjectives. We have 'smilt,' though wrongly spelt and not understood, in the glee, 'Hail, smiling morn!' which, without any imagery, is 'Hail, calm uncloudy morn!' A language is poor, not only when its words have lost the power of speech, but when their speech is confused and unintelligible.

'Soth' and 'Truth.'

What shall we say to the confusion of 'soth' and 'truth'? 'Soth' or 'sodh' (when shall we resume use of our letters for 'dh' and 'th'?) is verity. 'Truth' on the other hand is fidelity, and is verity only in the sense of being fidelity to it. 'Treow' is tree, and 'treowth' is truth; thus, tree is the root of truth, which is the expression of its qualities, of stability, uprightness, firmness, constancy, trust-worthiness, fruitfulness, majesty, support, shelter, and shade. It is a noble word. Has any language a nobler name for all these qualities combined? Yet we have ruined it by making it do a double duty, in which its expression of these qualities is silenced. 'Soth,' for which 'truth' does duty, is quite as noble a word as itself, but is utterly distinct from it in meaning. 'Soth' is derived from a participle of the verb 'wesan,' to be, which we recognise in our 'was,' and whose participle 'wesende,' being, is akin to the Latin 'sens' in 'præsens.' In accordance with this etymology is the following from Wedgwood in his dictionary under the head of 'sooth' : 'Sanscrit Sat (nom. san, acc. santam), being, is equivalent to " sens," " sentis," in " præsens," whence " asat," nothing, and " satya," verus.' Like 'sat,' then, in Sanscrit, 'sens' in Latin, 'sind' in German, and 'sende' in English, the word 'soth' means that-which-has-being, that which is. Could a more plainly speaking, could a nobler word be conceived for the expression of verity? No; and how do we treat it? We pronounce it as 'sooth,' and then throw it away in contempt. Then, taking 'truth' out of its place, we thrust it into the place of 'soth,' thus ruining both these magnificent words. If we took 'soth' back as verity, we might have 'sodh' as 'verus.' I cannot conclude without reverently remarking that 'Soth,' which is the name in one word of 'it-is,' is included in the name of the All-existent 'I Am,' in whom and by whom and for whom everything is.

'SPELIER.'

'To spêle' is to take the place of another; and 'spêlier,' from the verb 'spêlian,' to spêle, is substitute. The noun 'spêle,' pronounced as 'spell,' is in common use amongst sailors, who speak of taking a spell at the pumps; that is, of taking the place of another at them.

'SMITTEN.'

I bring this word into my poem in the compound 'sin-smitten.' It means defiled, and comes from 'to smitt,' not from 'to smite,' which ought to give 'smiten.' 'Smut' is the noun of 'to smitt.'

'SWELT,'

a short and strong word for perish. We have it in 'swelter.'

'STEF.'

Without poverty we have been beggars. We have borrowed trousers when we had a large wardrobe, and we have used the trousers as jackets. The Romans had 'litera' in the singular as an alphabetical letter, and in the plural as an epistolary letter. We have begged the word 'letter,' and have used it in the singular both for alphabetical letter and for epistle, which are as like each other as the clay at the bottom of a pond is like a brick house. 'Stæf' is in English the word for an alphabetical letter; and it is so because such letters, as used once by our forefathers, were Runic, consisting of stiff, long, staff-like lines. ' Stave,' the plural of ' staff,' is still used in musical notation to describe the staff-like lines on which the notes are written. ' Stef,' the form in which I have used the word ' stæf ' in order to distinguish it from ' staff,' enters largely into composition; thus, ' stefrow,' alphabet; ' stefcraft,' grammar; ' stefly,' literary. Let us leave ' letter ' to mean solely epistle, and let us take back ' stef.' Should we be going backwards? But going backwards, when one has wandered from his path, is going forwards.

' STIDH '

is a strong word for the strong mental quality of being sternly and severely stiff in mind, or resolute.

' SWETHM.'

We have no word for sweet-scent, and none even for ' scent ' but ' stinc,' which, perhaps from our abhorrence of perfumery, we have perverted into meaning foul-scent. The word ' smell ' does duty for the sense of smelling, and also stands badly for the scent which is smelled. It is, moreover, not English. ' Edhm ' is vapour, breath, scent; and, as scop, I have built, and humbly offer ' swethm,' compounded of ' sweet ' and ' edhm,' as sweet-scent.

' SWINSONG '

is swine-song, or what we name harmony; which word might, without loss of expression, be scammony. Let anyone, who has never listened to a herd of swine, clear his mind of ideas of ham and bacon, into which man converts a dead pig, and of hog's-wash and a sty, which man inflicts on a living pig, and let him be put into a room whence he can hear, but cannot see, a herd of two hundred swine *of all ages* at feeding-time, when they have only two or three troughs amongst them all, and he will acknowledge that nowhere in all nature is the whole gamut represented in such clear and rich notes as in such a choir. The pig has his faults, but is made more dirty than he naturally is; and no animal represents a full orchestra so well as he and his fellows do. It is to the credit of our honest tongue that it appreciates this fact. Our fathers, who fed their swine in the fields on acorns, found them clean animals, and respected them.

' SWITHER,' ' WYNSTER.'

' Swither ' is the comparative of ' swith,' strong. As applied to the hand or arm, it means the stronger arm or hand; and as applied to anything else, it means the side of it corresponding to a man's right-arm side; whilst ' wynster,' a sister word, apparently, of the Latin ' sinister,' means the side of a thing which is opposite to the swither. Whether or not our words ' right ' and ' left ' come from ' rectus ' and ' lævus,' and whatever they may mean as so coming, they are already in hourly use by us as ' correct ' and ' forsaken.' We know nothing of them as ' rectus ' and ' lævus.' When we say the ' right ' side or the ' left ' side of a house, we literally say the ' correct ' side or the ' forsaken ' side of it. Why should we unnecessarily make two words, in such constant use by us as ' right ' and ' left ' are, each stand for two utterly different ideas, each of which ideas is also constantly occurring to us?

' THENK.'

' To think ' is to appear, and its perfect is ' thught.' ' To thenk ' is what we call ' to think,' and its perfect is 'thought.' 'To thenk' is to make think or make appear; and that which is thus made to think is a thing; therefore 'thenk' is in reference to 'think,' as 'drench' is in reference to 'drink.' The connection between 'thenk' and 'thing' is somewhat that between 'reor' and 'res'; but, like 'res,' 'thing' is that which is made to appear in law; and so 'thing' comes to be a cause, or plea in law, and 'to thingen' comes to be to plead. By spelling 'thenk' as 'think' we have lost the beautiful connection of 'think' with 'thing,' we have lost the use of 'thing' as a legal cause, and we have utterly lost 'thingen,' to plead, in which sense 'thing' is so much used by our Scandinavian brethren; whilst we use, without understanding it, the compound word 'methinks' (it seems to me).

'THERRIGHT.'

The compounds of 'there' are very useful. We have 'therefrom,' 'therefore' (properly 'therefor'), 'therewith,' 'therein,' 'thereof,' 'thereout,' and 'thereafter.' Why not 'theretogens' for 'on-the-contrary-to-it'; and 'therright' for 'immediately'? We retain something like 'therright' in the phrase, 'All-right!'

'THROWERS'

are martyrs. 'To throw' is to suffer, and one of its nouns is 'throe.' What we call 'to throw' is properly to thraw; just as what we call 'to strow' is properly to straw. We have lost the connection of 'to throw' with 'throe,' and of 'to straw' with 'straw,' scattered grass, by our careless misspelling and by our ignorance of our language. The printer could set us right as to 'thraw' and 'straw.'

' THURBRIGHT '

is one of the many dropped compounds of ' thurh '
(through). It means transparent, and is transparent
in meaning, which ' transparent ' is not. For want of
' thurbright,' we have actually coined ' transparent.'
There is no such word as ' transparens ' in Latin.

' TWONNE '

is what I have modernized from ' tweon,' which means
doubt, and is formed from ' twa,' as ' doubt ' is from
' duo.' The Scotch have faithfully retained ' twa,' but
we have lost ' tweon ' by putting ' tweo ' (two) into the
place of ' twa '; and then, in ignorance of the existence
of ' tweon,' have borrowed ' doubt '; but few of us
know that ' doubt ' comes from ' duo,' whereas a child
would at once see that ' twonne ' came from ' two.' I
have added the second ' n ' in the word ' twonne ' in
order to give it an expression of reeling or unsteadi-
ness.

' TO UNNE '

is to acknowledge. Our old verb ' agan ' has been
modernized by us as ' to own,' but ' unnan,' our
equally old and worthy word, having no one to care
for it, has dropped into the same form, ' to own '; and
so, in contented ignorance of all this and of the existence of either ' agan ' or ' unnan,' we wonder, as well
we may, by what force ' to possess ' has made such a
stride as to stand for ' to give ' or ' concede.' I have
modernized ' unnan ' as ' to unne '; but ' unne ' already
exists as an old noun meaning favour. It might
stand as both a noun and a verb, as ' love ' does.

' UNTELLEND,' ' UNTELLY,'

are my renderings of ' innumerable.' Is the ' lic ' in
' luflic ' (which is the ' ly ' in lovely) like? It is com-

monly thought so, but can it be said that a woman or
a flower is lovely because she or it is like love?   Is not
' lufigendlic,' lovely, compounded of (1) ' lufu,' love;
(2) ' igend ' (from ' agan,' to own), possession, and
(3) ' lic,' the adjective form of ' læcan ' ?   And does
not the whole word mean love-possession-offering (if
active), or taking (if passive)? and is not ' amabilis '
compounded of (1) ' am ' (from ' amor '), love; (2)
' abe ' (from ' habeo '), have; and (3) ' lis ' (from the
root of '.licet '), allowing?   If these things are so, the
component parts of ' lufigendlic ' correspond with
those of ' amabilis,' and the two words express exactly
the same thing.   But, again, if so, we may easily replace all our foreign words ending in ' able ' and
' ible ' with words of our own compounded with ' lic.'

Still, we should much want an English form answering to the energetic Latin participle in ' dus,' and I
suggest our supplying this want from our discarded
noun and participle endings in ' end,' ' ende.'   We
should thus get ' untellend.'   We have a gerund, but
we never use it, for this reason, that by doing so we
should put the clock of speech back 1000 years to
correctness; rather than do which ridiculous thing,
we, when we have to say, ' I am to blamenne,' or ' a
house to lettenne,' utter the majestic nonsense of, ' I
am to blame,' or ' a house to let.'   We might have a
future participle answering to the Latin in ' rus,' but
I shall be thought to have lost my wits if, taking a
hint from German, I recommend ' loveward ' for
' amaturus,' about to love.

' WANHOPE.'

' Wan ' is a prefix formed from ' want.'   ' Wanhope,' want of hope, is therefore despair.   ' Wanspeed ' is adversity.   ' Wanhealth ' is invalidness.

'Wanhafness' is poverty. And countless such words could be built with 'wan.'

'WEEDS' AND 'WAEDS.'

We speak of garden weeds and of widow's weeds, and wonder what connection the two weeds have with each other. 'Bah! it matters not. It is merely a question concerning the English language. If we ask the question there is no one who has time to answer it.' The two weeds have no connection with each other. Garden weeds ought to be spelt 'weods,' and are a connection of 'woods'; widow's weeds ought to be spelt 'wæds' or 'waeds.' 'Wæd,' which we have in 'wadding,' seems to have been the name of coarse clothing, all in holes, used by the poorest people; and, as being such, 'wæd' is the root of 'wædl,' poverty, and of 'wædlian,' to beg, which we have in 'wheedle'; that is, to coax by pleading want. Widow's 'waeds' are coarse rough clothing (crape) made to imitate cloth in holes, and thus expressive of desolation.

'WILLES'

is voluntarily. It is the old genitive of the noun 'will,' and is literally of one's will; just as 'needes,' necessarily, which we write as 'needs,' is the genitive of 'need,' and means of one's need.

'WILLSOME'

is desirable, or that which carries somewhat of the will. We have handsome, lonesome, toothsome, and might build words without end with aid of the suffix 'some,' which implies part of a thing either in itself or in our knowledge of it, and very usefully qualifies numbers, as in 'twentysome,' or about twenty.

'WITHERWARDNESS'

is opposition, adversity. 'Wither,' as meaning contra, adversus (against, opposite), is a most valuable prefix. We have lost it, as such, by that contempt for our language which has allowed so many careless miscopies of it. There are two quite distinct words, 'hwider' (quo) and 'wither' (contra). We have taken the first half of 'hwider' and the last half of 'wither,' and making 'whither' out of the two, have quite lost 'wither,' contra, except in so far as we apply it to the shoulders of a horse. But few jockeys know that the 'withers' of a horse are so named from their being that part of him which is against or opposite to the collar of the harness. 'Wither,' as a verb, is in daily use by us, but without our understanding that it is merely in its meaning 'to oppose life,' that it means to speed death and to further decay.

'WIGHT,' OR 'WIHT.'

We say 'that person' when we mean 'that male or female.' Why not for the occasion use our old and in every way better word 'wight,' properly 'wiht,' which means man, woman, or thing? Why? Because we are ashamed of old English which is true English; and 'person,' a longer word, is now English in preference to 'wiht.' Ought this so to be? But is it wonderful that it is so, when so great is our neglect of our own mother-tongue that we are all hourly using many of its words and phrases in utter ignorance of what they mean; as, for instance, when we say 'odds and ends,' 'farewell,' 'world without end,' 'gooseberry' 'bridegroom,' 'that will do,' and 'methinks,' not knowing that these words mean ords and ends, or beginnings and ends, go well, age without end, gorseberry, bridegume or bride-man, that will avail or be

enough, and, it seems to me? Again, I say, ought
this so to be? Would it be so, if our scholars com-
posed a dictionary of words modernized from what is
called Anglo-Saxon, and if at our schools our children
wrote exercises in good English by the help of that
dictionary? No; but nursery governesses are the
professors to whom their education in this mere baby
language is entrusted; and at our schools the grave
masters exercise the boys in the more honoured and,
as they suppose, more important languages of for-
eigners and of the dead; so that the boys return home
with mongrel words above, or, rather, beneath, the
understanding of their first teachers, and, to say soth,
of themselves also. Aught and naught are 'any-
wiht' and 'no-wiht.' We use these words, and is it
not shameful that we are ashamed of saying 'that
wiht'? It is nonsense and unsoth to say that the word
wiht' and 'no-wiht.' We use these words, and is it
be lost by us are mere Anglo-Saxon words. They are
English, and are, or might be, made modern English,
and only unworthy faint-heartedness could prevent
them from being easily and profitably recovered.

'To Whirft,'

for so I modernize ' hwearfian,' to change, is a word in
sense and sound far superior to ' change.' It is the
verb of ' wharf,' which is a landing-place for the ex-
change of disembarked goods.

'Wyndream,' or 'Wyndrym,'

is rapture, or the being dragged or driven away by
' wyn ' (joy, delight), a word familiar to us in ' winsome.' Whether or not ' dream ' comes from
' dragan,' to drag, or ' drefan,' to drive, it means that

in which the mind and feelings are dragged or driven along in unusual emotion. In old English 'dream' meant (1) joy, mirth, and (2) music, melody, song. It is only by a late use that 'dream' has come to mean that in which the mind and feelings are drawn away in sleep. Our fathers spoke of 'dream-craft' as the art of music, and 'dreamer' as musician. But they pronounced dream as drêam; and by pronouncing it so we might still have the word in the sense in which it was used by them, leaving dream pronounced as we should pronounce 'dreem' to signify, as it now does, sleep-thought.

'Ze,' 'Zy,' 'Zine.'

I respectfully offer 'ze' for 'he' or 'she,' 'zin' for 'him' or 'her,' and 'zy' for 'his,' 'her,' or 'hers.' Before a vowel 'zy' would be 'zine.' In Latin a nominative to 'se' is not wanted; but in English the representative of such a nominative is as much wanted as that of 'se' is; and it is needless to say how much we need both representatives. The poor have already supplied for themselves a form for 'se,' 'suus.' Instead of saying: 'If anyone will call on me, I will give to him, or to her, this book, which he, or she, can take to his, or her, home, where he, or she, can read it at his, or her, own leisure, with benefit to his own self, or to her own self,' they would say: 'If anyone will call on me, I will give un this book, which ah can take to uns home, where ah can read it at uns leisure with great benefit to un.' The 'ah' here is evidently a form of 'any,' and the 'un,' 'un's,' of one, one's. These forms are better than none for the purpose to which they are applied, but I am not answerable for them.

' Losinth,' ' Loseth,' ' Takenth,' ' Taughth,'
' Loseds.'

What is there to prevent our using our past participles equally with our present participles as nouns? and why should we not be able to make abstract nouns of both of these? For instance, why should it not be possible to say: ' I regret my loseds and my losings ' ? that is, ' I regret the things which I have lost and my carelessness in losing them; for, in the loseth, I have lost much of my income; and, in the losinth, I have displayed great faultiness.' I see nothing except our despair of English that could prevent our doing this. We might with the greatest ease form abstract nouns out of any participles. Endings in ' ing ' would pass into ' inth '; ' ed ' would pass into ' eth '; ' en ' into ' enth,' as in ' takenth '; ' t ' into ' th,' as in ' taughth,' for doctrine; whilst ' taughdh ' stood for dogma. By these English noun-endings all our endings in ' sion ' and ' tion ' might be built on English stems; thus ' conversion ' would be ' geturnedh ' (the being altogether turned), and ' vocation ' would be ' calledh.'

' A Wilned '

means a thing desired; it is the noun of ' to wiln.' Let anyone, who finds fault with it, find its substitute. We say ' a desideratum ' because we lack such a substitute in English; but, in fact, we have lost that precious verb, ' to wiln ' (to covet or desire). Some Anglo-Franco-Latino-Greeko linguist will tell me that ' to wiln ' is Anglo-Saxon and that ' desideratum ' is English. ' Wilned ' gives, as an abstract noun, ' wilneth,' covetousness.

I have somewhat to say on English pronunciation, which is an utter ruin; but not as hopelessly so as some imagine, if only there is a will to restore it at any cost of trouble. There is, however, neither call nor room for my remarks on the subject here. If God still spares my life, now protracted to the age of eighty-five, I may possibly make the remarks elsewhere and elsewhen. And now, having justified my use of the words needing a glossary, which I have employed in my poem, and of which not more appear generally in five pages than often appear in five lines of Burns' poetry, I can only hope that my use of them may lead to the recovery of some of them. English will be the chief language of the world, and I would help to make it, what it would be if restored, the best language in it—a language worthy, and fully able, to carry the Gospel of the Hebrew and Greek Book of books into every land. As to the plan which I would suggest for making it all this, I ought to say something.

If then, you, my reader, hear anyone, unlike yourself, disposed to suffer panic at the mere idea of such an enterprise as the restoration of true English, I beg you to say to him this from me: ' Let not my enterprise startle you. I would implore you, be not angry; be not alarmed; faint not. I do not propose that you or your friends should in your whole lives use unwillingly any Old English words, such as those which I have dragged out of the dust of time, or any new words or forms of words such as I have myself suggested. Nor do I propose that your children should write exercises in what is called Anglo-Saxon. All that I propose is as follows: Firstly, I propose that our own language should be studied by many scholars, so as to be understood better than it now is. For, wonderful as the fact is, no one on earth understands English except as Anglo-Saxon. I myself, who am not professedly an Anglo-Saxon scholar, first found out from Dr. Bosworth's Dictionary its old beauties far too late in life to have been able to get more than such a smattering of them as I needed for writing this poem. Secondly, I propose that, after the language is better understood, an academy, formed of qualified deputies chosen by the universities, and authorized by the Legislatures of all English-speaking peoples, should be formed, whose chief work should be to study, reform, fix, and watch over the language; and one of whose first duties should be to modernize Anglo-Saxon, so called, words—a task requiring even more taste and judgment than scholarship; and whose next work should be to write a dictionary which would supply English forms of words replacing as many Anglo-Latinisms as possible. Where these forms did not already exist they might be got from German, Dutch, Danish, or other Teutonic languages. For instance, from German we might get ' self-standy ' for ' independent,' which word is a hollow shell. Furthermore, I propose that the youths at our schools should write exercises in true English by help of this dictionary. It does not follow necessarily that these children should in their talk adopt the old words which they shall have used in their exercises. It only follows that they might, if they chose, adopt them. The words might be confidently left to force their own way by their own worth. They would assuredly do this in time. By the establishment of such an academy as I suggest, we should help to bind together all the members of the English-speaking family in a closer union than even now exists; and should we by it, and by its work, have hurt our past literature? Scarcely any of it which is worth preserving; whilst we should recover much of our old writers which we have lost.

I have said enough here. The languages of the
earth are, as we quit it, passing away from us for ever.
We shall all be soon speaking that of either heaven or
hell. Reader, which shall I, which shall you, speak?
That we may both of us be speaking that of heaven is
the earnest prayer of him who has written this poem,
to the lessons of which, apart from its language, he
would affectionately draw your heed. Farewell!

OVERTURE.

ALL earthness, darkness! Every ray
Of earth-light, earthness! Every day
Of earth-life, night! but an earth-life's night,
A day, wherever is ghostly light!

From the sun and the moon mere mock-light beams,
That are light to alone the earth's day-dreams;
And sky itself, earth's heavenly roof,
A token mere of heaven aloof!

Earth's knowledge, the things that had reached man's
        mind
By light of the earth; and when there enshrined
Were, each of them, shaped by the shape of the cell
To which as its own it was taken to dwell;
Till there it, being by mind well wrought,
Became to the man his own made thought.
But each thing there, a likeness mere
In earth's mock-light of thing elsewhere.

The soul [1] of man, the man indeed!
While bides he from the fiends unfreed;
While abides he bound with his fleshly dreams,
And with shadows flitting in earth-light's gleams.

Man's ghost, the man! when the Hælend's [2] light
Has reached him, and when the Gospel's might
Has awaked and freed him from dreams of things
Which the Earth's mock-light to his earth-mind
        brings;

[1] For the right meaning of ' soul ' see Preface, p. 27.   [2] Saviour's.

When the man is dead to Earthy mood,
And he lives as born anew of God.

Man's lihhome [1] of body, limbs, and head,
Mere dust! whereof sin and death are bred!—
Blest, who to the dust of death lives dead!

But countless as dust are men; and they
Are all of them born as death's doomed prey:
And so with them each is it, as with all;
Each one is a soul, and is thus a thrall;
And fiends are their Lords, and God above
Would win to Himself their hearts' whole love
By His filling with light the murky gleams
Of their shadow-made earth-sun's mock-light beams—
With light, that light of the Holy Ghost
Which man, by sinning in Eden. lost—
With light, that light of the Gospel's plan,
By which God lives in the breast of man.

The noonday's blaze is that light's shroud;
As lightning's covert is the cloud.
As the surf-wave roars when its flash has come
To the beach where tarries its long flight's home,
So the roaming swell of the Gospel's sound
With a shout unlooses its light around,
When on some true man it has touched the ground.

Coming out of the east, from the west coming forth,
Coming forth from the south, coming out of the north,
A sound, a flashful sound from high!
A sound from far, a sound from nigh!
A thunder from heaven's every part,
That speaks in a whisper within man's heart!

[1] The whole body of a living man (flesh-home of soul).

To man it all is a call of might
To make from bondage at once his flight:
A call to man as the moan of love
Which God outbreathes from the skies above,
When sheaves of auroral light are spread
As fingers of love o'er Lapland's head;
And a call unto man as the thunder loud
Which He utters when off from the louring cloud
Light over Bengal in June resounding
Flies echoing, bounding, bumped, rebounding.

It shakes both heaven and earth and hell;
Shakes all men reached by its mighty swell;
Shakes Earth as the fall of a river on rock,
That half toward heaven's embrace from the shock
Springs back with a surf-wave's horror hoar,
Half sinks in the Earth with locked-up roar—
Shakes Earth as a rainbow, which from cloud
Comes tremblingly pledging love aloud
By every hue of its truth's white light
Turned out of its heart in its speech to sight.

It drops as dew; as the dawn it cheers;
As air it every-whither veers;
It wanders as clouds do, ready to rain,
By valley and hill from plain toward plain.
As a river it cleaves the salt sea wide,
And it climbs up each seaboard as a tide.
It flies as flieth the levinbrand,[1]
That flaps flame-wings over sea and land.
It saunters appealing as the song
Of bells in the breezes borne along.

Man's truth is assayed wherever it goes—
Truth whether to God or else to His foes;

[1] Thunderbolt.

For they who hate Him hate the shout
As call from all their self-love out;
And they who love Him welcome it
As help from what they hope to quit.

But as for the fiend, when he finds it nigh,
He looks at his haftlings [1] with heavy sigh:
Sith, albeit the most of them heartily fear
To be freed from the dreams which as fetters they
      wear,
And albeit, though hearing the call, ' Oh! come,
For your bonds may be broken, ye thralls! Come
      home,'
The most the more for that cry make
Those fetters faster lest they wake,
They some, when they hear it, slip from their bands
By lifting in Christ's name meekly their hands
To their Maker, their King, their Father above,
Who thus holds to them freedom, welcome, and love.

Then falls from God on these men light,
And through them 'gins to flow His might;
And into them, as their rightful Lord,
The Hælend [2] to hold them by His word
And keep them from being lastly lost,
Comes, comes by His Ghost, the Holy Ghost.
Their gaolers, their bolts, their doors give way;
They rise, and they live from that bright day,
Each one of them free from Satan's sway.

Oh, Gospel! thou that as God's own call
Thus loosest many a sin-bound thrall,
That makest man with such might free
As that wherewith the one word ' Be!'

<hr>

[1] Prisoners (have + ling).　　　　　　[2] Saviour.

Made all things erst from out of naught,
And left to them the shape it taught,
Why fliest thou fitful as lightning's gleam?
Why bidest thou not as the sun's staunch beam?
Wherefore moves thy light athwart this earth
As an angel's flashing arm, put forth
To draw the bolt of black night's den,
And ope its gate to some few men
But here and there, but now and then,
When like the sun thou might'st have in one
Broad sheet of light on all of them shone?
Why, Gospel! why?

     Then—oh, Israel! why?
Why Herald! whom it was bidden to cry
This Gospel and make this word of might
Bear over the world God's ghostly light,
Why shines it not as light of day?
Why comes not yet the daylight? say,
Why, Herald! why?

     ' Who asks?—but nay:
The asker first shall answer me.
And I, the Earth, cry, who is he
Who asks that crushed by the Hebrew's might
Be fiends who muster the shades of night?
Who calls the Herald of Dawn whilst yet
Those shades so thickly on earth are met?
What man calls Israel forth from dreams
Which bind him lest he awake day's beams? '

I call him.   I, the bard, who hear
His shout afar, his shout anear.

' Oh, Bard! forbear: thou hear'st no shout,
But echo mere that flies about;

For God to the men of the whole world wills
To speak in the echo from Jewry's hills,
Who spoke in the shout ere Israel
Asleep as in caverns dream-bound fell.'

Then over the Earth, upon fancy's wing,
My song, up away, to the echo's spring!
My song, up the echo, track by track,
To waken this sleeper fly we back!
From land to land, from stage to stage,
From realm to realm, from age to age,
Up the lines tracked out by the echo, fly!
Over olden Spain, Rome, Egypt, hie
To the cities of Greece!   From all these haste
To Jerusalem, thence to Sinai's waste,
To the mountains of Sinai, to Jacob's sons,
To the meeting of God with His chosen ones!

Here? nought but mist here!   Is it mist?
Nay, those are tents.   Tents? yet so whist!
Stay: haze from off me glides away.
Yes, hark! a murmur—see!—and—yea;
These are the Hebrews whom I seek;
That is their great Mount Sinai's peak;
Their wilderness, this around; and, lo,
The day is it, thousands of years ago,
When laws will be set them for weal or woe.

But a trumpet sounds!   By stroke of its blast
Every thought is laid, Earth's heart is aghast.

The four winds rise, have arisen, fly:
They clasp Mount Sinai, they sweep the sky.
The lightning's glances track their trail,
And spy rocks rent and strown as hail.

The fleeting heavens, black throughout,
Seem deadly still, as stunned with rout.
With a shriek each gust of the whirlwind, trying
To outfly the gust that afore is flying,
Springs out of its utmost speed; and soars
Beyond it in long and mighty roars;
Which, ere the cloud that it bears can fence
The mountain, warn away all men thence.
Yet fast in that wind do angels stand,
Each floating above his foot of land.

Gekinda,[1] lifting now her head
Up Sinai, sees her God with dread:
And dropping the rocks from the points of her crown,
But robed in a flame as her courtliest gown,
She stands on the mountain's highest peak
To listen to what He wills to speak;
Whilst smoke outbreathed by the panting ground
Through red lips opening all around,
And earthquake's roars from the depths beneath
Which rise like groans from the vaults of death,
Tell how the Earth abroad is biding
The things which will be soon betiding.

No wonder! that when Gekinda [1] felt
God coming, her crown did off her melt.
No wonder! that when He has come, she sees,
And faints in the wind as it from Him flees.

She quitted Sinai.   All things there,
As though hers never once they were!
No longer hers, the fire and cloud
Are there her Maker's sheen to shroud!
Wills He, whose word is the Earth's whole stay,
To rest His foot on this mount to-day?

[1] Nature altogether.

For He wills from the mountain's height to tell
Of the bounds within which would men walk well;
And the better to show men all these bounds,
He with laws will inhedge their wayfare's grounds;
He will lay down roads, and on both their sides
Set His laws as hedges and spear-armed guides,
That men not walking in ways aright,
Yet quite aright in their own self-sight,
May thus by their many law-leaps trow
How many a death they live to owe;
And, as guilty, may come to be led on the track
Of a better than Eden's lost happiness back.

Lo, men, your God!   With joyful thrills
Come, worship! love Him, as He wills!

What! failing of heart and a quaking of limb?
At whom?   At your Life-giver?   Quailing at Him?
Or but at His trump's rending Earth asunder,
At shriek of His wind, and His roaring thunder?

Oh, brethren! oh! for we shall die.
We hear our fathers' God Most High.
We hear His voice from out the cloud:
And yet we live, thus far allowed.
The voice is death; for who beside
Hath heard God speak, and not hath died?
Thou mightest live, Oh, Moyses, Guide!

Thou tell us, thou, what He shall say.
We flee; but thee will not He slay.

Their Maker allows their awe as right.
They flee from Him, winged with wild affright.

Yet why had they feared as death to stay?
Why felt they unlove's, unfaith's dismay?
His speech was in Eden life's own breath;
Why seemed it to these men that of death?
Does His Gospel dash to shivers and grind
Into dust man's body and soul and mind?
Men heard; and at once, as the Earth's great ear,
Filled Earth to its heart with their own foul fear.

Alone stands Moyses: appalled, e'en he!
He fears to stay, and he fears to flee.
He stands, though scarce can stand at all:
Yet strengthened by his Maker's call,
He climbs the mountain's quaking side
With lightning as his earnest guide;
Whilst rising wreaths of smoke jet-black
Hide step by step his lonely track;
And passes into the whirlwind's ring
Of gestilledh waiting on Heaven's King.

There sheen is veiled from angels' sight
By dazzling rays of sheerest light;
There light itself around that sheen
May not by man's dull eye be seen.—
No more! I stand adumbed; and hold
Hand over mouth, lest over-bold
I dare at fancy's bidding speak
Of Him whose might His wrongs to wreak
Wild fancy cannot ween, nor well
Could tongue shape words wherewith to tell.

My song! sound lidhly.[1] See, they gaze;
The smoke! the cloud! the lightning's blaze!

---

[1] Opposite to loudly.

My song! sound loudly.   Hark, they moan;
The whirlwind's roar! the earthquake's groan!
My song! trill, droop.   Lo, faints their hope;
The trackless waste! the warfare!   Stop!
Rise, sound, loud, louder!   More and more
Swell, boom! with loudest deep tone roar
Of the crash of the outburst of murmurings,
Which the wind in its howl's hubbub hoarsely brings.

A roll of smothered words!   'Gone!'   'Fled,'
'Forsaken,' 'Burnt,' 'Snatched,' 'Coming,' 'Dead.'

To the murmurers, whirlwind! shrieking, cry
As a Death in their fright's ear: 'Hark or die!
What! wait ye not for days on Him
On Whom wait countless Cherubim,
Whilst Earth's whole life passes by, as flight
Which meteors make in the wink of night?'
Cry that; then, Soul of the Whirlwind! bring
What words of theirs to thy folds shall cling.

I give you praise, my brethren dear!
For meekness much, for little fear.
Yet why the fear?   Ye stand in need
Of all good things on earth indeed;
And all deaths here around you feed.
But far around lies other sand;
And somewhere, too, is Canaan's land,
To which has gone your former guide.
These things all cheer you, as ye bide
In tears to see each dying day
Glide hopeless to its grave away,
And to see each night behind it go
As its mourner stricken dumb with woe!

Stags, hunted hither, will ye die
Like these your days?   Arise ye!   Fie!
What! know ye not a chief beside
This Moyses?   I will be your guide.
Have a priest of your own, and a likeness of God.
Let the priest bear his cross, and his crook-headed rod.
Let him wear at his back a fish-like cope;
With, as mitre, the fish's mouth wide ope.
And thus let us all go trimly back
To Egypt and home on our grief-worn track.

'Well said!'   'To the gods of old Egypt to whom
We bowed in our bondage mid melons at home!'
'Now, Aaron, a calf for us!'   'Aaron, we pray,
A calf, and Egyptian ritual's play!'

'Your earrings then!   Wood and more wood pile!
Now kindle a fire!   Now wait awhile.
Behold, the calf! and ye all may now
To God with help of an image bow,
In oneness with Egypt's rites, if still
Ye work as before my priestly will.'

The mount! the cloud! look! earthquake, flame!
A shiver creeps through all earth's frame.
That wrath be unsung!
Sing rather the coming, the wonder, the grief,
The cry, and the pleading, the prayer of the chief.
'Wherefore, Aaron, hast thou misled them?'   'Nay,
They misled their priest; but for us pray.'
'Oh God! their priest and them forgive!'
The prayer is answered: 'They shall live!'
The pleader has climbed the mount anew;
Again he is lost to his kinsmen's view.

Wait, Hebrews, wait! They wait. All well!
They wait. All well! And whilst they tell
Of God's great goodness—oh! what bliss
There is in merely feeling this—
Too happy they Time's tree to heed,
See thirty days so quickly speed,
That all of them pass as only one,
In which they are blent till all are gone.
Happy month! this month, this bearing bough
Of the green year's branch of Time's tree now
Puts forth and keeps with all its powers
The thirty days that are its flowers,
Until they fall as one whole day
Of bliss unbroken, fall away:
This month, this twelfth of the boughs of the year,
Which now in turn has the blossoms to bear,
Hath opened its thirty red buds of light
One after another; and fair and bright
At once have they all from the bough made flight.

The first red bud of the Time's new bough,
Begins, already begins to glow,
When the chief is midst his kinsmen found:
But with flash of glory-beams so crowned
That he hurls their gazings to the ground.

He is veiled; and with shielded gaze they brook
At the bearer of God's law's sheen to look.

Oh! who could have met with naked gaze
The flight of the spears of that sheen's blaze?
They alone whose look at its beams of light
Was with beams of love and of truth so bright,
That the force of its own faith's rays could pierce
Through the blaze with a flash of truth as fierce.

But Godward love and Godward trust
May not flash forth from men of dust.
They are theirs who, dead to soul of flesh,
Have as ghosts been born of God afresh.

Yet surely the law of God must move
The love of Him, since it bids the love?
Is therefore it not that mighty call
Which, carrying love and trust withal,
And echoing through the world amain,
Frees those that in bonds of sin have lain?

Oh, no! It bids from sin to flee,
It cannot make the sinner free.
Its call is ' Life to the sinless, Ho!
But death to the sinful, death in woe!'
And the Christless man, who feels no might
In himself to burst sin's bonds aright,
Still trusts to softness in God, and bides
Sinbound, albeit the call so chides.—
His thoughts back over his past life flit,
And meet spot following spot on it;
As it crawls along through time's green vale,
With its snaky folds and looks of bale,
And its each one spot, sin's unknown tale:
As it crawls along to a hopeless doom,
To the floorless pit, to the fire-lake's gloom.
And yet he trusts that God will keep
His life at last from that pit deep:
He trusts to a softness in God, and bides
Unhearsome [1] albeit the voice so chides.

Ha! where? for here is Sinai's waste:
The Hebrews whither? Oh, what haste!

[1] Disobedient (somewhat unhearing).

My thought has lured astray my mind;
My song has strayed; and, like the wind
Of the whole wide sky, from my fancy's glance
Has the landscape fled which it held in trance.
Time, time has been loosed.—My heart!—I stand,
Left all to my thought on Sinai's sand.
For to Hebron's hill and Babylon's towers,
Being loosed, Time rushed with Israel's Powers;
And Joshua at their head careers:
Now Judges amidst them rise, now seers:
Now further off rise mighty kings:
Isaiah tunes his hallowed strings.
The award of the doom, the doom from High!
The Assyrian's shout, the Hebrew's sigh!
Up! follow them, Song! thy slackness rue!
Thy speed to their own great speed be true.
Over ages forth as a seabird swoop.
In their up-flight soar, in their down-flight droop.
As a carol arise, and then sink as wail.
For arises or lurches their own flight's trail,
Down the trough of a wave, up a wave's crest high.
Overcoming, they shout; overcome, they sigh.
Being faithful to God, they arise and win;
But are worsted at once, as they sink in sin;
Then whelmed, they flee before each one foe,
And God's law follows them, crying ' Woe! '
And but their altar's murky breath
Stays day by day the scourge of death:
The shield alone of their altar's flash
Awhile wards off that law's dread lash.

For a dirge, this!—Often chased like roes,
They were cheered by Hope in all their woes;
But at last their Hope was slain by foes;

And their Hope she was tombed, and her winding-
    sheet
Was behest [1] of renewal of life when meet.
Be the dreams of thy slumber of death, Hope! sweet.
And they thus bewail her at her grave,
' To the death, oh! Hope, God's law thee drave;
But thy boast had been what life it gave.'
    And they weep, they acknowledge that sin had
      brought
    Them to this, that their God had against them
      fought,
    That His life-willing law had their Hope's death
      wrought;
And they smite their breasts where sins so throve,
That His law could but their life-right prove,
And attest it lost through lack of love.
    The dirge thus stopped!   Their own behoof
    Had asked that God should stand aloof,
    Nor thwart their seeing wrought that proof.

Hush, heavenly carol!   Hark!—nay, gone,
And wonder and wyndrym [2] left alone!

Thus happens it after a nightingale's song,
Or after the sun's having ruffled a throng
Of clouds in his setting, that beauty along
Through every sound and each one shape
Is found to have dashed, and made escape,
Amidst a spray of mazed delight,
Not caught by hearing or by sight.

Hark! carol again on the listing air!
Lo, angels amidst us, bright and fair!
Oh! words of life that as deeds so move!
Oh! living deeds that, as songs of love

---

[1] Promise.   [2] Ecstasy.

So blend in chords, wherein hlinns [1] most sweet
Of righteousness, peace, soth, mercy, meet!
'Good tidings to-day to men forlorn!—
In Bethlehem Christ, their Hælend, born!
All glory to God in the highest ones,
And peace upon earth in the men its sons!'

Yea, words! that as loving deeds are strong.
Yea, deeds! that as living words give song.
Oh, loving deeds! oh, living words!
Oh, mercy's song's ten thousand chords.
Arise, Hope! quickly thy grave forsake.
Thy Hælend comes.   From the grave awake!—
'Away with Him!'   What?   'Away! away!
Away with Him!'   Harrow! this thy day
Long looked for!   Awake not!   Oh, Hope—sleep!
'Away with Him!'   Clouds of heaven, weep!

Stern watchman!   Holy history!—
That dost from Zion's hill descry,
Say, what of the day?   It erst went well.
Say, what of the night?   Thy tidings tell.

The day? as dark as the brimstone pit.
The night? as black as the smoke of it.
'To thee, O Pilate, over us
Governing for Tiberius,
A misleader of men and a would-be king,
And the temple's and Cæsar's foe we bring.'
'No fault in Him, I.' 'Christ! death to Him!' 'Why?
What evil has——' 'Death to Him!   Send Him to
        die!'
'Fear, Pilate! to wrong that man of worth.'
'Art Thou then a King?'   'But not of earth.'

[1] Musical notes.

'To the Cross!' 'Your King?' 'Free Barabbas
      to us:
To the Cross, the raiser of Lazarus!'
'The blood of the guiltless?' 'His be laid
On us and our children!' 'Ye have said:
Then so be it.' 'Now from the Cross come down,
Thou Christ! and as King we Thee will crown.'
'In paradise with Me this night!'
The sun withholds from the earth its sight.
'My God! why hast Thou left Me? why?'
'Elias comes!' He cannot die.
'I thirst: It is ended!' All is done.
Earth quakes, but the life of men is won.
The veil is rent. The tombed arise,
'Not we, an Angel from the skies,
(His face, as lightning! we, as dead!)
Rolled back the stone. Our charge has fled!'
'Yet say men stole Him!' 'Mary!' 'Lord!
My dearest Rabbi! my adored!'
'To My Brethren! Tell them that I go
To My God, My Father, theirs also.'
'Why gaze ye, men? He so will come.'—
Now once rise, Hope! Rise! Thy home
Henceforth in heaven! and for aye
Thy foes away from thee! away!—
Jerusalem! where, where thy King?
Your King's return, ye heavens, sing!

Hold! Who with a strong world-weighted bound
Springs, hurling these idols to the ground?
Lo! Israel, led by Hope new-found!

He rises, herald high of God;
And thus he cries God's bann abroad:
Hear! all men! me your God; and heed.
For guilt on earth no more shall speed.

Too long forgotten and unknown
Have I a slighted stillness shown.
Idolators shall now have doom.
I leave to sin nor screen nor room;
Yet send My Son, and will forgive
Men who will hear Him and would live.'

The herald has cried that bann from God;
That Gospel has he abanned [1] abroad;
And thus to the world he further speaks.
' God forces your fear; your love He seeks
By this the Gospel of Christ, His Son,
By these good tidings to every one.
Have hope in Jesus, oh, men undone!—
For He, as your Hælend, of woman born,
Has midst you been dwelling, unhomed, forlorn.
Through Him, as Word of God, God's doom
Of death to you for Sin had come.
On Him, as Son of Man, in your stead,
With all your own sin laid on His head.
Has fallen, as He willed should fall,
That death to which ye doomed were all.
Having lived as sinless man sin-tried,
And as man sin-laden sinless died,
He, God in man, as free from stain,
By right has won man-life again:
And borne that life as man's away
To heaven, there to bide for aye.
And He thence beseeches you to strive
In the life He gives to you to live.
Live therefore from earth and selfness weaned,
And freed from your fell archfoe the Fiend.
Your every foe has He overfought;
Your hearts and your lives have by Him been bought;

[1] Proclaimed.

OVERTURE

Your wills may be made as His, and ye
Yourselves by His Holy Ghost as He,
Raised high by Christian love and awe
Above mere sin-forbidding law.
Live so, until at His call ye dwell
In glory greater than earth can tell,
In the realm of righteousness His home;
Whither sin and sorrow cannot come.
The bidding is to every one.
Take heed, it comes from heaven's throne.
Christ bids, beseeches, begs, and still
Awaits that ye shall do God's will.
From heaven to earth He comes once more,
Not, not as He ever came before;
Not, not as He once had come, to give
Laws showing how wrongly all men live;
Not, not to give, as He now gives, might
By which those laws may be kept aright.
He comes to meet and welcome all
Who here on earth shall at His call
Have heav'nward through His death-gate passed;
And—oh! He comes to bid that fast
That gate be locked against all who lie
Unfreed from doom the great death to die.
He comes on clouds with angels bright:
He comes with all His Father's might,
With magen [1] and with magenthrym; [2]
And every eye shall look on Him.
The man of sin, that lawless one,
Crowned, seated on an altar-throne,
And all Antichrists other and far less great,
Who against Christ rise with acknowledged hate:

----

[1] External might (means military forces).
[2] Majesty (the glory of military means).

And every godless man who stands
Aloof from God with folded hands,
Shall call on the hills their guilt to hide;
But even the hills shall not abide.
He has come in robes with His bloodshed red,
And the guilty world at the sight hath fled.
And——'

Why Israel's halt? Has his speech then flitted
As life from a body which soul has quitted?
Is the echo of his buried breath
As a shinhiw [1] roaming clear of death?

I stand in song on England's shore;
And hear, as I had heard before,
The shout, the shout of Israel.
It is the Gospel's mighty swell.
And shall that Gospel's cry of love
As but a death-song's echo rove?
Where, where is Israel, he whose dream
Holds daybreak back and its rising beam?

Ye Isles of Britain, Albion,
And Erin, will ye but look on?
Call, Britain! call the hour of night,
And blow thy shell with all thy might;
Arouse him. Over the dark waves cry
His name aloud to the hollow sky.
Shouldst thou, if he slumber, also sleep?
Nay, rise on thy rocks, and o'er the deep
Sing thence to the wind of the zeal, the awe,
And power, with which he will teach God's law;
As one, the doing which is rife
With health and haelth, [2] love and life—

[1] Apparition (shining-form). 　　　[2] Salvation.

A law which man can quite fulfil,
As being now the man's own will.
Wherever he be thy call may find
His haunt by the help of veering wind.
And since His crying Jesu's name
Will thrill with new life all earth's frame,
Cry loudly his own name forth to each breeze
That carries your barks bound over your seas,
Cry, ' Israel, where, where sleepest thou?
Night's watches await, Day loiters now.'

My song, thyself again cry ' Where? '
Hark! countless caverns answer ' Here! '

Then he slumbers! but he restlessly sleeps.
Like a deer he lists, he shudders, he weeps.
He forgets God's Gospel, forgets God's Son,
He forgets that battle which Christ has won;
But he hears God's laws still crying ' Sin! '
In his dream he flees their scourge and din
To death's very gateway, through which, with throes,
He quaking to God as at Sinai goes,
Unknowing a Hælend from Sheol's woes.

It ought to be day; yet darkness stays,
The darkness of earth-life's night of days;
And fast asleep the Hebrew lies;
But freedom's Gospel o'er him flies;
And billows of loud, but ghostly sound,
Still break with a flash of light around.
Where, where is Israel?—he, whose dreams
Hold back from the world its daybreak's beams?

Ha! those gray clouds! What? yes, they grow.
The dawn—that reddening streak below?
The dawn, indeed! The morn awakes,
The startled cloud its red wing shakes,

Rise, welcome light of day, arise;
From east to west fill all the skies.
I see that, like this light of day,
Lo! Israel springs from night away.
I see him risen from shameful sleep;
I see him wonder; see him weep.
He groans, he cries a bitter cry;
He prays, he peers up to the sky;
Then breathes his trembling prayer and song
Amid the proud world's faithless throng;
Messiah! God! Jehovah! King!
My own, my all in everything!
Heart-stricken, overwhelmed with shame,
Lord Jesus! dare I speak Thy name?
The more Thou dost my sin forgive,
The more I marvel that I live.
I live, but live in only Thee.
I live henceforth from unfaith free.
I live to Thee, by second birth,
Within a kingdom not of earth;
I live as Thine with a life above,
Forbidding laws to the laws of love—
With a life in which God's will is wrought
By Thine own through mine in every thought.

And may Thine Israel—may I, Lord!
Yet hope fulfilled Thine oft-said word,
That I shall with Thee in Salem live?—
If Thou canst indeed so far forgive!—
Shall live with Thee Thy praise to sing,
Whilst choirs of realms around me bring
Their hymns to Thee, my Salem's King?

Bliss—bliss too great almost for mind!
Too great upon this world to find!

Yet may I? Thou, my Hælend! come;
Be mine Thy chiefest earthly home;
There, whilst men all around me throng,
All voices follow mine along.
Be this the loud and blissful song:—
The Lord of lords, the King of kings,
By whom were made all men and things
That are and will be and have been,
The Bethlehem-born, the Nazarene,
The Lamb of God, His Holy One,
The Lion of Judah, on David's throne
Reigns, reigns; and for His Father so
Will reign till 'neath His feet sin, woe,
And Death lie—Death! that last dread foe.

THE INVOCATION.

Live, streaming torch! and though my shaking hand,
 Full of storm, bears thee through the gale and rain,
  Through foeship's bluster, and through friend-
   ship's tears,
   Yet live to speak amidst the roaring speech
Of that great fire, alighted in this land,
 Which once my fathers with their bones fed fain,
  When priests could preach with faggots to men's
   fears,
    Ye tongues of that fire's flame! oh, still beseech!
God of my fathers, hear!   Thou gav'st them life
To die for that flame's light: help Thou its strife!

·

BOOK I.

WORLDLY LIFE IN WEAL.

I.

SONG A.

AARBERT.

Once more have I, oh, my Aarwick! abode of love
And pleasure, to thee come, never again to rove—
To thee for the joys I lost when I left thee.   Hark!
      Methinks I hear thy hounds.
      How cheery those old sounds!
How fair is the landscape waving from off this park!
And all of the land mine own! oh, my heart it bounds.
      I hear a whispered call of ' Come!
      Come, welcomed to thy waiting home!'

ANTSONG A.

THE HOME.

Come! welcome! my greeting, heartily, Squire, I give.
Hare, partridge, and pheasant wholly for thee here
      live.
The fox in his hole here tarries for thee, and here
      Lurk trout, and salmon coy,
      Thy boat here swims in joy.

Pass merrily life 'mid horses and hounds and deer,
Nor ever again quit sweets that can never cloy
    In me, thine Aarwick, me, thy home.
    Come, waited for and longed for!   Come!

SONG B.

AARBERT.

My home! There is all in thee that a heart would pray
The most to have come, the least to have go away.
To take, and without stint, take of the boundless wealth
        Of pleasures stored in thee;
        To lie 'neath shady tree,
Or over thy breadth to gallop and breathe its health;
To fish in thy lovely lake, or to wander free
        By yon dear brook, I fondly come—
        I come, I come, my own dear home!

ANTSONG B.

THE HOME.

Come, welcomed with joy! Thy tenantry, far and wide,
Will love thee; the poor will pray that thou long abide
The Lord of the Manor, Squire of the neighbourhood.
        The wealth by thee here strown
        Will ever bide thine own.
Thy welfare will float on high on a brimming flood
Of that of us all; and I shall afar be known
        The home of bliss—a happy home.
        Long-looked-for Lord of Aarwick, come!

AFTSONG.

Aarbert.

My home!   I shall meet whatever I would in thee.
What not shall I meet? whatever I fain would flee.
Whatever on earth is bright am I now to find;
        For, oh, how much more bright
        The world is where a light
Is flashing from out the heaven in Milda's mind!
As swiftly as flies to her and to thee my sight,
        So slowly seems myself to come,
        My childhood's heaven—home, my home!

II.

Wrink *and* Aarbert.

Wrink.

If, Aarbert, you would do that little thing
For which I asked you, you would help me much.
An honoured name, and through the land a name
More honoured, sir, than yours I do not know,
Is in a bank a hoard of heavy gold
So broad and high as to shed yellowness
On all its vouchers, and to make them far
More willsome[1] than the weighty gold itself.
Now, only for your name, dear sir, I ask.

Aarbert.

Your fancy that my littleness, good friend,
Can prop your greatness, shows you scantly wise.
You hold the fancy still?   My name I lend;
And by the buttress may your wealth's pile rise!

[1] Desirable.

But, Wrink, I do this for the dear dead's sake—
Yes, partner: for your father's sake I do
This thing. So mark me well! No risk I take.
Be yours the bank's gains, yours its losses too.
No, no; I could not understand your book.
Ere danger ever reach you, warn me, nay,
Pledge but your word; I will nor read nor look.
Give back my name ere danger come. It may
And will come never, as right well you say.

III.

Aarbert.

Speed England! They that are born of thee
　　Love more their aarworth[1] than their gold.
Their minds as well as their limbs are free:
　　Their worth too dear is to be sold.

They spring to meet with undaunted heart
　　At aarworth's[1] call both loss and pain;
They feel joy thrill them in all the smart
　　Of their forgoing[2] shame-bought gain.

Enough for thee, were thy meed, dear land!
　　That such men are thy welfare's shield—
Men not afraid for the right to stand
　　On hustings or on battlefield.

For them enough were it, if their meed
　　Were but that they to win their wreath,
Climb needs by many a worthy deed,
　　Each leaving all past worth beneath.

---

[1] Moral honour.　　　　　　　　[2] From + going.

IV.

AARBERT.

(*A letter.*)

I write to thank you, friend most dear!
For welcome warm and thanely[1] cheer,
And all that at your home you said
And did to me when there I stayed.
You tell me that you wish to know
What here I do and how I dow.[2]
I live amidst my tenantry:
And they could say that so live I
With them and luck, that not a thing
Lack I not lacked by eke a king.

I live as country honour's guest:
I live at peace with all my neighbours:
From fret of evil-will I rest;
And sweeten rest by goodwill's labours.
I give old friends old wine to quaff:
I give an ear to him that crieth:
I laugh with all the gay who laugh:
I chase his sigh from him who sigheth.

In showing truth by saying soth[3]
I honour God and shame the Devil.
My busy pleasures brook no sloth.
I neither fear nor flatter evil.
I seize the rough by smoothest side:
I see the dark by bright side only:
My thoughts I never stoop to hide.
I love my thoughts when I am lonely.

---

[1] Noble. [2] Prosper. [3] Verity.

My wisdom keeps my welfare's gate:
And her I thank that I have known her.
All mine the best of all I rate:
All not mine bless I to its owner.
Whate'er I give, forgotten mine,
Becomes my joy wherever given.
Thus I, with nought for which to pine,
Have all for which I could have striven.

V.

AARBERT *and* ARNULPH.

AARBERT.

In this our world, good Arnulph!
There live uneasy people
Who are for ever grieving.
I hear them all day croaking
That man is born to trouble.
I cannot understand them!
To me mere life is revel.
The shifty times shift only
My ways and means of pleasure.
Spring, summer, harvest, winter,
Noon, evening, night, and morning,
Are each, when come, the choicest
Of all the times and seasons.
Hard work I find a pastime:
I know not aught unhealthy,
And naught I know unwholesome.

These men find joy in grumbling:
They take their ease in grieving:
And wonder when I cheer them
By laughing and by saying:—

'One half, sirs! of your troubles
Would leave you if you fought them;
The other, if you mocked them;
You say that you are rooted
Upon a ground too stony:
Grow out of it, oak-hearted,
And let your leaves and branches
Amid the breezes riot!
Then, though your tree lack peaches,
You yet may boast its acorns.'
They waive away my comfort;
I cannot weep to cheer them.

The more I make them happy,
The more are they made wretched.
They whine amidst the pleasure
That rollicks all around them,
They whine and cry—I hear them—
'A world—a world of trial!'
It is a world, methinks now,
Of not unjoyous trial.
There are a few bad people, .
Some murderers and such-like:
Were these all hanged, it would be
Without a speck of blemish,
Did not such dismal croakers
Keep off the sunshine from it,
And then cry, ' Lack-of-day's-eye!
A world of dismal shadows!'

ARNULPH.

Be thankful, oh, my friend, be thankful
That you and woe meet not each other.

 AARBERT [Book I.

AARBERT.

Now, when and where should I and woe meet?
Men never meet woe, meet her nowhere,
But when and where they far have wandered
From path of worth or path of wisdom.

ARNULPH.

Nay, Aarbert, nay; but woe strays often
Along these paths, and there men meet her.

AARBERT.

I know not that; nor should I know her
If there we met; but this well know I,
That as the worth of my forefathers
Won all their health and wealth and welfare,
So mine—my worth, I say, and wisdom
Shall keep their winnings, and shall leave them
As heirlooms to my own dear children.

ARNULPH.

Take this on trust from me, your elder,
That poor is he who holds his riches
As if his own, and thankless snatches
Each day the pleasure which they give him.
For at the call of Him who lent them
They put forth hidden wings, and quickly
Fly back to roost within His dovecot.

VI.

AARBERT.

As I look or here, or I else look there,
At the things that are, or the things that were,

The rebukes of Arnulph were trash, or both
Were in him all truth, in themselves all soth.
For my mother's talk would, as well I ween,
Have been more like his than my own has been.

VII.

Godard *and* Aarbert.

Godard.

Which?—Good or pleasure off from Time's gaunt
    palm?
  The gold of lasting good, or else the gleam
Of pleasure as it flits by, which?—The calm
  Upwelling from a mind with endless stream
In choice of lasting good is more than balm
  For wrench of soul from pleasure's sweets away.
Not only soothes it, Brother, all the qualm
  Of being torn from sweets of passing play,
  But flows as God-sent pleasure that will stay,
The pleasure which our Maker made our best.
  Whilst good itself, which is as gold, I say,
Buys lasting pleasure soon to be possessed,
  E'en if withheld awhile.   Rate not the gleam
Of passing pleasure worth the being blest
  With boundless bliss at end of all Earth's dream.
Death brings the wise man life, and to his breast
He brings unending peace—and he brings rest.

Aarbert.

I thank you, larned [1] Brother.   You have plucked
Bright flowers from the garden of your college
For this your speech's nosegay.   If not sweet,
The flowers yet are gay.   Nay, Godard dear,
Indeed I thank you; you have given me back

      [1] Taught (not learnt, see p. 32).

Some good old thoughts, which I had flung away,
But I begin to feel again their worth.
Old Arnulph has been talking in your strain
Quite lately to me.   I must mend my ways.

VIII.

AARBERT *and* WRINK.

AARBERT.

Where coiled a blue snake basks till the flash of its
Scales into flame bursts, so that its tracery's
   Stripes seem in fire floating, throughout which
     Blueness in every hue's wave flushes.

There halts as charmed, starts back, the Brazilian;
Quails, whilst the snake uncoils, and then down on it
   With lifted staff showers his beatings,
     Till he has slain what he deems a Death's glide.

This done, he jerks that deadly but loveliest
Snake off his path far into the underwood;
   Takes breath, and strides onwards, full often
     Eyeing with shudder the wayside bushes.

Good Wrink, if Maan[1] come charmingly up to you,
Shut close your love's gate, whilst at the wicket you
   Call, wary, up straightway your whole mind's
     Powers together around your reason.

Do reason's will, then.   Dash from you ruthlessly
That witch's charms.   If once you allow that they
   Pass through your love's gate they may whirft[2] your
     Weal into woe, and your hope to wanhope.[3]

    [1] Vice.   [2] Change.   [3] Despair (want of hope).

WRINK.

Forgive me, if I laugh, sir, at your fear.
But breathe it not, I pray you, to the walls;
Lest these should give its plague to men outside,
And work within the world's too ready mind
Unhealthiness of trust in this sound Bank.

AARBERT.

Wrink! yet a few calm words from me: list to them.
Speech faithful, whilst oft giving its hearer pain,
   Gives more of heart-aching to him who
      Utters it frankly in loving friendship.

Sail, sail about luck's stream, at the sides of it;
Lest far from shore wind fail you; and suddenly,
   Although you ply oars, you adrift glide
      Off to the falls of the mighty river.

Or, through the midstream sail; but unweariedly
Watch clouds; and steer well, trimming your sails
     ever:
   All winds are yours, someway to help you:
      Anchor at once, if they fall; take bearings.

WRINK.

That speech I praise, sir. I could not have made
One better. Go, with trust in this my word,
That you have laid down only those good rules
Of seamanship, which ever were my guides.

IX.

AARBERT (*to his son*).

   Sibriht! whatever you do, do that
      With all of your heed and all your skill:
   Both write your lessons and wield your bat
      With courage and hope and hearty will.

Run life's whole race with a bound of joy:
    What though to the goal you come not first.
Is sloth not dulness?   Be sure, my boy,
    That idlers of all folk fare the worst.
To lag and loiter with listlessness!
    Why, that is to drag unworthy life.
Let life run; ride on it; forward press
    With pleasure in racing, joy in strife.
Live out your powers, and they will grow
    In bulk and in worth by toil and rest;
And those who look on your deeds will know
    Your life is a struggle, not a jest.

X.

Aarbert *and* Wrink.

Wrink.   ·

Sir, you indeed do weary me; I hear
The same old croak from you each time you call.
What can I do to stop it, or to give
The ease you lack?   I know not, I lack time;
And in the Bank's behalf must put an end
To all this foolish talk.   Farewell, dear sir.

Aarbert.

Stop! hear me once more.   Honours are waiting you;
Great wealth is now yours: only be worthy them.
    Live not amidst gamesters in revels.
    List to the warning of one who loves you.

Fond seem your feres[1]: most charming they surely
        are;
Gay, witty, too.   You trust them.   I know that they
    Court but for your wealth's sake your friendship;
        Should you be poor, they would leave you quickly.

---

[1] Companions (from ' faran,' to go).

Ah! Wrink, your heart seems now to them, theirs to
　　you,
Drawn tightly; but next year may come finding you
　With Bank and heart broken and wealth lost,
　　Left to your sighs, and to lonely sorrow.

Wild life, its waste, mad riot, and recklessness,
Shake like a storm high houses, o'erwhelming them.
　Their inmates, then outcast, find shelter
　　Only in hovels amidst the ruins.

WRINK.

I must cut short this prating.　Fare you well!

XI.

AARBERT *and* SERVANT.

SERVANT.

Sir, I have heard tales very strange.　The Bank——
In whisper is it told me——

AARBERT.

What?　What?

SERVANT.

I cannot say, sir, for my tongue is tied,
But thought it might be loose to you, at least
So far as it has slipped.

AARBERT.

Here! take this letter to the Bank.

The letter.

Write, write at once some answer, or call on me.
What tales are these?　How far am I bound for you?
　I lent my name, trusting your honour.
　　Then were you rich; are you still so? are you?

XII.

AARBERT.

I now know what is heart-ache.
I now know what a pain means:
Have, oh! the lesson learnt, what
The grief is, which I mocked so.
God help me!   I in sheer love
Did what I am undone by.
Oh, Heaven! take the threat off!
Good Heaven! take the threat off—
Take off the threat of life's wreck.
I might lose much.   What might I?
What, if I lost my lands!   No.
No.   No.   Oh! how the wild thought
Went through me like a gunshot!
No, no!   Yet much I might lose.

XIII.

WRINK *and* AARBERT.
WRINK.

I hope, sir, that your mind is more at ease.
Great business at the Bank is calling me:
You will, I trust, not wish to keep me back
From duty there.

AARBERT.

          Farewell, good Wrink! I own
That you have not a little eased my mind.

XIV.

AARBERT.

I thought so.   Lies and slanders!
Mere soapy bubbles! hearsays!

Afloat in airy gossip,
And filled with breath of slander;
The young man, poor, poor fellow!
With what a long forbearance
He tholes[1] them! Why, he lets them—
He lets them drift. They pass him:
But then, the man is wealthy:
The man, though young, is forod[2]
In all the ways of business—
Not faultless, but a banker:
Bold, daring, most far-seeing
And wary. Gay? I fear so;
Gay—somewhat gay; but clever!
Hard-working and keen-sighted;
Withal, a great financier;
In short, a great and clever
Man: not without a weakness.
But, mark!—the soul of honour—
Trustworthy to the backbone!
Else, why do people trust him?
Whence, too, the careless bearing
With which he meets these slanders?
Yes; but with what a goodwill
He took the pains to rid me
Of all my fears! for, said he,
'This gossip, sir, is merely
The mould of lies, by gainsay
Of which in every hollow
You get, in each one feature,
The shape of all my state now.
The gossip shows me losing:
Stamped, therefore, on your trust, which
Its guilt, as wicked slander,
Ought merely to have heated

---

[1] Endures. [2] Experienced.

With anger, and have softened
To love of me and pity—
It shows me as all-winning!'
Dear Wrink! it does—it does so.
Most wicked are the slanders.
I knew that thus these hearsays
Would end.   But, oh! how slily
He told me of an heiress,
And—and of building houses—
I know not where—no matter!
New branches of his Bank; why,
He reckoned to a penny
The cost of those new buildings;
And spoke of ' reaping harvest
In springtide with the outlay,'
And, ' being soon in clover—'
The sly rogue! business phrases!
But all of that is nothing.
An honest man!—too gay, but
All right at heart.   I showed him
Mistakes of his.   He unned[1] them,
And praised my business powers;
But showed at once new winnings
He had forgotten.   Never
Had I my ears so tickled.
How droll it is when slander
Hurts only him who hurls it;
How funny is a bugbear,
When he no longer frightens.
Ha! ha! yes, I was frightened.
A deep shrewd fellow! cheerful
Is sunshine after thunder.
A clever, clever fellow!

[1] Owned.

I have indeed been startled.
Bright rays again are bursting
Upon the world around me.
Heigho! I know not why, but
Whereas this young man lately
Both gambled and lived loosely,
The bright rays seem to glitter—
They do—they seem to glitter,
As from a stage-play's footlights
Upon a painted landscape.

XV.

AARBERT.

He shirks me! and the world gives these tales trust.
It even eyes myself with froward look,
Most strange to me.   I find myself passed by,
As if I had no being, or were not
The Lord of Aarwick.   What can all this mean?
My very servants whisper of me, whilst
They scan me as a bench of magistrates.
Oh! how forlorn, when by its sickness touched,
Is wealth.   I seem of all men least to know
My own state.   Wrink can little dream how racked
My mind is.   What if in the tales be soth?
Bah, bubbles!   Here, this statue of me, too,
Wears look of strangeness.   It is ten o'clock;
Wrink told me thrice he should be here ere nine.

Marble! cold mocker, that wast by a sculptor
   With craft's whole strength wrenched out of stone,
      and hidden,
All in this statue's life, and shape, and stirring,
   Why jeerest thou at me, for that he boldly

Bragged that thy being in them made me deathless?
   I know that this my likeness, now thy prison,
Must become nothing but an offcast name's shape,
   But thou withal thyself, too, Mocker! braggest.
Other things earthen, as they fade and crumble,
   Sing deathsongs in the minor key of gleecraft.
Thou the while carolest that thou wilt surely
   Till time's end bide in youth's unfretted plumpness.
Vaunter! when fires, which have been said beneath us
   To slumber, shall be waked; and far more hungry
Than the lean kine, whereof King Pharaoh dreamed
     once,
   Shall eat up more than all the earth's fruit, eat up
Earth and man's works, his lore, his speech, his story,
   Thou, too, shalt swelt,[1] and shalt as soon have
     swelted
Quite as though crumbling at this hour, for time is,
   Thou sayest, naught to thee: and, lo! to even
· Wisest men all its rolling hours are merely
   Their works. To other men is time the nothing
Of a short life-play's show, and noise, and bustle—
   The nothing of a dream, through broken slumbers
Hugged, till death waken up the dreamer roughly—
   Or else the nothing of a death of searchings
After things which, when every search is over,
   Will like itself for ever quit the searcher.

XVI.

AARBERT.

It must have been by whelming work last night
That Wrink was kept from coming hither; yet
He should have written, oh! he might have come;
For I am harrowed by my fears, and have

---

[1] Perish.

To hide them from my wife.   He should have come.
How this young man has played with me!   Come,
        come,
You loiterer! he must be here ere long.

> Say thou the soth,[1] or speak thou less.
> Why tellest thou me, Cheerfulness!
> Why tellest thou my trustful sight
> That all is fair where all is bright?
> At noon the cloudless sky of blue
> Around the sun says, and is true,
> And also ruddy clouds at eve
> Say soth[1] which I may well geleave.[2]
> That smiltness[3] bides and will abide
> Till next has come an eventide;
> But when red clouds at dawning day
> Foretell a smiltness[3] that will stay,
> Do not they, like the bluest sky
> Around the sun in April, lie?
> Why tellest, therefore, thou my sight
> That life is ever fair when bright?
> Why cheatest thou me, Cheerfulness!
> Or say the soth, or speak thou less?

XVII.

AARBERT.

> Ye dark fears louring o'er me!
> Ye bodings of dark evil!
> Ye clouds of thought o'erspreading
> My soul's bright heaven's sunshine!
> Ye black eyes, wild and swollen
> Of fevered mind!   Ye watchers
> Within my mind, whose lookings,
> From all of mine aroundness

---

[1] Verity.   [2] Believe.   [3] Fair weather.

Of heaven-light, are meeting
Upon my state mine only,
O'ercharged with speech of all things
To me most black and baleful!
I know you.   Oh! I know you.
Ye all are each the likeness
Of woe fast coming hither—
Of woe my widowed welfare,
In blackest weeds of mourning.
How fondly, oh, how fondly
I basked in hope's bright sunshine,
Till one by one ye rose up,
Ye flushed as gloomy shadows
My cheery sky's all blueness!
I know that woe is near me,
Although as yet I see her
In only you; I hear her.
She must be, she is near me.
She is at hand; ye see her.
Her chariot is coming;
Her waggons wait my chattels;
The wild winds are her horses;
I hear the far-off rumble;
My heart itself cries, ' Ready!
Be ready, Aarbert, ready.
The thunder's wheels are rolling,
Are coming swiftly nearer;
The hurricane is coming;
The storm is nigh thee, Aarwick!
Thy trees and lofty towers,
Thy trees and lofty towers,
Pray down the bolts of heaven,
Give challenge to the whirlwind.
Ah! whither from my homestead,
Have I to flee forlornly,

Before the howling whirlwind,
Beside the roaring downflood,
Beneath the bolts of lightning,
Amidst the rising waters,
Affrighted, scorched, and blinded,
Unpitied, friendless, hopeless!'

XVIII.

AARBERT.

It is the thought of it, and not the thing.
The thing without the thought will never give
This dog one pang.   He will be anywhere
With food and shelter and his master's love
As happy as he is at Aarwick here.
But need I be a dog to have few wants?
Or would I be a dog to have no thought?
Can thought give pain to man, and can it not
Take pain away from him?   Yes; thought, I know,
Could either soothe my wound by meekness: or—
It could benumb its pain by help of scorn.
For me no meekness!   I have not as yet
Been tamed by scourges into lowliness;
As Godard has been: rather will I give
The meekness, and the wound withal, to scorn.
The wound is naught to me if naught I feel:
Naught, therefore, will I feel; but I will have
The wisdom of a stone, and on my wound
Will lay a death's calm—such as now is here.
How stilly is the world above my head!
How whist is all beneath!   My dearest ones
Are happy in unknowledge that a storm
Has blasted with a gun's loud boom my wealth:
Nor dream they that their past life's all of joy
Is being borne off like a dead wave's spray.

There is no downfall, and so stilly here
Are things that—Has there been a storm at all?
I but last week was lord of manors broad
And of this castle, in whose halls a guest
Had once been lounging, haughty, young, and gay.
He swore, he glozed, he talked of all his wealth.
Stay!—softly!—Let me not awake a change.
He was my father's great friend's only son.
And yet—I wished not—but—I helped him, oh!
And then—oh, right! oh, law! my all, my all!
I must not—no—I would that I could sleep.

XIX.

AARBERT *and* EDDA.

EDDA.

Papa, has something happened? for you look
So white, you frighten me.   Shall not I call
Mamma?   Do kiss me!

AARBERT.

What?—Go.   That kerchief o'er me!   Teaze me not.
Call no one.   Oh, my child! my darling child!
Now quit the room; haste!   Is she gone?   Oh! oh!

XX.

AARBERT (*at first alone, then* MILDA *also*).

AARBERT.

My thought will not take deadness; it will kill me
If still I bury it alive within me.
My brain, unload thee: let it outcome—loose it.
Say what is all this?   Homeless! what means ' home-
    less '?
I know not.   Who is homeless?   I am, I am.

I! Who? I—I am homeless. Who is I? Yes—
The past is ended. Poor, poor me! My manhood!
Another I, now! What means ' I am homeless '?
Just this, a beggar! Now you know the meaning.
You beggar! Nonsense! Will my friends say ' Non-
    sense '?
They must so. Aarbert—and the lord of Aarwick!—
' The wealthy squire—the lord of that rich manor! '
So—let me breathe. Not yet, then: dear, dear
    Aarwick!
Thou yet art mine. My fields at dawn to-morrow
Shall meet again to cheer my peeping windows:
The birds once more shall sing my waked joy—
    blasted!
Hahrr! They will sing their own bliss or my rival's.
Untruthful birds! will not one note be saddened?
Not one. But as for you, fair woods and meadows,
Park, lovely lake, and ye gray towers,
To all of whom I from my birth have given
My worship, care, and love, how nimbly will ye
Pass over from me quite away! Ye sicken
My head, my heart, my fancy. Go, go, rubbish!
I feel so sick. Ha, ha! my wounded feelings!
Ditch-drown my feelings! Oh, my wife, my children!
My children, they! their sun has set: their homestead
Is gone. The house, the lands, have passed to others.
My children's children! help me, help them, Heaven!
For only Heaven now a friend is left me.
Unless—ye lambs! there, there they are so happy
At play. Play on to-day, ye hallowed throwers![1]
Can ye forgive me, can ye ever, ever?
Can Milda? No, the shock will quench her reason.
If but my lands had been entailed! My lands will
Go rightly to the men at once who claim them.

       [1] Martyrs (throe, see p. 48).

I ought to die: and let these lambs be mangled
By wolves which howl throughout the world's wide
        forest
Of men?—by wolves which have already harried
Their fold and broken down its fences?—tigers,
Which in this jungle—this is worse than madness.
Is there no God, or have I nought to trust in?
Good angels, have ye left me?   Let not evil
Work into my poor will its way: Let not it
Bring down God's wrath upon itself within me.
Who comes? poor Milda?—I must tell her of it—
I dare not tell her.   Lamb!—I dare not tell her:
Yet must she know it.   Milda!—trust in Heaven,
For I am sinking.   Do you understand me?—
You cannot: we—this house—but what of that too?
She heard not.   Must I tell her?   She must know it.
Wife, drink this wine.   A beggar! evil, coming!
Say, have you heard me? for there seems an echo
Here, or my words grow shouts, I scarce can hear
        them.

Milda.

My darling, what has happened?   Oh, I feared it!
What, what is it?   Do tell me, dearest Aarbert!
Oh! what is it?   I saw that there was something
Not right; and I have wondered what it could be.
Do tell me, tell me, Aarbert!

Aarbert.

You understood me?   Did you hear me?——Milda!—
You feared some woe!—but the estates of Aarwick
Are not entailed!   So, now then, now, you know it.—
That fellow Wrink has done it. Homeless! beggars!—
I say that we are beggars, beggars, beggars.   Now
        then—

Ask Heaven to strike me dead; for I deserve this:
And give my deed a name.   Will no name span it?
Is it so bad as that, that you are speechless?
Oh, be not dumb! say something; sob, accurse me.

MILDA.

My own, my own, my dearest, dearest Aarbert!
May Heaven pour upon you all its blessings
And comfort with my own; and with my fondest
And never-flinching love.   You are my——

AARBERT.

Stop!   Bless me not.—Then I must cry and bellow.
My Milda, do not bless me: curse me: I have
Crushed all your life's hope.   Harrow not my heart so.
Say not a word, then; nay, not now, then, Milda!
Could you forgive me ever, ever? kindest,
My kindest—oh, I did not mean this, darling!
I was betrayed by—Let none—I—This weakness—
My kindest, kindest Milda! how more faithful
Than I!   But I will tell you all about it.

XXI.

AARBERT.

The house is left: the ties that bound me to it
Are snapped: the worst is known: the worst is over.
I feel so giddy; can it all be?   Aarwick
Left, left for ever?   Would that I were dreaming;
That these woe's pledges were but fever's fancies!
I feel so giddy; how has all this happened?
It is the time for thought.   How dreadful time is,
When left to thought like mine.   But how and where-
    fore
Came this, and whence?   It is too late to ask it:

The mischief has been done, is past undoing.
There, there, what mean that dirty yard? this lodging?
Strange things! how came I hither? shipwreck'd, ship-
    wrecked!
How came the wreck? that question must be an-
    swered:
Where is my note-book? Let me write the answer:
Harbour, left!—owner, fool, a fool!—the captain,
A rascal! Is the word clear? Rascal!—scudding—
Storm, storm—away, vile book! Tell not it. Hide it.
And so—I feel light-headed, and I shall be
Stark mad, I must be calmer. Breakers leeward!
Never mind whence it was, or how! Where am I?
Look there, look here; amidst forlorn men—Lapland!
Cold, houseless, stripped of all but clothing, shel-
    tered—
Heigho! yes, sheltered: I at least am sheltered
By gifts from some friends loving but—now severed
From me by seas of trouble. Gifts!—They reach me
Like snowflakes showered down by Heaven. I am
Thankful—They are my rich friends' parting gifts,
    and—
Need I then gifts? But I will try: help! Heaven!
In my pride's summer snow would have been hateful.
But it is sent to shield me. I am thankful,
Yes, I am thankful.—Gifts!—A hut of snowflakes
From my proud neighbours! I am thankful for it.
Love here may live with happiness. My loved ones
Will be the world to me and to each other.
Yes, home may find a shelter in a snow-hut
When wooden rafters and stone walls withhold it.
It may; and then my poor hut's inmates still may
Feel pride. They will, as Woe's acknowledged chil-
    dren,
As children of that mitred Queen, have homage

From all who fear her. Well, that thought brings
          comfort.—
My loved ones never more will have man's homage
For worth of mine, although they, for their own, may.
And will they in that snow-hut be as happy
As once they were in halls, where all that earth had
Was waiting on the pleasure of their bidding?
No: they will have their thoughts; and they will hide
          them
From e'en themselves. Who lost to them that Eden?
Who let run out the cable of our wealth's ship?
Half-witted scoundrel! who let slip that cable?
I did, none other, I did. Is there lightning?
The sky is blue. How strange it is that heaven
Is blue, yet earth so wicked. Gone for ever!
I did. With what a scourge of stormy weather
She, after she had drifted from her moorings
Has on a freezing sea been with her cargo
Lashed hither into Woe's ice-locked midwinter,
And hurled upon its floor of rocks, all lifeless!
Crushed, crushed, the stout old barque, all copper-
          fastened!
But summer even to this frozen stronghold
May haply come to loose the bars about us.
Ah-ha—ah-ha! and then may flee my loved ones.
Well! after that, what?—Then—then reft of canvas
And ship wherewith to catch the gales of heaven,
I yet may, as a rough hard-handed boatman,
Drudge on the world's sea, rowing to their masted
Ships richer men. If I can borrow of them
A boat—But what, if not? why, then—I know not.
Darlings!—what! all then lost? No, I shall still have
My good name, still my proud uprightness left me,
And therewith Heaven's blessing—still my good name,
And therewith men's goodwill—my name unsullied!

XXII.

AARBERT *and* MILDA.

AARBERT.

As you found happiness in all my weal,
  When I in it could merely pleasure find,
So now my grief you for my folly feel
  And, unlike me, are to my folly blind,
My Milda!—we were wont from Heaven to have
  Whatever good things Earth had to bestow;
But Heaven, since to those good things I gave
  Too much that love which I their Giver owe,
Now sends me evil things which you must share;
  Yet therewithal, lest you should share with me
The pangs they give me, sends with loving care.
  To you a mind which is from pride's fret free.

MILDA.

Great wealth had I, when once I merely thought
  Your own worth tenfold that of all your store;
    But since what then I thought I now have known,
      More wealth I now, than I had then, possess.
My wealth, by being to my knowledge brought,
  Is growing; and is now so much the more
    Than erst it was, as it is being shown
      By loss of all but you made not the less.

XXIII.

MILDA.

What!   Is this right?   It is a doom from heaven;
  It must be right.   Yet seemed it not quite righteous.
Which of God's laws then have we broken? which one?
  I would I understood it, why He sends us

Evil like this which is so more than most men's—
  ‘ Loves not He those whom He has lashed? ’ says
      Godard—
But this rod's lash has even wholly crushed us;
  Did not my husband well with all his riches?
Dare I thus answer Him who made me? Dare I?
  My husband tried, he tried to do his duty.
This is quite wrong; I feel it must be wicked.
  The doom bewilders; would I understood it.
‘ He is most good,’ says Godard; ‘ I must trust Him.
  He keeps me living.’ Dare I? He is righteous.

XXIV.

GODARD *and* AARBERT.

GODARD.

Poor Aarbert! how my heart is aching for you,
For you and dearest Milda and the children!
Take meekly God's upbraiding. May I say so?
He loves you, He has meant your welfare
In all this chiding; He will bless you by it.
And as for me, though I am poor, you know that
Whate'er is Godard's will be also Aarbert's.
Our little crusts shall be together hoarded
In the sound bank of love for one another.
But let me speak to you, do let me say it,
That God has bread far better than those crusts are—
The bread of heaven. Would it not be timely
To ask Him for it now? It would be, brother.
Do let me turn your thoughts from these great losses;
My roughness will be wholesome; let me turn them.
Methinks your ghost is hungry, and needs cheering.
I love her, Aarbert, love her very greatly;
Have not you starved her? You are feeling deeply

Your loss of world-wealth.   Are you not then fright-
     ened
By thought that, though your ghost has lost for ever
Her all of riches, you have never missed them?
She, not for earth-life, but for life unending,
Has lost so much of wealth, that these your losses
Of land seem losses more of children's playthings;
For she has lost almost her life.   She should be
Yourself, my brother! and her wealth should also
Have been your own; your worldly wealth was lent
     you.
She yet can live by eating bread from heaven.
If God had taken you from those your acres,
Instead of them from you, where would she now be?
Poor ghost! but now your night has left you;
You are awaked from life's dream; it is therefore
Her time for breakfast; give it her from God's Word;
And she, when fed, will lead your mind from earthness.
I know not better how to give you comfort:
It is my best.   Oh take, and you will like it.

AARBERT.

My brother, not just now.   I know you love me:
And it is meet that you should, as a parson,
Speak thus: but—and I ought to thenk [1] of all this—
And so I will, too, trust me, when my grief wills.
Meanwhile, I thank you for this gentle teaching,
And for your love.   I feel its comfort greatly.

XXV.

AARBERT.

Oh, Bankruptcy, I mourned thy robbing me.
But, lo! that many-footed worm the mob,

<hr>

[1] Think.

That creeping length of men of every rank
Who follow one another, that long worm
Ten-thousand-jointed, having at each joint
A mouth at whose cry quake its other joints,
Is barking forth that thou and I have leagued
To rob the world; that I for many years
Have fed the hungry outlay of my State
With what the poor had laid up in my charge
To pay their costs of sickness or old age;
That I have flaunted guineas as mine alms,
Each one of which was but the name of some
Two hundred pennyworth's of sweating toil
Laid up by starvelings in my gilded trust;
That I have on my hounds and horses spent
The thrifty chapman's[1] slow and hard-earned hoard,
The struggling farmer's scraped-together rent,
The maiden's dowry, wifehood's pledge to her;
And even that poor dole, which bowelless
Gaunt Death had tossed, as bootless to itself,
Off to the widow and the fatherless;
That through my stealing so much wealth, whereon
The honours of great households had been piled,
For tiers of lives, those honours with a crash
Have fallen—— Have I done these things? No, no;
Not one of them, not aught like one of them.
And yet have all these things been done through me.
I gave up to a rogue, a wicked rogue,
My honoured name; and did not watch the rogue,
As he was making it a vile decoy
For luring wealth into his robber's den.
For this wandeed[2] I gave my lands to those
Who had been robbed. The lands were not enough;
And then I gave my tears, the only things
Yet left to me. They pelted these with taunts.

[1] Tradesman's.   [2] Want of deed.

Poor fellows! I have wronged them very much;
And I forgive them. In their pain I feel,
They, not in mine; I therefore can forgive
Them proudly; for they step by their unfairness
To my low level from their own high ground.
But as for slanderers unwronged by me
Who grope in blunder's every wayside ditch
For dirt to fling, I give to these my scorn.
I stand above them, and above their ditch.

XXVI.

GODARD *and* AARBERT.

GODARD.

The rubbish, Aarbert, which on your unguilt
In this great bankruptcy is being blown
By a wild storm of outcry, strikes me, too,
As here I stand beside you. Had we stood
On lower ground the rubbish would have passed
Over our heads not touching us at all.
Should not our knowledge then of many faults,
Which we indeed have, and of much unworth,
Teach us to take a stand beneath this storm,
Which sweeps along the level of the world?
It is our pride alone, which lifts us up
Into its range. Were not it wise in us
To leave the pride then to its world, to quit
Them both, and in a heav'n of lowliness
With Christ live lower than the world's ground, till
We live in heaven far above its height?
A Christian, waiting for a better world
Than this, has need of nothing more than food,
Lodging and clothes here. God assures him these;
And he enjoys at ease what more he has.

Aarbert.

What! Wise, say you, to quit the stormy world?
I know not whether once I might have liked,
And might have fitted on another man
Your reasoning, as worthy and Platonic;
But I am wounded, Godard! and I now
Cannot in even play of loosest speech
Fit it at all upon my state of grief;
Nor can I wear unfitting what so much
Presses my bruises. Whilst my pride is hurt,
Your comfort, lo, is that I kill my pride!
I never did a thing for which my pride
Should die; and should I kill it? If it cost
Me grief or care, so much the more will I
Love it so costly, and well worth the cost.

Godard.

Aarbert! the cost is greater than the worth.

XXVII.

Aarbert.

My mind is a Sun.   It fringes so with light
These slanderous clouds that they are glory-bright,
And thus that their will to wrong works out my right
    My mind were a Sun, although were I a slave.

My mind is a King.   Its doom, if it should say,
' Well done! ' would enough of honour on me lay;
Nor could it in saying, ' Ill-done! ' take away
    What honour, in dooming, it as kingly gave.

Let, therefore, my mind to all its brightness cling!
Let, therefore, my mind reign ever as my king!
Let never it crouch to be a creeping thing!
    Let never my mind become its honour's grave!

XXVIII.

AARBERT.

Oh, Bankruptcy! thou fell and deadly weed!
By what means hast thou gotten so much speed
As thus to choke the gasping fields of trade?—
From out the richest soil upsprings thy blade.
Thou thrivest by the trader's husbandry.
Heaven's rain and sunshine feed and ripen thee.
Thy root is deeply sunk in right's own ground.
Fair-dealing wind broadcasts thy seeds around.
And thus by help of God and man they mar
Time's harvest near thee, and beyond sight far.

XXIX.

AARBERT.

The arrows, striking at my breast, fall blunted
From off the breastplate of my proud self-knowledge.
Yet does their rattle on that breastplate pierce it,
And reach the heart defying them.　Moreover,
As round about me lie those fallen arrows,
The reek of their heap's witness is loud venom
Which slays my good name.　Oh! that name once
　　given
By God's self, once to me at birth, once only—
My good name, that which was from Him a passport
To all my neighbours, wheresoe'er I journeyed—
That dearer thing than life, my life's whole beauty,
Is dying even in their keep; whilst daily
The foul heap reeks.　My good name, oh, is dying!
With fevered flush and dying look at heaven
It breathes the air thus poisoned by the muchness
Of witness from those slanders though unrighteous

And dies within the keep of all my neighbours.
I thought that wrath was ripened into hatred
In but the venomed veins of fiends or vipers.
Can these be men, who fear to give me challenge
Within the law's fair tilt-yard; yet outside it
Behind its fence with deadly slanders shoot me?
If they be fiends, short rest have they from out of——
Hush! they are men; and I am man—I also.

XXX.

AARBERT.

What hateful feeling crawls with a tooth of venom
From those late thoughts of mine that I now am
        raking?
I kill, I kill that adder with utter gainsay.
Let not me harbour curses as e'en mere feelings.
Should man to man his brother do deadly mischief,
Unfelt, unknown, and thus by the man unwarded?
My feeling's curse by Heaven was heard with sorrow.
But Godard knows not aught of it.   I am thankful.
I hate his strange geleafs;[1] and have yet full often
To look above myself at the mind which holds them.

XXXI.

MILDA.

My husband! how most wicked are these slanders.
I quite geleave thus much of Godard's teaching,
That the Almighty, though we see Him never,
Yet reigns; and in the world with love and wisdom
Arights at last the wrongs of all who trust Him.

[1] Beliefs.

XXXII.

Godard *to* Aarbert.

Would these your losses, my brother, of wealth in the
    world ever fret you,
    Were heaven's wealth to you more than the world's
      whole wealth?
Would you, with heavenly wealth by you prized,
    brother, give it to get you
    This world's for thousands of years of unflagging
      health?   .

Would, would that, having the better and heavenly
    riches, you rather
    Rejoiced in these than at loss of the earth's repined;
Would, would that, soon to be hieing to heaven the
    home of the Father,
    Your love were less in the ties of the earth entwined.

XXXIII.

Aarbert, Milda, Sibriht, *and* Edda.

Aarbert.

Amidst the Poor will henceforth, Sibriht, be our lot—
    The wards of heaven! They, with worth and under-
      standing
As great as ours, live nigher heaven than we.   Let not
    Our gentleness, which curtseyed o'er wealth's sea,
      lie stranding
Here on its shoals 'mid breakers!—Gentleness is
    might
    Of strength within the check of love more mighty
      hiding.
It is a ton weight, falling with crush feather-light.
    It is a tiger's wary stepping as if gliding.

Stout bones and brawny muscles move its fleshy touch
  Of softest feeling.   It is cheerful, yet hates folly.
It truckles not to man, although it fears God much.
  It loathes, though pities, weakness—e'en of melan-
      choly.
Its power is yclad with lowliness.   Its wit,
  Though keen, is kind, not ever comic, coarse, or
      bitter.
It is frank, open, true, and loyal.   Honour governs it.
  Its rivalry is fair.   It shuns loud noise and glitter.
Learn it from God, Who checks with sand the tide-
      wave's tread;
  Whose lightning points the trembling needle north;
      whose showers
Of snow are hurled by nipping frosts on green life's
      bed;
  Who at His own cost quells with goodness Evil's
      powers.
From woman learn it.   Softer and less armed, indeed,
  Than aught that breathes, so strong is she in utter
      weakness,
That man, no less than babe, is of her help in need.
  It grows from woman.   'Tis herself, whilst, veiled
      with meekness,
She wrests from man proud homage. Oh, it is her own
  Self halo-crowned with coarsest works of love;
      which ever,
Like sparks of glory, fly from her, none having shown
  The least of might her mighty charms from her to
      sever.
It is that meek gethyld[1] wherewith she reigns as
      Queen
  Of Earth, beside man, crowned its King with
      strength and boldness.

<hr>

[1] Compassion, patience.

In man or woman, whilst it glows, it is love's sheen;
  And is fair courtesy, when stiff with deadly coldness.
But gentleness knows also how at duty's hest
  With grasp of steel to seize the means of fiercely
      wrecking;
Whilst its love halts from giving to its strength arrest,
  And whilst its reason's law alone is its self-checking.

MILDA.

My children! fallen as we are from all
  Of Aarwick's rank and pleasures, each of us
By zy [1] behaviour ought to make the fall
  Less painful to the others.   We should thus
Much lessen it.

SIBRIHT.

          Although, my mother dear!
  We lose the park, we have the road and fields,
And shall be happy.   Have I waked a tear?
  Why, many a joy the rambling through them yields.

EDDA.

Yes, happy, dear mamma!   Have not we here
Papa and you?   We should be anywhere
Happy with you and such a cosy home.
Days bright as Aarwick's often to us come.
We read nice books, too, here.   The one read last
Was about ships.   Now, list! were you to cast
A deep sea's lead into our happiness,
The—the——

SIBRIHT.

          Line's knots would prove it fathomless.
But, mother! since you into it will heave
No lead, you must, to gain such proof, inweave

[1] His, her (suus, see p. 54).

Into our speech your faith; and get the proof
From out the pattern of that warp and woof.

AARBERT.

God bless you both, my children! and reward you.

XXXIV.

AARBERT.

A goldfinch?   Yes.   Well caught, a very goldfinch!
Why, how it pants!   It fears me—me, the stricken,
The hunted down: as if I could have hurt it!
Why, even in my haughty days I never
Wronged willes [1] aught.   You wicked bird! to fear
      me.
These goldfinches sing well in cages?
Yes; what of that? poor fledgling!   It this morning
Was wholly free within its nest—so sheltered,
So blithe, so cared for, so allowed.   Poor fledgling!
I now might steal its little self and plunge it
Within the self of this great world.   I hate this
Great world, which, like an ogre, eats its children,
And calls the deed love.   Goldfinches are singers—
They do sing very sweetly.   Now, I wonder,
Could not I keep the songster, yet not do it
The least wrong—not the least wrong?   No, I could
      not,
I know that well, and so—heigho! this morning
It left its nest.   My nest needs much to cheer it.
But now this songster's nest—where hangs it?   Some-
      where,
Somewhere.   My own first nest was foully pillaged;
And what I now have is so bare and cheerless—
Heigho!   Poor bird, poor bird! thy nest.   The chirpers
There soon will follow thee to this wild woodland,

[1] Willingly.

And they will be at home here; thou too wouldest
In this free land have found the home thou seekest,
If I were not to steal, I mean, to take thee.
Yes, for the sake of thy sweet song hereafter
I mean to give to thee a varnished cottage
For all thy days.   It must be so.   My parlour
Is dark and dismal; and my banished darlings,
Who sit there all day long will need some cheering.
It must be so: I cannot help but do it.
But thou must love me.   What! why look so fright-
        ened?
Cannot I feed thee?   Have I wronged thee, birdie?
Didst not thou seek my path?   Was I the seeker?
Wast not thou straying here athwart my pathway?—
Ha! would I rob this goldfinch of its good name,
To make my stealing of itself more rightlike?
How Might, ere slaying Right, thus ever drags it
Off to its own plea's shed, made out of touchwood
From every rotten tree on which rains mercy!
I stand as Might here; yet shall Right have surely
Its life from me; and so that I may know it,
I fairly at the bar of that great Deemster
Who sits for God within me, that Inwitness,
Will stand.   I seized this bird: I found it straying
All ownerless athwart my path, the highway.

All ownerless?   Its Maker owns it.   Straying?
It was at home: it lodges here in freedom's
Large inn; I broke into its home and stole it,
When it, aweary with its life's first outflight
Of hope, here rested, unaware of aught that
Could have awakened eye-lust: little bilwhit![1]
It never costened[2] me.   It crossed my pathway,
Indeed; for though it knew not what was foeship,

---

[1] Innocent.   [2] Tempted by allurement.

Or why it feared, it, when it saw me, hurried
At fright's worst hint, with much ado and bustle,
To put its eyes beneath some heather's shelter.
Then it did naught amiss, and I am guilty! am I?
Have I to this no answer?—Yes, albeit
The bird was at its home, and not enticed me,
Its running drew my chase; and, ere I reasoned,
I found that I had taken from its freedom
The life.   The life is lost.   Its life of freedom
To luck is forfeited; and thus is left me
To choose if I shall keep its freedom's carcase.—
This plea is rotten.   Let the bird go, Aarbert!
I must; I fear so.   Stop! I have another
And better plea; I overlooked it.   Blockhead!
I but half knew my heart's brief.   Yes, the pleading
Is sound.   How wildly I till now have argued!
In nothing have I guilt.   My plea is clearly
This, that I hold the bird by right of lordship;
For man is lord of beast and fowl—I, lately
The wronged, and the bereft of all that——   Folly!
This is mere foolish talk.   Come, little songster!
I mean to gild thy cage; and thou therein shalt,
Through even winter's dearth, be feasted.   Just so.
I hold the right, and lose my time in scruples.
Besides, what boots thy freedom?   I will slay it
For thy behoof.   Forsake thy lowly life, then,
And live within my parlour out of danger——

Where I shall gar thy life be thy mere watching
From prison all thy herd of mirths outside it:
Where I shall gar thy life be thy mere passing
In woe from all thy share of weal untasted;
Where I shall keep fast-bound thy love of freedom,
That love of thine which is, of all earth's metyards,[1]

---

[1] Measuring rods.

The largest and most finely marked for telling
The pain of bondage, up to whatsoever
Pitch-tightened are the bonds: where I at daybreak
Shall hear thee sing a call to thy far fellows,
And shall await their answer; none shall give it:
Where I shall come up loving thee and courting
Thy love, whilst thou art pining and yet singing,
And loving only those free birds out roaming
Through uncaged air amid the light of heaven.
Wherever drops of dew and leafy greenness
Can catch their wings: nay, where, the more I love
          thee,
The tighter I shall make the bars about thee;
And these, which will be bars of brass or iron,
Shall stand about to smite thy flight against them;
Until thy nerves grow calm through utter hopeleast;[1]
Until thy swoop becomes a well-trained flutter,
That has its mirth withdrawn to eke my own mirth;
Until thy bones themselves, which all are airy
And full of flight, grow tame and fond of hopping,
And till thou sing out loudly for the breathing
Of all that stir-love which I thus shall smother—
Until, if thou wert loosed, the birds thou lovest
Would for the honour of their own free feathers
Hunt down a songster so undone, so fallen
From freedom's proud self-bearing.   Little goldfinch,
I could have given thee such love; I could have
In one gulp drunk thy helpless life's whole sweetness.
Quit my hand—fly; I have as yet not wronged thee.
Fly further.   So! I now am free as thou art:
And henceforth shall my thoughts be with thy carol
Blent in the blue-roofed and green hall of rainbows.
Fly further yet.   Now stay, until I bless thee.
Live long! live free! live merry! live, antwhether[2]

----

[1] 'Hopelessness.   [2] Notwithstanding,' in spite of.

Mock sportsmen who may make thy song their target:
And live, antwhether landlords who may grudge thee
Thine eating what is theirs and thine together:
Live, too, antwhether women who might set thee
Stuffed as their best of beauty on their bonnets.
Thou canst not fall to earth without God's knowledge
Sweet psalmist of the glade, by Him appointed
To thy high bardship at all landlords' charges.
May He then keep thee! I will share thy sweetness
In no whit lessened by my sharing largely.

BOOK II.

I.

AARBERT *and* MILDA.

AARBERT.

News, wife!   Now shall your mind beneath its weighty
Thought's tread shake, as the rafters of a house do,
Where huge, heavily-beating and steam-driven
Cogwheelworks with their whirling arms of iron
Thump, each thump with a thud like laden waggon's
Drawn o'er stones of a roadway built on arches.

MILDA.

What wreck's load are your hints behind them drag-
    ging?
What news mean you?   My fears are by your merry
Eyes mocked.   Aarbert! the fears are fed and frisky.

AARBERT.

This kiss therefore shall take the fears from off you;
Pay back straight to me one of yours as forfeit.
Prawst, godfather and fondest friend of Godard's,
Though fond never of me, I know not wherefore,
Died last week, and has left to him his money,
House, lands, even the whole estate of Prawstsel—
Worth half Aarwick's estate.   The news is startling.

"

How much more, then, is that which is to follow!
Dear good Godard, whom all the lechs [1] have often
Warned most earnestly not to stay in England,
Means, God willing, to quit it; and is going
Soon far southward—I fear, from what they tell me,
Too late going for hope of his there being
Lungail-healed. [2]   It is sad.   And he has asked me—
Guess what!—asked me to live in charge at Prawstsel,
Send one-third of its rents to him, whilst keeping
Two-thirds net for my stewardship.   His goodness
Outstrides thanks; they can never overtake it.
What storm-clouds do I see around you gather?
Whence this rain from your eyes in hope's mid-
          harvest?

MILDA.

Dear, dearest Godard! I indeed am grieved
To hear you speak so sadly of his health.
I much had hoped to see him well again.
And Prawst, too, good old man!   I am most pained.
You thought him not your friend, but such he was;
And we, for Godard's and our own sake, too,
Must speak of him with only thankful love.
The world has been indeed most loving; yes,
The stream of life that flows in all men's veins
Is but one river, trickling down time's rocks
By drops that, in their fall from point to point,
Keep each its roundness somewhat selfishly;
Yet always, elsewhere than at such points, glad
To meet in deeds of blessing and goodwill.
The more I love my fellow-beings all,
The more I find in them for me to love.
There is much goodness, Aarbert, in the world.

[1] Physicians.   [2] Lung ailment (consumption).

I hope my thanks may match its average.
But as for Godard, what a man is he!
And what a brother!   Dearest fellow, thanks!
Oh, whilst I thenk [1] of his ill-health, and then
His going far away for so long while,
A wish to weep in sorrow or in thanks
Is choking me.   My husband, I do feel
For Godard so much pity and such grief.

II.

AARBERT (*in self-talk*).

Dear, dearest Godard—lucky, lucky man!
Ah! only for my wife's and children's sake
I take this; it is like an alms to me.
But is he not my brother?   Yes, he is,
My younger, and the gift is much too large;
It weighs me down.   Yet must I take it.   Oh,
It would have been my bliss to give it him.
Say, Heaven! by my whole life's deeds sun-eyed
By Thee, and say, too, by its darkling thoughts
Pierced by Thy stars' sight—say by all of them
How rather I would give than take a gift.
No marvel that to give is sweet!   To give
Is lordship's right, the privilege of kings;
To take is but the shift of bounden need,
A bondsman's lowly duty.   Who to man
His mate would willingly be sold by want
A bondman, both to take a gift and pay
Thanks endless?   Hum! my sore is there, is it?
May not a man, then, love his bond to pay
Thanks endless? No?   Then does the freeman hate
The bond by which he freely binds himself?
Loves not the lover his free bond to love?

[1] Think.

The lover does so.   Hate I Godard, then?
No, Heaven help me! no, I love him, oh,
I love, I love him!   Yes, I therefore like
My love's own bond to give him endless thanks.
Though he has been so raised up, I so sunk,
I love him.   Dearest Godard, brother, friend!
Him whom I sent to Oxford; whom I gave
His vicarage, and welcomed at my house,
Whenever fancy brought him, till that time—
Name it not!   He has been upraised, I sunk;
I love him.   I am glad to see his weight
Borne lightly on the chariot of wealth,
Along the highway, up to courtly halls;
Whilst I upon my back bear forth from sight
My load of sorrows by some narrow lane.
Alas me! lucky Godard!   It is hard.
I cannot take this gift.   I must.   I won't,
At least, I would not.   Could I freely bend
My will so far to my lot's level?   No.
It must be taken.   What! to have my poor
Downfall arrested by my brother's youth,
Which saucy life's wave lifts above my age?
And then for me, that was the wealthy Squire,
To be through life, for but one slip of mine,
Thus made my younger brother's underling,
To cringe to him who ever cringed to me?
Cringed Godard?   No; he gave me honour's thanks,
All glowing from his love.   What thoughts are these?
I should not dare to show them.   God has willed
To lower me; my mind should now be low.
Meek, worthy, loving, honest Godard!—he,
My brother, too—my own dear loving brother, too!—
And who is now so ill.   Oh, hateful pride!
How loathsome art thou, Pride!   Hide, hide thyself.
I reasoned well erewhile, but reason rids

Not man of pride.   I hate it—hate myself.
Can this be Aarbert who has had these thoughts?

III.

MILDA *and* AARBERT.

MILDA.

Why, Aarbert, when I drew the bolts of slumber
That held thine eyelids, showed they to my wonder
The glassy brightness of thy mind's two windows,
So dimmed by streaming mist that they could scarcely
Give welcome to the cheery light of morning?
I pray thee tell me why that mist within thee
So blinded thee, whilst all the world around thee
Was flashing back in joy the beams of daybreak?

AARBERT.

I had been dreaming, I had dreamt, my Milda;
For up to midnight and beyond, while midnight's
Darkness, unmindful of the cock's crow, lingered,
I had been muning [1] how unworthy, hateful,
Unclean and small was pride, when o'er me slumber,
As darkness through that night's darkness, settled;
And with a soft hand loosed me from the knowledge
That chained my mind to past things.   I was quickly
Amongst some shadows, floating at my leisure.
In one of these I stayed.   It was an empty
And large hall.   It was mine.   I had a feeling
That there was something wrong about and in it,
And that I ought to leave it; but, in trying
To do this, found before the door some hindrance.
It seemed a heap of life there in the twilight's

[1] Meditating.

Gloom darkling.   I saw a face of some kind 'midst it,
And scanned this; but I could not from its shifty
Features catch one of them, so quickly flitted
Their short gleams, mingling one within another.
Sounds from the living heap I heard, however,
And lo! they were the words of someone speaking
The very thoughts that then were passing through me.
I thought of other things, and, lo! each thought came
In words distinctly back.   I shuddered.   What was
The speaker?   No good being, no one friendly!
I seized the door to pull it to me open;
What seemed my foe, whate'er it was I knew not,
Withstood me.   Then my will was fired with anger.
I pulled the door with all the might of madness.
It, with as wild a will, a will of madness,
Withstood me still; and so I gave up striving,
And stood bewildered, as before a being
Stronger than me, who, entering my mind, had
Seized my thoughts, making them its own.   My mind,
     which
Had all been whole and like a ship that off her
Dashed the big waves that leapt at her as fellows,
Here as a mass of stolen thoughts was more like
A wreck's planks flowing as the mates of water.
Long stood I, cowed.   At last the living heap rose;
And that which lived was all upright before me.
It was myself! my very self outside me!
We gazed at one another, I, astounded.
But soon I looked with fondness.   With like fondness
It looked on me.   I found that whatsoever
I did, it did at once; and still it gave me
My thoughts in words back.   Soon from out the heap
     rose
Other shapes slowly; these were each myself too,
In all my lifetime's moods of scorn, of anger,

Of haughtiness, of self-content, or vengeance.
They moved.   I sprang aside to let them pass me—
But whither?   There had been around me changes.
The lofty hall had grown into a temple.
And my grouped selves were as a pride-bent, stately
Stepfollowth [1] marching up its long nave eastward;
They marched, by twos, on slowly as the priests do.
My fond gaze, therefore, with the greater pleasure
Still tracked their steps; for these priests, true and
          holy,
As you know, Milda, since they so have told us,
March in church not at all for their own glory,
Well knowing always that to show themselves off
Where men had met to worship God were treason.
But now I looked about me.   In the niches
Of the great temple and upon its windows
The images of heavenly men and women
Were asking with the holiness of beauty,
The meekness of looks downcast, the assurance
Of marble, and the sinlessness of whiteness
The worship of my gaze; and whilst I noticed
That they were thus not flinching 'fore high heaven
From such a calm and stately show of worth-look,
Their daring woke within me fellow-feeling.
I caught their courage and my pride rose quickly.
At once a blast of wind, as if behind me,
Bore me off gliding to the temple's altar,
Behind which on a pedestal it set me.
Myselves marched onward.   Kneeling at the altar,
They gave me worship, singing but my praises,
And each in order telling some past thought mine
Of pride, of anger, self-content or self-trust,
Whilst each one thought so sung was duly ended
With these words: ' Still I do both well and rightly.'

[1] Procession.

I knew how, when, and where each thought had
   passed me,
I oft had worshipped thus myself. At last I marvelled
And thought thus: ' Here then stand I as my own
   God.'
The thought came back in loud words, uttered
By all myselves, and those words through the temple
Pealed echoing almost in tones of thunder.
I looked; the sky was black, the sun was lurid;
The temple's floor seemed whirling, so that all things
Seemed drifting there into a pit amidst it.
Those lovely statues, foremost! I could feel that
My pedestal was sinking. With some mighty
Bounds by the standing walls I left that chancel,
And, rushing to the temple's door there fled it.
Then sat I weeping, for my having yielded
So oft to the small sin of pride within me.
I cannot understand my dream, or wherefore
Its black sky, and the pit within that temple.
I soon will brush my sin off; there is power—-
That of the priest—to help me in so doing.
I never yet have sought this; I will seek it.

MILDA.

A fearful dream! When wearied mind and body
At night-time slumber, angels good or evil
Come in for talk with the lone ghost, and take her
Away from those tired sleepers. Godard tells me
That when, as in a holiroom,[1] thus lonely
She sits at night, God's self with her talks often,
Or sends her shapes of warning. Would I knew Him,
For I am sure that He is good, dear Aarbert!
Moreover, Godard speaks of having evils
Within him such as Christ alone can drive out.

[1] Sanctuary.

Your brother told me how, but I was restless,
And stayed not long enough to understand him.

IV.

Aarbert.

As once by holy Mother I was dubbed her knight
  In church, and at her font there unned [1] her sway,
So now I with her banner, and red-crossed aright,
  Ride forth my first one dragon foe to slay;
And, feasting in her bowers or in else her bright
  Grots fasting, as she bids me praise or pray,
I hope to have the strength from her and heart to fight
  Against each comer who would stop my way.
She girt on me my sword, and she in every plight
  Shall guide me, and be trusted as my stay.
By help from her I fight, and I, throughout death's
        night,
  Shall, resting in her blessing, wait for day·

V.

Godard *and* Aarbert.

Godard.

You trust in an ecclesia, which methinks
Is that of Rome, a gathering of priests
Mistaking lore mistaken from long-linked
Mistakes of a mistake of Peter's lore;
And holding fast the chain of their mistakes,
As if were its unbrokenness a proof
That they were linked with Peter's self by it.

[1] Acknowledged (owned).

A better proof that they are not so linked
With him or Paul is the un-Pauliness
And the un-Peterliness of the lore,
Which after all of their mistakes they hold.
Your trust should, Aarbert, be in Christ.   His own
Ecclesia (or in England's speech) gelathe [1]—
That great gelathe of those together-led
By God's self, and by Him enrolled in heaven,
Which here is in the wilderness of men,
Who know her not as once they knew not Christ,
But which Christ knows, He never has forsaken.
Yet not in even her her children trust.
They trust in God, and in the Son of God.
They trust, moreover, in God's holy writ,
Not in their thoughts of it.   The Holy Ghost
Gives them its meaning clearly as to things
Needful, and as to these their lore has been
Thus the same ever in those Glathemen [2] all.

AARBERT.

Ah! you take, Godard, from me all my prop; yet
Give me none other.   You have nowise helped me.
Yet, as God's Priest, you might have helped me
    greatly,
Had you, as largely as have many others,
Priestly assurance, showing priestly power;
Such an assurance as the priests of Rome have.
Nought is your Bible but a book to me; and
How can I trust in it, or there find helper?
Faith in weak Laymen, whom the Holy Mother
Feeds at priests' hands and theirs alone, is wholly
Faith by them gathered from the priest's assurance,

---

[1] Ecclesia.   [2] Members of the Ecclesia (Churchmen).

Shown in the boldness of his words; a Romish
Priest would say: ' I will, if I shrive thee, loose thy
Sins from thee, making thee as having not sinned.'

GODARD.

I dare not say this.   Read in history
   How lowly was of old the Christian knight.
Read how, by rule of Pauline chivalry,
   He, armed with merely hope as helmet bright,
The word of God as sword, broad faith as shield,
And love as breastplate, sought earth's battlefield.

Read how he there, a thus-armed ghost, as flame,
   With flame of God's own Holy Ghost inlit,
Bestrode his steed, which was his fleshly frame,
   Sitting its rider o'er the pomps of it:
And praying meekly, whilst he boldly fought;
And giving praise, whilst wilning[1] it in nought.

Read how he then was hindered by his steed
   In all this lowliness, and had with rein
To curb and stay it, and to guide its speed;
   For pride was flowing through its every vein;
And every thought in it bore earthly lust,
It reared, it pawed, with wayward will's self-trust.

Then read how, riding to his life-war's end,
   He forced the steed to help him in his aim
Of fighting fleshlife, and the world, and fiend.
   And all that pride of theirs which Christ o'ercame—
That priestly pride, that speaking in God's name
What God spoke not, and would, if spoken, blame.

[1] Desiring, coveting.

VI.

Aarbert *and* Milda.

Milda.

I little like that Jesuit with whom
You seem so often to have lately walked,
Straying from Godard's and from Arnulph's track.
He shirks, as even Glengly says, the road
Marked by the Bible's sign-post ' Heavenward.'

Aarbert.

I like his leading less and less, although
It wins me with a wizard's might along.
He leads me onward through enchanted grounds
Which, when by Glengly's help I climb again
To that highway, I thence see all are quagmire.

VII.

Arnulph, Aarbert, *and* Glengly (Costna *coming
up*).

Glengly.

See, Costna comes. Beware of him. I fear
That you have listened, Aarbert, much too oft
To that most zealous Jesuit. Beware!
For he will meet you, handling playfully
The rapier of his lore; and seeming e'en
To strip the bosom of his own geleaf [1]
To the sharp point of your misliking's sword,
Till you strip yours; when, gently numbing you,
His sophistry's baned sword will sting your mind's

[2] Belief.

Sheer nakedness.   He then will lead you off,
With eyes bedimmed by bane, toward the edge
Of this our Anglican faith's garden here,
Bestrewn with Romish flowers of ritual.
For at its Romeward edge the garden lacks
A wall of hindrances; the wall has slipped;
And whilst the ground here merely slants, it there
Sinks with a leap into the popish gulf.
Hear, Heaven, as to Costna's faith.   God speaks
By dooms.   All kingdoms and all commonwealths,
Whatever means or want of means were theirs,
Of whatsoever race of men they were,
And in whatever clime they were on earth,
Have, as they have been Protestant, been raised;
And, as they have been popish, sunken down.
Not in the rule that these things should be so
Has there been ever breach.   The rule is thus
As sure, as are the laws that guide the stars.
But here he is!

Costna.

Ha! Aarbert!   Here amid blithe friends in talk
As to the rules of tennis, whether ripe
Somewhere for bettering, or—nay; but as
To whether in the State be not some wheel
Faultless which ought to give its room to one
Of later build!

Aarbert.

Sir, I would rather chaffer
Words as to such a wheel, than as to things
Whereof we know, whose worth at most to me
Is less than that of their asked price in time.

Costna.

Is that so? Your young brother, as I hear,
Has had dark reasonings with you. Take care.
No warrant has he as a priest. His sect
Has grown to be a wreck. It has thrown off
Some hundred sects as splinters from its schism.
Lose not the lore which I instilled in you.
There is on earth but one gelathe, and that
Is Rome's. The splits from it are therefore schism
From Christ. Its chief is on St. Peter's throne,
A king with power in heaven, earth, and hell.
He, helped by Blessed Mary, Queen of Heaven,
Can ward away from men the wrath of Christ.
His priests, too, can, by warrant of writ holy
Read aright, offer Christ as sacrifice
For sin. Such things no other men can do.
Outside the one gelathe is there no hope
Of heaven, no forgiveness, to man's soul;
And clearly not mid Protestants, those men
Of cheerless faith. But I am glad to know
That many, Aarbert, of your countrymen,
Though Godard be not one, alas for him!
Wish to come back to us. I tell you, sir,
Your love of holy writ and of God's day,
Your Sunday-schools, your hospitals, your strength,
And well-earned welfare, claim our thanks to God.
And yet we thank Him for your passing now
From all that you have been apart from us.
Some of you kneel before our crucifix;
And some before the blessed Virgin kneel.
Some of you speak as Priests. Alas! that speech
Is play at priestwork; all your work as Priests
Is worthless, for you cannot change good bread
Into the living flesh and blood of Christ.

Who had them once on earth.   You Protestants
Have not a priesthood; yet you, robed as priests,
Outdo our rites.   This makes us hunger for you.
Since we agree that as St. Peter's heir
The Pope is King of kings and Lord of lords,
Why stand you from His sway aloof?   Oh, why?
Come wholly to us.   There may haply be
Some faulty ground of ours, not having yet
The Holy Father's notice, which ourselves
Can quit, that we may nearer come to you.
Call Him your Father; unn Him as your King.
Untruth to Him is that one only sin
For which there is in hell no cleansing fire,
And no forgiveness; since it cuts off souls
From any way to heaven.   Take your faith
From only Him.   Faith Catholic alone
Has in all kingdoms, and at all times, held
Its sameness.   You can therefore trust in it,
And it will guide you to the Bible's meaning.

ARNULPH.

Aarbert! your brother tells you that in things
Most needed for man's life through Christ the best
Guide to that meaning is the Holy Ghost.

COSTNA.

As speaking by the mouth of each of you?

ARNULPH.

No; but as speaking to the mind of each:
So that each one may know the meaning, and
May utter this, but not as law by which
He binds the mind of any other man.

COSTNA.

Come, Aarbert!   I so oft have through my lore
Led you that you must wish to pass it.   Come!

AARBERT.

Not so, dear Costna!   I have been indeed
Your scholar, and have followed your tall teaching,
Although, whereas it was too near mine eyes,
I could not view it well, or know in all
What thing it was which I was following,
But I have since then seen, as you have guessed,
Its cloud-capt height cast wholly to the ground
By the bright sun of heaven; so that now
It lies below me as mere length on earth,
Thus darkened, and the more I scan its shape
In this dark shadow's answer, I the more
Mislike it.   Sir, its limbs, its head, and all
Its body, if I so may speak, I mean
Its doings, goings, teachings, and whole state,
So hurt my look that I would wish to see
No more of them; and fear to trust myself
Into the power of so grim a guide.

GLENGLY.

No, Aarbert! we will go to neither Rome
Nor cold Geneva; but will warm our faith
With the mild glow of worship Anglican,
Amid the pomp of rightful ritual.

VIII.

GLENGLY, AARBERT, GODARD, *and* ARNULPH.

AARBERT.

Godard! I tell you, though to your great grief,
That I from Costna, you, and other men,

Hear now against the faith of England, now
Against Rome's, that which gars me loathe all faiths,
And hold that pomp is worship's better half.
Your faith is shifting. Whether England's glathe
Be sister or be daughter unto Rome's,
She will be Romish; she will deck herself
With gold and scarlet, jewels, pearls, and lace.

GODARD.

I hope not so: her churches till restored
To fever-flush of sickly art were all
With fond love whitewashed from its death, and still
Herself as yet in them stands hale at heart.

GLENGLY.

But Godard, I, although I like not Rome's
Gelathe, yet like her churches thus bedecked.
I like them dark with smoke of incense; dark
With window-stains that give earth's hues to light
Of heav'n nor let it show earth's paltriness
Too flashingly, I like her images
That win, like players in a playhouse, awe.
My awe is merely that which I have felt
In such a house; but man is made for awe,
And wants some trickery to bring this forth.
When churches Anglican then settle down,
As do the Roman, in the very depth
Of worldly wants, I speed their sinking thus.
Most glad am I that, whilst their tiny spires
Point heavenwards, their naves with earthy sweets
Are crammed full, and their transepts are stretched
        out,
As our good Mother Earth's dear kindly arms,
To clasp all comers to her loving breast.

Aarbert.

What matters, if we good and happy be,
What are our faith and style of worship?   Yours
Suit you, and Costna's him; so also ours
Suit us, and all are in their own way good.

Arnulph.

Aarbert! do yours suit God?

Godard.

Why, Aarbert, feast in Church your fleshly eye?
   Why there sip sweets that sweeter are elsewhere?
Since to live fleshly-minded is to die,
   Why not, then, die where earth is merrier?

Come to Christ, brother!   God will welcome thee.
   But come to it as ghost to worship Ghost,
Who hates a worship bright with trickery,
   And loves men least when they love that the most.

As for that jewelled harlot who to kings,
   Rich men, and leaders holds her golden cup,
You, if you thence sip wine and sweetened things,
   Must drink her boast and all its madness up.

She boasts of oneness: it is offness mere
   From all not one with her.   She boasts of peace:
The peace lasts only during lifetime here,
   And needs blind trust in her not meanwhile cease.

She boasts that all her children hold one faith:
   One faith is by them all not held but said;
And faith, which through them she in one age saith
   Is faith from hers in other ages strayed.

She boasts of helping order; but the strength
  Of evil in the help slays order's life.
Not one realm ruled by her has not at length
  Been full of misrule, restlessness, and strife.

IX.

AARBERT, GODARD, GLENGLY, *and* ARNULPH.

AARBERT.

Nay, Godard! trust no more the jealousy
Which tells you that I like those Romish Priests
Who aim to rule the kingdoms of this world.
Costna no longer is a friend of mine.
I dread those Pontiffs, though I like their pomps.
I loathe the silly and the lying tales,
The murders and misrule of Rome's gelathe.[1]
Yet were it well, if we could gain her strength
From even evils like hers, were they stripped
Of all the sting and bane to health in them.
Might not a stingless evil work out good?

GODARD.

Is there an evil which has not a sting?
Is there an evil which banes not the health?
Is there an evil which is not accurst?
No, nor is there an evil which brings strength.
Nay, more: to do an evil that a good
May thence come, bringing to the doer strength,
Is but to do the evil twice, and twice
To call and bring God's wrath to crush the strength.
God works out good from evil which is done
By any foe of His; yet surely gives

[1] Ecclesia.

The evil-doer what woe evil earns.
Rome feigns to shelter from that God-sent woe
Those who do evil for her good.   For this
Most evil deed woe doubled waits herself.
What though she from the evil wards awhile
The woe by means more evil; that woe grows:
Yet only by those evil means, those stings
Of evil, as you call them, could she do
Evil without her losing strength at once.
And who could do it otherwise, if she could not?
What men could, copying the masterpiece
Of Satan's wisdom, hope to better it?—
That wisdom earthy, soulish,[1] devilish,
Whose crimes, although to crush her at the last,
Are for a while allowed to be her stay?

Glengly.

But England's churches even now with gain
Have copied those of Rome in things which you
Call evils—they are filled with images.
And, see, I pray you, they thereby have grown
Already more, and stouter, and more strong,
By being fed with them and ritual.

Arnulph.

Churches thrive often in a starved gelathe.

Godard.

Oh, Glengly! if I thought that aught could gain
Net strength or soundness through the wilful breach
Of one of God's laws, not one word of His
Would I thenceforward heed.   Now, God forbids,
With the most fearful of His earthward threats,
An image in a church.   So understood

[1] Sensual (see p. 27).

The Jews; and they, to help their faith, had none
In synagogue, and none that met the sight
Of more than Priests in e'en the temple's self;
Whilst God by Christ's death brought to naught e'en those
Which He had willed should in that temple stand.
Moreover, the gelathe of Christ, whilst whole
In all her outward shape, and whilst He dwelt
Within her outer wholeness, when she thus
Well knew His mind, so loathed aught looking like
An image in her churches, through her first
Three hundred years, that, even in her fourth,
Good Bishop Epiphanius, having seen
With wonder in a church a curtain smirched
With a fair shape of Jesus, tore it down
In wrath and horror, bidding men to wrap
A rotting corpse in it.   Can our gelathe [1]
Thrive, therefore, whilst, against the laws of God—
As written by Himself with threats, as read
By all the Jews until Christ's time, as read
After that time by Christians all for quite
Three hundred years in which Christ guided them---
She lets fond, foolish men set images
Upon her churches' windows and behind
Those churches' tables?   No!   Be sure that God
Will answer with ill-speed that deed of theirs.
The winds of speed may waft idolaters
From rightful worship's haven; but the storms
Of wanspeed [2] wait to sweep them through the seas
Forlorn and freightless.

GLENGLY.

We worship not a crucifix's stone.

---

  [1] Ecclesia,   [2] Adversity (want of speed).

GODARD.

But if you worship with its stony help
God, He forbids this as idolatry.

GLENGLY.

That I allow.   But stones may rightly teach
What to revere and worship.   They are books
To those who cannot or who will not read.

GODARD.

Ah! ah! I know.   Mere sophistry, my friend!
Mere sophistry! the once strong, boasted child,
Now old and cloakless, begging, lame, and deaf,
Of Gregory's proud Hope; soon after birth
From which Nicea's second council smashed
Its lustihood by rule that second-rate
Worship be paid to images as shapes
Of unshapes having first-rate worship.   This,
As you allow, is sheer idolatry.
For stones, when worshipped as are Gods, are Gods,
Not idols unto those who worship them.
Idolatry's growth knows no stop.   Its eld's [1]
Death-guilt is to its naughtiness of youth
Assured; as God knows, Who forbids a man
To make an image for his worship's use
As ornament, or teacher, or aught else,
As much as He forbids him worship it.
True Christians loathe its use.   Lactantius
In the three hundredth year from Christ's birth, wrote:
' All pictures are forbidden in a Church,
Not only heathen, those of saints are too.
Where pictures are Christ's worship cannot be.'
Augustine wrote, ' The force of images
Is but to crooken souls.'   What says our own

<hr>

[1] Old age's.

Beloved gelathe?   ' No preaching of the Gospel
Or other stay or means can help against
Idolatry where images help worship.'
But what says God?   ' Near where thou makest thee
An altar shalt thou not set up an image;
For this the Lord thy God hates utterly.'
Will our gelathe cast ever forth again
Her pictures from her churches?   They, alas!
Are now the country's idols.   You mislike her.
You want a new gelathe.   Oh, might we keep,
But cleanse her—keep her cleansed, although we lost
Her Rome-stained churches!

ARNULPH.

I pray you, Glengly, mark me as I sketch.
Christ's gelathe, that of all the newly born
Who are, or will be, or have been, by God
Into the fold of Christ ' together-led,'
That great gelathe, known only by Himself,
Whose one and only Head is Christ in heaven,
And whose All-Teacher is the Holy Ghost,
Is guileless and unworldly; full of love,
Of hope and mercy, trust and holy joy.
She lives unveiled before her God, and lives
Therefore above the need of earthly helps.
She takes her faith from only holy writ.
She worships naught but God; and worships God
With naught of brightness from a tricksy flash,
But with the brightness of meek, cheerful love,
And thankfulness.   She loathes a worship pompous,
And likes to pray within walls clean and bare,
That she may pray with cleaner faith.   She stands
On only God's stay here, yet stands she fast.
Of such was the dear glathe of England once.

Now look with me at Rome's gelathe.   You see
Her guileful, haughty, worldly, stained with blood,
Unholy, lusting for both gold and sway.
She hates the Bible; worships many things
Other than God, and worships God beneath
A veil of rites all steeped in earthiness,
With, 'twixt His jealous and her own fond eyes,
A grove of God-forbidden images,
Such as herself deemed heathenish, until
After four hundred years she loved them much.
She lives on earth coquetting with earth's kings;
Lives but by earthly helps, grasps all of these
Or good or evil, sets aside God's laws
And overrules them with her own at will;
Yet for awhile she floats, and tightly floats
Over her waiting death's gulf, buoyed by e'en
Her very hollowness of skill-wrought worth.

GLENGLY.

I want not either of two such gelathes.

ARNULPH.

No; but the one you want, nor standing thus
All ghostly on the ghostly rock of Christ,
Nor floating thus all worldly on a sea
Of worldliness would on a quicksand lie
Where neither heaven nor earth would give her stay;
And there would wait till broken up by storms,
Or till Rome's Priesthood took her off a wreck.

X.

Aarbert, Godard, Ankirkly.

Aarbert.

Lo! here is Godard.   You can get his answer.

Ankirkly.

Godard, I grieve that you mislead your brother.
The great gelathe of Rome holds all the Fathers
And Councils General.   It holds, moreover,
That Pontiff-king, the Pope, whose sway is needed
By Christendom, whose lore in undefined things
He also yet may mould to meet our pleasure.
Then if both we and such as we will Rome-shape
Our own mislore, the whole great world of Christians
In oneness with the headship of Rome's Pontiff,
May, with a crushing force against outsiders,
Await with him in joy Christ's second coming.

Godard.

Has Rome's Chief Pontiff reason thus to wait this?
Then where is seven-hilled Babylon, which once was
O'er all earth reigning, and was seen from Patmos
About to be the faithless Bride of Jesus,
And ghostly harlot of the Earth's kings, selling
To them for earthly power of theirs Christ's ghostly
Power, and making all the Earth's realms drunken
With her drugged wine of harlotry, and being
Drunken herself with blood of Christian martyrs,
And sinking then at last in flames for ever,
With all of hers, not leaving trace behind her,
As soon as Christ was seen on Zion standing?

I ask for knowledge; where is that great city,
The seven-hilled o'er earth in John's day reigning,
And being, when Christ came, to sink thus wholly?
She not as yet has so sunk: not as yet has
The Lord come.   She is standing somewhere: where
  then?
And where is but in her, the man of sin too,
Who lived in Paul's day, waiting somewhat's passing,
Which then was known, and being to be crushed when
The Lord came?   All has passed which barred his
  being
Revealed.   He somewhere lives: and where, then?

ANKIRKLY.

I know not.   Who can understand the Bible?
My faith is from the teaching of the Fathers.

GODARD.

But mine is from the Bible which God's children
Well enough understand, and which has told me
That St. John saw a ten-horned, seven-headed
And scarlet theor,[1] ridden by a woman
Arrayed in purple and in scarlet, decked with
Gold, costly stones, and pearls; who, whilst her right
  hand
Held out to all the world her whoredom's golden
Cup of idolatry and filth, was titled
On forehead: ' Babylon the great, the Mother
Of Harlots and abominations earthly.'
That St. John saw her drunk with blood of martyrs;
That he was by an angel told that she was
The city seven-hilled o'er earth then reigning;

---

[1] Wild beast (in Greek, ' thērion ' ; in Old English, ' deor,' whence
Derby and Durham).

And that St. John foresaw this city sunken,
Together with all hers, in flames for ever.
In God's Book she and hers are foreseen sunken;
But she has not so sunk yet; she is standing.
And where is she if not at Rome?   Yourself say!

ANKIRKLY.

Who gave the world its Bible?   Rome's gelathe did.
Who brought this Bible into England?   She did.

GODARD.

The world had erst the Bible from its writers.
And Christians, long ere Rome had claimed all Chris-
        tians
As hers, both made that list of these men's writings
Which bears the Bible's name, and brought the writ-
        ings
Hither to England, as our Holy Bible.
Augustine hither brought Rome's anti-Bible
Of teachings from her then much mistaught Fathers,
Together with that saying of his Master's,
Even of Gregory the Great who sent him,
He who shall call himself priest universal
Foreruns the anti-Christ.   In ten years' time came
Boniface, that forerunner.   In three hundred
Foul years whereafter, men more foul or wicked
Than popes breathed not upon this earth, by witness
Of cardinals, and Rome's gelathe's self chose them.
Moreover, she was taking, or had taken,
Back under Christian names the rites and statues,
The feasts and much too of the lore of Pagans,
For. sake of that same oneness now so wished for.
Was Christ, who guides His own gelathe, then guiding
Rome's?   Surely not so: She was anti-Christian.

Gregory's anti-Christ and anti-Bible
Of Christo-pagan lore were brought to England
By your Augustine, smothering Christ's Gospel,
And God's own Bible's teachings long here settled.

XI.

AARBERT, GODARD, *and* GLENGLY.

AARBERT.

If Rome's gelathe and that of Christ lie where
Arnulph, methinks, once rightly showed them each.
Then that of Christ is founded on a rock
Cut sheer away from all on lower earth;
Whilst that of Rome as steadfastly is founded
Beneath the rock upon the lowest ground
On which earth-loving air can press its kiss:
And twixt the two grounds merely is a slope,
Which yields no rest by one fixed stay of thought
On level and unyielding utterness—
On utterness of all unworldliness,
Or else on utterness of earth's whole helps.
I do beseech you, Godard, not to fear
That I shall stand upon the lower ground,
Or on the slope that yearns down toward it;
But hope not ever my acknowledging
That on alone the slope and lower ground
Are found those flowers fair of ritual
Which I acknowledge that I greatly love.

GLENGLY.

Godard, I take upon myself what blame
You give your brother's love of ritual.
For from my own heart into his has passed
That burning love; so what you have to say

Against it will you please to say to me.
Yon sun will soon be setting; will you, sir,
With evening's calm, unhasting mind set forth
Your reasons why such love as ours is wrong?
Lo! here a quiet nook!   Shall we three sit?
The seat is cosy.   Now then, Godard, thresh
This thing out here, until the flighty chaff,
If any of unsoth in aught I said to him,
Shall fly away from underneath your flail
Of reasoning and leave me grain on which
My love shall have the right to feed at will.
Aarbert shall listen; but on me alone
Shall fall your chiding, if it fairly can.

GODARD.

In heaven worship is no player's plot.
   Good angels redden not their zeal's own glow.
Love shows not off herself, and soth wears not
   Fair mask: she loves her fairer face to show.
Of cold things ceremony most is cold;
And no man paints his rubies or his gold.

Can earthness higher than it rises raise?
   Can Godward feeling, as it 'neath thee flows
From carvings, gildings, stains, and priestly plays,
   Buoy thy ghost Godward high above these shows?
Must not she quit all earthness to arise
To heaven's mercy-seat beyond earth's skies?

Why this church-garnish?   Has thy drawing-room
   Been searched by God?   Has He with hungry look
Been begging worldly things for chasing gloom
   Of ghostliness from Church's every nook?
He asks thy best, and weenst thou that if these
He sees thy best things, thee as His He sees?

Is't Christ who wants the garnish?   He has died
   To earthiness, and lives He to earth's glory?
Or have His earth-poor for the rubbish cried?
   Need these see stones to know His Gospel's story?
Are not God's poor less babylike and blind
Than are the world's rich both in mood and mind?

If thou believest with thine eye or hand,
   If guns must roar that tales of war may reach
Thy wits, or if, ere words thou understand,
   Thy flesh must to thy mind their meaning teach,
Yet God has gifted poor men otherwise,
They love His words and look on stones for lies.

What hangs from off thy neck?   Men would-wise
         scorn,
   And men self-righteous stumble o'er Christ's cross:
Christians from earthlife by its wrench are torn.
   But that toy!   Brings it thee an earthlife's loss?
Bears not it earth's stamp?   Does the earth-King care
Of what a shape His own stamped trinkets are?

Christ's cross, if thine, is that thou diest in Him
   A felon's death for evil by thee wrought.
Thy carved cross is the cross of felons grim
   Who put to death thy Hælend.   It is nought
But Pilate's cross and that of priestly Jews,
Of Abbas and Barabbas and such crews.

If with mind nailed to Christ's stern cross indeed
   Thou wend without the world's camp, and live there
His death to earthness, thou wilt never need
   Bear shapes of Roman gibbets everywhere;
Which witness, whilst thou wearest them in pride,
That such art thou as those by whom He died.

But on thy duty laid athwart thy lot
  Do thou thy fleshly length and breadth outspread?
That what of earthlife in thee likes them not
  May hang on these until that thing be dead.
For clear of earth-mist by these crosses' death
Thou freelier wilt breathe sweet heaven's breath.

XII.

Milda *and* Aarbert.

Milda.

Lurked last night in the bowers of your brain,
  Ere locked by sleep, that thief of night's rest, Care?
Or into them had that rough burglar Pain
  Burst afterward? or did I thence but scare
A dream? when, hearing uproar through your frown,
I woke you, and put thus the uproar down.

Aarbert.

I was in church where men, as priests attired,
  Were worshipping with all a stage play's arts
In costumes gay and quaint: sith they desired,
  For bettering of worldly people's hearts,
To have them where men's worship would be warmed
By seeing it in tragic style performed.

The church amidst an abbey's ruins stood.
  Man's skill was shown off in its fretted stones.
The window's stains showed off man's self as good.
  Brass outlines honoured there man's buried bones.
Man's bowings there to God with pomp were done;
And with a waive there worshipped everyone.

There graven images were raised as teachers.
　There candles gleamed to show a ghostly light.
There pastors were of rites and manners preachers;
　There altars held up flowers to God's sight;
Whilst incense toned down daylight for a wheaten
God's being there made flesh, adored, and eaten.

I left the church, and, looking forth, beheld
　The abbey; it had been unroofed when mind
Sought heaven's light.　Its pillars all lay felled;
　And in its wall's rift stood mid howling wind
An old man; him would I have passed aloof:
He stopped me.　Pointing to the shattered roof,

' So wrecked,' said he, ' are realms where idols preach:
　Where word of man undoes God's holy Word;
Where priests bear rule, through what they wrongly
　　　teach;
　Where kings wield priestcraft as their shield and
　　　sword;
And where the people love to have things so.
Whence comest thou, and whither wouldst thou go?'

MILDA.

My husband! whence this dream, and why, and how?
From Godard's chidings in your sleep awake?

AARBERT.

Such church I oft have seen.　I make a vow,
On keep of which my very life I stake,
To crush my pride and most that pride whereby
My singing there God's glory was a lie.

MILDA.

Oh, Aarbert! Pride, which, more than evil, is
The king of evil, cannot by a vow

Be overcome; nor can such hopeful words
As you have uttered daunt him. So at least
It seems to me; but I am woman weak,
And you are stronger. As for me, I unn
That when I have defied him with such words,
I soon have found that it was he hiself
Who put the bold defiance in my mouth;
And that he never with a stronger grasp
Held me than whilst he crowned me with the hope
Of being his o'ercomer and his Queen.
Whenever I have led against his walls
My whole armed powers, he has cheered me on;
Has aimed my weapons at his weakest points;
Has been the soul of my most bold assault;
And thus, by leading me against his might.
Has ruled my own. But this I say as one
Who has by failing found her weakness out.
I know that you are stronger than your wife.

AARBERT.

Now, Milda! are you quite against my weal,
And are my foe. Pride! I will harry thee
From any home in me; so help me, Heaven,
As I will do this. So then, to begin:—
Too wrathsome am I; thou shalt nevermore
Lay me low henceforth by mine angriness.
Upon the keeping this my vow to God
I stake all right to hope of reaching heaven.

MILDA.

War is the life-breath of the better self
In man or woman, Aarbert. I myself
Am not without some knowledge of the war.

The feather of my cheek has often blocked
Your hurry's too straight path to evil things,
Which, being in a line with your eye's sight,
Were so foreshortened that you merely saw
Their winsome face and heard their speech.   Now, I
See from aside the body of this vow:
It meets you as an Eden's angel-snake—
A helper sent you by the fiend to seize
You either by proud hope or reckless wanhope.[1]
Why ask you not for Godard's help?   He fights
With evil as it comes.   He says that best
It is to crush an evil by God's might;
For then God rules the heart that crushes it;
And that the might of God is dealt to faith
And prayer when needed by them; but that vows,
Though overcoming by the might of pride,
Other things overcome not so Pride's self.
He oft has told me of this Pride: he says
That in man's mind there is a tower built
Upon the hill of honour by the fiend,
The king of evil, and that this his tower
Is named man's pride.   And Godard says that when
The troops of evil have been driven out
By good from other places in the mind,
They win within it shelter, and do thence
With more of power often rule the man.
He says that some men stoical, although
From lust of honour, wealth and beauty free,
Are there by Pride's whole power often swayed;
That Anchorites, barefooted and coarse-garbed.
Have also in that tower oft been forced
To pay as toll to Satan, king of evil,
The most of all their fasts' and scourgings' winnings.

---

[1] Despair.

AARBERT.

Though be thou, Pride! a stronghold's tower built
On highest ground within the realm of mind,
Where good and evil ever are at war—
A tower, which is by the choicest troops,
The life-guards, of the king of evil held;
And unto which, if driven in by good
From that realm's weaker parts, all evil flees
For shelter from the utmost might of good:
My whole soul, standing at thine iron gate,
Hurls challenge at thee; for although thou be,
Thou oughtest not to be in man at all:
Nor canst be ever in a stalwart man
Like me, in whom is will that thwarts thy mood.
Therefore I, having sworn that by my might
I will for ever bring down thine in me,
And having staked upon the vow my hope
Of heaven, now shall surely keep it whole.
The thing is done.   I overthrow thee, pride,
And, henceforth lowly, am of fault all clear.

XIII.

AARBERT *and* MILDA.

AARBERT.

I wonder, Milda, that you see not well,
That I must overcome by this my vow.
Know not you that the will of man is free?
And that he, as he wills, can do the right,
Or do the wrong?   By that my will I did
My duty when I chose, and, when I chose,
I left it undone.   I have often slipped
In carelessness, but not in weakness once.

When found you weakness in me? Now, this pride
To which for pleasure I have yielded me
Too often, and for which I now so blush,
Is one of feeling. Can my will not quell
That feeling? You will see. I tried at first
To quell the pride with churchy ritual;
But there was in the churchiness much pride,
And so I failed. So shall my will not fail
To-day. Do not you see this, Milda, now?

MILDA.

May not there be some pride in this your will?

AARBERT.

No. If I will to be not proud, my will
Is lowly. Surely you must needs see that.

MILDA.

I cannot reason as do you by words;
I only can by means of daily things.
I know this thing that I have often willed
To do aright, and yet have done awrong.

AARBERT.

I never knew you do one thing not good;
Your reasoning is therefore bad. No, no:
There is no evil in you, Milda, none.
Why cover you your face with both your hands?

MILDA.

For that upon the glass of this your praise
I am so black and foul that it is meet
For me to hide a thing so hideous.

Aarbert.

Dear, foolish Milda.   Well now, we shall see.
I go into the town here; fare we well.

XIV.

Aarbert.

That slander!   Oh, that snare! that stumbling-block!
  The broken vow!   The deep-stained robe of pride!
The ditch!   God's truth there like a sharp-edged rock!
  And the stain branded with a rent so wide!

Can any deep-drawn sigh bring back the dead?
  Can any primrose soap make dirt's self clean?
Can black be brightened into white?   Can thread
  So sew up rent that it shall not have been?

I never now can say I have no stain:
  I cannot say again I could have stood:
I never can unfallen be again:
  Nor can be, as my vow had made me, good.

XV.

Aarbert *and* Milda.

Aarbert.

When man first rises to flee a sin that loves him,
  And that had ruled him by his love's own will,
The charmer, rising in all her power, proves him
  With tenfold wiles, and so she holds him still.

Then when he finds her to be a fiend that seized him,
  That she might lure him into endless woe,
And finds the charms, wherewithal she so much
      pleased him,
  To be the witchcraft of a deadly foe,

' Thy gift this, Wisdom? ' he cries—' the gift of seeing
 A traitress life-long in my fond love hide,
From whose embraces I lack the means of fleeing?
 Away thy gift and thou—nay, both abide! '

MILDA.

  Ha! learnedst thou that song of me?
   I knew and sang it long ago.
  No, never sang I that to thee—
   I sang one like it, running so:

Song.

When woman rises to leave the faults which love her,
 And whose charms oft had given her delight,
Those faults rise also to keep, or else recover,
 Her love with ten times all their former might.

Then, when she feels that they each are but a fever,
 Which woos her soul for Death, her suitor grim,
And feels that, since she is loath that they should leave
  her,
 Her soul must marry, and be marred by him.

' Thy gift this, Wisdom? ' she cries—' the gift of feel-
  ing
 That faithless friends in my warm friendship hide,
To give me hurt which they hold me back from
  healing?
 Take back thy gift—stay, Wisdom: let it bide! '

BOOK III.

WORLDLY LIFE CROSSED BY CHRISTIAN LIFE.

I.

Godard, Aarbert, Lesgeleaf, *and* Milda.

GODARD.

Something I see by your careworn face has been fret-
    ting you, Aarbert!
What is it? Where is your sore? What is it ailing
    you thus?

AARBERT.

Yes, I indeed have a mind's sore; but why lingers
    your sailing?
Sickness, I fear, gains ground now on your linger-
    ing steps.

GODARD.

Yet shall I tarry till winter is nearer; for, brother, be-
    sides what
Business stays me, my love yearningly clings to
    you all.

AARBERT.

Ours not less to you fondly. You ask me what ails
    me; I answer,
Knowledge of ailing; a fall into the wist that I fall,
Deeming, as ever I did, that I stood by a strength of
    uprightness,
Whence by my sheer free-will, never in weakness, I
    sank.

Last week staked I my life on walking clear of a fresh
 fall
 Into an old fault mine, wrathness, arising from pride
Wounded; for I will acknowledge that, stung by the
 taunts of the poor men
 Here by the bankruptcy robbed, oft have I into the
 fault
Hurried: on that same day of my staking on walking
 from fault free,
 Life-everlasting's bliss, into the fault did I sink.
Now have I tried what strength I had boasted, and
 now for the first time
 Clearly have seen that the strength merely in fancy
 was mine.
Now, antwhether[1] my whole strained powers, have I
 for the first time
 Sunk into sin, and have thus utterly fallen from
 hope.

GODARD.

Brother, when Adam was good as his God first made
 him he sinned, caught
 Sin-love, and gave it as plague down to his children
 for aye.
Thou hast been born in the plague, in its weakness,
 and death, and uncleanness;
 Therefore, whereas having health, strength, and the
 blessing of God,
He fell into the plague, canst thou, plague-stricken
 and weakened,
 Stand? No; never hast thou borne thee uprightly
 an hour;
Neither shalt thou from his sins' fall, even in worship
 of God, rise,

---

[1] In spite of.

Till by the new birth, asked erst at thy christ'ning
    for thee,
Then, too, granted against thine own faith's taking the
    gift up,
  Thou shalt have Christ's life thine, thou shalt have
    Christhood in full.
Thou, though striving with God, hast been walking as
    righteous before Him,
  Rating Him wrong in the strife, charging its guilt
    upon Him.
Whilst thus warring against Him, what one deed has
    been quite good
  Out of thy whole past life's? All have been leav-
    ened with sin.
Now first fallen hast thou into sin's death? Out of
    the death thou
  Never hast stood; thou there fallest from sin into
    sin.
Thou art as guilty almost as the guiltiest man in the
    whole world.
  There is a measureless gulf sundering guilt and un-
    guilt:
Small is the span over all guilt. Grieve for thy sin-
    fulness, therefore,
  More than for some one sin; ask for a grief unto
    life.
Jesus has paid by His death that death for thy sins
    that thou owedst;
  Paid by His life's good deeds those that thou owedst
    to God.
Waste not time, then, on vows of living uprightly, but
    ask life,
  Which at the font stood once given to thee on thy
    claim.

Christ's indwelling in men by His Ghost, and their
  dwelling in Him, too,
  As does a branch in a vine, that is their Christhood
    in full;
That is their life full-gained. When thou, no longer
  by self ruled,
  Yieldest thee up as His branch, bearing from only
    Him fruit.
Then shall His will be thine own; and thy well-doing
  therefore shall not need
  Ever the threat of a law, ever the spur of a vow.

Lesgeleaf.

Store, Aarbert, every word of the answer which Go-
  dard has given.
  What he has said to you now oft have I told you
    myself.
Only leave all to the Hælend, forgiveness and heaven
  are then yours:
  Light is the labour of trust, easy the task to geleave.
As by the death of the Lord's being reckoned as yours
  you are rightlike,[1]
  So are you righteous by Christ's righteousness reck-
    oned your own.
As by the chorister's surplice the youth stands clean
  in his foul clothes,
  So in your sinning you stand cleansed by the robe
    of the Lord.

Godard.

God mend your teaching! Call it never mine!
Christ's holiness can hallow only those
Whose faith has made them one with Christ; these die
His death, and in His life live righteously.

[1] Justified.

The surplice o'er them of His righteousness
Has never foulness neath it; He will hide
No living sin.   He neither hides a sin
Till in His death dead; nor is wholly one
With sinners till, by living in their lives,
He gars their deeds be righteous like His own,
Till having o'er them laid His righteousness,
He works it into them.   Then, though arise
Foulness from up the flesh in which they live,
They cast it off them as it rises up
Before, by being their willed thought or deed,
It can become as foulness part of them.
Their own willed works are clean; but they are theirs
Only by being wrought in them by Christ,
And all their worth and honour thus are His.
Such men have sin, for they have guilt of sin;
Such men have sin, for they have flesh, which is
Sin's self; but such men sin not, for their will
Is kept by Christ, in whom they die to flesh,
And float above its luring them to sin.
By not their works, by faith they live in Him;
But this is faith from which His good works flow.
If Jesus died, as being you, and you,
As being He, are dead as He to sin,
To pride of life, and lust of flesh and eye,
How can you sin or keep unrighteousness?
You, if you sin, abide not one with Him;
Or else, as biding one with you, He sins.

LESGELEAF.

But Anglican and Roman priests would say
That any man who walks in sin, but means
To quit it, is by their great sacraments
Brought close to heaven, through whose gate he will,
Unfleshed, pass free from sin by faith in Christ.

GODARD.

As twixt an earthy tomb and heaven's gate
Is no Bethesda's pool, where souls may drop
Their sins and win the life of holiness,
So without holiness shall none see God.
Sin leads nor through nor up to heaven's gate.
Oh, narrow is life's path, and sin's broad way,
Even where hugging one of those two walls
Which mark off that path narrow, leads to death
As much as where it furthest quits the path.
Yet to touch one of those two walls, although
Upon its outside, is a restful thing
To some, who by the broad way hope to reach
Life endless, through some heaven-fitness won
In death by sinners.   Many Protestants
Keep alive, hidden from their better knowledge,
A hope of heaven-fitness thus sin-won.
This heaven-fitness nor good works, nor faith,
But righteous qualities alone can show—
Those of Christ-likeness and sheer ghostliness.

LESGELEAF.

We enter heaven then by having Christ's
Righteousness wrought within us by our faith?

GODARD.

We are made rightlike by mere faith in Christ;
And are, as rightlike, welcomed here by God
On earth; but righteous are we made by Christ's
Righteousness wrought in us; and only as
Thus righteous shall we welcomed be to heaven,
With all our guilt washed off by blood of Christ,
And all our sin by water from His side.
Cleansed we, when flesh-rid, shall have nought to hide
But that which lowliness would keep from show.

MILDA.

These reasonings are new to me.   My mind
Is shy before them; therefore I shall wait
My husband's leading them to me in talk,
When he has known them better through your speech.

GODARD.

Alas! poor Milda! for the reasonings
Bring you the Gospel.   If you die without
The Gospel's haelth [1]——

MILDA.

                    God is merciful.

GODARD.

You had a garden at your Aarwick once
Full of plants beautiful and yielding fruit;
But in it was an evil weed which grew,
And quickly would have choked the ground.   You
        bade
Your gardeners to dig it up by root
And burn the root.   You thus were merciful—
But only to your garden's fruits and flowers.
A cobra once was gliding up a bed
Where slept a child; its nurse was merciful—
But not to both; she slew the murderer.

MILDA.

Yet will I trust God's mercy, for I dread
And hate all wrangling, and I clearly see
That Aarbert will withstand your teaching long.

GODARD.

Lo! how your wife has put into your hands
Her life, and as you seem to stand in twonne [2]

____
[1] Salvation.   [2] Doubt.

Whether or not to do God's bidding, halts
Herself; then, turning towards Him the back
Of all her heed, turns toward you its face.
What if He take that answer as her last?
Oh, Milda! love bides ever; mercy bides
But through the hour of hope.   Trust not that hour;
Live rather by the Gospel's love for aye.

II.

Milda, Godard, *and* Aarbert.

Aarbert.

Godard, I cannot understand your teaching.
How is the stain, which is by guilt in one man
Left on the law's roll, washed away by life-blood
Taken from some one other man quite guiltless?

Godard.

Jesus is not some other man than we are
Each; He is all men; all men's is His bloodshed.
He is the Son of God and Son of Adam,
Holding within Himself by faith the fleshly
Being of Adam's children all, and also
All of the ghostly life of any of them.
Therefore is He the heir in full of Adam's
Doom to a death, and of his hope of heaven,
After the death.   And yet His own death touches
None of the men who shrink from oneness with Him.
So that His death is to the men it touches
Death as if theirs for all their own sins, through Him
Paid in a wise in which God takes it from them;
Whilst it is death, which these same men, as being
One with Him, pay before they pay their grave's
        death—
Death of an earthlife numbed; without which dying,

Though it be not a part of His in worth, yet
Naught would have pardon of their sins bestood them.

AARBERT.

Jesus, you say, was sinless.   How can therefore
God have, as most High Deemster, slain Him guilt-
    less?
How can He even have allowed His dying
Thus?   Can His guiltless Son's foul death have'
    pleased Him?

GODARD.

Jesus indeed was sinless; but the sinless
Bearer of Adam's sin and death-guilt; bearer
Also of all the sins of Adam's children.
And for the sins upon His head God slew Him.

AARBERT.

Yet can I not see why God sternly asked that
Death from us men which Christ in such love paid
    Him,
How can have vengeance more than mercy pleased
    God.

GODARD.

God, as all-wielder, needs is all-avenger,
Merciful all, these both together always.
He is in all things, not in merely some things,
Utterly good, and quite as true as loving;
Nor may His mercy clear His debts of vengeance.
Truth in Him claimed the death which Christ in
    Adam's
Name has been paying, and the death's truth pleased
    Him.
He, as I showed to you, is not man merely.
He is in God, God; what in God we know not.

But we know this, that there is one God only,
And in His slaying Christ, His Son by Mary,
He at His own cost somewise slew Him therefore.
God was in manhood in the death thus paid Him.
Jesus as God, but also Son of Mary,
Son of a woman, was nor wholly God nor
Wholly was man; He thus, as God-man, could be
Seamer [1] betwixt our God and us.   Had He been
Merely a man His death had not for man's stood,
But at the cost of charge that some unguilty
Man had been slain for guilty men; and had He
Merely been God He could not have at all died.

MILDA.

Must I, dear Godard, understand these answers
To Aarbert, ere I understand the Gospel?

GODARD.

No, Milda! ten times no!   Heed not these answers.
As not from God come cavils to His Gospel,
So not to anyone who takes His Gospel
Without the cavils, come from Him the answers.
Thrice happy you, if you with trust will take it
From Him unladen with its proof's faith-helpings!
But Aarbert asks for these; and I must show him
That none for which he wills to ask is lacking.

III.

GODARD *and* AARBERT.

AARBERT.

Godard! I fain would follow all your teaching:
But it outstrips me.   You have learnt at College

[1] A mediator, one who, between divided beings, unites them, as a
thread unites sundered pieces of cloth.   Seam and same are distinct
words, yet akin to each other.

Things which I never knew, or have forgotten
Wholly, if I in mother's days had known them.
I am a threefold being, understanding
Little my ownself; how much less the Being
Therefore of God, my Maker?   I will pass on.
Why may a man not make by better doings
Fullest amends for all misdeeds before them?
How can you say that Greeks and Romans, such as
Socrates, Epictetus, Aristides,
Cato and Cicero, were life unworthy?
What! does the Mussulman, who fasts nor mockfasts,
Bows to the will of God, and hates all idols—
Does the Hindoo, hook-hung, who racks his body,
Never by good and worthy deeds earn life-right?
Such are the men whose lives I would have copied.
Such are the deeds I would have wished mine own
        were—
Deeds of a life's self-sacrifice and gainsay.

Godard.

Mean you by Sacrifice your self-denial,
Whether of pleasure or aught else, for gaining
Good to yourself or others?   Then I unn such
Sacrifice worthy; yet a deed not earning
Life in the least.   The man has not lived ever
Who by his deeds won right to keep life given
Erst by his God.   The very best of Heathens
Lose, and have ever lost, a life by living.
God has alone the right to rate the duties,
Earning a right to life.   Man's greatest duty
Is to the God Who gave to him his being,
Keeps him, and showers o'er him daily blessings.
Is there a man who always did this duty?
Is there a man who always loved his Maker
More than he loved all other things and beings?

Is there a man as good as God made Adam?
No: there is therefore none that earns a life-right.
If by your sacrifice you mean your giving
God by your forfeits some amends for evil
Done by you, God for such amends ne'er asked you.
What is the worth of such amends?   Are losses
Borne by a man God's gains?   Is man's pain ever
Pleasure in God, unless it gar man love Him,
Showing his love by good deeds which are welfare?
Can a man's fasting be itself God's feasting?   '
How can a sacrifice of God's gifts please Him?
How can in any way be gain or goodness
In the mere casting quite away some goodness?
Sacrifice all is bad in man, unless it
Bettan [1] the sacrificer's own life.   If then
You by the sacrifice mean self-denial
Made for the bettanness, how could it make you
Better until you were in Christ?   In Jesus
Man has a ghostly and a fleshly being,
Therefore a higher Being and a lower.
Now, it is good that he should crush the lower
Being for better living out the higher;
But a mere heathen has in Christ no Being.
So his self-sacrifice is naught but crushing,
Bootlessly for his gaining aught of ghost life,
Some of the evil in his fleshly, which is
Also his only, Being.   Low and evil
Lusts will abide with him, His pride will rule him
Only the more, the more he sacrifices.
Pride is array of life against life's Giver,
Pride is the blemish of man's lower Being.
He, that in Christ so lives as to be nothing
Out of him, yields self-sacrifice more thorough,

[1] The old word was betan.

Costlier far to flesh and blood than Plato's,
Made in a life of bliss and wealth and glory.
Never do men so please their God as when they
Happily live a life like that of angels,
Loving and trustful, lowly, meek, and hallowed.

AARBERT.

You yourself showed me, and with praise, Christ's
        having
Lived and His having died self-sacrificed for others.
Since for the sins of others, and to make men
Good as Himself, He sacrificed His own life,
Why for my own sins may not I do likewise?

GODARD.

Simply forthy[1] you cannot.   Sinners cannot
Copy the sacrifices made by Jesus.
His was the death in flesh of one who, being
Sinless and thus all worthy of a life, was
Also, in ghost, life's self; and after death could
Come to a flesh-life back, and bear it heavenward,
Stripped of its earthness; breaking, as He went,
        death's
Barriers all away from those who, being
One with Him, followed or were soon to follow.
Sin and a death cannot be sundered.   Sinners
Therefore may not outlive their death nor quit it,
Nor by it earn the smallest thing.   They merely
Pay by it what they can of death still boundless.

IV.

AARBERT *and* GODARD.

AARBERT.

If, if I rightly had laid the salve, dear Godard,
Of God's law over my deeds, it would have healed
        them,

[1] Because (for, this, that).

So far as this, that I now should not be mourning
That wound of worth in me which has so much
    shocked me.

GODARD.

Well said, my brother; but deeds you know are only
The skin outlying the shape of all the inlife
Of thought and will in a man; and health, though
    seemly,
If but skin deep in a life that all is ulcered
Within, is merely the hectic flush of beauty,
Which hides a death that is burrowing beneath it.
To lay God's laws as a salve on man's mere outlife
May thence rid sores, and to man's eyes make him
    seemly;
Yet, whilst the life is with God-hate inly ulcered,
The salve works only the keeping in, and therefore
The keeping up, of a taint of death throughout him.
The laws should not be a lecsalve laid on smoothly
To heal up every breaking forth of deep sin:
They rather ought to be drinks for hurling outward
The deep sins into the sight of those who have them.
Indeed, they all are in two such lecdrinks[1] made up;
Each less forbidding the show of outward illhealth,
Than bidding inwardly better health. The first one
Is law that man with his whole self love his Maker;
The next, that like as himself he love his neighbour.
These two work less on the outlife than beneath it;
And each so little agrees with all it finds there,
That thence it hurls to the man's affrighted knowledge
That show of sin in himself which you bemoan so.
He sees how weak is his will to love arightly,
With allself, God; and, with as-self, man his neigh-
    bour;

[1] Medical potions.

And straightway goes to the great Lech, Christ, to
    heal him.
For Christ alone can at all in man heal sin-plague.
God's laws show sin; they will never heal the sinner.

V.

AARBERT *and* GODARD.

AARBERT.

Your sayings long have lain in my mind's store,
    dearest Godard,
As lifeless statues; now, with a life of bones and
    sinews,
They move, but move as beings that, gaunt and all
    but fleshless,
Are strange withal in midst of the homely thoughts
    there dwelling.
My old gethoughts[1] give not to them any friendly
    welcome.
I all through life have trusted that, if I paid my Maker
As much as well I could of the deeds He asked, He
    surely
Would not then ask the lave[2] of them ever to be paid
    Him.

GODARD.

And could you ever pay to your God one debt of
    duty
With any heap of deeds by yourself done, Brother
    Aarbert?
I pray you tell me now, are your deeds His own mint's
    money?
They are at best well coined from the metal of your
    badness—

[1] Opinions, or summed thoughts (together-thoughts).
[2] Remainder (left).

The pewter, silver-like, of a rebel's show of fealty.
You hold not one good mite that can help you pay this
        duty.
God claims your wealth as that of his bankrupt
        debtor; all that
You are and have He claims.   If you pay Him these,
        and, standing
Before Him as no longer your own, but bought by
        Jesus
Away from fleshly mind, from your world-love and
        from Satan,
He will forgive you all that you up to now have owed
        Him,
And life of Christ will through you work out hence-
        forth your duty.

Oh, it is much to give my all up freely.
Well can I see, by what you now have showed me,
This—that to God I am a bankrupt debtor—
See that I cannot pay Him all my duty.
That which I cannot see is, why He therefore
Asks me to pay it all up.   I have always
Hoped that my yielding, for the debt's unpaidness,
Life on the earth, had washed me clear from owing
Such of it as, by harm from Adam gotten,
I was without the means of ever paying—
Hoped that by paying what I could of duty
Here on the earth, I then should have at Edrist[1]
Heavenly means of paying to my Maker
Duty in full, and taking stand in heaven.
Now, to my grief, you say I owe, for even
Duties unpaid, and quite beyond my paying,

[1] The Resurrection (after-rising).

Death in Gehenna.   What! Gehenna's utter
Death for the debts which were beyond my paying?
No, you have never meant that God is dealing
So with me.   If, indeed, He is so dealing,
Idle is all my aim to do my duty.

GODARD.

Though do the laws of God ask either duty
Or a Gehenna's death of yours, yet surely
Not by the will of God you pay Gehenna's
Death for the lack of that your pay of duty.
Jesus has paid in full the death of all men
Being in one with Him, and He will give you
Means, by His working through you, of your paying
All of your duty; this I showed you plainly.
Here is your hitch—that you mislike God's chosen
Way of your paying Him; you shrink from Jesus,
Therefore you shrink from life: for you indeed are
Not with Gehenna's death now merely threatened.
Into the pit, whose bottom is Gehenna—
Into that pit of death you have already,
Brother, been plunged.   You cannot stop your sink-
        ing—
Cannot arrest, without Christ's stay, your sinking
Down in it: for its top is earth-life's ailing
Even from birthday's cries of pain; its bottom
Down in Gehenna lies.   And as to plea, that
Idle is all your aim to do your duty—
If at the doomsday you before God make it,
Thus will He answer: ' Steward of the powers,
Trusted to you at birth, you say that you were
Helpless, and say moreover that you feared me,
Reckoning me a hard and harsh task-master.
Why were you not, by helplessness and fear, then
Driven to cast yourself upon my mercy,

Pleading your helplessness, and asking power
Better to do my bidding—power better
Unto my rightful gain to spend my money?
These were at least some deeds of faithful duty
Which you had might to do, and then your doing
These would have surely from my mercy won you
Power of doing more.   You missed the doing
Things which you might have done with fear to help
          you,
Backed by the thought that you yourself were help-
          less.
Great was your helplessness; your sloth was greater.'

VI.   ·

Aarbert and Godard.

Aarbert.

Godard!   He made me; boundless is His might;
Well can He take away my sloth, take all
Evil from out my heart—my frowardness,
Fear, and unfaithfulness.   Why lets He me
Sin to the death to which He dooms me thus?
What if I lack the faith to fear His wrath?
Can it be guilt in me that I lack that
Faith which I never had from Him at all?

Godard.

Nay, you have quite enough of that same faith
Given you.   Not the gift of faith you lack;
That which you lack is will to take the gift.
Knowledge that God has made the world is faith
Given to you that He can mar it all:
Knowledge that none flee earthly death, which God
Doomed them, is faith that from Gehenna's death,
Doomed by the same God, none but those who seek

Shelter in Christ will flee.   You thus have all
Faith that you need to fear God given you.
Then, in your knowledge that He spares your life,
Clearly He gives you faith that He is love.
Therefore He gives you faith for loving Him,
Whilst He is giving faith to fear His wrath.
Either and much more both of these His gifts
Ought to have garred you pray for mind and heart
Thoroughly changed, and bent on what is right.
Surely the prayer would not have been unheard.
Why have you not so prayed?   You nilled the gifts.
Is it a fitting thing that now you claim
Mercy and life from God in not His way,
But in your own?   He gives them as He wills:
Yours is to take them, or by not His will
Die; but your sloth forbids your taking them.
They, as you know, would ask that you should live
Wholly to Him by strife with everything
Hindering you; you rather choose awhile
Pleasure on earth, in living not to Him.

AARBERT.

Sloth! then I scantly, brother, have understood you;
Scantly am understood by yourself.   Pray listen.
Oft have I done amiss, but have wished and striven
Always to do aright.   Do you mean to say that,
Though I have wished and striven to do my duty,
Death in Gehenna, utterest death, is doomed me,
So that I need, my life being lost, another
Rather than any mending of this my old life?

GODARD.

Aarbert, although you mostly, I unn, have meant well,
Death is a wage well-earned by your sins; you cannot

Live by appeal to æright.[1]   You nor have striven
Always with all your power to do the right; nor
Would it have aught availed you in thus appealing
That with your utmost power you so had striven.
Done have you not the right, as you were bidden.
God, who upholds His laws by a truth unswerving,
Neither will loosely let them be overleapt, nor
Weakly will give to any who overleaps one,
Even although that one be the lowest of them,
Right to a life by having overleapt none other.
Therefore for one deed wrong by you done, albeit
That were the only wrong one, and you in doing
That one had wished it right, and had even made it
Right to the mark itself of your best endeavour,
Lost is the life which God to you erst had given;
Since it has swerved aside from the utter rightness,
Biding in which alone it had then its being.

VII.

AARBERT *and* GODARD.

AARBERT.

Your reasons merely shift and backward draw
That bar athwart my mind of which I spoke;
Here stands it: why does God not give me heart
To ask of Him a better heart than mine?
I needed not the Bible's help to know
That seed of good lore, scattered by His love,
Falls some on good hearts, some on evil hearts.
But God made every heart; why made He not
All hearts quite good? or, since He made some bad,
How can He, being love and truth, hurl men
Bad-hearted into endless pain from fire

[1] Justice (eternal right, from ' ae,' akin to Greek αει, always).

Unending? Has He mercy less than mine?
No, therefore am I all the more amazed.

GODARD.

Aarbert! beware. You speak with breath of His,
Yet with a daring of unwisdom, which
His boundless love alone has length to span.
The goodness of our God, Who lets us live
From hour to hour, though sinners, overlaps
The range of sight, which is a speck in it.
To know His mercy we must know His might,
His holiness, His doings, and His deeds,
His knowledge, and things other dark to us.
All goodness known is He; nay, more, from Him
And from His works our only knowledge comes
Of goodness, beauty, rightness, everything.
Not only throughly good are all His works,
They are the shapers of our thoughts of goodness.
When by your mercy's height you measure His
You merely show yours naught. And yet His truth
Is boundless as His mercy; and to keep
Them both as whole as did His utterness
Of goodness need, His fellow-feeling bore
The shame and pangs of Christ's death for our own.
He bore thus far with sin. You cannot rate
The cost to God of His forgiving men.
You said that He had made bad hearts. Oh, no!
He erst made nothing bad: He made man good,
But free to make himself at life's cost bad.
Some things He made for life and honour; some
Not so. You ask me why He gave to man
A free will; why He gave to him the means,
Of knowing evil, at the cost of life
To one unfitted for the knowledge; why
He, being good, let any evil be.

I know not by one hundredth thousandth why.
I know that evil is the bound of good;
So that, by knowing evil, man knows good.
The shape of goodness is to man's eye made
Only by all the evil bounding it.
No eye but God's can trace it as it lies
Within its being's whole and uncarved block.
Moreover reason shows me that were naught
Evil there would be naught to bring forth much
Of goodness, such as mercy, help, and hope.
Were nothing wanted, nothing could be given.
Were there no depth, or toil, or ugliness,
There would be neither beauty, rest, nor height.
Indeed, man's very greatestness comes forth
Through evil, whilst he overcomes its might
By Christ's might, and in overcoming it
Arises through his manhood's death up e'en
To angel-likeness. Other good I know
From evil coming. Evils on the earth
Make up a glass, where man can see himself
In all his sin and in its hideousness.
They make up, too, a school for heaven-life,
In which man learns to loathe the sin,
And love the heaven-life. Thus evils, though
They boot not travellers to hell, are helps
To pilgrims who are going heavenward.
Are you of these? Be thankful for them then;
But if you say you are a castaway,
A Being made for meanest use, then thrown
Into the pit, a Being reft of hope,
I answer that your own mouth utters that
Doom to death hopeless; for you heard it not
From God. Oh, Aarbert! fear your fear. Dare not
Mistrust the loving words of God to you:
' Whoever comes to Me him will not I

Cast out.'   That word ' whoever ' clasps yourself.
So live that evil may be good to you;
That good and evil, both of which alike
To some are curst, may reach you blest alike;
That coming from your Maker and your life
They neither of them may be death to you.
Thus evil undoes much of evil's work,
And is the light of hell around the shape
Of good, and is a worker forced of good;
But it was not by God made.   Sin alone
Is evil sheer, and sin is the unmaking
Of that which He made good.   Sin, sin alone
Is that which He made not.   His long delay
In crushing it is lengthened life to sinners
That they may sue His mercy.   He at last
Will crush both it and them, and whilst withal
They ask why He allows it.   Even now
Is evil sinking into death, wherein
It will be quite stamped out; for Death will be
God's last foe crushed.   Quit, quit it!   You have
      asked
Why, having left to man free will to do
Evil, He dooms its doers to the dread
Flame everlasting's everlasting pain.
Who gave your question? who has told you what
Gehenna is?   What know you of the doom
Awaiting buried babes or men born witless?
Keep God's writ holy.   Fear to hurt His name
Among men foolish to their own great hurt
By cutting to your fancy shapes from out
The warnings which He chose to leave as clouds.
He lacks not aid to clear, He wills the clouds.
He wills not that His words be stretched, drawn out,
And twisted into thread for being spun
To thoughts that have some other words as shapes.

This well we know, that whatsoever God
Does that is right.   To know a deed as His
Is to be well assured that it is good.
For He is Holy, good, almighty, wise,
A loving Father, though avenging King.
Whatever God has written that is right.
But let us, since we know not well His deeds,
Nor all the meaning of some words of His,
Acknowledge that we know them ill.   Enough,
That well we know Him in His sway love's self,
Yet all-geburning[1] fire to that great sin
Of trampling on His love's appeals for love!
We know the rack, the thumbscrew, and the fire
Of even priestly power; yet Christ who knew
Them all, and well knew what was hell, said, ' Fear
Not man; but I will show you whom to fear,
Fear Him who kills, and casts His slain down Hell;
Yea, fear ye Him!'   They who fear not that Hell
Which surely as the grave will overtake
All sinners, and will end for some of them
In but Gehenna, would not fear a life
Of everlasting agony in flames;
Their thought of which would faint in recklessness.
Oh, brother, cavil not at God's high dooms,
Nor strive against Him, as a minnow might
Against Niagara, if swimming up
Its rapids, he by force would stop their flow,
And thus arrest the roaring waterfall.
Your asking rose from out of things less known
By you than those of the far Pleiades;
And earth's unknowledge answers you right well.
All evil angels, all good beings, know
Him righteous; but He clears Himself to none.
He makes it sure that sinners, by their own

_____
[1] All-consuming.

In-witness stern, have well been told their guilt;
Although, by ceaseless hearing it, their heed
Has to the sound been deafened.   Blasphemy
By fools, earth-brained like neats,[1] will in the pit
Be smothered in its stench as rottenness.
It will not shock the sweet air.   Breathe it not.

Aarbert.

I will no longer gainsay, I will take
Your teachings to my trust; I clearly see
That I must gain God's pardon and His peace,
And on His terms.   If only I could gain them!
His terms you say are that I give up all
For Christ, as He has shared with me His all.

VIII.

Aarbert.

I cannot give it.   Godard drives me on
Too quickly.   Oh, my own mind, give me help—
Thy whole help!   Where—where, after every change
Through which both thou and I have from without
Been driven, where, oh where, at last am I?
(My own mind, help me; thou must help me now.)
By Godard's rating here, upon the flood
Where worldlings drowning lie in dreams of sin.
My life here floats within that ark of faith
Wherein, when christened, it was laid.   It floats
Not light with ghostliness and needs must founder.
It is an ark-life in the Christian fleet,
And yet not of the fleet—not written down
As one belonging to the Hælend's fleet—
That fleet of ark-lives whose one life is His,

---

[1] Brute beasts (ne + wit).

This is it: where and what I am.   Alas!
I dare not earthly die, nor can I live
In Christ-life ghostly; I must halt for thought.

IX.

GODARD *and* ARNULPH.

ARNULPH.

Your words have to your brother's inner self
Not pierced.   They lie uncovered on his mind;
And there he shows them, as mere things to catch
An eye's glance.   They have not within his own
Knowledge so sunken as to be your levers
For moving to one deed his settled will,
And yet he pines to have his will so moved.

GODARD.

I know—I know it.   God, and not poor I,
Can move him.   But, dear Arnulph, we may move
Our God by Christ's prayers carrying our own.
And will you not, my brother in the Lord,
Pray for him?   Do so; let us pray at once.

X.

NOTE.

The terms 'ark-life' and 'ark-fleet,' or 'ark-life-fleet,' which appear in the following ode, and in several others like it in the poem,
are, of course, not words, but technical phrases.   The odes in which
they appear are written with imagery suggested by, rather than taken
from, the stories of the ark of bulrushes in which Moses was laid
when an infant, and of Noah's ark.   In the imagery every Christian
is a human being who has been placed by the baptismal covenant in
an ark of life, floating over the world's sin-death-flood, and floating
as an ark-life distinct from all its fellows, yet being within an ark-
life-fleet.   Throughout this fleet there is but one real life : it is that
of Christ, its captain, and in the baptismal covenant the Christian
vows that he will receive Christ into his whole ark of life-being, so

that his life shall be wholly a part of Christ's. If the vow is fulfilled by the Christian, his ark-life floats buoyant over the flood of sin, and its name is entered on the book of life in the ark-fleet. If the vow is not fulfilled, the ark-life founders sooner or later.

The ark-life-fleet floats until the flood has passed away, although the captain, of whose life it consists, has gone before to the New World, and the ark-lives, which are not only in, but of the ark-life-fleet, pass one after another to Him in that world. In the meanwhile, the people of this world are floating with pleasure in their flood of sin-death, until they sink in it one after another. Each ark is imagined to be furnished with two hopes—one a raven, as worldly hope, and the other a dove, as hope heavenly.

I need hardly say that in the Bible Noah's ark, and its human inmates, really represent the Christ-life in the world of all nominal Christians together.

AARBERT.

Where am I? what am I?
A hopeless, hapless
Wretch floating
Upon the flood of sin-death here,
As its waters brood over the pit of Gehenna,
Bottomless!
Floating within an ark,
Faith-built and woven
Once at the christening of me!
Floating as an ark-life
Amid the fleet of life,
The Hælend's life;
But not as of it!
A wretch estranged from God,—
Far from forgiveness—
Without peace with God made.
Hast thou then
Left me quite, Peace from God?
In childhood asleep as in guiltlessness
I kept thee;
In manhood I awoke and found thee gone.

A wave of worldly trouble
Had overflowed me!
Then I straightway sent for thee
A dark hope, a raven—
For thee, my childhood's peace, for thee—
For thee—it was a raven
Which I in manhood sent for thee!
She brought thee not, nor came she back.
I knew not why, and wondered much;
Watching, peering, looking long-while,
Till I—
I looked within me.   What?
Nay, merely a speckle of sin's mud!
It seemed a speck, and next to naught of it.
I now know that man's flesh is earth all,
And that whene'er there is a leak
In his ark-life of bulrushes
The life is all a mess of mud.
But little knew I then of that;
And, as to my wee sin, ' Bah!
I will rid me of the speckle.'   And I
Blew at it jauntily
With a breathing of ritual.
And then I vowed to wash it from me,
Or forfeit all my hope of heaven.
But I washed it with the sin-flood,
And it fouler than ever was.
' Sorrower! sorrower!
Hast thou no other
Hope yet left thee?'
' What is thy name, oh breath of heaven?'
' My name is Peace; my breath the Gospel;
My bidding, send the dove, that hope, oh, send her,
That dove to fetch me!'
I thanked thee,

Breath of peace wilned![1]
I saw that all my worldly troubles
Were but the foam-sheet of a flood
Of sin-death,
Which was over the pit of Gehenna beneath me;
And fain I sent that hope
Forth on the errand.
Over the death-flood flew the dove,
Alas! meanwhile
My heart shrank back
From Him Who holds
And gives thee, Peace!
Therefore He withheld from me the pledge of thee
Lovingly, faithfully: thou wouldst
Fain have o'er the billows to my breast come;
But to my proud mind
There could be no peace.
I love my will, I love the world,
I love my pleasures more than God.
I willen[2] not Christ live in me.
Nor will to float buoyant with ghostliness.
Thou canst not come.
The dove went, she came back, without thee.
Woe! woe! woe!
My hope, lo, has come back without one
Token of thee, or a token
Of my fleeing the sin-death.
My mind is sinful, and it willens not thee.
Thou mayst not come,
Until I shall be Christ's.   Oh, thou must
Stay away, stay from me.
This bale have I to thole
Until then.
Naught has been left to me now, naught

[1] Desired (participle of to wiln or willen).   [2] Desire.

But to be forsaken by thee thus quite,
Until then.
Woe! woe! woe!
Therefore from me stay, thou calm, blest,
Dweller in Paradise! stay from me.
And must thou not come?
Oh, must thou stay?   Peace!
Still aloof!
It must be, thou must
Leave me to my earned lot.   No!
It must be, thou must
Stay away, stay from me,
Leave me to my earned lot, no!
Shunnest thou my life, then?
Lost, lost, lost,
Lost life!
Dark clouds lour now;
Wild waves roll high;
Death is from between their lips
Yawning for me, but
My hope abides;
And all that is within me pants for thee,
Oh, Peace with God, my God.

XI.

AARBERT *and* GODARD.

GODARD.

You are unhappy, Aarbert! for you want
A feeling of forgiveness and of peace.
You will not steal the feeling, as do some:
You will not cheat yourself.   You are too true
To bless yourself with feelings of a peace,
Not given you by God; but when He says,

' Come, and in Christ have peace,' you shrink from
      Him.
You want forgiveness in the sin you keep
Of standing off from Christ; your want is bold.

AARBERT.

I cannot give my fleshly mind up.   I
Am flesh, and flesh is worldly; and to give
·It and the world up were to give up life.

GODARD.

It were to take up, not to give up, life.
Your life you have already given up.
My brother! you are dying at this hour.

XII.

AARBERT (*a letter*).

Godard! if all men are sinners, and God be so true to
      His law's threat,
   How, having threatened to men death if they ever
      should sin,
Still has He choice left whether to slay them or not at
      the doomsday?
   If He forgive them the death, death will they never
      have had.

GODARD (*a letter of reply*).

Oh! how oft shall I tell you that God not threatens us
      death now?
   Men have already the death; new is the life that He
      gives.
Never forgives He a sin unpunished, although He is
      Love's self;

Oft has He said that He clears never the guilty at
    all.
That same death which in Eden to Adam and Eve He
    had threatened
    Came to them there. In their first sin did their
    dying begin:
So that their children are born sin-loving, unmaying
    avoid sin,
    All of them sinking in that death which to Adam
    was doomed.
Christ to them now gives life. Their first life lost is
    for ever.
    Not that life is the one now to them given by Him.
Not as in that life earthy and weak will they live in the
    new life;
    But will as children of God live in it likened to
    Christ.
As they moreover have now not threat of a death, but
    the death's self,
    So have they now life's gift rather than hope of the
    gift.
He by His death to the flesh and its sinlove e'en from
    His birth's hour
    Never to God's stern law forfeited life of His own.
So that with life in Himself, He, as being the children
    of Adam,
    Died, whilst also as God keeping His heavenly life.
This is the life by Him given to those who are shar-
    ing His flesh-death,
    God's life, which in His own to them comes by a
    birth from the Great God.
Having a share in His deaths, they are dead to the
    world and to sin now,
    Whilst they are now in Him born newly as children
    of God.

Like seeds sown do they die; but their dying will end
　　at the edrist.[1]
Like sown seeds do they live; then will their life
　　have a shape.

XIII.

AARBERT.

Is it so that Christ has died my death and given
　　Life to me even His for ever?
Is it so that, since I now am one with Jesus,
　　God is to me as Him a Father?
Is it so that, I shall soon, as one with Jesus,
　　Share in His joy and all His Glory?
Is it so that, I am heir to better things than
　　Eye ever saw, or ear heard ever?
Heir to things so great and good, that mind has never
　　Wrought them by thought to hoped for Being?

XIV.

AARBERT.

Like as a man who in sleep walks down some cliff to
　　　its last ledge,
　　There is awaked; stands, looks upward, afraid to
　　　go back;
Looks with as great fear downward; sees where les-
　　　sening neath him
　　Rocks are as pebbles; and where billows, as
　　　dimples of smiles,
Mock at his dread of a leap down; even as he in his
　　　wanhope[2]
　　Crouches, arouses his strength, springs from the
　　　ledge of the rock

[1] Resurrection.　　　　　　　　　[2] Despair (want of hope).

Into the sky, falls clear of the steep's crags, strikes on
     the deep sea,
  Sinks in it, climbs it, and swims; so in my wan-
     dering waked,
I from my pride's high perch will leap to the mercy
     beneath me;
  Will in the foam of that sea fathomless swim for my
     life.

XV.

AARBERT.

 I cannot take my stay away from earth,
· Although the stay be merely on a ledge
 Jutting from out a grudging cliff's dead wall.
 It is the only stay that I can feel.
 I cannot slack my hold of that, nor leap
 By faith from all on which I here so rest.

XVI.

AARBERT *and* MILDA.

AARBERT.

Milda, my Milda! more than ever lorn
And worsted am I.   I have left one half
Of what I was.   Undone are half my old
Thoughts of things.   Half of what I had been built
Is loosed from that knit wholeness which was I;
And, lo! I am another man, with yet
My old self barring my new self's whole life.
I feel that I must flee earth's death, and cannot.
I cannot quit my hold of earth; nor——

MILDA.

Why flee you?   Wherefore quit you aught of earth's
But that which is unrightful in it?   What!
Are not earth's rightful pleasures given us
To love?   May not we give our hearts to them?
To taste them with no zest of hungriness
Is, as it seems to me, to slight their Giver.
Says Godard then indeed that you should quit
Tight hold of earth's love, and love something else
Better than what has here been given us;
And that the Gospel asks this?   I must unn
His Gospel is to me all foolishness.
But, no; I must be foolishness to it.
He is so good!   I often talk with him
Apart from you; for then to my short sight
He nearer brings the showings of his lore.
In what he now has said to you I see
Mist merely; I enjoy the lovely world
With thanks; and love it, love its people all;
Nor know I aught that I can better love.

AARBERT.

He would have said that you may like this world;
But so much more must love things heavenly,
That unto these alone on earth you live.
Now that is what I cannot, cannot do.
Milda, I must again have talk with him.

MILDA.

Godard is still in London; for his ship
Has to be chosen, and his outfit bought.

AARBERT.

Then thither must I write to him again.

XVII.

Godard (*a letter*).

Oneness with Christ does indeed mean all that you
    say; but of all that
  Nought can within you be wrought but by His
    working it out.
Go to Him even in this your lack of it, go to Him
    straightway;
  Ask it, and ask Him to come working it out in your
    heart.
What! is it harder to yield you to Christ than to Hell?
    You have yet choice.
  Will you be Satan's or Christ's? Will you to
    heaven or hell?
Whence is the frowardness, brother! that so much
    hinders your taking
  Pardon, that hinders your thus yielding you wholly
    to Christ?
Lust of the flesh and the eye are, with life's pride, out-
    come of flesh-life;
  Flesh-life never is aught else than a hatred of God.
Up to this hour has it grown in you; now is upgrow-
    ing your ghost-life;
  Therefore do these two growths struggle within you
    for sway.
Either the one or the other may thrive; but they both
    of them cannot;
  Thrift of them both in you means thrift of the life of
    the flesh.
Flesh-life's tree is a life-tree sprung from the earth-
    ness of Adam;
  Christ-life's rather a tree sprung from the ghostness
    of God.

Flesh-life's tree is a bramble that bears sin's thorns.
  You may prune them;
  Others will grow in their stead. Kill them by kill-
    ing the tree.
Let at the root of your flesh-life Christ-life grow; and
    the Christ-life,
  Fed on your heart's love there, quickly will starve
    it to death.
Pruning the thorns from the bad tree whilst it is thriv-
    ing is far more
  Painful than starving the tree, wasting its life at the
    root.
Death to yourself and the world will be pleasant as
    soon as you feel life
  Heavenly thrilling your heart,. filling you wholly
    with joy.
Ask for the life, and at once, why linger in going to
    God's throne?
  Ask it, and pray Christ come working its growth in
    your heart.
List to the call of the Hælend, ' Come to me! Bide in
    me!' Let Christ
  Bide in you! Surely He gives power to do what
    He bids.

XVIII.

AARBERT *and* GODARD.

AARBERT.

Oh! Godard, how can I ask that from God
Which, were it given to me, I should hate?
I should in asking for it feel the prayer
Unheard. My brother, help me. 'Ask,' you say,
' For will to love God; ask for heavenly life.'
I oft have asked, and am without them still.

GODARD.

Ask then again and yet again, and till
Doing so proves that asking wins them yours.
Never has God turned off a suitor meek,
Who for His Holy Ghost's most needed help
Prayed, if he waited that for which he prayed.
Never has Christ, Who pleads for man, cast out
Any who came to Him for help in prayer.
Therefore, my brother, you must ask, still ask
God for His gifts, and wait to have them; nay,
Ask for a faith that they are yours; for yours
Surely they are, when you with faith thus ask.

AARBERT.

I will, I will thus ask Him as you bid.
But leave me not just now; I lean on you;
And if you take from me your priesthood's stay,
The upgrowth of my heavenward life will all
Be from its climbing spilt upon the ground;
And as a pool of wavy leaves will lie,
Like a tall ivy wrenched from off the oak
To which its thousand weaknesses had clung.

GODARD.

My brother, hear and heed these words of mine.
If not one other breathed by me you heed,
Yet heed for ever these my words to you.
Lean not on me, or any arm of flesh.
For cursed is the man who trusts in man,
In angel or in aught of heaven's or earth's,
Instead of trusting in the Lord his God.
I am a Prest,[1] an Elder, not more priest
Than other Christians are.   God pours His gifts

[1] Presbyter (see p. 41).

Into the very hand of every man
Who trusts in Him through Jesus Christ our Lord.
There is between God's Son and every man
Who takes Him as his High Priest, no mid-Priest.
All they who boast as middle Priests to stand
Betwixt them are mere priests of Antichrist.
Their boast is that of pride, e'en Satan's sin.
I pray you loathe from your soul innermost
All such mid-priesthood. But moreover loathe
Priestcraft. It is the craft of Satan's self.
True Christians all are Priests; and pray down gifts
Through Christ, in measure of their faith in Him,
Or for their own or for each other's needs.
You know that I am bidden go abroad
For health. I cannot stay to teach you more.
Lean, lean on Christ, Who is the one High Priest
Of all our priesthood, whether we be Prests [1]
Or not; and set you running free some thoughts
Which I have left you. Hunt them to their homes;
And where they lead you, you perhaps may catch
What knowledge God would give you. Pray to Him;
And search His book. Aarbert, I fear for you.
Poor men and children, men unskilled to read,
Heathens, and even outcasts oft are found
Dying to self, to Satan, and the world,
And to God living. Proud men, worldly-wise,
And rich men, too, are found so doing; but—
But only as a wonder-work God-wrought.

AARBERT.

Yet pray for me, dear Godard! will you so?

GODARD.

Yea, with my heart's heart will I.

[1] Presbyters.

XIX.

Aarbert.

Oh, that my love's look might with thy truth, bright
    sunflower! henceforth
  Follow the lead of the light beaming from heaven
    above!
Oh, that the hues which my God's love would to me
    give as His own were
  Over and into me now wrought by the speech of
    His light.

XX.

Aarbert (*a letter*).

So have you left us at last?
  Yet wisely went you, dearest Brother,
Off to a sunnier clime.
  May health on balmy breezes meet you!
Since we are parted by seas
  Which nill that words of mine should cross them,
Look in your heart for my thanks;
  Our hearts are one still: Read my thanks there.
But from your foreign abode
  Look hither, too: in home's sky hovers
Light from the hearths of its love;
  Whence rays, as star-beams, track the truant's
Every step, to await
  Their being by his look found faithful.
Talk with me much by the ships.
  Your flight has left a gap which nothing
Earthly can fill, and a blank
  On which can naught of earth's be written.

BOOK IV.

WORLDLY LIFE AND CHRISTIAN LIFE CROSSING EACH OTHER.

I.

AARBERT.

What thoughts did Godard leave me?   One of them
Looks sternly at me to be called to mind.
It is that I, a man of fleshy soul,
Must have new birth, and be a ghostly man;
If I would flee the fire which is at last
To burn things earthly up with earth itself.
This is a sword-girt thought that will not brook [1]
My slight—a thought, pushing, that stidhly [2] holds
Its large claim forth.   Another thought of His
Looks frowning from behind it, and thence shows
That I must, as a ghostly man—a man
Of Christ-kind, not of Adam-kind, live dead
To this doomed world, the Devil, and the flesh.
Dear Godard!   These his thoughts ask much of me.
Now let me count the cost of what they ask:
My having not on earth, but up in heaven
My home, and having there my chiefest wealth;
My being here a pilgrim, with my soul
And body held by Christ; my being dead
From fellow-feeling in their worldly life
With many whom I love and daily meet,
Until my life becomes rebuke of theirs:

[1] Endure.   [2] Resolutely.

My drinking with numbed taste the sweets of earth
And relishing but heaven's. To pay these costs
Were death indeed to all that now I am.
How any man can pay them cheerfully
I know not. Some men do so. Godard does.
He seems, and what he seems he is, quite happy.
Nay, more, it is from out the paying them
That springs his happiness. The thing is strange.
I wonder whether I shall ever know
By some means how the paying them is done
Without a pain, which evens that great deed
With loss of earthly life. But not to pay
These great costs is to pay the greater ones
Of loss of heaven, and of life for ever.
Must one or other set of costs be paid?
It must. I cannot pay these fearful costs.
I must pay one or other of them—which?
I was at ease when once I knew them not,
Nor thought of them: I was in worldly peace
When I was worldly. Would I then go back
To earth-life, sleeping into hell? No—yet——

II.

AARBERT.

Thought! I fear to let thee lead my mind
    Through thy caverns hollow;
Though thou whisper I shall 'yond them find
    Sunshine if I follow.
When in answer to thy words I say,
    ' Lead! I will be braver;'
Though I, fain to quit my wonted way,
    Would and will, I waver.

Thought! I fear thee. Show me what is right;
   Need be that the rightest?
Though thou brighten for me what is bright,
   Must thou make it brightest?
When from off my wonted ways I rise
   Briskly at thy rally,
Though I fain, as willing to be wise,
   Walk with thee, I dally.

Thought! I fear thy roughness and thy zeal;
   Fear thy haste, thy power.
Though in pushing me thou wouldst my weal,
   Pushed, I sink, I cower.
When thou raisest me to hurry me
   Into caverns hollow,
Though I rise, it is to fight thee, flee;
   Then I thee would follow.

III.

Aarbert.

Where, whence, whither am I? Oh! I am backwardly
Near, more near to a steep's treachery staggering.
How soon sunk have I down thus to be grovelling
Here, whence wisdom awhile beckoned me up with
    her!
How short while from my youth's pathway of earthli-
    ness
Faith's wings bore me aloft up to my heaven-home!
Blocked paths stay me, alas! here, as I heavenward
Climb God's mountain afoot. Faith would have
    carried me
Past those blocks had I dared trusting myself to her,
Dared quite slacking my grasp's hold of the world be-
    neath.

IV.

AARBERT.

Dragged from flight heavenward on faith's wing down
   To crawl up over earth-love's hill of rocks,
I shall yet sing that I, as ghost, have flown
   Again by faith high over all earth's blocks.

And between whiles shall be my song: ' Thrice blessed
   Is he who nigh to heaven, like the lark,
Floats on bright sunbeams o'er his earthly nest,
   Until from death's dark thunder-clouds a spark

' Parts his two selves, and they asunder bound,
   The high-born up, and to, the realms above;
Down the self low-born to the nether ground—
   Each thither where its home and country are.'

Oh! the thought cheers me, that I not as yet,
   Although by earth-love down-drawn, am enthralled
Whilst my heart's wishes are on freedom set,
   Whilst I by bondage am but chafed and galled.

V.

MILDA *and* AARBERT.

MILDA.

So early from the feast!   Not yet had I
At all of time thought.   I had left to you
To bring me your return's time—(This I see
Has outrun that of my mind's watch)
And was in restful pleasure, midst my work
Beholding you, as you were soon to come
With a quick step befitting brows that bore

A wreath of flowers from the evening's mirth,
Or, that at least, brought back the sunny joy
Which, when you left a sunset to your wife,
You carried with you glowing with her love
Off to the supper with your merry friends.
Where have you hidden now that wreath, or those
Bright rosy looks?   I see not one of them.
You must have been at some great gathering
Of lofty minds, and caught its show of height;
Or else you would not stand there, like a mount
At mid-day; which, with collar of linked clouds
And look of smothered thunder-rolls of care
Anent the world's weal, cannot see the glance.
That out of the poor sunny home beneath
With all its might yet idly courts his heed.
If down from some great Witenagemot
You now have not come, why that knitted brow?
Why so? my husband! wherefore so? I pray.

AARBERT.

From not above, but from beneath I come,
My Milda! when I into this my home
Bring clouds; and when I bring them so indeed
They dwindle, trust me, and then quickly dwin [1]
Beneath your loving heart's rebuke of them.
Your sunny joy, which cannot steadfastly
Behold awhile the darkness of my gloom
Ought not to catch a knowledge of it, whilst
It flees and hastes to hide its dismalness.
I tell you, sweetest darling! that my foot
In stepping o'er my threshold carries me
From a dark, sulphurous and busy mine
To daylight's freshness blowing still o'er time

[1] Vanish.

From off my childhood in my mother's home.
It lifts me upward to a heaven of peace,
And trust, and knowledge free from evil's touch;
And sets me treading upon holy ground.
Lo! gone is now the gloom; and with my head
Uncovered with that ugly cap will I
Say where and how I got it.   We had dined:
My friends had drunk much wine, which loosed in
        each
The arrow of his bow's bent; fun and wine
Filled all.   I shunned the grape; and being stung
With wish to preach to them of heaven's worth
And better things than were their best, said, ' Friends!
The guild, to speed which we have met to-day,
Was framed on wisdom's plan by freedom's leave;
How much we owe to freedom!' ' Much!' they cried;
And so we praised it.   They sang songs with jokes
That told the goodness of all kinds of freedom;
Whilst I, much loathing some of these, yet needs
Sate listing.   Now we sang in turn at call;
And as the call flew round and came to me
I caught it; then I hurled through air this strain:

Song.

Breeze of evening! born of freedom,
    Tarry, prithee; take my lays;
These to light, and those to darkness,
    Carry whither wend thy ways.

Light! abide on lands of freemen,
    Cover them with glories all!
Night! above the homes of bondmen
    Hover like a dead man's pall!

But how shall the light, if both it see,
Know which are the bond, and which the free?

And how shall the black-eyed night, too, tell
Where freemen abide, and bondmen dwell?

Say thou the free, O breeze! are men
Whose lives away from folly's fen
Flow forth like rivers quick and bright,
That, filled to lowest depths with light,
Are mirrors whereon all descry
The pattern of things heavenly.
And there they live, O Light, where seen
Are men arrayed in heaven's sheen.

Then say, the bondmen are, O breeze!
The men whose lives of luxe and ease
Are each one like a reedy pond
That tells of earth and nought beyond.
Their pools, their place, their sleep, their slough,
Are for their highest hopes enow:
And where men live in pleasure's graves
There know thou, Night! where dwell the slaves.

(End of Song.)

My friends, who restlessly had heard my song,
Stoned it with jeers [1] slung out by voices strong.
But they asked for another, if fitlier sung;
To the winds then I this for it heartily flung.

Song.

Fly, O freedom! tell thy lover
    Where thou dwellest on the earth.
Cry that in his heart thou lodgest—
    There, and there in only worth.

[1] Mock-cheers, ironical cheers.

Men unworthy say their freedom
    Dwells in laws.   Where dwelleth she
When to change the laws each freeman
    Sells himself if bribed he be?

Bribes will buy the man of pleasure——

My friends here stopped me. They misliked e'en
    more
What now I sang than what I sang before;
And whilst some cried, 'Your preaching, Aarbert!
    cease,'
Old Bradwater began a song for peace.

Song.

Our mirth, O master! prithee spare
    Whatever woe betide,
To-morrow be the day for care;
    To-night the feast abide!
If even now you let us patch
    On mirth's unwelcome rent
A rag of peace, its nearest match,
    We all shall be content.
The morrow we will then put off
    To quite another day;
For day as well as night should scoff
    At care's arrest of play.

He stopped.   You stop, said I, too soon:
Thus ends the song of the buffoon:

    'The time will come, alas! alas!
        When stayed shall be the feast;
    And when both day and night shall pass
        In care or thought at least.'

And, friends, e'en now what peace have ye?
What peace belongs to you or me?
Are want, and woe, and wastings wan,
And ache, and plague, the peace of man?

Then Clegge, or if not he, I know not who,
Rose shouting loudly and with thick speech too:
' Down with this bother all and wretched strife!
Preacher, hence! troubler of the feast of life!'
Next rose up Wrohtly.   This man, once afraid
To speak one word before me, grimly said:
' His zeal is burning with a dullish haze,
But with some chafing's heat to give it blaze,
The bankrupt will behave most merrily,
And this good feast shall then go pleasantly.'
Whereto I answered, having stared agape,
' I take my speech off, but I leave its shape.
These drunkards know that I no longer here
Have house or land, but am a steward mere.'

MILDA.

Poor Aarbert!   Now, in looking on your wound,
I too have one; and mine is taught by pain
Much wisdom, which its lips are opened wide
To preach: what! if the wisdom be as cheap
And thin as air; the weightless air you know
Has more than gold's worth to the life of man.
So listen to the speech your little wife's
Poor fellow wound in meekness makes to you.
When into folly's clump of trees you walked,
And standing in its midst began to notch
The sickly boughs there with a pocket-knife,
Whilst yet within the clump a drunken wind
Of revel raged with force enough itself
To snap all boughs too weakly, did the trees

Not after well-known manner of the earth
In hurling at your head those wounded boughs,
Which so were driven by the gusty wind?
But oh, my husband! had you to that clump
Been called to do the work you took on you,
With nor fit tools, nor skill in woodman's craft,
Nor smiltness [1] from the hour which ruled your task?
The whole wide field had begged you choose your
      path:
Its Lord had never given you or charge
Or means to lop the boughs of those His trees:
And was it wise in you, my husband dear!
To make your way to that one clump, to cut
Its sickly branches to the heart, and stand
Beneath its wrath, when, by the gusty wind
Hard pressed, it was so likely to seek ease
In hurling at your head that deadness which
Your knife's unfeeling edge was marking out?
Have not you badly wrought another's work
At your own hiring, and at wages large
Of only sorrow paid you by yourself?

VI.

AARBERT.

Yes, for work wrought and even overwrought,
And by which taunts to me and jeers were brought,
Grief in full pay was not the wage I sought
          Or wished, poor me!

Well was once said of me, ' Ah! overmuch
Righteous, how strains he to achieve by touch
Work of long lifetime! not a strain for such
          As him '—as me!

[1] Fairness of weather (smilingness).

I shall heed less all other people's weal,
And with old Time shall also mildly deal;
Freely he grants what from his grasp no zeal
        Can wrench—ah, me!

Time, who frets fetters, ay! and rocks away,
Time shall crush all that would my climbing stay;
Time shall work out for me by night and day
        My task—for me!

VII.

MILDA *and* AARBERT.

MILDA.

Ah! Aarbert, we had not too many friends
To lose! and this new quarrel with our kith [1]
For sake of righteousness will cost us loss
Of some of them.   It may to me cost those
Few buds of better life that bloomed in me;
I feel the bloom much withered by this blast
Of winterness.   But those poor buds of hope
Had, I acknowledge, merely in me bloomed
On staves of thought cut green from Godard's talk,
And driven into my mind's fallow ground:
They therefore were but sickly.   Had they there
Been blooming on young trees of rooted life,
They would have lived throughout this nipping frost,
And would have thriven rather than have thus
Been by the wintry witherwardness [2] killed.
I fear that e'en in both of us the glow
Which had been forcing better life is chilled.

[1] Acquaintances.   [2] Opposition.

AARBERT.

Fear nought, till it has come out of the shell of it.
Lo! lads, into a wood passing at eventide,
See trees standing as fierce robbers in wait for them,
Hear leaves rustling, and catch some of their shiver-
 ings.
Lo! men, passing at night fearfully, haltingly,
Churchyards, spy in their nooks things the uncarth-
 liest,
Mild gleams, flashed from the moon, seem to them
 glyderings.[1]
Fear nought. Evil is far; shadows are near to us.

Fear nought, till you have learnt whether you need to
 fear.
Lo! wrecked sailors in boats mid the Atlantic's swell,
'Faint, fagged, hungry, athirst, row in affright whither
Some good ship is unseen coming with help to them.
Lo! brave soldiers throughout hundreds of battle-
 fields
Live, though many a wild bullet has shrieked for
 them.
Death shrinks oft from the bold, seizes the cowardly.
Fear nought. Evil is strong; stronger your will may
 be.

MILDA.

Your words are cheery; yet I fear we both
Have slidden off from Godard's trust in God;
And in ourselves are trusting now the most,
When self in us is showing least of stay.
Forgive! I should have said that I had slipped.

[1] Apparitions.

VIII.

Aarbert.

Watching, self-curbing, into training putting
Deed and thought, I shall be for heaven fitter;
And by this strength-work of my ghostly powers
                        I, as they grow great,

Shall in their might up to the block which barred my
Heavenward climbing—to the block which time is
Crumbling, rush forward; and the rush shall sweep
      me
                        Over its hindrance.

IX.

Aarbert.

A crafty plan as well as righteous this is
Of doing strength-work as the means of climbing
With greater ease the uphill of an earthly
Life toward heaven.   Better plan than Godard's !
For by it climb I by a circling pathway,
With surest speed, at not the cost of flying
On wing of faith from off the earth's stay wholly.

X.

Aarbert.

After all said, and after many thoughts
Anent this world and life here, I have come
To this gethought:[1] These worldly men on whom
I have been looking down from Godard's clouds,
Although not living high above this earth
In clouds as he does, nor like me on earth

[1] Opinion (summed thought).

More wisely living by the rules of training,
Are quite as good as he, and better men,
More loving and more cheerful than myself;
Broad-minded men are they, great-hearted men,
Men so unsparing of allowance large
And lofty, that they reckon naught as wry,
Or evil in the hungry commonwealth,
Unless it be such thing as robbery,
False witness, murder, or adultery.
That Hell! why even its mere whispered name
Is to their goodness shocking; as a thing
Which has a hateful evil-willing look.
Yes, yes, they are more hopeful men than I,
More loving and more worthy to be loved.
Their hearts send all men with themselves to heaven
And not a line is there that tells of guilt
In all that story-book of pleasant thoughts,
Which at a glance is read from off their round
Mirth-kindling wholesome faces, no, not one.
Sadness and gloom! Ye sins in long black cloaks,
Who came to me as mourners for my sins,
Avaunt! Ye much dishonour Godliness,
Whose face is cheerful. But not thou, avaunt,
O bright world, I have lately rated thee
A sandy waste with green oases stocked;
I see thee now an Eden full of fruit
Scarce aught of it forbidden. Could I spurn
Those charming forecasts and those brightest hopes
That freshly crown each dawning day of thine,
The noon-like riot of thine earnest life,
And all thy lore, which, as a sunset sky,
Shows back in every shape and glowing hue
The glory of thy life of burning deeds?
Could I forswear thee, oh, thou ever new
And young world! world of revelry and rest,

Of rain and sunshine, frost and blossoms, speed
And wanspeed,[1] strife and hazard? no: these all
Are more than mine are of me; and at once
In taste, in foretaste, and in after-taste,
Are as my being's self.   And could I swear
That thee I love not with my whole heart?   No,
Nor does thy rule of worship ask but that
I bend the knee, and bow myself in church
With lowly awe, then yield me all to thee,
Soul, body, mind, and strength.   Thee must I love.
I cannot gainsay but that I to thee
Would live, as once I did, if so I might.

XI.

AARBERT *and* MILDA.

MILDA.

Oh! that in heaven now my life were hid
  From eyes here!   I should not be missing then
  The friends from whom our quarrel with these men
Will keep me back; and should of grief be rid.

AARBERT.

Were hid in heaven! and from earthly eyes!
I know not what you mean.

MILDA.

Nor I.   I am unhappy; and my heart
Said, Aarbert, what I know not with my mind.
What said I?   Nay, but let it pass.

-----

[1] Adversity (want of speed).

XII.

AARBERT *and* CLEGGE.

AARBERT.

Well met, my good friend! Sir, we parted last
With too much willingness; but meet again
With more, I hope—not more than most is meet,
If you forgive the thing that parted us,
When from good fellowship I fell away.
Forgive my breaches of good manners then.
I would be now your scholar if I might.
And since my mind has not arisen quite
To an uprightness making it a staff
On which my bearing of myself may lean,
I now would ask you to uplift my mind.
Sir! would you, with your known goodwill, set forth
How best, according to your view of things,
A life may pass uprightly and with proud,
Well-mannered, lofty mien amidst the thorns
And flowers, and o'er the pits and mounds
Of changeful things that wait it, as along
It glides o'er this most charming world of ours?

CLEGGE.

Sir, I will set it forth right willingly,
But I am weary. Walk we to yon bank!

AARBERT (*in self-talk*).

Oh, can have, in my dying, time been deemed by me
  The means of my recruiting my lost health? Oh,
      can—
Oh, can have, in my fever, strength-work seemed to be
  As good a thing for me as for some healthy man?

Oh, can have men, with mere untaught minds seemed
    to be
  More wise than Godard, who is heaven-taught?
    Oh, can—
Oh, can have men ungodly good been deemed by me?
  And dare I sin to God to please some fellow-man?

CLEGGE.

I now am ready.—A greater question
    Could not be asked me.
Have you, a man of the world, forgotten
    That life's uprightness
Is kept so long as in rolling downhill
    The life's self carries
The set and fling that it had at starting?
    My friend! these held it,
When erst it into the world came bowling;
    And so will hold it
Whilst still they bide in it, sway, and guide it,
    As they at first did.
Whilst thus they sway it, it keeps its being's
    First worth: and dashes,
Antwhether[1] outer assault and inner
    O'ertoppling bias,
Through scrub of hardship, and slush of pleasure,
    And folly's molehills,
And clash of rivalry, too, a hundice[2]
    More trying to it,
Till, though with some of the earth's mould laden,
    And though marred also
With show of many a dint, it reaches
    With ease and glory
Its rest at bottom of time: and boldly
    From righteous heaven

---

[1] Notwithstanding.   [2] A hund times (hund is a form of hundred).

There claims reward, as a life unfallen
    From seemly bearing
Throughout its running.   A life like this is,
    Methinks, worth living.

XIII.

AARBERT.

Reward claimed?   Hum!—For what? for that a life
Of rolling downward in its self-will's ease
Has reached its lowestness within the grave,
So much in oneness with its rolling down,
Instead of rising by the might of Christ
To higher life in heaven, that God in wrath
Has let it hold itself from other fall?
Can I have made so bold a claim as this?
Did ever I live thus, not staying me
From aught but from a fall from living down
To that low bottom of a flesh-life's bent
Of pleasure, which is lower than the grave,
And is below the hope of life beyond it?
Can I have ever had at Aarwick Clegge's
Low cow-brained eyes, that feed on earthness, whilst
His kisses crop the earth?   How I have grown
To manhood's bearing, and its heavenward look!
Poor Clegge! I blame not.   He is what was I.

XIV.

AARBERT.

My ghost! my better self! my higherness!
    My fleshly being's pleasure and its pain
Shall have henceforward all my care for less
    Than thine shall, that thou mayest through me
        reign;

And that my Ghostly Father me may bless.
　And thou, not lusting earthly sheen to gain,
Thou, being strengthened by my care of thee,
　Thou, being free by birth from world-love chain,
Thou, quite from lust of aught of earthness free,
　Thou, staying me from ride in folly's wain
Mid idle bustle, pomp and revelry—
　From ride which worldlings, for their hour, love
　　　fain—
Thou, crowned Christ's under-king within my breast,
　Shalt rule within me by His might and main,
Shalt bring me greatness, honour, joy, and rest,
　Shalt rule till other self in me is slain,
And thou art I.—If ruled by Christ thy guest
Who is thy life too, thou wert self-possest.

XV.

AARBERT.

Yet, though this world be but a moorland,
　　And I, in living
Above it, do so well—yet—there is
　　Much flight of knowledge
Above the moor; which mind high-flying
　　Might, like a falcon,
Have swooped on.　May I not then love it
　　For that large flight's sake?
Still love it, whilst in chase of wisdom
　　I live above it?
Or, put in thus:—Though not an Eden,
　　The world has in it
Full many worthy trees of knowledge,
　　Whose fruit is pleasant;
The fruit is fair, and not forbidden,
　　May not I love then

The world for such fruit's sake, such only?
　　　　I wonder whether
No pleas could force my loving worldly
　　　　Life for its lore's sake,
For not its own sake; oh, no! not so—
　　　　For but its wisdom's.

XVI.

AARBERT, UDWITA, LISTA, *and* WYNLIFFE.

AARBERT.

Why, here they are, the very men to tell me!—
It is most strange, my friends, that I have met you.
You catch me tracking out in thought the wayfares
Of life to see which one of them trends highest;
And you, methinks, are just the men to guide me.

UDWITA.

Lista! will you give answer to our friend?

LISTA.

I will, but I would hear your answer first,
Or, why should Wynliffe not be first to speak?

AARBERT (*in self-talk*).

Oh! can have I, plague-stricken, thought it right to be
　　Behaving just as though I were in health? Oh,
　　　　can—
Oh! can have been the Hælend's help held light by
　　me?
　　And will I for my haëlth trust another man?
Oh! can have been this world so much loved still by
　　me,
　　That I will for it forfeit heaven's bliss? Oh, can—

Oh! can have I, although in sins dead, will to be
  Unchanged?   Will not I be in Christ another man?

LISTA.

Come! no more backwardness!   We waste the day.

WYNLIFFE.

You know my thoughts, old friends, of higher life.
The highest life must needs be that of wisdom;
And wisdom is, as said the wisest man,
For man to eat and drink, and to enjoy
The good of all his own works.   If you list
To me then, Aarbert! you will loose your mind
From careful questions, wherefore you were made;
Or whether, if you drain without a fear
The cup of worldly pleasure, as it comes,
There is a hell for you.   It wiser is
To flee such questions, and be merry now
Without them.   What to you this morning is
The you of afterlife?   Let that ‘ you ’ burn,
If so it is to burn; and laugh to-day
Over its groans.   Enjoy yourself to-day.
Set yourself hard to hope that there is not
A hell; but if there is, when in its flames
It will be soon enough to writhe.   Meanwhile
Time is the enemy of life.   Keep this
In mind, that life can show no greater skill
Than in the manner of its killing time.
Which should be done by drunkenness of mind
In things like gaiety and novel reading,
For time and thought are the two foes of one
Who lives for pleasure.   Pleasure is their death.
Let pastime be your wisdom’s aim! and when
All time is past be aftertime for thought,

Together with the pastime's earnings all!
If there be aftertime and earnings there.
My pleasure-love, you see, is that of one
Who, loving wisdom also, has his eyes
Wide open to his walk on every side.

AARBERT.

I thank you; but I cannot love your pleasure.
You show her deadly secrets.   These the world has
Within its knowledge, but looks never at them,
Whilst kissing her.   Are you a wisdom-lover?
Oh, Wynliffe! yet I thank you for your frankness.
Do you love even knowledge? when the knowledge
Which you have kept is that a life for pleasure
Is stay within a frosty world's unwaked volcano,
For sake of warmth arising from the oozy
And slumber-forcing lava there, and when you
Have thrown away the fruit of that your knowledge,
And nill the knowing that unwisest is it
To bask in that volcano's warmth and slumber?
You, my poor friend, enrich me with your knowledge;
Whilst yourself, having it, have not its riches.

UDWITA.

A life for pleasure is the lowest life;
Paths thither then through lowerness must lead.
You ask me which of all the ways of life
Tracks highest ground.   I fain will tell you, friend!
For now you speak, as spoke your wiser youth,
And show yourself a would-wise man.   A man's
Most highly rising path is that which seeks
The house of knowledge; and, in treading which,
The mind is leader of each wayfarer.
You, if you choose the path, will from the world

Win breadth of honour, and will from yourself
Win honour boundless.   Now, I pray you, look!
The march of mind and of the worshippers
Of knowledge tracks that path.   It shall be yours
And what, if you awhile be not beside
The leading mind and at the March's head,
You will at once have place there; for you know
That he has caught by head and horns the bull,
Whose tail he tightly in his strong grip holds;
And he, who grows, may claim to have the youth
Of all the greatness ever reached by growth;
And he who makes his first step up the hill
Of highestness, is nearer to the top
Than he who half-way up it makes a stop.
You nod; to what is further you shall bow.
Come! let me lead you.   Take a step or two
In knowledge.   Know you how the leopard won
His spots?   This is a thing of nearest sight
To men of knowledge: he must erst have had
Armour-plates; which when bony food grew scarce,
Dropped off, and somehow left these spots on him.
But this is reasoning to eyesight's glance.
We shall find things more hidden as we go.
A furlong's march in knowledge is to know
Thus far, sir, that a thing grows out of that
In which it is; and yet within it grows,
By taking itself forward; and withal
Grows thus by might within itself, and so
By but its own might: for you know that nought
Wholly outside a thing has life within it.
If naught is in me but myself, my growth
Is clearly by my own self's might.   The ground,
You see, is hard beneath us; let us walk.

AARBERT.

I seem within a wood.   The ground, I hope,
Is hard; but it is rich with undergrowth
Of leafy thorns, whose love's fond catch holds back
Rags torn from off my reason's having quite
In whole, come hither; so that I can scarce
Say I am wholly up to you in mind.

UDWITA.

Leave now the wood, and we will come at once
To thought of that great might by which man grew
From mist, and is to grow to angelhood.
Sir, wise men know not surely aught of aught,
Nor e'en that there is aught; and therefore all,
Who know aught more than this know less than
        naught.
But insofar as well is known by man,
Some Being must from mist, or else the mist
Must as a Being have from something else,
Once made that spray of life, from which then sprang
Those great forefathers of those mighty worms
From whom, still rising up the steps of life
Through froghood, doghood, and then monkeyhood,
We men have wrought ourselves in bone and limb,
In eye and heart, in liver, brain and nerve,
According as we wished at times to grow.
You follow me I trust.   Well, since to grow
A hand forth asks much time, my scholar needs
To have the strongest faith in unseen work
Of past time's may-have-beens: and, to be strong,
Such faith has need to be his slave with might
To work his will with every other thing.
The times of which we know, give not a sign
Of have-beens which from beings vary much:

But I can bid faith give to time what age
I will.   Why not an age of one hund-thousand [1]
Millions of years? and I can ask the time
To speak from off the standpoint of that age.
Then must the man have brows of inch-thick brass
Who can step forth to gainsay what Time thence
Shall, in the honours of his white hairs, say.
If faith shall tell me, as from hoary Time,
That men were maggots when the Time was young,
Or beetles, nay, were seeds of gossamer,
What fool so saucy as to gainsay that?
Our teaching as to growth is out of reach
Of all irreverence.   I pray you, then,
To trust it with your fondest love and hope.
It is not shallow-clear, like that which shows
The stones at bottom of its flow; which flow
The wary child of wisdom should withstand,
With foot set firmly upon every stone,
If he would keep the ground which he has taken.
Our teaching has a depth too great for that.
My scholars, awestruck at its misty depth,
Give it a free flow, saying they have now
A law to thought for further knowledge—dark,
But therefore of a depth all fathomless.

LISTA.

My friend Udwita's cunning Fancy
        Has stepped within him,
Into his idle Reason's workshop,
        And there is framing
Such wares as much amaze that craftsman,
        And more the dealers
Who buy of him, and ne'er before had
        Such wares from Reason.

[1] Hundred thousand.

I followed, whilst my friend walked over
　　　His warehouse, showing
His stock; but, after some short walking,
　　　With thought behind him,
My heed came hither back to wait you.
　　　His faith is folly.
The faith of wisdom waits the witness
　　　Of sight or hearing.
If back to your own self you now have
　　　With loose mind travelled,
Come, start with me, and you will know then
　　　What life is highest,
And whither wends it.　Come, hope whispers,
　　　Of soon our seeing
Old shapes of thought unrolled as mummies,
　　　From rags grown rotten,
To freedom's air and light.　Thus wakened
　　　By breathing freshness
They will, ashamed like things of darkness,
　　　No longer hidden,
Slink from their outlines down to powder,
　　　Which, flying off then
With the first wind, will leave behind them
　　　Merely their traces
Upon the eye of gazing wonder;
　　　Till these quit wonder
And fade e'en thence to white forgotness.
　　　So come on, Aarbert!
No path of life can run so rightly,
　　　And none can raise you
So high as that which rises, climbing
　　　The hill of knowledge,
Where Earth, our mother, that great teacher
　　　Most sure and trusty,

Holds locked in strong rooms up for study
    Her books and records.
There Moses is rebuked by quothness
    Of land and water;
And thence as witnesses moreover
    Rise godlike beings
From underground; who, till now hidden,
    Are telling secrets
Of other-world-life. No As-beings
    Are these. We feel them;
We know that they are living with us;
    We talk with—hear them;
And they are but the newest, latest,
    Of this hill's showings.
Then, come! Be 'midst the first in seeing
    When air, which hurries
In living things their life, and hurries
    To death things dying,
Shall, helped by light, prove full of deadness
    Your very Bible.
Quit old lore's ruins, haunts of creepers,
    And homes of mummies;
And let me show you why that Book should
    Be much mistrusted;
Or shall this tract at leisure draw you
    From trusting in it?

AARBERT.

I thank you. I will surely try its strength.
My friends! although I give you thanks unfilled
With my whole trust in all that you have taught,
Yet take them as a casket made of love.
In such a golden casket give I you
An answer, friend Udwita. My dear sir!
As a man's lowliness, in his account,

May not with falsehood underrate his worth,
So may his folly's speech not bear against
His worth false witness. You have earned our
      honour,
And proved yourself much more than maggot-born.

Udwita.

No praise, sir! at my mind's cost. Sir, I say
That we must true be to the shifty times.
We must, sir, for our own sake, walk behind
This age's nation-big and booted legs.
For whilst the age walks right athwart the trend
Of old thought-ways to that of later ones
More meet for its strong youth of later wisdom,
The men who walk not with it needs are bruised.
Is it a wider thing for mind to clasp
That flowers have from God a might to give
To seeds the might to give to flowers again
What shape they choose out with their herbal mind,
Than that at first were flowers made from naught?

Aarbert.

No, but an asking which would step before
Yours is, Has God to flowers given might
To work new shapes out with a herbal mind?
Chooses a husband whether boy or girl be born?
God makes and unmakes; and none other can.
And unto that which He has made He gives,
As pleases Him, both life and might; but these
Are, even in its very using them, His own.
Had aughts which He had erst made changed their
      shapes
By their own might or will to other ones
They would have thus far made themselves; and earth,
Made on plans countless, would have all been chaos.

But order shows that change of kind by growth
In any of them has been made by one
Might and will only.   Even while such change
Is wrought by might of God's laws, it is God's
Own Self and He alone who works that change.
Laws on things powerless no further work
Than lawgivers work through the laws.   Thus, friend,
You have not proved that by the will and work
Of maggots you have into manhood sprung;
Nor can you claim these worms your forefathers.
Friend Lista!   I will, as I told you, try
Your tract's strength.   I do long to climb your hill
If I may climb up heaven's too.   But though
On heaven's hill some earth-hills may be climbed,
No hill but heaven's may to heaven lead.
I well will try your pleas for my mistrust
Of that good book which is best guide to heaven.
Forgive me, if the embassy of words,
Which, in my answer comes to you, shall wait
A meeting of some thoughts of mine, grown gray
In watching this great question.   For the thoughts
Gave honour to your speech, when heard by me;
And now would give it more by putting rank
Of worth upon the answer ere it starts.

XVII.

AARBERT.

Oh, can my soul's sore canker yet be thought by me
　　A freckle on the outside of its health?   Oh, can—
Oh, can my Hælend's leecraft [1] yet seem nought to be
　　For me, and only something for some other man?
Oh, can the balm of Gilead be still by me

---

[1] Medical art.

Misliked, for that so thoroughly it cleans? Oh,
    can—
Oh, can I have health given me, nor will to be
    Hale, lest I so be changed, and be another man?
Oh, can be yet my dying soul advised to be
    Mis-spending time by living as in health? Oh,
    can—
Oh, can be still the leech [1] of souls despised by me,
    The Godman Healer, slighted for some other man?

XVIII.

GODARD (*a letter*).

Whilst from my window o'er the waves I see
The mere blue sky, my brother hid behind it
Seems listing to my last fond prayer to him
To lean on Jesus, and to rate God's Book
As best of Teachers, yea, the very best
Of glosses on all glosses on itself.
If Aarbert still is listing so, the words
Which I am shipping to him will breathe through
And make the old prayer louder. Then I said
That that Book is the only light on earth
Which shows things ghostly, and that it to him
Shows them whose faith is an unprinted page
So smeared with love's good feeling to the light
That it can take the light's writ to itself.
I said, moreover, that the ghostly things,
Ligraven [2] thus on leaves of faith in man,
Set forth how God would drag him from his death.
I said this then to you, my brother. Now
I tell you that such leaves of faith in man
Are fellows, leaf for leaf, of leaves of thought
Within him, whereupon his own self tracks

---

[1] Medical man.   [2] Photographed (light-graven).

Sketch of his being and its wants.   When first
I saw that thus my own self's showings matched
The Bible's, wheresoe'er these bore on me,
I laid the showings each beside its fellow,
And bound them all up in a book of love.
But looking down then upon earthly things,
And knowing that their outlines and their lines
Of bearing to each other are God's writ
On earth to guide me from without, as He,
To guide me from within, had on my faith
And reason written, I had hope to find
That that writ's showings matched my faith's and
          reason's.
I therefore, taking copies of the writ
On fresh leaves, placed them also in my book,
Each by its fellow.   Then I read, and, lo!
The Bible and the earth and I gave each
Clear quothness, and the quothnesses agreed;
Thus proving that the Bible's writer wrote
Also myself and all the earth.   I rose;
I walked; my heart was burning with new life.
Yet when I looked around me on the world's
Scoffers who, much too slothful or too proud
To ask from God the gift to understand
His Bible, cannot see its tallying
With earth and with themselves, and so quite miss
One mighty proof that it has come from Him—
When on these men I looked, and thought how God
Gives often after not before men's faith
The fulness of the many proofs of soth
In what He tells them, lest, untrue to Him
And even upon evil bent, they learn
The proofs, and, through more knowledge of their
          sin,
Sin at more cost to their poor souls in Hell,

My praise sank into childhood's stilly awe;
And having once been not less blind than they,
I worshipped meekly with a child's whole trust,
As chastened too by that His will so stern
And yet so wise, so full of very love,
So truthful e'en to those untrue to Him.
Learn, Aarbert, learn to love this Holy Book.
It is to highest knowledge of the earth
And to a right self-knowledge that great key,
The use of which is given by Him alone,
And given to but those to whom He gives
Sight ghostly. Ask these gifts: without them you
In strife with evil, will be crushed by it.

XIX.

AARBERT *and* MILDA.

MILDA.

How strangely has an answer to your friend
Been placed within your hands! What brought about
This timely warning? Is there One indeed
Who, even in our wanderings from Him,
Is unseen tracking us? How awful seems
His nearness now! This letter should awake
Thoughts which have, Aarbert, slept in you since last
You saw your brother. In the thoughts are wrapt
Your answer to young Lista, are they not?

AARBERT.

They are so; He who will not meekly ask
Sight ghostly is by love held back from it;
And nor could take my show of ghostly things,
Nor give against them show which I could take;
For I see that in them which he sees not.
The unfaith therefore of my friend must bide

Still as a hollow.   Since it is a hole,
I cannot pluck it out, and since the air
Of merely reasoning is in the hole,
There would be. were I 'gainst his reasoning
To breathe mine, wrangling mere of wordy winds
Within the emptiness of his unfaith.
The Gospel, could he take it in, would force
Its own self's being clenched.   That emptiness
Would then be stomach's hunger; but, alas!
Lista lacks stomach for the Gospel's sweets;
And sees he that myself have fed on them?

MILDA.

If only Godard had been here!

AARBERT.

Oh, me—me! tenfold more the fool than Lista!
Must I say over still for evermore
And yet not know them, yet not know them all?
The reasons why I dare not love this world
For e'en its wisdom. that as-wisdom, which,
Talking as if earth's God were naught on earth,
Is Folly grown stark mad, and in the gown
Of Wisdom raving out of Wisdom's chair?
I know that earth-life is a railway-run,
An ownership of seat upon a car;'
Nought more to even those who love the world;
Whilst hell and heaven are the wither-ends [1]
Of this run.   Train to hell I dare not take,
Although the cars be filled with all that yields
An hour's sweet pastime even to a scholar.
I know that I must take the train to heaven.
When, when will I cease luring these, my friends,
To talk all this my knowledge out of worth?

[1] Opposite ends.

XX.

Arnulph (*a letter*).

Lista, I write instead of Aarbert.   He has
Shown me your tract: and, having told me also
Speech of yours bearing on it, he has prayed me
    Give you an answer.

Oh! but how shaped shall be my answer?   If it
Shaped be as truth bids, it will vex you; yet if
Not by truth shaped, it will be trash.   Let therefore
    Truth from me please you.

For your love's giving him the tract he thanks you.
For the tract likewise would he send you thanks; but,
Taken in wholly by his mind, it never
    Reached to his mind's trust.

You have not shown to him the Bible's wrongness;
But have well shown that it is read arightly
Only when looked at by the light its own self
    Gives, and with right sight.

Those, your new kiths,[1] that seem as gods, are angels,
Dealings with whom have been, of old time, treason
High to God, partnership with fiends hell-waiting.
    As to your lore, that

Earth itself gives to holy writ a gainsay,
'Tis an old tale, but not of Earth's own telling,
That the earth gainsays holy writ.   Freethenking
    Science has told it.

Ah! but this science is a lying painter.
With a loose brush she daily gives a pleasant
Change to her sketch of the unknown, and boasts it
    Steadfastly each day.

[1] Acquaintances.

As a sure likeness, by the measure taken.
Though her last touches of it mostly please her,
Yet she lacks never on her lip a faithful
                    Smile of fuldoneness.[2]

Be her last sketch whate'er it may, she sets it
Down beside that of Holy Writ, and where they
Tally not says that hers has there proved Holy
                    Writ's to be quite wrong.

If, by time, hers is as the wrong one shown there,
Softly she rights it, and as much as ever
Boasts herself trustworth.   Holy Writ when teaching
                    Heavenly things used.

Earthly speech, faulty as it was in earth-lore,
Which it taught not; but when you, Lista, gainsay
What of things heavenly it taught, and put your
                    Guesses against that,

You, my friend, gainsay what our God and Maker
Vouched for.   Fear having after death to answer
For the lost souls who shall on these·your guesses
                    Slip to the pit's pit.

Ought you not more to bear in mind your danger?
Much has been held by you as known, of which yet
Proofs have lain underneath the dusk that that has
                    Merely been fancied.

Much has been branded by you proofless which your
Reason's self ought to have well proved.   Your rea-
          son
Shows your hand lifted by a life behind it
                    Utterly unseen.

                    [2] Satisfaction.

Reason, moreover, sith the lives of men are
Flitting, whilst others in their stead are coming,
Shows an unseen life, out of which the seen must
　　　　　　　Spring and have being.

Reason, too, shows that, since are seen in all things
Order and plan, they are by that Self-Being
Governed no less than they were made, though He is
　　　　　　　Never by man seen.

But the Self-Being who has made men claims their
Love; and since some of them withstand and hate
　　　Him,
Yet on earth speed, they live, as reason tells you,
　　　　　　　After an earth-life.

Lastly, this Being must, as God, have given
Sight of that after-life; and nowhere is it
Given as fully or as well, says Reason,
　　　　　　　As in the Bible.

XXI.

AARBERT.

Oh, glorious sunshine! fearful is thy light
As it is veiling fire which blazes now
Within this earth, and waits there eagerly
The goodliness of all earth's outward show—
As it is veiling that fierce fire in hell
Which waits all those who, earthy, pass from earth
Ere earth's thin crust is reached by fire.　My flesh,
Wilt thou abide this burning? wilt thou stay
Me from my rising from thine earthness up
To Christian ghostliness, till thou thyself,
At Christ's touch, rise up like a seraph's lihhome [1]
To be the sheen in which my ghost shall dwell?

[1] Flesh-home (a man's whole body whilst his soul is still at home in it).

BOOK V.

CHRISTIAN LIFE SOUGHT.

I.

AARBERT.

Book of God!   They to whom thou givest sight
   See stamped upon thy lore His warrant's seal,
No other book can shed a thine-like light
   On heaven and on man's best way to weal.
I take thy tellings to my utter trust,
   Though but of ends of things which here are not;
And though thy writ be dim beneath time's dust,
   My trust in it is bated not a jot
By boast of check from past life's ashes mere.
   Not mine to paint thy sketches, or clip down
Thy models to what seem the right ones here,
   Those models shaped to things by me unknown.
I know scarce aught of what beyond earth lives;
   And God knows better what the best I ken.
I therefore will be lowly.   Since He gives
   Earth-knowledge for but earth-use unto men,
I will not sit in doom, thou holy Book,
   Upon thy dooms; nor wrest them, that by thee
My evil life may have unevil look.
   Show righteous God, though thus unrighteous me;
   And earth-life reft me ere thou reft me be!

II.

Aarbert.

Oh, Art! oh, Hlist![1] by man befriended fain
  Why help ye witches, that are man's worst foes?
In thraldom pining he through you should gain
  More freedom: thraldom more he undergoes.
Queen Freedom's Daughters! Why, why hurt him
      so?
He came your lover, let him harmless go!

Fair Art! that catchest for his jaded mind
  All flitting beauties, every flying charm,
Why let old Priestcraft, that hag hateful, bind
  His ghost and soul with chains, and do the harm
Which she is doing with those mighty wiles
Wherewith thou snatchest loveliness and smiles?

Fair Hlist![1] why let that imp of night short-brained,
  Called Freethought, build around man's mind a wall
Of earthly knowledge, which from thee she gained?
  Why let man's mind be tombed in earth from all
Beyond earth? Thou! whose eye o'erruns the star,
Why let man's sight be else than free and far?

III.

Godard (*a letter*).

Your story of the wounds, which your true love
To God's writ bore in shielding it from foes,
Has grieved me. Lista is but one of millions,
Who hate the word of God: but in your heart
Let that word rule, and it will keep your heart.
The Fiend, who thwarted it in Eden erst

[1] Science.

With gloss and gainsay, brands with hate of it
All who are not God's children on the earth.
Nought recks he in what ranks they stand of faith,
Or of unfaith; if but they bear that brand
He knows them his, and you may know them thus.
Some of these Bible-haters, the mid-priests,
Write over it a gloss which shapes God's words
Into their own, and gives His speech to men
What meaning e'er they will: and some, the men
Of Freethought, smear its writ with utterness
Of gainsay's blot.   Now, these two sets of men
Hate much each other, but the Bible more;
And so they work together: for the Fiend
Works through them evenly against that Book.
He with his swither [1] arm hurls priestly hate
At God's Word: Then he with his wynster [2] arm
Hurls at it freethought's hatred.   But that Word
Abides almighty not the less—abides
Whatlike it came at first from God's own mouth;
And keeps all those who keep it at their hearts.

IV.

AARBERT.

Song.

Hope! Dove, heavenly Hope!
Cheerer of the Sorrowful!
Thou whom I had sent from me
Forth, that if amid sin's flood,
Haply thou didst
Spy a mountain
Of mercy, whereupon thy feet could rest,
Thou wouldest for my faith bring thence

[1] Right (stronger).   [2] Left (Latin, sinister).

A Token
Of peace;
At what time I first saw my life's ark away cast
Loose on that deep flood—
Saw and was fear-struck,
As in, and not as of,
Christ's ark-fleet there—
Being estranged from Him amidst His fleet
On the dismal gulf
Of the flood of death,
And was being there
Afloat by my not leaking to the full:
Not floating by my buoyancy as ghost
As those were who
Were ark-lives of His fleet.
Hope, Dove!
Finding nowhere
Rest, thou camest
Back, and anew then
Forth I sent thee.
Home again thou straightway flewest
Quick-winged with joy,
Bringing to me by thy beak a newly-plucked
Leaf from the hilltops,
The leaf of an olive, a loving
Green pledge
Of the merciful forgiveness
Of the misdoings of my whole life,
Which from my Maker thou hadst gotten.
I held the green leaf;
I held its pledge, that
If only I indeed gave
Mine ark-life wholly
Up to Christ as
To the Ark-fleet's Captain,

If I would have His life all ghostly
As my own for aye,
And not have earthness fill mine ark-life's veins,
I should with ease float
O'er the flood of foul sin
To the realm of peace which
I so by thee sought,
By thee, Hope, Dove!
Thee.

Antsong.

What, what thrillings of joy,
Even unto wyndrym were—
Even unto wyndrym—mine!
Joy, which I had not felt, till
I, outlooking,
Saw the token,
The pledge that in thy mouth, O dove! thou thus
Hadst brought to me of God's rich love,
And mercy,
And truth.
But those thrills from thought came; my heart shrank
        in weak faith
Back from my own life's
Sinking in Christ's life.
Afar, anigh, around,
Huge billows rolled.
I was in terror of my losing life
In the flood; for though
I was not there left
Without help to drown,
As always are the children of the world,
But lodged within an ark that was amidst
Christ's ark-life fleet,
Mine ark was not by Christ's
Life filled.

Tops of mountains,
Each an island,
Peeped from the flood, bore
Trees of olive,
Stretching o'er the death their branches;
And all showed peace.
Therefore I upon the billows sent thee forth
Now for the third time—
I sent thee to bring me another
Leaf back,
For the helping of my yielding
Me to my Lord, Who in His manlife
Went into death within the sin-flood,
That He, all sinless,
Might give men God's life—
Might there be as an ark-fleet
Of lives for ever
Free to all men,
Who would yield Him lordhyld.[1]
Then flewest thou for such dear pledge that,
If I indeed willed
To live no more as Adam but as Christ,
I should, as ghost-full,
O'er the sin-flood's death float
To the home of life where
Love dwells, and whence too,
Thou camest, Hope,
Dove!

Aftsong.

Longwhile hast thou been gone, Dove.
Hope! Dove! Hope!
I have longed ever since
Thou hast gone; I have longed

[1] **Allegiance (hold to a lord).**

Ever since thou hast gone—
Have longed for thee.
Therefore would I fain have
Trusted to the loud hoarse
Bluster of the bold winds
That were lawlessly ranging
O'er the waste of the waters,
Who showed off their own bird
As thee—
Their raven as thee! They called her thee, but her
Beak was with the garbage of the flood foul.
She fed and floated upon things
Which Death would soon engulf from her—
The peace of which she knew was but a peace which
Had no stay.
The wild bird!
I knew her well before I knew thee.
Heavenly Hope! come, thou, come!
Bring to me—cheering me,
That other
Branch of an olive-tree
Off from the mountain-tops
For which I sent thee:
Bring it, bring it! Oh, that token
Of peace were peace itself—were peace
To me.

V.

GODARD (a letter).

My brother, I will give the answer
    For which you ask me.
How lags your bark of life in sailing
    From out Sin's harbour!
The ground there cannot hold an anchor.
    Your Earth-hope's cable

Is but a brittle chain of breathings.
    You hear the breakers
Which roar from rocks around, and well may
    You feel uneasy.
You pray for peace; you hate its Giver;
    Your prayer is selfish.
You cannot have peace, till is anchored
    Your life in Christ's realm.
Your port of peace is in His kingdom;
    He there awaits you.
The peace, when you have come to Jesus,
    Will come unsought for.

VI.

GODARD (*a letter*).

You ask me what the faith that haels [1]
    A soul from death is.
Hear what it not is—not such knowledge
    As fiends with fear have
Of sin and death, and of the gospel
    Of Christ, man's Hælend;
Nor such a knowledge as is gotten
    From lore or reason.
It comes not needs from mumbled prayer and
    A splash of water.
It is a thing by God's self given
    To those who love Him.
It is His gift to but His children—
    The meek and loving—
And with it He to these gives also
    His words to feed it.
It is that trust of love which rather
    The heart than head has,

[1] Saves.

The lack of which proves lack moreover
　　　Of love and lordhyld.[1]
It is that trust which love gives ever
　　　To worth as homage,
And gives in whole to God as being
　　　The One all-worthy.
It is the trust by which men, gifted
　　　By God to love Him,
Both see and feel as things whatever
　　　In words He shows them.
It is assurance that His truth will
　　　Not fail, however,
Man's trust in Him may fail through weakness
　　　Awhile in trial.
God-given faith is more, however,
　　　Than mere a feeling.
It is a clasping of the things which
　　　The mouth beseeches.
It is the after-prayer of waiting
　　　What prayer has asked for.
It is the breathing and heart-beating
　　　Of restful worship.
It is its name—geleaf.[2]　Geleavers
　　　In God do leave their
All, piled together in His keeping,
　　　And trust Him wholly
And lovingly therewith; well knowing,
　　　That since He loves them,
He well will work out all things for them.
　　　It is a Christian's
Self-leave to be to Christ's shape moulded,
　　　As God-begotten.
It is the very self of Christians
　　　When thus begotten.

---

[1] Fidelity to a lord.　　　　　　　　　　[2] Belief.

It is their Christ-life’s might and magen.[1]
    It is man’s lifeness.
It more than look is sight.   It rather
    Than thought is knowledge.
It holds far more than has; it also
    Less lives than quickens.
It even wills instead of wishing
    When God is willing.
Geleaf is more yet; it is more than
    A feeling’s working.
It grows to be the mind’s gate ghostly;
    To be that andget,[2]
That living gate, which, nobler far than
    Mind’s other andgets
Of touching, tasting, smelling, hearing,
    And fleshly seeing,
Gives ghostly things a way of entry
    Through walls of fleshness
To the poor ghost locked up within them
    In earth-night’s darkness.
It is the ghost’s blue eye; that eye, which
    Lies like a filmy
Blue vault of heaven stretched betwixt her
    And boundless ghostdom;
And down through which, as all the roof that
    Her walls of flesh have,
God o’er her sheds His dew of blessing;
    And rains His shower
Of light in bright words, burning largely
    Enough for faith’s sight,
Though some are star-points which no farspy[3]
    Makes ever larger.
Through this her living roof of blueness
    She sends her praises

[1] **Means of might.**   [2] **Mental faculty**   [3] Telescope.

And prayers to God, and gets His answers.
    The eye, if slighted,
Grows dull and horny; then in darkness
    She sits forlornly,
Walled up in flesh, where sin and death come
    To sit beside her.
But God all holy is her guest whilst
    She keeps it living;
And then she does His will almighty,
    And works with power;
She knows the mind of Him all-knowing,
    And glows with wisdom.
Yea, faith is power drawing power
    From God in heaven,
By which a man, whilst like the lightning
    It flashes through him,
Does meekly all the will and pleasure
    Of God, antwhether [1]
The let or lure of flesh, the world and
    The whole of Hellware; [2]
By which he grasps the gifts God helps him
    To ask and wait for;
By which his ghost can roam to places
    Afar and see them;
Can search the vaults wherein lie hidden
    The Been and Will-be,
And can in each one read the book that
    Its shelf holds darkling,
By which he moves earth's laws, and forces
    Its highest rulers,
Although unwitting, nay, unwilling,
    To give whatever
The Lord has made his own, whilst praying
    In lonely chamber——

---

[1] In spite of.   [2] The inhabitants of hell.

Woe them, though throned. who wrong God's praying
  Though poor geleaver! [1]——
By which, by which—— But where are they that
  Have marvellously
Wrought through geleaf? and Aarbert merely
  Asks what such faith is.

VII.

AARBERT (*a letter*).

To Aarbert's friend, Udwita, and through him
To their beloved and loving Lista, these:
My friends! great wrong I did you in that hour
In which my knowledge was the innkeeper
Of words of yours betrayers of your weal.
I give these guilty words up for gedoom [2]
To that which sits as Deemster in the breast
Of each of you, and there I charge their guilt
Of being lies against the Book of God,
And being treason to Himself, the King
Who more than all can work you weal or woe.

VIII.

AARBERT (*a circular letter*).

From Aarbert to his old friends all, God's speed!
Oh, still beloved, my fellow-travellers!
With whom o'er what in youth seemed sunny paths
I walked in magic's day-dreams, now I write
To warn your lives away from them.   The paths
Lie in a ghostly night amid foul swamps
Where fen-fire flits o'er death-pits bottomless.
If any of you, by the fevered breath
Of rotting marshy life envenomed, still

---

[1] Believer.   [2] Condemnation.

Are dreaming, wake!   and see, it is the hour
Of midnight; and what seems afore you flash
Of sun's light is indeed the fitful gleam
Of witchery.   But I have found a lamp
By which a man in this benighted world
Can pass without a risk these gleaming swamps
To that far cheery home in other life,
Where welcome and a ready home await.
The home is far away, and I, forlorn
And cheerless, all as yet, am merely starting
To reach it.   Will ye, if ye are not yet
Upon the way before me, have the help
Of my good lamp, and come with me along?

IX.

AARBERT.

They glide away.   They leave me, one by one.
Oh, how there comes a damp like that of death,
When many of man's world of kith and kin
Have left him; and he, mid his friendships' tombs,
Stands in his long life-evening's hush and gloom,
With his bereaved love finding nought in touch,
And shedding warmth on emptiness, until
It coldly faints.   Thou carest for me, God!
I pray for my old feres[1]: may they yet hear
Thee speak as love in my late call to them.

X.

AARBERT.

How sad, and yet how glad is he
    Whose growth of mind has cast its shell,
    When, hid in rock from billows' swell,
He lies forlorn amid life's sea:

---

[1] Companions in travel (fare).

Till, whilst he braves the billow's jest,
 God over him new armour fits,
 When, sad no more, the rock he quits
To find again in life's surf rest!

XI.

AARBERT.

I would not frozen lie again;
 My limbs are thawing, I awake;
 Mine ease of numbness grows an ache;
But life is burning in my pain.

Nor would I sleep again death-sleep;
 The trance has left me, and I live;
 My sweetest dream I gladly give,
That I my bitter thought may keep.

XII.

AARBERT.

Whilst, O my mother, Holy Writ
 Was, ere thy heavenward flight,
Read daily by thee, how on thee and it
 Fell holy light?

As dashed into a thousand deeds
 Falls daybreak on a town;
As dashed into the growth of grassy seeds,
 The dew falls down.

On me, alas! that light from God,
 Whene'er I read the Book,
Falls like the moonbeams that are splashed abroad
 On rippling brook.

Like daybreak on a rocky plain
　　It falls on me.　On me
It falls like dew on dying leaves, like rain
　　On rootless tree.

God giveth light to even him
　　Whose eye, howe'er it gaze,
Can catch nor ray, nor e'en a glimmer dim
　　Of noonday's blaze.

The sun's bright beam has might to thrill
　　Through rocks as through the waves;
The rocks no might have to let sunbeams fill
　　Their sealed-up caves.

The sunset's dew has might to give
　　To grass a life renewed;
The mown-down grass has not the might to live,
　　Although bedewed.

And thus art thou (whilst o'er thy grave
　　At dawn the daisy wakes,
Or whilst at passing of an earthquake's wave
　　Thy grave's self quakes).

Still lying with thy powers lorn
　　Beside thee in thy death;
The whole earth's life is being waked by morn:
　　Thou sleep'st beneath.

But shalt thou thus without quick ear,
　　Without a flashing eye,
For ever there neath morning's levelled spear
　　In slumber lie?

Although may not live mown-down grass,
　　Nor may be rock inlit,
Thy grave shall give life entry, thou shalt pass
　　Clear out of it.

Thou, filled with light, shalt look abroad
　　Again at outer light;
Thou shalt again have power from thy God
　　To win back might.

And could not God to me too give
　　Such might that I, who now
Am dead to Him, should, reading this Book, live,
　　As yet shalt thou?

A thought, thou scatteredst as seed
　　Within me long ago,
Climbs like a woodbine up my manhood's heed
　　To tell me so.

It was where rows of elms abreast
　　Seemed daily to have come,
Like henchmen honouring each welcome guest
　　Who sought our home.

My father homeward drove his steed,
　　And seeing thereabout
His wife and child, came nigh to catch his meed—
　　A smile, a shout.

I looked at thee, and then at him;
　　Thou pleadest for my ride;
I rode, but, glancing back with careless whim,
　　I thee espied.

I saw my mother weak and wan
　　Left all alone.　I knew
Her toilsome walk was to an ailing man.
　　We stopped; I flew;

And I was caught by thy sweet kiss;
　　My love was fondly grasped
Within a greater love than mine; my bliss
　　In thine hung clasped.

We sauntered listening along
    With footsteps growing slow;
The earth and heaven sang their even-song
    With mantling glow.

Upon a harp of slanted rays
    The sun struck chords full loud;
The welkin shook and waved with peals of praise,
    Cloud rolled on cloud;

The earth's own hushed, but deep and clear,
    Voice answered heaven's strings:
The evening's stillness echoed, ' Love and fear
    The King of kings! '

The landscape into awe was stilled;
    The birds sang psalms; and then—
Whilst strains as soft as angels' earth-song thrilled
    The breasts of men—

Then saidst thou, ' Aarbert listless saw
    These very clouds when white
At noon, from which he now can, thrilled with awe,
    Hear speech of light;

' Yet was as full of light each cloud
    That whispered in noon's sky,
As these are which of God and heaven aloud
    In all hues cry.

' Dear child! ere reading holy writ
    Look upward, and beseech
That God would stir the living lore in it
    To quickening speech! '

My mother! now I understand
    These words.   When I was tost
Into the godless world, I lacked thy guiding hand,
    Thy faith I lost;

But God has never lost the prayers
      Thou breathedst for thy child;
His love has led through manhood's thousand snares
      My footsteps wild.

And so His mercy leads me still:
      He shows me duty's tasks;
And names my mother to my stubborn will
      As one that asks.

He stoops in pity's love to twine
      Thy bidding with his own,
And takes it done for Him, when done as Thine,
      And His, too, known.

XIII.

AARBERT, GODARD, *and* MILDA.

AARBERT.

What! Godard here!   Right welcome home again!
My dearest brother!   Welcome, welcome back!
But how—but how is this?   You seem—you wrote—
No letter—you are pale.   Do tell me what
Has brought you.   Had you not my last month's note?
You seem much ailing.   What to me has brought
This joy in seeing you—this—brother!—pain
In seeing you so—wan—with travel faint.

GODARD.

Aarbert, I had your note, and much I ail.
Yes, I am wayworn and have travelled far;
For I have, on my road to heavenly health,
Passed that of earth, and I have come to find
Some sleep within an English house of dust.
Let not this saying shock you.   Earth awaits
All men; and, brother, Christians cannot die.

MILDA.

My dearest Godard, let me straightway send
For the good lech.   Your bedroom longs for you;
And a warm supper comes to cheer you soon.

GODARD.

I thank you, Milda.   Call the skilful lech;
And till he comes sit still to hear the words
Which I have brought to both of you from God.
My breathings all are numbered.   I must give
His errand; take it as from Him through me.
My sister, I shall speak to Aarbert, but
What of the warning in my speech you need
Is yours: and it is spoken with my love
To you and him, and with for both of you
My prayers.   My brother, take this from your God;
He tells you you have stayed aloof from Him;
Your eyelids to His Gospel's light are sealed;
Your heart is cold to all its tearful love.
Your life on earth is ever held from Him
At but a twinkling's lease-tide, which may end
Without more warning when he wills; when that?
A man unskilled to read, nay, more, a child,
A heathen often, under one day's light
And love from God as great as you have had
For many years, will give Him heart and life.
Oh! He will have you.   How then?   Crushed by woe?
If so, the woe will on your earthwardness,
Not on your Godwardness, at all alight;
And it shall win you, though at death's thin gate.
Oh, Aarbert! Aarbert! must it win you so?
My brother, I am going.   Let us meet in heaven!
Seek God, and then the holy Frefriend[1] still

---

[1] The Paraclete (Lord-friend).

Will bide to teach you.   Read your Bible much.
Man's words at best are names of living things;
The Bible's words are living things theirselves,
Far easier of being understood
Than are man's teachings as to what they mean.
The Holy Ghost, who wrote them, speaks in them,
And shows their meaning as can no one else.
That book will guide and cheer and strengthen you.
Read, mark it, learn it; prove by it the words
Of every man who comes to teach it you.
Hold naught on trust which even I have said.

XIV.

AARBERT *and* MILDA.

AARBERT.

My own, own Godard! what would not I give
To see his health recovered!   That is lost.
But if he might have lived for some few years!
My God!   Oh, spare him, spare him, woeful day!
He dies, and this unworthy I yet live.
Make—make me at all cost his follower.
Oh, what a jewel in our fear lies loose!
But it is God's, and He will keep it where He will.

MILDA.

Poor Godard!—nay, rich, rich, and we the poor!
My heart is rent, my life is withered up.
Ah, woeful day indeed!   The world knows not
What worth it soon will in his lost life lose.
He yet is with us.   Oh that hope could keep him!
I wonder whether prayers can keep a soul
Half fled from earth's hope.   Godard would have said,
' Not wonder's prayer could keep it; that of faith
Assured might.'   Would that I could pray for him,

As he would pray for me, were I so ill!
How earned by us his chiding was!   How strong
Were his appeals!   Hear how he coughs.   Poor
    Godard!
Oh, I, like you, have stayed from God aloof.
Go you to bed; I sit with him this night.
How golden time is, whilst his life's hours shine!

AARBERT.

Nay, half the night: the other half's watch mine.

XV.

AARBERT *and* MILDA.

MILDA.

The lech says now that Godard yet may live
A year or longer, if his life escape
The bleak winds which, as ambushed archers, line
The passes of this wild month.   Much he hopes
That in the covered wain of home's defence
It may, in fleecy armour, pass the month.

AARBERT.

Oh, may it! may it!   I shall hug the hope.
To prayer!—for I have too much talked—have prayed
Too little.   Come; he yet may live awhile.

XVI.

MILDA *and* EDDA.

Mama, dear uncle soon will go away
To Jesus.   He this morning told me so.
And I am going some time afterwards;
And Sibriht too is going, I geleave.
Dear Jesus! I so love Him!   Do not you?

MILDA.

I wish to do so; and you ought to say,
Not, ' I am going.' but ' I hope to go.'

EDDA.

Why, dear mama, when Jesus bids me come,
And when I wish so much to go to Him?
I love Him, and am quite, quite sure of it,
That He will take me, since He bids me come,
And you will come, and so will dear papa.

MILDA.

My darling! has your uncle talked with you
And Sibriht much about such things as these?

EDDA.

Oh yes: all through this month, when we have read
The Bible to Him.   I so like that Book,
It says that all my sins are washed away.

MILDA.

It says they may be washed away; and you
Can only say you hope that they are so.

EDDA.

Mama, mama, I know they are!   Why, look!
The Bible says they are.   Besides, I know
They must be so, for I have prayed to God;
I prayed to Him this morning in my room,
And told Him I was sorry for them all,
And asked Him to forgive me for Christ's sake.
They are then washed away, you see—quite, quite,
And Jesus now will make me a good girl;
And uncle says that He will keep me so;

For God says, Trust in Me, which means that He,
Almighty and all-true, will keep me then.

Milda.

My dear, you understand not what you say.
Oh God, have mercy, mercy, mercy, Lord!

Edda.

What did you say?

Milda.

Ask not, but take your hoop and have a run.

XVII.

Aarbert.

Book written as with a sun's bright beam
    In ink of sheerest ghostly light,
That flashes through earthy wisdom's gleam
    As through the gloom of pitch-dark night,

The wisdom of earth aloof at thee
    Stares blindly like a cavern dark
At flame in its midst; which, woulding see,
    It mocks in seeing but a spark.

Wherever on earth appears thy blaze,
    The gloom around is like some grot,
Whose empty and wide eye-socket gaze
    Beholds lit torch, but knows it not.

Mind heavenly meets thine each one ray,
    And draws it home to it to shine,
As that of a bright and open day;
    And oh! that more such mind were mine!

XVIII.

AARBERT.

Gone! the room empty! and how empty seems it!
How, oh, how emptier the world around it!
Even care's pangs, which are the joys of love, have
                    Left me alone now.

Gone, my dear brother! even gone for ever.
What a woe death has, since the dawn, been working!
Nought can unwork it; he has broken that which
                    Nothing can mend now.

Yet has death done his very worst, and merely,
After all, burst a jewel's casket open:
God has that jewel.   He has wrecked a prison:
                    Fled has its inmate.

Godard has fled, as in a ship's escaping,
Only her masts loom with their every sail set,
Whilst a bright track's wreath is the last which watchers
                    Saw of her hull's flight.

When, aside drawing from thee daylight's curtains,
Thou, as night's blackness, through this chamber stalkedst,
Treading down tenderness's careful nursing,
                    Slayer of all men!

Flinched my dear brother from thy dagger?   Did he?
Failed his faith once?   As he had boldly waited,
Fearless he met thee.   We have seen the battle,
                    Fought by him, won too.

Thou indeed smotest at the heart his earth-life.
And the life rallied; and again thou smotest:
But his ghost, mightier in Christ than was his
                    Body, o'erfought thee.

Soon his gaze told us of the looming nearness
Midst thy dark suite of one of Christ's own angels
Bright and armed, waiting in his glory. Then did——
                    Where is my brother?

Gone with him! know I not that look?   Yea, he has
Slipped from thee.   Though thou hast as spoil this earthen
Mould which I loved so, it is not his self, but
                    Merely his likeness.

Take it.   Dear Godard is no longer in it.
Ah! he seems speaking from it. What? He tells me:
' Yield to Christ all of thee! For heaven's life's sake—
                    Yield, and be praying! '

Will I not yield? Will not I pray? My brother,
Wisest and truest! Oh, I will! I never
Knew thy worth so as I do now, when I have——
                    He is at home—home.

Why do I grieve? He is at home. That word ' home '
Answers grief. Heaven be my home henceforward!
Oh, me! Home! His was ever but a Christ-life,
                    Flitting to heaven.

Nevermore, brother, oh, my faithful brother!
Now shall I hear thy loving voice of warning.
Never! how helpless am I! Not a thing thou
                    Badst will I not do.

Take, O Death! take away this image. God-like
Was the life dwelling in it once, and loving
With the love which is from the heart of Jesus,
                          Beaming on all men.

Take it! I know that Godard's self awaiteth
Till an archangel by the blast of trumpet
Sound the call, ' Edrise! '[1] when will e'en his body
                          Float up in glory.

What will that glory be? a glory like his
King's, who will give to him this welcome: ' Well-
     done!
Good and true bondman! enter thou thy Lord's joy.'
                          Into the joy, Death,

Thou shalt not enter. Oh! that I might follow
Godard's each footstep thither with my children,
Milda, yea countless others! Hear this prayer mine,
                          Jesus in heaven!

XIX.

AARBERT.

My Father's halls are up in heaven;
    My home beyond these skies.
My heart it clings to what is earthy;
    And what is earthy dies.

Wrecked is the world's weal. Men from off it
    Drop into earthy waves.
Earth's hills are but a sea of billows,
    A stormy sea of graves.

----

[1] Rise again (ed = after), float up in glory.

But wrecked is earth's woe.   Souls of men flit
    Thence like a sky-wide gale.
They leave the woe to be their children's.
    They flit as a told tale.

How we had hóped to live together,
    Dear Godard! unto eld.
Your life's blade then was green and growing;
    It lies beside me felled.

It lies amidst whole fallen kinrens [1]
    Of men, once hale and blithe,
All mown down, kinren after kinren,
    By sweeps of Time's great scythe;

Of men whose lips were sealed from blessing,
    Whose hands were dashed from toil,
Whose gallant hearts beat fast and fainted,
    Whose minds sank midst their moil.

Man's earth-life is an endless quitting
    Of all things which have come.
To even earthlings shunning heaven
    This earth is not a home.

It is the very home of fleeting,
    Where naught may long abide;
Where what is good and strong rests only
    On groundless hope of pride.

If envy ever showed me greatness,
    There passed by Change and Chance;
And lo! in Envy's place stood Pity
    With meek, upbraiding glance.

_____

[1] Generation (run of kindred).

If ever Wonder showed me Beauty,
  And I then praised its sheen,
Soon Wonder's self cried, ' Oh, how wan is
  The cheek where glee had been!'

Then wherefore longs my heart, so jilted,
  For rest beneath these skies?
My heart it clings to what is earthy,
  And what is earthy dies.

XX.

AARBERT.

There at that churchyard whither Death had borne
      him.
There, and where both had into earth together
Plunged, I stood brotherless; and thence I called up
            Thoughts of my lost one.

Everything gave me them: a stone on which he
Lately sate talking with me caught my glance, and
There I saw, heard him; with him thence strolled
      homewards,
            Lost him, and sighed, wept.

Hundreds of miles would I have trudged to get one
Walk with him more. I thought of past ones, locking
Each in my heart up like a book of stories,
            Left as a keepsake.

Whilst I stood weeping over things there—weeping
Over things smallest in the past, that least seemed
Worthy one thought, when I so richly had them
            All in his own self;

When I could slight him, I could wrangle with him
Through the long day; and then at bedtime clasp his
Warm and dear hand with the sure hope to meet him
                After the sun rose—

Whilst I stood thus, where he had often cheered some
Poor bereaved mourner like myself, the sun set.
Stillness came nearer then, and spoke of good deeds.
                Some of his unknown

But to ourselves.   I was in thought lost wholly,
When a slow rustle to my feet came gliding.
Nay, it was nothing but the breeze of evening
                Bearing the earth's sigh.

Stealthy breeze! thou that with a leaf-like rustle
Garredst flesh shiver in me, I am coaxing
Time to come back with the past life of one who
                Sank in this churchyard.

Take, then, man, take, then, from my sigh his answer.
Time is no trifler.   He is ever dragging
Earth from fresh deaths through newer life's own
      dyings
                Off to the world's death;

Whence will start kinships, aye, and kithships newly.
Men, on earth living, are the seeds of beings
After earth.   Nothing do they show of what they
                Will be for ever.

As the men now are inly fair or ugly,
Ugly or fair will be their outer shape then;
Since to themselves it will be fitted.   Earth-lost
                Shapes are for aye lost.

As the tale also of their earthly life shall
Give its stern quothness or against or for them,
So will their home be either hell or heaven.
                    Linger no longer.

Earth alone here is.   Unto life's or death's home
Godard's whole past has with himself hence flitted.
Is he not one of very life's own household?
                    Linger no longer.

Hence from these tombs! and, as thy brother liveth,
Yea, as earth lives, which is from death now drawing
Back his dust, live! achieving right to stand his
                    Brother in heaven.

Hence! for not here, but at the end of earth-life's
Path is thy brother.   By it hope to meet him.
Loose me.   Life beckons; we have loitered, each one
                    Bearing the Lord's charge.

Breeze of wise evening! I will, as thou biddest,
Go; the more fain, for that my brain is fevered,
Whilst the cold shiver of an ague thrills my
                    Body and each limb.

XXI.

Aarbert *and* Milda.

Aarbert.

Out of the grave has a gourd of fresh wealth over us
        grown now.
Under its shadow we might in the heat of our earth-
        day have rested

Pleasantly, but that the gourd's root feeds on the death
    of our lost one.
Milda! the shade thus far to me seems more gloomy
    than cheering.

MILDA.

If one feeling have I but of loss which seems to en-
    gulf all
Near me, the feeling is dread of a woe that is looming
    behind it.
Thought of a gain have I none; but am atfore [1] that
    which alarms me.
What is it?   Fear I the wealth, or the loss of my fear
    of it rather?
Though we may mock earth's power, its wealth when
    thriftily spread out
Into the world's all shapes with the thinness of gilding
    and colour,
Quickly will win us away still further from Godard;
    and sorrows
Then will be sent us as offsets; one great joy will be
    yours now,
That of your paying in full whatever is left of the
    bank's debts.
Oh me!   God was your brother's joy as well as his
    whole wealth.
I have at least from him learnt to be wretched in being
    without God.

XXII.

MILDA.

I said it well, that there was woe foretold me
By that strange cloud upon me looking dumbly.
My darling Aarbert!   Spare him to me, Heaven!

---

[1] In presence of (coram).

XXIII.

Aarbert.

Death! have I talked with thee day after day,
  Nor known so deep thine arrow in my breast
That now, though thence I cut the shaft away,
  The forkhead yet will, as thy pledge, there rest,

Whilst thou behind me climb'st day over day
  Time's stairs to my last month; to catch my breast
In that month's bedroom, worn by wound away,
  And panting on its bed for breath and rest,

And there to watch my fever night and day,
  Till it has wasted quite my stricken breast;
When thy rough hand will dash her work away,
  Pluck forth thy pledge, and in its stead plant rest?

XXIV.

Milda, Hulda, Arnulph, *and* Aarbert.

Aarbert.

Well leapt! Not yours, sir! No. My own gold bought
      bought   .
That horse. Poor man! you lost your all. I know it.
I must sell Aarwick. Who are you? My wife!
Ha! ha! But what! has she acknowledged you?
Is she dead? I forgot it. Packs of lies!
Have you come here to die?
King Death is a shadow
That married young Life,
And strolled o'er the meadow
With her as his wife;
Till they came to a grave dug deep,
And were bedded and fell asleep.

Know you that song?
Deep! deep! Stand back! A gulph! We shall fall in.
Is that the sea there roaring in on us?
How the surf thumps the beach! Fly! Loose me,
          sir!

MILDA.

Good Hulda, run to fetch the lech; run, run!
Nay, you are lame; stay, I will go; watch here.

HULDA.

Trust me, dear lady. Sir, drink this. Now, hush!
Speak softly! Let us stand awhile aloof.

ARNULPH.

It is the mind's fret at that bankruptcy's
Large pack of yelpings at his covert which
Withstands the soothing voice of drugs to it.
How his mind rambles! That the world has wronged
        him
His tombstone may at last know; but a thing
Grievous is knowledge bought with loss of that
In whose behalf alone it has its worth.

XXV.

ARNULPH, MILDA, AARBERT, *and* HULDA.

ARNULPH.

Have not you borrowed many hours from sleep,
Milda, in these last fearful weeks of watching?
Beware of wronging Sleep, the friend of health,
That health which you would lead to Aarbert back.

HULDA.

He wakes. It is time for his new lecdrink.[1]

[1] Medical potion.

MILDA.

My darling! you are cooler, and your look
Is brighter. For this mercy thanks! The lech
Has told me that he cannot see the face
Of Death here now; and even that its back
Is gliding out of sight. He leaves with you
And Hulda, who is waiting on you now,
The head-nurse, Stillness; and he greatly hopes
That your soon-growing strength will honour her.

AARBERT.

I! I am well; I am strong. Thanks, thanks! I have,
        Milda, seen
    Strange things, have wandered away to a foreign
        star.
No, no; not wandering now, but wandering much
        have been.
    Do let me speak. I have roamed from you all afar.

The fever, seizing my mind, and reeling along death's
        shore,
    Had borne it off to the fields and the bowers sweet,
Where dwells the shade of my buried youth, and I held
        no more
    A mind; 'twas carried away by my fever's feet.

When swooned the fever, my mind came back to the
        brink of death,
    And whispered: ' Shallow as bloom on a cheek is
        health;
Man's life floats loose in the floating cloud of his
        looser breath;
    And yet that life is the chief of his earthly wealth.'

Then begged I life of my God as that which had so
    much worth
To me a sinner, whereon to me came in dream
An angel, bidding my ghost to fly with him forth. We
    forth
    Flew therefore up by the path of a star's bright
    beam,

Until we came to the star's self. There I around with
    awe
    Looked back for earth and its glory. He showed
    me then
A spark like that from a forge; and said that the spark
    I saw
    Held all earth's women and children, and hosts of
    men.

The fleets and armies of volks[1] all swayed by its
    thrymful[2] kings,
    Its wealth worth millions of souls, and its works
    whose worth
Is priceless—nameless, and all the rest of its awful
    things,
    Launched their whole glory through each of its
    twinkles forth.

Its mainlands, islands, and seas, its ranges of moun-
    tains rife,
    Were all at large on the point of a pin spread out.
We homeward flew: so he said, ' Thou livest; and sell
    thy life
    No more although for the bulk of this speck of rout.'

MILDA.

Enough, my husband! you must more be calm.
What God has in your illness said to you

---

[1] Nations.   [2] Full of glory.

Must be for afterwork; you have to-day
The work of doing nothing.   Thanks to Him,
For having spared you, and in you myself!

ARNULPH.

To God thanks, Aarbert! for your earthly life,
Thus given back, and for the better life
Which soon will be His larger gift to you!
I now would by your leave in prayer with you,
The nurse, and Milda, shape due thanks to meetness
For the large taking of these gifts from God.

BOOK VI.

WORLDLY LIFE FORSAKEN.

I.

AARBERT.

With a ' woe-worth thee! ' earthy World! I greet
   Thee, Foe mine ever deadly! that with blaze
Of magic sheen hast had the might to cheat
   My will, and lure me through thy stronghold's maze
Of streets; although I well the while did weet
   That men, there treading thine unfaithful ways,
At beck of pride or greed or pleasure sweet,
Were slipping one by one with death-drawn feet

Down pits, which, diving under thee through night,
   Quit thee and neath thy wall in flame-moat meet.
Oh, there was time when I, by faith's keen sight,
   Could at thine every crossway see the street
Which would have led me lifeward on aright;
   And when I would have fled with footsteps fleet
O'er bridge that overleaps thy moat's ill plight.
But whilst I wished to pass, if so I might,

That moat, that lake of flame wherewith is bound
   Thine outer wall, thou spread'st mirage bright
To stay me. Clouds with blackness fore me frowned,
   Or made through all earth's glory-shapes their
      flight;

And neath me loathsome things, that crawled the
     ground,
  Showed heavenly loveliness by witchcraft's light.
My steps were tangled in thy spells around.
My will was in thy charm-wrought pleasures drowned.

I have been lifelong following in thee
  Sheen ever fleeing me, or faded found.
But slowly sinking seem I now to be
  With lung-ail[1] through a rift here in the mound
Of time, which, as thy wall, imprisons me.
  Already through the rift I hear the sound
Of roaring everness, and frighted see
The moat's fire. Could I be from Death's hold free,

If down this grave I slipped throughout thy rail?
  His moat would catch me: none past that, can flee,
But over drawbridge made by Christ, man's Bail.
  Let, let me reach the bridge! or, mid thy glee,
Thy feast's glee, hear from out the moat this wail:
  'Lost! all good, lost! A lower life I dree
For ever. As a blighted wreath I trail
Life's hopes. Their blighter thee, oh, world! I hail.'

Kill thought, that fireworm! weary out the pain,
  And shame, and unrest of this flaming gaol!
Or at least send me dreams and lies again!
  No: thou hast left me. Oh! at that I quail.
I wear thy mischiefs linked into a chain,
  Which thy rust eats not—I who, clad in mail
To fight the fiends who forged them, might have—
     fain—
I strove with them; but now I sink here slain.

---

[1] Phthisis (pulmonary disorder).

II.

Aarbert.

At all my past life, then at thee,
　　At it again—at both I look;
Then shut mine eyes that night may cover me,
　　Great Doomsday Book!

Thus hidden from myself I lie,
　　My hiding-place, God's sight.
My very mind and flesh are but His eye;
　　His look is light,

Which writes on thee whate'er He heeds.
　　The ligwrit[1] which that look has wrought
Is thus the story of my lifetime's deeds
　　Within thy thought.

And in thy page's brain will bide
　　That dread thought, till at day of doom
It forth as speech shall in thy mind's flash glide
　　Throughout geroom.[2]

III.

Aarbert.

Unmeek, unloving! ever putting forth
　　An evil-hurried foot with daring speed
　　To meet that woe which meets all evil deed,
As welfare meets all welfare-meeting worth!

---

[1] Photograph (light-writ).　　　　　　　　[2] Space.

IV.

AARBERT.

Self-standingness [1] as self-life—this, the core
   And bark, the leaf and stem, too, of that tree
Of guilt, which, from my heart through every pore
   Of brow-sweat branches!   I have built in me
The shrines of idols; I on holy lore
Have fed my pride; have brought, like Cain of yore
   To God my fruits of work as freegifts all,
Thus striking from account the boundless score
   Of works I owed to Him; have held, as small,
Sins each as great as death which Christ once bore.
Is mercy for my life-long guilt in store?

V.

MILDA *and* AARBERT.

MILDA.

Would I could comfort you; but comfort none
Have I myself.   Our fear is as to what
That book of God's great doom may say of us.
Spake not dear Godard of a book of life,
In which whatever name was written down
Was that of one who had a pass to heaven?
I would our names were in that blissful book!

AARBERT.

Would, would that they were so!—that aught would blot
   blot
My deeds from doom's great book!—that it forgot!—
That ink would strike them there, and they were not!

---

[1] Independent.

The cloud has passed by, he that sate thereon
Has with his sword in sheath of thunder gone.
But only breathing time I thus have won;

That at full speed I may, athwart the field
Of earth's sin, reach the shelter Christ would yield
Beneath His lightning-catching iron shield;

Before the sin-avenger come again,
To cut my sickness down, and me in twain—
Before my soul forsake my body slain,

And pass from earth to wait the dreadful tide,
When Christ no more with shield on earth shall bide—
When even He on fiery cloud shall ride—

When through the hour-glass shall have slipped the
　　　sand,
And ruthless doom shall take the flashing brand
From war's more rough but mercy-slackened hand.

VI.

Birtnoth *and* Aarbert.

Aarbert.

Birtnoth! it is most loving thus to come.
Our youth-sown friendship never died in me;
And at your call its root has at a bound
Sprung into stalk, and tendril holding out
Its clasp to your good fellowship.　Oh yes,
My fellow-thane! we both of us, nay, more,
The country all has lost a friend indeed,
A teacher matchless.　I have lost in him
The brother of my body and my mind.
I thank you for your greetings and for all
Your loving wishes.　I have better health
In some things, but in mind am not at ease;
And I could tell you——

Birtnoth.

It is the thing!—the leaven of that thing
Within my thoughts it is, which works as yeast
And gars them so to well up in my mind,
That from it they will overflow in speech
To other ears, if not now caught by yours.
Pray take my speech in, though in foamy hints
At its first outflow, charged with zealous haste,
It burst upon you hoarsely from my grief.
You once to me showed such a height of mind,
And so strong truth to duty, that I grieve
To see your goodness seem undone, and this
Before the taunting world. My friend, my friend,
The world has seen that you are not at ease;
That you have bowed your head beneath your own
Self-chiding, and it listens when the gloom,
That reeks from you where'er you walk abroad,
Unns[1] fire of knowledge smouldering beneath.
I will not ask you what it is that burns
In your inwitness, but would quench its heat.
The ghost in each of us is by the mind,
And more so by the witless body oft,
In all their lusts for wealth and pleasure wronged;
And since these two our wrong-doers are each
A mere astondness[2] of ourselves, we see
No wrong of theirs, and need another's eyes
And gentle hand to set things right in us;
Then, when right, we with loftiness of worth
Can meet the world's eyes with our own again,
And even eye blue heaven's look with look
As bright and unaware of cloudy guilt.
If I might help you win back ghostly health,
Sir, I would boast my pleasures passing yours.

---

[1] Owns, acknowledges.   [2] Outstandingness (branch).

I pray you spare then my endeavour's life,
Till it has dealt with your great sores of mind.
And firstly let me, as your friend, say this:
That you do well in feeling shame and grief.
For such right feeling takes away shame's food.
But furthermore you ought to show in works
A proof of your beruing [1] your misdeeds;
Such works would win you heavenly health again.
If in that wretched bankruptcy were deeds
Of yours not quite forgiven by your heart,
You now that you have wealth may——

AARBERT.

Hold, hold, sir! what will you say next of this?
But hold there; draw the bridle of your speech,
And let my answer overtake its haste;
For it ahead runs through the hedge of soth
And over-rides my ownings.   I will show
Marks, and you then shall know my rightful grounds,
Across which you have galloped in a mist.
I swear, sir, that by that foul bankruptcy
Of which you speak, not one man so was wronged
In money, none so wronged in name, as I.
Besides loss naught I ever gained by it;
And all its loss I gained; for I have paid
To all my fellow-losers every loss,
And they have but lost losses.   No, my wounds
Of mind are not from sin of mine to man.
You say that I have fallen; so I have.
You say that I am changed from what I was;
You say this well; I am a man quite changed;
And I have sickness more than you have thought,
For I have sores of sin-plague unto death.
But therefore set me down as past your skill,

[1] Repenting.

And fear to lay a lancet's easy edge
Or e'en the finger of a probe on mind,
The workings of whose wheelry not a thought
Of yours can track.   The bluntness of your knife
Would bruise its cogs and hair-springs.   Do not try
To cut out aught from mid them or to mend
One of them.   All of us, the soundest men
Are in the mind unsound.   Man's flesh is quite
Blood-poisoned; and its fever makes his mind
Unsteady.   It is better with us when
We live in not the flesh, but in the ghost,
Which is the heaven-born and heaven-homed
Higherness of our else low selves on earth.
The ghost itself, however, oft is bruised;
And for the looking at its bruise one needs
A ghostly sight.   Sir, have you this?   Well, yet,
I was not sound when once you thought me so;
Nor ail I now where most your speeches grope
For ailing.   List! you may by hap have felt
Such things as I shall speak of.   It is so;
My soul is troubled.   Yes, but there is One
Within me mending that which erst He made.
His skill is sure; and boundless are His means;
His work is thorough; and, indeed, dear friend,
His leecraft [1] is my life's last fondest hope.
Whereas the surgery of undue blame
(And all my friends are surgeons to the mind)
Would come to me not blessed by hope at all.
For raw and touchy wounds of mind, you know,
Are heated by such mauling; yea, they feel
Affronted by it; and more sinned against
Than sinning: wiser also than the salve
Which hands, too much enfranchised, and too brisk
Of men who are apprentices, to skill,

[1] Medical art.

Lead up to heal them of their festerings.
The wounds are ruffled by the bungling salve,
And show but anger at its aim to soothe.
Have you, too, felt this? Then indeed you know,
That when so mauled, the wounds shed many a tear
From their self-pity, whose rank bitterness
Frets their sore edges; and they spread so much
That, whilst the dapper freshmen who have made
These wounds plot more mistakes, death's under-
　　　taking
Of all the surgery is called in. Sir,
Man's knife can never cut sin's canker out.
I pray you therefore hide from me your tools.
You used them lovingly; but lay them down.
Forgive me; I have in my wound's behalf
Been brandishing a branch of speech unleafed
Of wordiness and quite unflowery
Against your well-willed haste to meet its sore;
But pray forgive me: I am sinful man,
A weak man. What! there yet is that in me
Which, at the smart of twitting taunt, breaks loose
To wield a battledore, and send the taunt
Back like a feathered cork as light as down,
A shuttle fledged and pointed for return.
Awake not up that fiend in me, with whom
I have through years been struggling for my life.
As you have man's flesh, wake not that—nor—
Birtnoth!—nor yet be startled off from me:
Nor take away your friendship. Well, farewell!
Since fare you will, you must so, but, farewell!

VII.

AARBERT.

Oh! that was wrong to God and to my friend.
Have I more knowledge of some higher things

Than he?   Yes, both of us had on our knees
For that good knowledge begged; but, having asked
The more of it, I was the beggar thus
To whom the more was doled.   Not much was that:
The knapsack of my mind held earthly thoughts,
And had for heavenly knowledge little room.
What of the knowledge I could take I had;
And with my crumbs I should have fed my friend;
For all of these were love's free gifts to me,
As one of men.   But I have to my friend
Tossed both the knowledge, and the knapsack, too,
And all the earthliness within the sack.
I tossed my bag of knowledge at his head—
A heavy bag, though filled with lightest crumbs.
Wretch! I did toss my bag at him, until
He wore the blush I should have rather worn
For such unloving dole of love's free gifts,
Such fling of wisdom in unwisest words.

VIII.

AARBERT, LATEINOS, *and* EDDA.
EDDA.

Why, here you are, papa!   The Rector asks
To see you.   Here is my papa, sir, here.

LATEINOS.

Dear sir, good-morning!   I have broken through
Your leisure's fence, I fear.   Your daughter showed
My way, perhaps, too rashly.   You must now
Forgive us both.—I thank you.—Then I stay,
Trusting the unearned welcome which you give.
Farewell, my child!   Come when you will to me.
My duty chides me, sir! that I must unn
Myself a stranger to you; but in soth

I now have for a long while wished this day
Of sweet amends to come; and overlong
Have fasted from the pleasure it bespeaks:
For I, your parish priest, although you stray
To churches other than the one where gifts
From heaven, through myself and me the most,
Wait you, have oversight to give you still.
Would I could give it, and give insight too,
To all of whom I have the holy charge,—
As touching that, allow me, by the way
To tell you—since I touched it by a chance—
You greatly lose in keeping from me back
Your inward likeness.   I have that of men
As well as that of women and of girls
In this my parish, and should hold it locked
From others' sight; and if you gave it me—
Not now I ask it—not unless you would—
But in good time.   I see that you are moved.
I had not hoped so soon to stir your heed
To this great duty.   Since I so have done,
I will say this, unclothing you of check
In giving that your inward likeness whole,
That I shall by your gift of it have means
Of being, what I wish to be, your friend.
I feel for you; I hear with pain the talk
Of all the town here, of—of—well!   Had I
The gift of that your likeness from yourself,
I should have means of smoothing out the shape
Which your unhappiness, as you must know,
Too freely hands about; and which, alas!
The rabble, full of dismal talk of you,
And chiefly as to that sad bankruptcy
And all its flighty deeds—well! well!   But if
I may behold the fret of that grim shape
Which your inwitness bears about, I soon

Shall smooth it of its ruggedness with paint
Of absolution, which would make you like
One that had never had life's beauty marred.
And oh! how I have longed that something might,
In my first call upon you lead to this.
I like your zeal, but shall we slowly speed?
Show yourself fully, as to God; and when—
My son, allow, I crave, a few more words—
When you unclothe a sin, have faith assured
That I shall not betray your trust in me.
Just one or two thoughts more, before you answer!
Besides my loosing you from guilt of sin,
It shall be mine to borrow from the world's
Wardrobe of many suits of speech, a cloak
For your sin, showing it a deed in which
Other men wrought with your right-minded hand.
Pity, a mistress of the robes, will ask
The bulging cloak from Hope; and then your sin,
Although it was till shriven, a skeleton,
May, as if large and fleshly, having halt
From over-flesh's weakness, walk abroad
With smile of kinship to the passing works
Of this unsteady world.   Besides, dear sir,
It is well taught that there are cases where
Misdeeds make Love their debtor for mild doom.
Your alms were great, and——

AARBERT.

Though, my bold sir! who call yourself my father,
    Whilst I to God alone have ghostly sonship—
Though, my bold sir! you are a priest, what warrant
    Have you for claiming thus my inward likeness?
All are God's priests who have a share in Christhood;
    And Christ alone amid them has High-Priesthood.

You among priests are but a prest; for though you
  Have claimed high-priesthood o'er us priests un-
      prestly,
Holy Writ gives you to the rank no title.
  Since, therefore, Jesus only has High-Priesthood,
Whilst the mere presthood you have more than I have,
  I nill to strip to you my bandaged bosom.
Why have you asked this?   Holy Writ has bidden
  Us all to strip our sores to one another;
But the deed's shieldness [1] is that so we strip them
  Before a throng of gazers, grieving with us,
Praying too for us, whilst to them our brethren
  We strip our shame.   You yield me not this shield-
      ness; [1]
Nor to you grant I power such as knowledge
  Of all my sores and weaknesses would lend you.
Well you know how has been such power wielded
  By wicked prests [2] who passed as sacrificers.
Ask you this, hating what you ask, and fearing
  The sin-plague-wound's breath, when its mouth
      you open?
Christ alone heals that wound; and, as all-holy,
  He well can do it harm-free.   Oh! His balsam,
Made at life's cost to Him, indeed could heal me.
  He gives both health and haelth [3] in that balsam.
Earth for His love has not a name; none other
  Than He could thole my sores: I would none other
Nurse than Him.   No one is so near as He is.
  I tell Him things which I could not have told you.
Would my sin's lowness make you lowly?   Would my
  Pain at your stripping it become yours?   No, sir.
Could your mind cleanse me?   No; it must itself have
  Been fouled by dabbling's with the filth of others.

---

[1] Protection.   [2] Presbyters.   [3] Salvation.

As to that bankruptcy, the tales are rubbish;
  And as to alms, mine—Rector!—he has left me.
Should I run after him? No; nothing can I
  Unsay. No; let him go! But I am sorry.

IX.

AARBERT *and* ARNULPH.

ARNULPH.

What kind of thing is it which bows thee, Aarbert?
I pray thee drag it from thy neck awhile,
And know it, that thy friend may give thee help.
Or stoopest thou 'neath weight of that foul sin
Whose other name is flesh-mind, and whose grasp
Of worldlings is a loved and sweet embrace?
If so, thou needs must to the flesh-mind die;
And must in Christ's life be of God new-born.
Or, art thou bowed by thought that thou hast done
Wrong to thy fellow-man? Then, as thou canst,
Thou needest to aright the man.   I deem
Aarbert unguilty willes [1] of such deed.
Or, bendest thou beneath the gloom set up
By wrong which other men have done to thee,
Such wrong as slander?   Then must thou of that
Gloom rid thee by forgiveness of men all.
Shun gloom.   It is the child of married Pride
And Hate, and is the brother of foul Fear.
Oh! shun them all; for they have deadly guilt.
Now, which of these things named by me, or else
What other thing is there thus bowing thee?
Look closely; and give answer, not to me,
But give it to thy God, whose liss [2] alone

[1]Willingly.

[2] Absolution (loosed-being).

Should bring thee peace of mind: and give it, too,
Through Christ thy High-Priest, who will feel with
   thee,
And will, as one with thee, be thy new life.

AARBERT.

I know not. Slanders some. although their own
   selves
Lie lightly on my knowledge of them, bow me
With their ill-will's weight. Oh! but I am loaded
With much sin, Arnulph! and this drags me down-
   ward
Into the gloom you spoke of—wounded pride and—
And many other things of which I cannot
Now speak to you. I cannot rid me of them.
I sink, and still, in rising from the gloom's pit,
Sink back in it. I know no evil fully
Wrought into deed mine, since I quitted childhood,
To any being, in the breach of honour
Or chastity or mercy. Yet do many
And great sins through my law-clear mind keep leak-
   ing
To heaven's sight. My mind has taken knowledge
Of all of them with greedy gaze of loathing,
Until it with their fret has grown unhealthy.
The rabble, looking at their own lives' worstness,
As the grim likeness of the things which grieve me,
Give hatred to me for them. To my Maker
The evil of my life is. He has stricken
Me—He, none other! And His stripes, His only,
I feel; I earn them. Would that He would clear me
Of sin at all cost! Would that He would scourge it
From out of me with tenfold His past scourges!

Arnulph.

My friend, He cannot scourge it from you; you are
Sin's self; you need in Christ a change of Being.
You love Him not; and why? You cannot love Him
Until you, as a sinner, fear Him—till you
Do quake for that as, bidding you to trust Him,
He binds Himself to keep you in your trusting,
So, in His bidding that you fear Him, He is
Self-bound to crush your welfare in your sinning.
When you fear sin as wedded into oneness
With hell, you soon will feel how great God's mercy
To you is; you will love Him, and will gladly
Ask His forgiveness. Are you ripe to ask this?
Then ask it with whole trust that you will have it,
And rate it lowly love to boast it yours then.
For He is by His own truth pledged to give it;
And as you have it you will have new being.

X.

Aarbert.

Oh, Thou by me more wronged, my God, my Father,
Than I by any other being could be,
I wonder that a man can live so wicked
As I am—I who am with all sin leprous.
For every deed of mine hath been sin-smitten.[1]
My best deeds bad have been; my bad deeds count-
    less;
I strive against sin; Thou, my God, Thou knowest;
But it abides, and all my strife is bootless.
I should have loved Thee with my whole of being,
For all I ever had of good Thou gavest,
And I have wholly to myself lived. I have
Lived free from Thee who givest me my breathing—

[1] Tainted.

Lived making as a God my own law. Have I
A word to say against my doom to hell? No;
I ought to be there. Thou hast till now spared me,
And Thou hast bidden me to ask forgiveness.
Oh, wilt thou therefore give it me for Christ's sake?
Give, give me, give me in Thy Son new being.

XI.

BIRTNOTH *and* ARNULPH.

BIRTNOTH.

I hear that Aarbert, our old friend, than whom
Breathed not a man once prouder, worldlier—
You know how long he scornfully withstood
His good wise brother's preaching—now at last
Raves as to sin, and says that he hiself
Is no whit better than a murderer;
Pleads guilt of everlasting death, and cries
For mercy from the calm and stilly heavens.
In soth he wears an unrest's guilty look,
Bespeaking need of mercy much from God.

ARNULPH.

If you had felt with Godard, you would feel
With Aarbert. Godard pitied both of you;
His heart was full of rest as yours is. Yours
Is that of stillness in the world's strong grip;
And well did Aarbert when he left such rest.
In his not having reached to Godard's rest
Of stillness in the grip of those still heavens,
He has done worthily of all your pity.
I know men strong in a full-blooded faith
In their own selves, whilst strongly in the world's
Grip held too. Never faints that faith; no, though
They snatch all chance of sin. Their stride is bold;

Their heads high; great their peace; their guiltless-
          ness
Unstain of guilt-look.   These you deem good men.
E'en the faith-faintness, known as evil shame,
Is no sure proof of some one sin.   It earns
The scorn and loathing paid to faith-lack's fear;
Yet is it sin of often those the least
Guilty of aught but pride, and too great love
Of man's praise, and a want of faith in God.
The gloom of heart-change tells but grief at sin.
When a man proud as Aarbert is—a man
Into this world-life canker-rooted too—
Is being wrenched from it, whilst quivers still
His one half in it, and his other half
To heaven's claim is given, his mind is all
A tatter of torn thoughts and weaknesses
Unknown to some men who, whilst giving up
Themselves to heaven, were lowlier.   To these
He is a wonder; to the world he seems
Mad, and most surely mad is he or it.
But not so surely he is so.   I watch
With prayer and awe my friend's mind.   Look on him,
I pray you, with more loving lack of knowledge.

XII.

AARBERT.

Why, aching heart—why, why, O heart, thy scare?
  Speak; murmur not, thou dull ache; though
          through rift
Of all my hopes, speak out!   ' Has Christ a share
  With him who, after having had inlighting's gift,
Sins wilfully?. Will God that sinner spare?'
  Oh me!   ' Prayer hopeless is but mockery.'
Oh me!   ' Thy misdeeds huge and countless are.'
  Oh me!   I know, I know it; I must flee—

I know not whither.   I must cast off care,
    Drown thought in riot or in bus⁺le's din,
And follow—I shall but as most men fare.
    Oh, lost me!   ' Aarbert! '—who is that within
Who called my name out?   'Aarbert, dost thou dare?'

Help me, Lord Jesus!   Is it thou?
    My all is from the fander's fan
Fast flying.   Help me, help me now!
    Am not I Thine?   Oh, I am man.

But was the voice from cut my breast
The Lord's, and was it not mine own?
I know not—oh, I know not.   Past
Forgiveness!   Satan holds me fast.

Christ's am I, otherwise men good and evil,
Devils, good angels, He, the Lord, my Hælend,
God my loved Father, hell, and earth, and heaven,
                                All are against me.

Turn not Thy face from me away.
Lord Jesus!   Thou hast bought me; Thou hast
        seen.
Oh, whither, whither do I slide?
Thou knowest all that I have been.
Wilt Thou forgive me—— What, Lord?   These,
Were these words Thine?   They were.
No—yes, they were.
My Lord! my Lord!
And these words follow them.   My Lord!   He sees.
My Lord!   They were Thine own.
But were they?   Yes, they were.
Where is the Bible?   Here they all are, here.
They all have been sent to me.   Then Thou hast
        known.
Thou seest me.

This holy writ,
Every word of it,
I take as answer to my prayer.
This sword, which flashes all around mine eyes,
Has loosed me from my every fear, has cut my
      chain,
This flaming sword gives me to be
No more the lost, no more the bound,
But now the loosed; and once again,
No more the lost,
But now the found.

Lord Jesus, keep me, for I quake.
I dread, Lord!   Hold me fast, for I trust in Thee.
Am I forgiven?   Am I quite?
But what, if not?   Hell! hell!
I scarce can breathe for fright.
Who?   Milda, you?   I will unlock the door.

MILDA.

Why bide you in this dingy room all day,
Mine Aarbert? What is troubling you? Your look
Affrights me.   What is it?   Come, tell your wife,
What keeps you in this lonely room away from us?
We know your worth, and love you.   Let the world
Say what it will.   Is not our love enough
To cheer you?   Won't you come, or let me stay?
Do let me stay with you.   No? will you not?

XIII.

AARBERT *and* MILDA.

AARBERT.

My wife! my Milda! thanks be to the Lord!
   The war is ended.   I have made my flight

From hell's whole powers. By God's mighty
  word
Their chain was sundered from me. By that
  sword
My way was through the fiend-king's armies cleft.
  I fought. My strength was often in the fight
    Spent. Once I felt almost of hope bereft.
    But, looking upward, with my last hope left
To Christ, I cried forlornly, ' Be my stay;
  My own Lord, help me! ' Whilst I spake, ther-
    right [1]
    Came words that carried all my fears away.
    They back were rushing, when you at mid-day
Found me; and ever since then I have been
  Struggling for life itself in battle's plight.
    My foes flashed all their powers fore mine e'en,
    The wrath of man, earth's pleasures, and its sheen.
Came warning, ' Look on Me! ' Then Christ alone
  As a sheer ghost unearthly grasped my sight.
    As sheer ghost gave I Him myself. Thereon
    My battle was His own. My fight was won.
For whilst I prayed the Holy Ghost of God
  Upbore me, and mine earthiness felt light.
    The hosts of evil shrank, as from His rod,
    Before my path; until, as men dryshod
Walked over Jordan, I had passed along
  O'er peace throughout them. Oh, how fair, how
    bright,
    The world was! I was full of joy and song.
    But word came, ' Foes behind the darkness
    throng;
Keep watch and pray. Lo, I am near thee; stand! '
  They came, I shook, I felt one qualm. The might

---

[1] Immediately.

Of God's word through me flashed. As levin-
brand,[1]
Cleaves cloud, I them. They stood on either
hand.
And I was left with Christ. My brain did reel;
The ground seemed hallowed, all was new. Delight
And wonder thrilled me. I was fain to kneel,
But could not speak. I could but weep and feel.

MILDA.

Oh Aarbert, Aarbert! what has happened now?
You yet are ill. Your weary mind needs rest.
I have not stopped your speech, for I will bear
With all my love's strength somewhat of the woe
That burdens you. I pray you now be calm,
And we will get the lech in. By his help
And God's great mercy all will yet be well.

AARBERT.

Joy! Milda, joy! The peace, the joy,
Which nought can nim[2] and nought destroy!
My freedom from the power of the fiend is won.
The sway, too, of his dukes in me is quite undone.
Evil-hope, Evil-fear, Evil-shame, Evil-trust,
Evil-thought, Evil-pride, Evil-love, Evil-lust,
Each of them a chieftain who has wrought upon me
woe,
Each my soul's deadly foe!
And thus it is the day for thankful song;
And this it is, of which in thanks I sing,
That now I to myself do not belong,
But to God through my Lord,
Made a priest, made a king,

---

[1] Flash of lightning (thunderbolt).   [2] Take away.

Born of God through His word!
My life He only is,
And my life is wholly His;
And what is His He well will keep.
I was mine and lost; I am His and found.
I rath [1] was mine, I His am rather.
Was chained by the world, to Him am bound—
To Him, my Hælend!   Him, my heavenly Father!
O day, come never to be gone!
O deeds, by nought to be undone!
My aching joy for ease would weep.
Dearest Milda! also come,
Welcomed to the angels' home.
Feel a forgiven sinner's bliss.
That is mine; and that is this,
That on earth I can live with my Father above:
And I soon shall in heaven live with Him,
Where all is good, and all will stay,
With but its betters and the best,
In the halls of the holy, the halls of love,
Which are thronged by the glory-clad cherubim.
In the homes of beauty, bright and fair,
Where life is health and love is air,
Away from sin, from death away,
In the sweet abodes of sheen and rest,
Of light and soth,
Of right and troth,
Where Jesus reigns in every breast.

MILDA.

I cannot follow you, my husband!   Here
You leave me, Aarbert, and are out of sight
Upon some dizzy perch, that more by thought

______
[1] Willingly (the positive of rather).

Is trodden than by foot of man.   Beware!
Oh! where are you?   I cannot understand
Your feelings.   Stay!   These high-wrought hopes
          may faint.
My reason claims that I, at every step,
Should follow it, but here it cannot go.
Your talk seems wild and witless.   Can you mean
What you have said, and as you said it all?
Oh! you have made me wretched, thus apart
From you in mind.   But I have been unhappy
For years, whilst I, with flow'rs from every path
Laid on my stilled behaviour, hid the death
And burial within it of my joy.
And have you found the peace you talked of?   How?
And are you sure of it?   You seemed to speak
So wildly.   Oh, then I must flee to prayer!
I, even I, might——   Pray for me, do.

<h2 style="text-align:center">XIV.</h2>

AARBERT.

I now am happy.   Oh, I now am free!
The choice is made, and the trial was past, when I
Gave myself to Thee—
To Thee, my God! my Father!   Thee, my All in All!
Lord Jesus, hold me—hold me fast; for I
Once was Satan's thrall;
His world was the owner of me.
Thine am I, my Hælend, Lord!
Thine, my every wish and word,
Thine, my every deed and thought;
And now be mine Thy war with evil fought!
Life to me ever be
Work of Thine within me wrought,
Wayfare mine, wherein is sought

Thy holy, happy, happy home,
To rest at last in which I pine,
To bide in which I yearn to come,
And which I even now call mine.
My God, in only heaven be my home henceforth
Love I none as Thee I love!
Reckon I nought as having worth,
If to be held without Thy love,
If to be held from Thee away!
Happy day!
Happy, happy, happy day!
Angels greet me from above.
Whatever shall on earth betide me,
Lord Jesus, ever stay beside me,
Thou to say when, and what, and Thou,
Too, to say whither, and where, and how,
I am to feel, or thole,[1] or do,
I am to speak, or bide, or go.
Thrice blessed bonds that bind me to Thee!
Let loose by the sword
Of Thy holy Word.
I am thine,
From tie to the world for ever free,
I am Thine, Thine own,
My all in every thing,
My God, my King!
Oh, Thee to know, forgiving me,
My Father! and to know
That I am one
With Jesus Christ Thy Son,
As a branch in a vine,
And then to be sure that I by Him am known,
This—this indeed is life,
Is endless good,

[1] Endure.

Is end of pain, of toil, and strife,
Is peace that may be felt, not understood.

XV.

AARBERT.

Earth!　Earth, so bright, so gay, so sweet!
Could Milda though but faintly know
The joys I know that cannot fleet,
The sweets I know that cannot cloy;
If only this she knew, that naught
Of thine at its best can once bestow
Peace like mine now or like mine joy,
How dull wouldst thou by her be thought!
How chilly she soon would feel thy glow!
The charms thou holdest forth
I dare to hold
At but their worth,
By the dying told—
At naught.
I spurn thy joys;
For they start with leaps both long and high;
But soon they limp from sigh to sigh.
I scorn thy toys.
I dread thy beauty as a thing
That often flits as soon as seen;
That flits away on Death's black wing,
And leaves behind his baneful sting;
And in life of Christ, life heavenly,
That chariot of love,
I would from love of thee,
And of thy joys
And beauties, flee
To the joys full of glory, and the beauties full of sheen
Of the realm of bliss.

Whilst these to me, coming from Jesus above,
Entice, call off, drag, whirl my love away
From an Earth like thee that canst not stay;
From an Earth like thee arrayed in sin;
From an Earth like thee that, whilst arrayed in this,
Yet seemst to be an Eden both without, within,
Treacherously.

XVI.

Birtnoth *and* Arnulph.

Birtnoth.

Well, clearly madness is in many men
At home.   Then from our evening's talk I draw
That Aarbert, our poor friend, would seem to you
Wise if he steeped his whole life's joys in tears!

Arnulph.

Of tears I spoke not.   Let us calmly talk.
We trust the Bible.   With that trust in it,
I know not how we could be wise in steeping
Our joys as Christians in the worldly joys
Of those whose life is foeship unto God
In growing wrath from Him; nor know I how,
If we be striving as we should with sin
Within ourselves, the world, and those dread fiends,
Each one our stronger, in the whole of whom
Hunger-pangs force their feeding on our woe,
We else can be than sober and oft sad.
Is Aarbert sad?   He has full many mirths,
And will, I hope, have many thousand more,
Of which, alas! you know not aught as yet;
For these as yet are far above your reach.
No earth-joy matches one alone of these,
The joy of loving God.   If Aarbert wins
This, you will have small need to pity him.

XVII.

Aarbert *and* Milda.

Milda.

Joy, Aarbert, joy! your joy can I quite share now;
And bid you share one like to it, e'en mine own.
Oh! mine is welling forth with an overflow,
Oh! mine is overflowing its selfhood's wall.
Oh! mine is into the stream of yours self-poured.
You must have been praying for me—Ah! I thought
I felt at the time, I knew that it was so.
In my bower, and there
Before that throne where mercy meets us all
By whom through Jesus it is sought—
Oh! Aarbert, at that seat of mercy, where
Not even I could plead with idle breath,
There knelt I begging life, as having earned a death
Until was blocked mine upward gaze
By a misty head, that, with a frown
Rose turbaned with the shades of night,
That in jetty folds were around it curling.
Upon that turban's browband were
The world's bright glories, each a gem;
And witchery's light was flashing over them.
It was the Fiend-king's head.
And the locks of his hair, as they rolled from it down,
Hung o'er me like thoughts whirling
Upon a restless bed;
And from his lips there flowed a stream of speech,
Whereon swam flocks of fancies, his strong elves.
These soon took wing and settled themselves
Around me all; and then so wrought
That a hundred landscapes met my sight,
And a hundred wains began to alight;

And as, one by one, they started each,
In one or other wain my own
Rapt fancy rushed with an elf away.
Our wains were some of the wildest dreams.
So I roamed with the elves to mountain streams,
And coral isles with surf beset.
We roamed through plans for coming years;
We flew through hopes; and flew through fears.
We flitted—whither—I forget.
At length their hour with me had passed,
And all my troubles and my sin at last
Sank with me into sleep.
I woke up, kneeling, and with headswim ill,
And looked around me dazed and chill;
And strove to pray.
But, though, whilst reading God's good Book,
I got from it the sounds of print,
Yet nothing out of these I caught;
Nor could mine eyes so worldful take up aught
From out it with their crammed though greedy look;
They could but shed their worldly load in tears—
They could but overladen weep.
And so went slipping all the day.
Then came a crawling whisper saying,
' Arise from off this bootless praying;
God helps you not, you see His mind;
Your wishes are as idle wind.'
But I knew that the Fiend was nigh me still;
And I knew that from him had come that hint;
And I knew that God is love.
And the more with tenfold strife I strove,
I hoping, trusting, waiting, prayed,
Until I had, I had my will,
For God had heard my sigh;
For He with help was nigh;

For He was near with aid.
Mine eyes, with sightless look,
Were fastened on the open book,
When flashed a verse as with a spark,
Which running left a fiery chasm deep,
Deep, reaching unto hell.
Another flashed. Then all around was dark.
But down that chasm still I looked, and still
I saw it to the lurid lake wherein fiends dwell.
My sins before my frighted mind were brought.
As I saw hell-fire, I saw myself within.
Rushed into me dear Godard's lore.
His many long years' daily reasonings
Of earth and hell and heavenly things
Passed whole through some great hours of thought;
And crunching, one by one, my old mind, stood
Instead of it in every part.
I did not know my old self; nor
Could else than wonder how I never saw
Things now so clear as what he then had taught;
I wondered how the world had filled my heart.
I now could see that God all good,
Who slew His only Son
For bearing sin though sinlessly,
So hated sin
That I, who sinned all day, had not one claim to live.
But I saw my Lord on sin's accursed tree—
Saw Him accurst on that unholy tree,
Hanging for me the wicked woman me;
And I prayed that God would therefore me forgive.
I pleaded that my life was won
By Him on whom was laid my guilt;
And I forced my prayer up, up to where He stood.
Then, whilst I pleaded there that He had spilt
For me the flowing blood,

For me the water's flood,
All my fears,
And all my sadness
Went off in tears,
But those of gladness.
And there was in my heart peace, rest;
And I was to my hope's height blest;
And then, oh, Aarbert, then the bliss.
Which nought of earth gives, even this,
To know Him faithful, and to know
That I was now indeed God's child,
No more to be by sin beguiled,
But held in lordhyld [1] by His love—
To know all this, and know yet more
Than all of this laid up in store
For me and for the race of men,
I found, and well
I cannot tell
What this will be when found above;
But this I found, as felt I then,
Was life, was bliss, was heaven on earth below.

AARBERT.

I thank my God.　We more than ever now
Are one, dear Milda!　You have not withstood
His love so longwhile or so stubbornly
As I did, when through Godard He besought
That I would pass the gate of Christ to Him.
I wonder that I live to speak of this.
But how more quickly than or you or I
Godard self passed that open gate to Him!
It was at Oxford, ere you knew my brother.
I like to read the story from my mind;
And you, I know, will like no less to hear it.

[1] Allegiance.

He had been wont to ask his day's bright hours
To glide away down Isis in his boat,
Leaving their sunshine's glory on his skill
As oarsman, whilst he begged each night to keep,
Until the birds began their morning hymn,
Sleep from his reading, and to leave the sheen
Of lamplight on his brilliant scholarship.
He asked for more than health had strength to hold.
And when his prayers were granted (for he shone
As oarsman and as classman also) health
In anger fled the boy; and then a chill
Seized him, and brought him to the tomb's gate, where
Sate Death, who tried him for some fourteen days,
But loosed him with the fine of half one lung.
A gospeller soon found and spake to him
Of after-life. Dear Godard heard and did.
No seed of Gospel knowledge sank in him,
That sprang not up into a rooted deed.
He asked forgiveness of his sinful life,
And took the whole forgiveness. Then he cleared
All hindrances as cobwebs from his path,
And started heavenwards in trim as man
That, having died at heart a felon's death
With Christ for sin to God, was living, too,
With Christ a hidden life in heaven. He made
All things of his about him fit at once
Into his state of newness; saw them fly
Before his faith into the fitness all;
Won peace, and in a fortnight showed his friends
His life's great change. A show that asked of him
His whole sheer thoroughness of truth and will;
For but to know him was to love him much;
And in his college some dear friendships cracked
At strain of that bold show. I smiled at it,
And thought him frantic; but myself was mad.

XVIII.

Milda.

My God! I sought Thee.
Then Thy holy Word
Came to me, and I became to Thee
A daughter; and then
Came life and light to me, indeed,
And then indeed to me came joy and peace,
And then came blessedness beyond my earthly ken,
But which by hope was brought.
By that good hope and Thee its guard,
My love is quite from earth set free;
And heavenward, heavenward,
Soaring in the joy of new release.
Oh, my Father! Oh, my Lord!
I sought; but thou the while wast near;
For Thou hadst found me ere I sought.
I called; but Thou hadst heard my need:
Ere I called Thee Thou didst hear;
Came Thy help before my call.
Now I all to earth am naught:
Thou to me art all in all.
Oh! I feel so happy, I have not a care.
All my care on Thee is laid;
All my debt to die is paid.
How my Hælend! how could I
Ever thank Thee worthily?
My God! my God!
Nought from me through life's trials sever
Thy loving aid!
Wilt Thou forsake me? Wilt Thou leave me ever?
For faithful His crook, and faithful His rod!
And will He leave me, leave me ever?

My Hælend! by Thyself my trust on Thee is stayed.
I trust Thy pledge of endless truth to me;
I trust, I do put all my trust in Thee.

XIX.

AARBERT.

I sate within my thought's cell in a crowd,
  And heard a whisper, ' Who most loved should be? '
  I thought of that which had been done in me:
Mine eyes swam, and I heard my breathing loud.

My neighbours saw not, heard not, whilst I strove
  To quell my thought. Then prayed I, as I sate,
  ' My loved, my all-loved God! not here ask that,
Lest here I shout my worship and my love! '

I dared not trust my mind. I kept me calm,
  With all my feelings bubbling. In the strife,
  The toil, and turmoil of the day's hot life,
When I was chafed, men knew not whence my balm,

My yearning cry was ' When will evening come,
  That I may loose my every thought and word
  In worship's wildest joy? ' and now, my Lord!
Have come the hour, and joy, and Thou, and home.

BOOK VII.

CHRISTIAN LIFE CHOSEN.

I.

AARBERT.

Hope! Dove! twice by me sent forth
From the ark-life of bulrush-canes,
Wherein I was, when christened, laid,
Under vows made for me
That every cane of it
Should be buoyant with ghostliness—
Under vows made that I should float amidst
That fleet of ghostly lives,
Which is summed in the life of the Hælend—
That fleet of ark-lives,
All of them buoyant with faith and with ghostliness.
Hope! Dove! twice by me sent forth,
Thus for a token of peace
From God,
Thou at the second flight
Broughtest it.
I could not take it;
For I hated God.   My vows had been naught to me;
My veins were full of earthliness;
And I lacked the faith to have them filled
From the mighty rushing wind of God,
Which bloweth where it listeth,
As the life of the Born-of-Him.
I floated midst the fleet, but not

As of it.
I floated on the flood of sin-death, there to founder.
Therefore I sent thee
Forth for a third time,
Forth for my faith's help,
To bring me another
Green leaf's token of peace.   Thou
Flewest for it.
Hope, hope! since then
Have I with great joy
Yielded me wholly up to Christ.
My name is on His book of life.
Mine ark-life is filled with Him.
Therefore have I the peace itself.
Oh! I have a peace that never more will wane.
One that will yet greater and yet greater grow.
Greater, greater, through the ages.
It is the peace of quick stillness
That is in Love's embrace breathing,
And with a flame of life's power
Within itself aloud roaring—
Of a delight by none else known,
And with a voice by none else heard.
Now I hold it, here I hold it
Mine.
I do already in my Lord's life hold it
Mine.
And need I therefore now to bid thee
Bring its token back from the hilltops?
I need not, I want not, that token.
Yet come thyself, Fast-flyer!
Come back,
Hope, Dove!
Breathing of the flowers,
Dripping of the dew, which

Thou hast on the mountains,
Ranging by my faith's side,
Met.
For I am longing, oh! so longing to be
Over the floods and far away—
There upon the mountains,
Heavenly, evergreen, far away.
Bring me of the dew there,
Come!
But, nay:
Why should I bid thee
Come to me hither—
Come to abide here?
Wherefore should I tell thee
To come and thence,
To bide and here?
Stay, and I will follow thee.
Stay, dove! stay
Upon the hills, upon the hills of peace
The everlasting hills—
Within the homes of peace
Upon the islet hills.
Tarry for me till I thither
Come to find thee.
There abide mine,
Bide afar there.
Why should'st thou
Abide here on wrath's flood awhile buoyed,
To glide off at last hence to love's ground?
Be yet there, O Hope, Dove!
Tarry for me
And I will follow thee.
For even now I have thee there;
Yea, even now my ghost is ranging those green
          mountains

The homes of peace beside thee;
There even now and with the Hælend,
The Captain who has gone before His fleet,
By faith beside thee,
My ghost is ranging,
Now, and ye shall range there till I find thee
Mine own in Him and in my Heavenly Father
As all of good for ever,
My wide-winged Errander, my Dove,
Hope!

II.

THE FIRST BROTHERSMOOT[1] OF ARNULPH, AARBERT, *and* MILDA.

AARBERT.

Life begun now by us in Christhood, Milda!
Should be unselfish and unworldly, hallowed,
Lowly and loving.   For myself I daily
                    Utter the fond prayer:

The Prayer.

Be not my life a self-tombed well of pride;
Be it a rill of love, which no stone wall
Can check from flowing like a brook that fain

Quits selfness, deals out wealth on either side,
Often looked down upon by cliffs too tall
To be refreshed, and speeds all grass and grain;

Yet onward hastens eager to abide
Lost in the sea its home that coral hall,
Nor stayed by hill nor loitering on plain;

[1] A meeting of brothers (in council), as witena-gemot is a meeting together (in council) of wise men.

As unning [1] thus that, roving far and wide,
Mists from the sea had fed its flow when small
With mountain dews, and feed it still with rain;

Whose drops, aleaping from the winds they ride,
Cheer it when ripples from it loudly call,
When both its banks like parchèd lips complain;

And on yet hastens, till tide after tide,
Sent by the sea, come meeting it with all
It ever lost by love's unslacking drain;

When, full of flow, it bows itself to glide
Off to its source; and with an easy fall
Age-hoary rests in love's own boundless main.

Let thus my life flow!   God be still its Guide!
Let it not hoard its smallness, or be thrall
To aught that bars its way by loss to gain.

MILDA.

Also mine, Aarbert! such a life as that be!
Life that glides onward as a stream, enriching
All in its reach, and is in self-loss ever
                        Gathering greatness.

Oh, the great life of one who loves his neighbour
Is a life streaming through a beauteous country
Under bright sunshine, giving countless riches,
                        Gaining them thrice back.

ARNULPH.

Every life, friends! that in a love to other
Lives, is out cruising in the king of love's yacht,
Buying up shares in them with fellow-feeling
                        All for the good King.

[1] Owning, acknowledging.

Feasts on rich blessings and has draughts of angels'
Mirths from gold chalice which the King's hand
      gives it;
For that through buying thus a share in other
            Lives it may buy grief.

When it buys grief with fellow-feeling, having
Not enough worth to buy it all, the King's self
Comes, at call, buying up alike the griever's
            Heart and his whole grief.

But the King always has at gift His gospel,
Showing how woe is, as His Father's scourging,
Means of His working in the wights [1] who thole [2] it
            Weal everlasting.

There is one woe whereof a share is never
Bought by love's cruisers from its wretched holders,
Sin.   From that woe may be their love, however,
            Bought by the King's love.

III.

The Second Brothersmoot [3] of Aarbert, Arnulph, *and* Milda.

Aarbert.

Sweet, next in sweetness to that talk at night,
Which Christians, speaking in the wordless lyden [4]
Of thoughts and feelings to their God through Christ,
Have, whilst they throw themselves into His arms,
And know that they are fondly to His breast

---

[1] Person.   [2] Endure.   [3] Meeting of brothers in council,
               [4] Language.

Clasped with a joy far overflowing theirs,
Is their talk one with other, whilst their thoughts,
Then being into speeches struck by Him
Who is the harmonist of all their minds,
Plump on the chords of answer's many yeas.
We much enjoy these talks with you, dear Arnulph,
My brother!

ARNULPH.

Pleased you more are not than I,
My friend, that we have thus each other's help
In holding up the swinsong [1] of this talk.
Then pray we that we all may well be tuned
To one another and to God's sweet Book;
That so the sonnets of our speech may be
Such as were those which Godard's mind poured forth.
For he was altogether a strung lute,
Through whom thought passed in tuneful melody
As breath from heaven.   Again then to that breath
Let us hold out our minds all strung to catch it!

AARBERT.

Thought! that, when as lightning flashing
    Through a mind with Christ-lore bright,
Art in brightest noonday dashing
    Cloudy dulness into light;
And that, when as lightning blazing
    Through a dark ungodlit mind,
Art in very night amazing
    Maze, and making gazer blind,
Lighten when the sun is beaming!
    Clear from all its cloud my day,
Lighten not at night! Thy gleaming
    Then would only blurr my way.

[1] Harmony.

Arnulph.

Sunny thought, that beams on sparkling
    Holy Writ, to worldly mind
Draws up clouds of mist; which, darkling
    There, fly wildered, tost with wind.
Oh, the thrill! when, after sipping
    Cloud, the mind to God draws near;
Through the cloud is lode-fire [1] slipping,
    Light is flashed forth, mind is clear.
Mind! with mystic knowledge reeling,
    Would'st thou be from darkness free?
Meet the cloud of God which, wheeling,
    Turns to flash forth light through thee.

Aarbert.

Thought! that, when as war beginning
    Neath the flag of Christ, art strife
Which to living soul is winning
    Back from evil more of life,
And that, when as war neath flying
    Flag of fiend with evils might,
Art a strife that unto dying
    Soul is winning death outright,
Fight, when God is eke attacking
    Evil in me; else take heed
Lest the evil, through thy lacking
    Might, should by thy warfare speed.

Arnulph.

War with evil is unending
    War with death; and thought in this
War is striving to be rending
    Out of death's grip hope of bliss.

[1] The electric fluid (leading fire) as in lode-stone.

Oh! the wyndrym [1] of the striving,
    When the mind sees, God-led strife
Winning and the spoil arriving
    Won by Christ to warring life.
Thought! to mind of Jesus clinging,
    Take to thee, in war His might.
His the battle! thine the bringing,
    Life His spoil from overfight! [2]

IV.

The Third Brothersmoot [3] of Aarbert, Arnulph, *and* Milda.

Arnulph.

Oh! more than Adam-born, begotten thou,
My brother Aarbert! even as am I
By God's word, so that of a ghostly kind
We now are, though from earth's womb through its
        grave
We not yet into heaven's air are born
To live as angels there, how well by that
Word living are we nourished in this world,
Within the fleshness of our mother earth!

I eat and drink of Christ's wórd, when the bread
    And wine which tells Him lifeless is my food;
When I take into mind His body dead,
    And when I take to mind His poured-out blood,
There is no more a dead Christ; but He wills
    Thought of His past death kept up by man's mind,
And this His will my mind most fain fulfils.
    It keeps as feast the thought He left behind,

[1] Rapture.   [2] Victory.   [3] A meeting (in council) of brothers.

That He the Lamb of God for man was slain.
  Then, whilst with friends I share that thought, I
      feed
Upon His life in Heaven, where again
  He lives, and is the all my life can need.
My life here feeds on His there—His is there
The only life I could have anywhere.

AARBERT.

I eat and drink Christ's life into mine own
  When I am looking at its shape and sheen,
As these have by God's written word been shown:
  For whilst His life is by my faith there seen,
My faith's eye, fastened on that Holy Writ,
  And quick and eager thence to know His shape,
Is by the light of heaven traced with it;
  Till, shamed, all else from that life makes escape.
Then does my whole mind, from behind the eye,
  Catch that fair shape; and with such love behold
Its beauty, that its own old features die,
  And others like His start out where its old
Had been.   These are not only over me,
But through me wrought till I am all as He.

ARNULPH.

Now, call your thoughts back, Aarbert! let them track
The run of holy life through some its ways.

AARBERT.

Since on this earth God erst made all things good,
  Yet all their goodness warped is by His foe,
The speed of all things here, unless withstood,
  Is to a man's unholiness and woe.

I therefore, that I may that speed withstand,
  Live here unearthly, with but Christ my Lord,
And Christian brethren, as in Robber-land;
  And live in merely tents here by my sword,
The Word of God, with heaven's foreign life
  Within me. Thus, though daring every death,
I fight unharmed. I hold throughout my strife
  The Holy Ghost within me as my breath;
And have my Hælend as my life, my health;
And keep my heaven-home. There, all my wealth!

ARNULPH.

As I was once made rightlike in God's sight
  By my faith's sharing Jesus' life and death;
So by my letting through me flow Christ's might
  Am I made righteous by my loving faith.
I never by my own best works could make
  Such righteousness as His mine. His is stored
In Christian manhood; and when that I take
  Is through me wrought by Christ, not merely scored
To mine account. When Christhood has been quite
  Formed through me, Adamhood is in me dead,
And Christ lives, filling me with heavenly might.
  He, as my power, and my will, and head,
Works out my works. Can they unrighteous be?
All works are holy, when the Worker He.

MILDA.

One thought I hope that I shall never lose.
It is a thought of Godard's, and is this:
I cannot lay my sins on Christ, and deem
Such laying as my riddance of the sins.
The sins of all men, when He died, were laid
On Him; and now can they, if one with Him
In life and death, live free from sinning more.

Or, when they sin, they, knowing that their guilt
Is laid on Him, can through Him ask forgiveness
And power again to live in Him sinfree.

ARNULPH.

God cannot clear men sinning, though they mourn
Their sin, and pray it be in Christ's blood washed,
If so they mourn as not the less to sin.
By what they be at day of doom will theirs
Be hell or heaven, though by what they then
Have done, and now are doing, will their state
In either place be better or be worse.

MILDA.

Our meeting ends then.　It has been
Delightful to us all, I ween.
Much cheer to me has been your lore.
Such meetings, Arnulph, many more,
Attuned to this, be, as you say,
Our joy on many a toward [1] day!

V.

THE FOURTH BROTHERSMOOT OF AARBERT, MILDA, *and* ARNULPH.

AARBERT.

Arnulph, I feel that I have overrated
Much the wrongs done me, and have blamed in people
Faults which I, knowing more myself than others,
　　　　　　　Most in myself find.

[1] Future.

ARNULPH.

Made alike all, and all alike marred also,
None of us spy in our neighbours' wrongness
Root of whose growth they would, if searching closely,
        Not in themselves see.

Nor is one millionth of the wrong which each man
Does to God ever to himself by man done.
Even those wrongs which to their fellows men do
        Done are to God most.

Yet they, though wronging Him so much—though seeming
        seeming
None so wrong ever to each other as they
Seem to Him always, are by Him forgiven—
        Ay, and beloved too.

Oft as they plead for His forgiveness; therefore
They the forgiveness of each other owe Him.
When a man wrongs me, he is asking of me
        Mercy in God's name.

MILDA.

I my own self am never wronged; the only
Foes I have, Aarbert! ever had, are those who
Wronged you; but I have, as I feel, been never
        Worth having others.

You are withal to me a shield. Had I been
Wronged, my forgiveness of my poor wrong-doers
Would have lagged far behind my bounding pleasure's
        Haste to forgive them.

ARNULPH.

Good! I would rather have a hedgehog nestling
At my bare breast, than I would nurse mine anger.
Wrath at wrong done to us should never outlive
        Evening's last prayer.

VI.

The Fifth Brothersmoot of Aarbert, Milda, *and* Arnulph.

Aarbert.

What is there good, which Love is not, dear Arnulph?
Love is life, honour, faith and hope.   Oh, love is
Truth and soth, largeness of the heart, wealth bound-
  less,
       Blessing and bliss too.

Love is life's strongest of all bonds and motives.
Love will build that which knowledge merely puffs up.
Order and love together dwell.   Love's joy is
       Heaven's own heaven.

Arnulph.

Love is life's glow.   It is a people's money,
Which, as from all of them it still is passing,
Is by all gotten.   Men are one another;
       They are a built man.

Milda.

Love is Christ's badge.   Though He for each one
  man died,
As for each only; yet He died for all too.
Off from each other men have hope not any;
       Off from the Lord none.

Arnulph.

Love is not fondness that will cocker children.
Love is not weakness that for peace will ever
Yield a word's worth of Holy Writ's right meaning
       Up to a foe's wrench.

Love is no breastfellow of guile's [1] or hatred's,
Nor is love aught which, under love's name, snatches
Bliss without giving in its stead a blessing
                    Having a like worth.

Love is not someone's giving up his whole wealth,
Ay, or e'en life, for other people's welfare,
But is his giving them the goodwill forcing
                    Forth from him such gifts.

Love does not faint through fear of check; love's
        uptide
Overflows soon the falling stream of shyness.
With a goodwill, which is by no force ever
                    Daunted or slackened.

AARBERT.

Dwellers in love like that of holy Jesus
Dwell in God's self, and have in all life's changes
Peace. Then what clearness to the sight does love
        give!
                    Lookers for evil.

Having eyes spotted with it, shed on whiteness
Spots, and walk lifelong as in filth by dirty
Fancies smirched. More than even love, when
        fondest,
                    Hate is geleaf-light. ˙

MILDA.

How it keeps guessing! and how often wrongly!
What has guilt's look is often not guilt; what is
Guilt indeed oft has come of things outside, and
                    Even above men,

1 Credulous.

Things perhaps old, and by themselves forgotten,
Known to but God; which, had we known them also,
Might, as we frowned upon the men, have softened
　　　　　　　　Some of our hard looks.

ARNULPH.

Jesus so loved them, that He died as Godman
For the most guilty of them.　Man is always
Haloed with greatness; whether he on heaven's
　　　　　　　　Road be or hell's road.

MILDA.

Love is worth nothing if it can be beaten
Back; it flows forward with a force almighty
Forth from God's life; and in its own life finds from
　　　　　　　　Him its reward paid.

AARBERT.

Had I, whilst cleaving to my standpoint tightly,
Taken love's peep from that of those about me,
I had more known them, and had gained more knowl-
　　edge
　　　　　　　　As to myself, too.

ARNULPH.

Neighbour-love always, oh, my friends! is self-love.
Lovers of thousands live a thousand lives out;
Which may bring griefs, but they are griefs joy-
　　bearing,
　　　　　　　　They are a king's griefs.

Nought but sin working in me brings such grief as
Kingly love's sharing does not soothe and lessen;
Nought but sin wilful in my friends can make my
　　　　　　　　Love for them joyless.

VII.

AARBERT.

Lord God! True and Almighty! Whose bidding
        man
Put whole trust in Thee pledges Thy keep of him!
No foe fears he if Thou felt art as friend by him.
Faint heart, sorrow, or shame never can whelm any
Man whose trust is in Thee.   Evil, until it has
Thy leave, never can work harm to him.   When it has
Gained that leave, he has lost wish to escape from it.
Thy will mine be.   It works all for the best to me.
No harm e'er did a wound dealt by Thee deal to me.
Not such wounds do I fear; all that I fear is sin.
No chance happens to those who are with Thee in
        one.
Where stern duty would lead, marked is my path by
        Thee.
There no danger I know.   Evil is none in it,
But that only which Thou willest allow be there.
Oh God, Keeper of men! they who unslothfully
Use what helps in their reach Thou hast already put,
Leave helps other than these all to Thy care of them.
Wealth, joy, courage, is theirs who have their trust in
        Thee.

VIII.

THE SIXTH BROTHERSMOOT OF ARNULPH, AARBERT, *and* MILDA.

ARNULPH.

Oh, almond's blossom! as the worth in thee,
Whilst thou in beauty bidest on thy tree,
Is that thou there dost o'er an almond brood;
Yet bitter almonds are a baneful food;

So mind's whole worth is in that from it forth
Springs love; yet holiness gives love its worth;
And if mind's fruit be but unholy love,
The mind and love, though blooming, baneful prove.

Milda.

Oh, rose-bud! slighted as a ruddy ball,
With glories folded up and hidden all,
Yet kept in wholeness which is beauty's health,
And trimmed to open in their time their wealth!
As God has propped with green leaf-buttresses,
Thy shrouded life of hallowed lowliness,
So keep He now my Christ-life's hidden sheen,
Until in heaven it is open seen.

Aarbert.

Oh, dewdrop! pilgrim over leaf and flower,
Or anchorite that passest there thine hour,
Self-gathered from all earthness, and alone,
And bright as though some spark from out thee
　　　shone,
Till, the sun rising, calls thee. I, like thee,
Would on my leaf of earth live loose, and free,
And holy, till I hear God's loving call
From earth's poor everything to heaven's rich all.

Milda.

Oh, daisy! shutting thy meek, hallowed eye,
To every star that decks the darkling sky,
Nor gazing till thou seest thy sun again,
E'en as the beauty of thy petals plain
Were less, if petal from a gayer flower
Were set mid those that are from God thy dower
So all earth's other beauties worth are less
To me than that of mine own holiness.

AARBERT.

Oh, peach-bud! grafted upon plum-tree's stock
So closely, that ye both together lock
One into other, and become then one;
Whilst either's wholeness still abides undone,
And each is holy, though nor plum nor peach.
I, too, and Milda, married, though we each
Partake the other's being, yet remain
Both whole and holy, since no longer twain.

ARNULPH.

Oh, holiness! for more of thee we sigh,
From whom High God His title takes most high;
For more of thee, without whom none may live;
For more the worth and beauty thou dost give;
For more of thee, sith God on earth can rest
In but one temple, that of hallowed breast;
For more of thee, how all-worth unto us
Mean earthlings, that art God's chief glory thus.

IX.

The Seventh Brothersmoot[1] of Aarbert, Milda,
and Arnulph.

AARBERT.

My God! my Father!
Lived I once, taking Thy best gifts all day,
    Like some fruit, which is bitter, whilst it hourly
        Is being ripened by Thy summer weather;
Whose sun beseeches fruit its thanks to pay,
    Not even bitter-sweetly, much less sourly,
        But mellowly and sweetly altogether?
                        Yes, alas! once.

[1] Meeting of brothers in councils.

MILDA.

My God! my Father!
Lived I once, although daily blessed anew,
  Like some land which is barren still abiding,
    Whilst still it drinks by day food-laden showers;
And whilst it quaffs by night Thy blessing's dew,
  Whose cheer keeps asking with such gentle chiding
    Some thankful bloom from its so fostered powers?
                          Once, alas! yes.

ARNULPH.

My God! my Father!
Blessed by Thee daily, did I once yet live
  Like some trees which, although on rich loam
      growing,
    And though on sunshine, rain, and fresh air feed-
      ing,
Yet, when the time for fruit comes, merely give
  By leaves, and more of their own wood a showing,
    That all Thy tilth of them at all is speeding?
                          Alas! yes, once.

X.

THE EIGHTH BROTHERSMOOT OF ARNULPH, MILDA, *and* AARBERT.

ARNULPH.

This morning, Father, Thine to us, be Thine
From us as morning of our this day's thanks!
And Thine this day's life new to us from Thee,
This day be Thine from us in life of love!

AARBERT.

How freshly sings the morning that Thy love
Broods ever over us in cloud or mist;

And, morn by morn, is found in drops of dew,
Gems of gift, blessings, strown along our paths!

ARNULPH.

Thine earth has waked. Thy sun makes heard the song
Of flower and fruit, the breathings of the trees
And greensward many-tongued, whilst man, the
        world's
Priest, offers up the tunefulness in praise.

AARBERT.

This earth accurst, thus being by Thee left
Full of such beauty's carol, what will be
Our new earth? Fancy knows not. Will be there
Rocks, rivers, mountains, dales, and flowery meads?

MILDA.

Yet ghostly, all! no mouldering, no death,
Around its flashing city's golden streets,
And pearly gates and walls of all-hued gems!
There will the happy and the blest be found.

ARNULPH.

Maker of all things! that new earth, the more
Glorious of the two! and yet the less,
In that here Jesus gave His death for man's;
Here gave He man a life—His heavenly——

AARBERT.

Our God! in goodness reaching to our needs
The nearest One of Beings to us each;
The furthest from us in Thine utterness
Of goodness, far beyond our praise's reach!——

MILDA.

Our God! The life to all who burn with love,
And death to only those who, being touched
By Mercy's torch, become not loving flames!
Most merciful and not less righteous King!-

AARBERT.

Our God! The so forgotten, slighted, wronged!
Upbraiding with but sunshine, rain, and food,
And love through earth-life! Yet, afraying most
By meekness more than that of all Thy meek!——

ARNULPH.

Our Father! watching till hope's latest hour
The wreck and wreckers of what Thou mad'st good;
Yet watching also for our own poor love.
By only Whom our heart's love can be filled!

XI.

AARBERT *and* MILDA.

AARBERT.

My little daughter and my son
　　Were kneeling at my Milda's knee;
I waited till their prayers were done,
　　And then I blessed my hallowed three.

How gifted is in head and heart
　　My Milda, watching life's well-spring,
To aim the life for God at start,
　　To check its early wandering,

And still to guide it, whilst, a rill,
　　It splashes down life's mountain side,
To flow until its waters fill
　　A valley's coil with fitful tide.

MILDA.

Mine Aarbert to my bairns and me
　　Is under God the shield and stay.
Their guide am I, and mine is he;
　　And ours is Christ throughout our way.

Then, withal I to them have shown
　　Our far-off home at sight's best hours,
My show of them is Aarbert's own;
　　His guide is mine, and theirs is ours.

XII.

AARBERT, MILDA, *and* SIBRIIIT.

AARBERT.

O'ershading heights which God, ne pride, has made,
　　So stream with blessings that they not annoy.
By putting here His light and there His shade,
　　He o'er unevenness spreads wealth and joy.
If He, then, raising you to earthly height,
　　Should rain His gifts there on you, dear my boy!
Let not pride keep them in a lake's store tight,
　　Till fulness come your thirst for them to cloy;
And Hate's eye scan your height. Loose, let them
　　　　forth!
　　God's gifts are all for stewards to employ;
Nor should be any of them robbed of worth
　　By being greed's own wealth, or pride's own toy.
Seek highestness; but let mere height-love raise
　　Your hope! God's blessing cares not to convoy
To higherness a hope's proud search for praise.
　　Hope led by height-love is a climber coy;
But pride is to a hope the rashest guide.
　　I saw this guide once up a steep decoy

One of Hope's daughters.   Woe, the wife of Pride,
  Watched both.   The steep was panting to destroy.
They fell.   Hope shattered found! near where she lay,
Pride seen in Woe's arms now her own for aye!

SIBRIHT.

My Father! I by God's good help will aim
With all my might to reach the goal of worth;
And if one worthier than I shall reach
Its honours, passing me, I shall be glad
To know myself his friend, and feel him mine.
I meanwhile not at all at what I am
On the back-flying racecourse fain would rest.
I hope to use aright God's gifts to me;
And lowlily to thank Him for them all.

MILDA.

No lass wore ever hrail [1] so fair
As that which life-clad lilies wear.
No flowers have a living dress
So fair as faith, love, lowliness.

While now, with lamp betrimmed and burning,
Thou waitest for thy Lord's returning,
Thou needest, Edda, this attire,
This bridal robe of living fire:

And if thou shalt, with lamp in hand,
Glide off from earth to sheol's strand
Before He come, He wills thee seen
There too in this His robe of sheen.

---

[1] Clothing (night-rail=night-clothing).

XIII.

The Ninth Brothersmoot of Aarbert, Milda, *and* Arnulph.

I.

AARBERT.

Oh, praise Him! Let us love Him till
  Our love arise, and higher raise
Our hymn than air to waft may will,
  Till love to heaven take its praise!

MILDA.

Who entered manhood's life to break
  Its sin-love's chain, and set it free;
And passed through manhood's death to make
  A way for men from death to flee.

ARNULPH.

Thy praise, O Lord, for slaying Death,
  Would lost within Thy praiseworth stay,
Though Earth's and Heaven's air were breath
  Of men's and Angels praise for aye.

CHORUS.

Come, sinners! No more sinbound sigh!
  Be freed by Him, and being freed,
Come, praise Him! calling, ' King Most High!'
  Come, praise Him! calling, ' Friend indeed!'

2.

ARNULPH.

Oh, praise Him! Whom? e'en Heaven's King
  The King of kings, the Lord of lords.
Our lives His praises so should sing
  As to outpraise our praise's words.

Milda.

Who rose a room in heaven to dight,
 To which we sin-free might arise,
And sit with God and angels bright
 Above these blue and starry skies.

Aarbert.

Thy praise will, Lord! by all who live
 Be sung with joy around God's throne,
When Heaven's kings their worship give
 To God and Thee, and You alone.

Chorus.

Come ye, His poor! bring thanks for this:
 That ye will, as His brethren made,
Share both His being, home, and bliss,
 In glory that will never fade.

3.

Aarbert.

Oh! praise Him, warriors in His ranks!
 How praise they Him?   Their deeds do there
So shout His praises that their thanks,
 Though loudest breathed, seem whispers mere.

Milda.

Who gave for life to them His life;
 And now to live within them strives,
That theirs should likewise aye be strife,
 To live out all in Him their lives.

Arnulph.

Thy praise, dear Lord, they louder still
 Are singing, whilst resounds their thought,
That but by Thine own work and will
 Throughout them were their good deeds wrought.

CHORUS.

Come, all ye kingdoms!   Praise the King!
　Ye islands! cry His name abroad!
Come, Africa! Come China! sing:
　Praise, South and North! the Son of God.

4.

ARNULPH.

Oh! praise Him, brethren, till ye live
　Within His home of light and glow;
And then until the praise ye give
　Shall endless prove the praise ye owe.

MILDA.

Who will in heaven let you view
　His glory by His glory's rays,
With wonder waking wonder new,
　And praise that ebbs on flowing praise.

AARBERT.

Thy praise, dear Lord, Thou help me tell!
　In whom is all my hope but Thee?
My life is that in Thee I dwell,
　It is that dwellest Thou in me.

CHORUS.

Come, all my being! all my frame!
　Come, all my strength!   Come, all my heart!
Give glory each to Jesu's name,
　Bear each in praising Him your part.

XIV.

Aarbert *and* Milda.

Aarbert.

Sang not we last night praise in many a word,
  Whose greatness we were lacking means to fill?
And did our hollow praises reach our Lord,
  Though wafted toward Him with utmost will?

Milda.

In words though hollow, yet made up of love,
  All praises reach Him if they so unclose
Their truth that toward Him around, above,
  Beneath, they ray forth like an opened rose.

XV.

Aarbert *and* Milda.

(Singing before a large assembly.)

Milda.

I heard a bird amid the trees;
  And who will do the bird this wrong,
To take his thoughts as being these,
  And chide as if were his my song?

' Dear grove! in which we built our nest,
  The nest we feathered so with care;
I would have lulled thy leaves to rest,
  With evensong throughout the year;

' But soon will flee thy leaves outright;
    No grub or berry bide for food;
And then my life will follow flight,
    And leave thee, too, thou dearest wood!'

Aarbert.

If bird there be that, like a man,
    So foolishly doth make his moan,
Let that bird take, as this man can,
    My answer to a lackwit's groan!

Should leaves be lulled by that one's breath,
    Who makes his woe, then makes his plaint?
Who sings his ease, yet knows its death;
    Has faith to know, to do is faint?

Nay, songster! wherefore are thy wings?
    To bear thee till on wintry earth
The bird shall die that there now sings?
    So keen the blast! so dread the dearth!

Let earthlings stay; but is there not
    A clime wherein abides the spring,
Nor overcold nor overhot?
    Canst not thou thither wend on wing?

Cling not to earth; arise, take flight;
    Stoop never to the earth beneath,
Unless thou stranger-like alight,
    For halt as on a lonely heath.

Then, up again! and onward fly,
    Well taught by Him who thee has sent,
Where lies, although unseen by eye,
    The fair land whither thou art bent.

What, though thou weary wend thy way,
　　Forgoing [1] all the goodly things
That bid thee fall, and mid them stay
　　Like others that, like thee, have wings?

Fly, fly!   The winter comes apace,
　　For what hast thou or strength or time,
But to flee death in this doomed place,
　　And win thy life in yon fair clime?

[1] Forgoing is frogoing, and a different word from foregoing.

BOOK VIII.

CHRISTIAN LIFE AT START.

I.

Aarbert *and* Milda.

Aarbert.

Song 1.

Thus far have we upward come
On our heavenward way,
Milda, by might
All Christ's.
I in my own small strength once climbed
Up God's high hill
By steadily putting foot
On each of the blocks to my climbing there;
And thus I, by even their hindrance, rose.
But when I reached a cliff where, these
Blocks being high,
Climbing is stopped,
Unless in mighty faith
Wholly to the Hælend pilgrims yield
Life, limb, wallet, and very staff withal,
Heart there quite faint forced me to halt.

Antsong 1.

I therefore besought and won
That in strength for a while,
Half of it mine,
Half His,

I by the steps of those high blocks
Might climb that hill.
But whilst I was climbing thus
By grasp of the earth, to the earth I clung,
And lessened His heavenly strength's good help:
So, since the cliff allowed my path
Little and less
Breadth, till at last
It nearly cast it off
Into the mid heavens, there I slacked
All tight hold of its stay, and felt at once
Strong arms seize, raise, carry me past.

Milda.

Song 2.

It is even so, Aarbert: I climb,
As you are climbing,
With ease by the power of Christ
My heavenward path, though rough
Always, and often so blocked,
Narrow and steep, that it stops
Every climber having
Mere man's powers;
For even when
The path is grooved
In the wall of a rock,
And becoming so narrow a ledge in its side
That needs there I slack hold of earth quite,
And fain trust my whole weight on Christ's strength,
That strength not once fails trust of my all
To Him.

Antsong 2.

Be it, Aarbert, our glory and joy
That thus to heaven

We climb by a strength not ours,
But wholly by that of Christ.
Ours is the might of a man,
His are the powers of God.
All of us may by faith have
Christ's strength's help.
We need it much;
For oh, how oft
Is our heavenward path
As the slippery ledge of a cliff that anon
Will sink quite in flat rock, whose steep side
Afloat soars from sight lost in dark clouds,
Whilst far low down sunk also from sight
In gloom.

II.

AARBERT, MILDA, *and* LESGELEAF.

LESGÉLEAF.

Aarbert, I bring to you a friendly wish.
It is, that you would for your own sake breathe
Your worthy protest against Popery
With, in its words, less sound—with, in its words,
Dear friend, not so much loudness. We must fight
God's battle so as not to waken wrath
Too much in those with whom we fight, and thus
To put the battle's outcome into danger.
Your foes are strong men, and a wise man's fight
With strong men should be full of wary thought;
With ceaseless eye at peace, and with a show
High-minded of allowance, where they push
Their fight. But how behave you here? Have you
Been liberal with darkling things of faith,
Which your foes hated in you, and which you,
By dropping them in darkness, would not miss

More than an old oak does the pith which time
Steals out of it?   Have you known how to yield
Such things of pithy weight up, to your foes?
Or, there, have you stepped forth to meet your foes,
When men of high rank? and been gentleman-like
And thankful for their courtesy, although
Of course unfriendly?   No; these courteous men
Are fearless and unflinching; yet you hold
Your faith's flag, that one thing of yours accurst
By them, unfurled!   You shrink not from your faith's
Clashing with that of men so mettlesome!
Their rule of war is this: ' Dare, ever dare! '
Should yours become like theirs then?   Frightful
  thought!
They give way not an inch; the greater need
Is therefore that you yield the inch to them,
And barter cheaply some good ground for theirs.

MILDA.

In our own strife for earthly things a peace
Ought to be sought by us at all pride's cost.
Moreover, whilst we may not bid, God-speed!
To those who stop or mar the faith once given
To Christians, and must rather strive against them,
We so must strive against them as against
The dupes of our own deadly foe the Fiend.
This I acknowledge; but whereas your rede
To Aarbert shocked me, woman as I am,
I tell you from the mind of Holy Writ
That of the faith, left once to us in trust
By God, we may not sell the faintest show
For peace with man at hint of either fear,
Or hope, or love.   That faith belongs to God.
And Aarbert's strife on its behalf with e'en

The mightiest men cannot endanger it;
Although it might his holding it, were he
Not held; but God will hold him.   As for me,
Though woulding not in strife for it to hurt,
I would myself be hurt to fleshly death
And utter earth-loss, rather than forsake
One whit of it, or have my protest for it
At all toned down by frown of man.   Our peace
With one another, made at cost of truth
To God, is war by all of us with Him.

LESGELEAF.

Your boldness, lady, more befits a preacher
Than one who bears the brunt of earthly life.

MILDA.

You are a man, sir!   Let me blush for you.

AARBERT.

My wife has given to you, Lesgeleaf,
Her husband's answer.   Take it with these thoughts:
God and one man are an unfearing army
Wherever stands a Christian!   Our bad speed
In protest for the Bible's lore is first
From those of us who fear God's foes, and next
From those who speed their rights as Protestants
Ere strife for God's right that that protest speed.
Had we been, like our fathers, ghostly men,
Unworldly, soon would our foes been like
Those of Elizabeth and William, dust
Before an unseen gale, which bore ourselves
On a career of glory, striving all,
Without let, earnestly for that old faith
Entrusted once by God to holy men.

III.

AARBERT.

Keep me, Lord, when I do my best and when
    My very best I thole [1] and dree; [2]
When from sin furthest I do feel, keep then
    The worst sin—Pride—from me.

Thine, the might; therefore is the glory Thine,
    May through me straightway rise to Thee
Loving friends' praise of me! for, held as mine,
    It would be pride in me.

If myself spy within me good. I ought
    To thank its Giver.   Let me see
Theft and mean lie in but a passing thought
    Of pride at good in me!

Praise from Thee, Christ! from Father, Thee, all good
    That praise my glory ever be!
Though, alas, that too may be also food
    Of pride that lurks in me.

Life and life's wealth I to Thy goodness owe.
    I should, if I bethought me, flee
Sin as death; then would never pride, I trow,
    Pride even costen [3] me.

Would it not? keep me!   If the keep Thou quit,
    I shall at once bend worship's knee
To the mean thing, this very me, to it,
    Whom pride will mock there—me.

[1] Suffer, endure.   [2] Act, sufferingly, enduringly.
[3] Tempt by seduction or alluring.

Keep me, Lord! therefore. Keep me day by day,
   Until I am from trial free;
Till I quit earth, till all of earth away
   And pride go far from me.

IV.

AARBERT.

The fight is won. The danger past is and the sigh.
Upon the wave of routed battle floats on high
My flaming banner. Rest from overfight is nigh,
And iron peace shall as the battle's statue stand.

V.

LATEINOS, ANKIRKLY, AARBERT, MILDA, COSTNA,
WROHTLY, *and an open assembly.*

LATEINOS (*to* ANKIRKLY).

Lo! here is Aarbert. At the parish church
We idly look for him. I never there
Found him at hour of morning sacrifice,
The eighth o'clock. But then, as I am told,
At that most wholesome hour a Protestant,
Who has his will, is in his bed asleep.

ANKIRKLY.

I fear that he has heard you.

LATEINOS.

If so, then he has heard some wholesome words.

AARBERT.

At that good hour the eighth o'clock I lead
Worship for all my household at my home.

You haply wished me not to overhear
Your speech.   The air has brought it to my heed
With challenge of my answer.   You are grieved
That at your church I do not share with you
The breakfast of your morning sacrifice.
Our Lord has left no breakfast to be eaten,
Nor has He left a sacrifice for sin
Which men can either make or show to God.
Making your sacrifice as part of Christ's,
You say that Christ made not an end of His.
Showing your sacrifice to God as show
Of Christ's, you say that one made by Christ
Has by His loving Father been forgotten.
In either way you wrong Him.   He has left
A supper's tokens of His death to us,
With charge that we should show them to the world
Until in life He came to earth again,
When men would need no more the show of them.
Moreover, when to show these hallowed tokens,
He clearly told us by the time of day
At which he held the supper—day's ninth hour—
That at which afterwards He died; at which
Withal the passover's foreshow of it
Was given, and the Paschal Lamb was slain.

ANKIRKLY.

The Eucharist was in Tertullian's times
A sacrifice at after-midnight oft.
It therefore then was quite a morning's feast.

AARBERT.

The tokens in those times of danger oft
E'en after midnight were in caverns shown
At a belated supper, which asked night
To hide and shield it.   When four hundred years

Of the then mystery of lawlessness
Had wrought, the fathers, whom you boast forbade
Christ's supper, bidding after sleep, instead,
This breakfast, which agreed in time of day
With naught of Christ's, but which was timed to
    match
Feasts to the upper heathen gods, all held
Ere mid-day; and before which feasts men made
A sacrifice; but I, not having mind
To breakfast in a church, or anywhere
Sacrifice, like Lateinos, shut my ears
Against the chiming of his parish bells.

COSTNA.

What mean, ' This is my body, this my blood? '
Christ by these words changed bread into Himself,
His Godhead, ghost and body, blood and bones,
Whilst yet He sate at supper; and He bids
Us priests to do what He did then.   By these
Words, therefore, we His priests—we, mightier
Than are archangels, call Him down from heaven
To lie before us on a plate, disguised
As bread, and in a cup disguised as wine;
And there abiding, as if merely bread
And wine, to undergo the sacrifice,
Be given as food, shut up awhile in pyx,
And dealt with otherwise, as pleases us.

AARBERT.

Against this lore does England pay Lateinos
To make the protest of God's Holy Writ,
Which tells us that Christ's sacrifice was made
Once by Himself, not ever to be made
Again by Him, and far less by another.

You, when you make up into what you say
Is living Christ your wafers, which may then,
As Christ, be charged with poison, rat-eaten,
Grow mouldy or be carried through a waltz,
As in a snuff-box, or be lost in ditch,
And there lie helpless, make up wheaten gods.
And when you say that Christ has given men power
To drag Him down from off his heavenly throne
At will, and then to sacrifice Him thus,
You say what, not as faith soars over reason,
But bolts as folly neath it at the check
Of scorn.   You would yourself deem that man mad,
Who, if his lawyer, placing in his hands
A freehold's title-deeds, said, ' Take and pocket,
For this is your estate! ' should, pocketing
The deeds, make claim that he within his coat
Had a house, fishpond, some twelve hundred trees,
And seven thousand acres of good land,
Besides the live stock feeding on the grass.
Yet is the papal lore, which you would shove
Past our allowance now, more branched with hooks
On reason's check than would have been that mad-
      man's.

ANKIRKLY.

To you the church is not the house of God?

AARBERT.

God's house is not the church, but the gelathe.
There Christ is, and Lateinos turns his back
On these to seek Him on a plate of bread.
Ankirkly, is not your large heart of love
For lack of guidance by a Christ-taught mind
Trying to bring within a circle those
Who worship God, and those who bow to idols,
Which God hates; and who needs fly back, the more

They are together drawn?   Will you have Christ
Within your circle?   How can He stand there
With men who claim to have Him on a plate
Within the image of a piece of bread,
For the mean uses of fresh sacrifice
By them?

One in the Crowd.

The sour old Puritan! why hear ye him?

Aarbert.

I know not who you are; but this
I know, that I would wish to have you as my friend.
If I am Puritan I am not sour;
If sour I cannot be a Puritan.

Lesgeleaf.

I know the gentleman who spoke to you
As Puritan, dear Aarbert.

Wrohtly.

What! here, the bankrupt?   Puritan no less,
  Since knowledge wrought is knowledge great, the
     man
Who, having outdone worldly wickedness,
  Then fights it—fights as but a traitor can.
  Cheer, friends, the mighty bankrupt Puritan!

Enjoy our world, sir, as a hero may,
  Then hoot it with a talk of moth and rust.
Taste all our sweets, but make wry face, and say
  You live for heaven; and since live here you must,
  You give us courtesy but keep your trust.

Bradwater.

Hush!   Wherefore shout so loudly, man?

MILDA.

Most wicked slanders! which from this back-seat
I needs leave answerless. But Aarbert sits
Still as a rock, against which swelling waves
Dash; and, with then the rock's allowance calm,
Go trickling back in foamy wrath's content.
I wonder whether my weak voice could reach—
But no; I must not, if I could, be heard.
I cannot in the hubbub hear those men.
What mean their angry looks, and all that noise?
Some other man seems now to rail at him.
He speaks—what? He is answered. Yet again
He speaks. He buries in his hands his face.
He is not well. Oh, Aarbert! But what now?
Two other gentlemen are quarrelling!
Something is wrong. Friends, let me pass you by.

FRIENDS.

Sit still, good lady! See, your husband sits.

MILDA.

He must be ill, he must be. Something hard
Has struck his head. Do help to make a way
For me. Oh, friends! do help.

FRIENDS.

You cannot pass to him. But lo! his hands
Are taken from his face, and you can see
That he has not been hurt at all.

MILDA.

He rises like an angel, full of peace
And love to all men. What! and going home!
He has forgotten me. Yet all is well.

VI.

MILDA *and* AARBERT.

MILDA.

You fell not.   How I watched your strife's career!
And how I longed to waft you this my cheer:
Take meekly on your whiteness that black sneer!
     There shamed and starkly shown up let it stay!
Outlive all slanders!   Let them float and feed
Upon the air through which they love to speed.
Till they and those who hurl them, and, indeed,
     That air itself, shall pass as wind away!
God knows your life as one of love and soth,
Of death to earthlove and to sinlove both,
And that you live His steward not in sloth,
     His soldier fighting earthness, not in play.

AARBERT.

Alas! I have not earned the praise which you bestow.
  My morning's prayer had scantly to me drawn
     down might
From Jesus; and I swam without God's blessing's
     glow
  That folkmote's stream of trials into all its plight.
Then came the trials' billows up my pride to over-
     throw;
  Until my self-trust and my strength went quite
     away.
The need of Christ's help shall I not forget, I trow:
  For streams of trial oft athwart life's goings stray;
And, when unlooked for, meet high mind to lay it low.
  Half over those of this stream to its further bank
I well had swam; when, seeing how row after row
  The waves were overpassed by me, I did not thank,

But thought thus: How my brawny arms each billow
        mow!
    Then was it that no more Christ held me; and a
        squall
Of stormy wind began upon the stream to blow.
    My strength was quickly broken by the billows all.
And I could see that I was drifting on their flow
    To those rock-dotted rapids wherein deaths are rife.
So, looking up to Christ, I said: My sin I know
    With sorrow. Hael me, my Lord! my Strength!
        my Life!
He therefore seized me; and although my speed was
        slow,
    I reached dry land here, where I prayed Him as be-
        fore
That He would keep my trust, nor need to me to show
    My weakness, if I swam such trying river more.
I said: 'Oh, keep in me the trust which Thee I owe!'
    And, as I spoke, I looked back. Shaken into
        waves,
The stream was rushing like a landslip of rolled
        graves.

VII.   .

AARBERT.

For that I will not, Father, bend my will
To the meek stowing of this slander's wrong
Within my cheerful love of Thee and those
Who wrong me, does it fester as a thorn
Within me. Make my still proud life so meek
That it shall hug the thorn as fellow flesh,
And live at peace with it!, To choose my lot
Is Thine: and mine it is to love it then.
Not much were there for man to choose betwixt

Lots whose unlikenesses have but his hour
On earth for show of them; and are but those
Of evil's more-or-lessness. What makes each
Quite good is that its bearer loves it well.
My heavenly Father, teach this to my deed!
Then take my love of griefs allowed by Thee
As my fond duty. Take it wreathed each day
With my fresh kisses of Thy holy will.

VIII.

ARNULPH *and* AARBERT.

ARNULPH.

Good day! my brother!   I but now have heard
How greatly was your Christ-life's meekness tried
Last week.   You fell, arising from the fall.
So ever should we falling twist the fall
Into self-lowering for such a rise.
Have you felt much yet of that inward strife
Arising from the Christian's twofoldness?

AARBERT.

No sooner had I
Been christened inwardly,
Than I, by the peace of my mind betrayed,
Thought that my rest had for aye been won.
Bewrayed by passing peace of mind, I said
That I felt that my battles all were done.
And done indeed is that great fight,
Which I in alone the Lord's great might
Have fought with fiends, the powers swart,
The powers of darkness, who stood athwart
My quitting their kingdom for that of light.
But now, alas! that fight I find
Was but the first in deadly strifes

Whose last one's end will be my life's.
My fleshly soul, at so much cost
From those swart powers so set free,
Hates, hates the freedom she had won:
And, loving the thraldom she had lost,
Is at war with my freedom-loving ghost:
Is at war with myself, then.   I am she.
My fleshy soul, which erst was I,
And hopes she so again may be,
Is at war with me.
Peace I now have none
Out of Christ; though in Him boundless peace still I
        find.
I but have been, in all my breaking
The chain of dreams which bound me, waking
To battles in mine own self every day beginning;
To battles which I shall be winning, and so winning
Life's greatness; or I shall be losing, and so losing
Life's self; and left me now is but the choosing,
Or to fight or else to die.

ARNULPH.

The glorious fight of faith! that overfight,[1]
In which each Christian, strong through Jesus' might,
Strikes off him as a ghost his flesh's death,
And lives by God's word as her food and breath!

AARBERT.

Moreover, my fleshly mind,
Which erst was a bondslave of my soul's—
This my soulish mind which, when
My ghost crushed my soul's sway
Through Christ's might, to whose ghost
She then became a wife,

[1] Victory.

Did at once pass along with her mistress as part of the
      spoil
To be the new Queen's maid,
Therefore to be mine,
Often awakes to the war in me
Things of greed, and things of strife,
Things that creep, and things that fly,
Lusts of the flesh, and lusts of eye,
Pride of life,
Butterflies, beetles, moths, and bats,
Scorpions, spiders, slugs, and rats,
All of them out of my flesh ruin's holes.
Heigho!
So these try often thence to come,
Some on foot, and some on wing,
Crawling some, and flying some,
Some to smear, and some to sting
The poor ghost, that
Pale queenly anchoret.
And if, still beating, still beset.
She sink in sleep,
Worn out with toil,
Or not as Christ's abode—if she forget
That Christ must keep,
Bah! ah! ah! ahh!
One here, another there,
A third some other where—
And shudderingly——
For she to heaven with none of them can go.
For she hates them with a hatred's strife
Which is the breathing of her very life—
But soon she hears a whispered word.
It is a loving call.
It is the voice of Christ, her loving Lord.
Whereon she tells her grief that things were so

Faring with her, and with heavy sigh
She through Him asks His Father throned on high
For whole forgiveness, and that He anew
Would free her from her loatheds, which afresh
Did so beset her in her house of flesh:
And that He burning out of it their food,
That so they might be starved with all their brood,
Would be her guest once more.
Then—
As when—
As when upon a grassy plain,
With the quickening might of a morning's glow,
And the freshening life of its bath of dew,
Day breaks with a ruddy hope again,
Afresh on her falls a cleansing flame,
Around her again is cheering light,
Within her is felt the Frefriend's [1] might;
And her faith, once more unlet by shame,
Can boast of what gifts God gave her before;
Her hope, once more set free by liss, [2]
Can take His pledge of endless bliss,
Of everlasting peace and health,
Of a sheeny robe of lowliness,
Of the rank of highborn holiness,
With endless joy and endless rest,
Amid the Good, amid the Blest.

ARNULPH.

She dares hold her hope full of God's pledge of all
　　　this?

AARBERT.

For albeit shadows may by stealth
Creep o'er her in her fleshly cell,

· The Paraclete's.　　　　　　[2] Forgiveness (the being loosed).

Though still that cell
For a few flashwhiles
Be overspread   .
With a web of the flight
Of thoughts that hate, and thoughts that hide,
This ghost, I tell, dear Arnulph! thee,
This ghost through Christ (I tell it thee with smiles)
From welcomed foulness wholly free,
Nay, less befouled from day to day,
Nay, growing holier,
Nay, growing daily like her God her King,
Dead unto sin, to all of earthness dead,
Shall bide in honour borrowed of Him, honour bright
In even the house of flesh now filled by her;
Until she, no longer a prisoner
In that her fleshly cell,
Nor there in strife with foreign foes,
Nor slighted there and weak,
Shall in body more worthy of Beings holy,
Of the free, and the fair, of the loving and lowly,
A ghostly body clad in whiteness glistening
Or in hues of the rainbow like to those
Of the gem of the earth or the sea's red shell—
Shall not within a world accur'st not there
Not where the Proud and wicked are the strong
Shall amid the mightiest and those most meek
Shall in greater wealth than earthlings seek,
Shall amid good things which eye has never seen,
For ever midst them to abide,
Shall crowned with an overfight's flowers of light,
Amid good things of which no dream can tell,
So clad, so crowned, in so much bliss,
As one of the rays of the glory of Christ's great bride,
As daughter to God alwielder dwell
Thus surely, though not here.

Shall, oh! with Christ for ever dwell
As this, and thus, and more than all of this,
With God and Christ and angels bright,
Elsewhere! elsewhere!

IX.

AARBERT.

Hope! thou that flashedst o'er my youth's night forth
  In brightest sheaves of rays auroral, till
My sky was wholly streaked, and south and north
  Mingling garred reel my reason and my will
In the wild glory of what yet was night!
  Then seemed thy sheen, where'er I looked around,
To fill the earth with heaven; and my sight,
  Borne forth upon it, only back did bound
From sky, that glass which bars unghostly gaze.
  But now my sight by thee has pierced this sky
To heaven's self beyond the starry maze;
  And far on thine auroral rays shall fly,
Till through the window of their flash I see
  The bright ones who will soon edrisen [1] come—
See Christ's own self; until my sight by thee
  Shall reach New Salem, that, that blessed home
For those who love Him. Flash then, through these
      skies;
  And on to heaven flash! Cheer thence mine eyes!

X.

AARBERT *and* MILDA.

AARBERT *(speaking for both)*.

Lord Jesus, Word of God! our life, our All,
  Our Hope, our Strength! If we may, free from
      blame,

[1] Risen again (aft-risen.

Call Thee the Branch, we so to Thee will call
  For more and more of life by that great name,
And say, Lord God! Who, stooping from Life's
      Tree,
  As deathless hast in man's death stricken root,
And sprung up death-barked thence; that graffed on
      Thee
  Men, cut from earthness, should be each Thy shoot,
Give, give to us, who through Thy bark of death
  On Thee art grafted, more of life from Thine,
And ever breathing through us life-sap's breath,
  Feed us, as branches fed are by a vine.
Feed us from heaven! For Thy root hast Thou
  Uplifted quite from earth's mould. More and more
Uplift our wills then, that no longer now
  We willen [1] bear such earth-fruit as we bore;
But that, as boughs of Thee the Tree of Life
  Who hast no part in earth, we may from lust
Of aught but heaven live. Oh! let the knife
  Top all our shoots, which down would root in dust!
And such our fruit be all, as love, faith, hope, and
      trust!

XI.

Aarbert.

On! onward! on!
The wreck of earthlife now behind me left!
Staved on the breakers earth-hope's every boat!
Of every stay but that of Christ bereft!
And on the deep by but His might afloat!
On, onward, with from Him
More might to swim!
On! onward! on!

____
[1] Desire.

On! onward! on!
The tide against me flowing!   If I swim
With all my strength, well!   If I slack my strength,
I drift from off the coast.   My every limb
Loses or wins the race throughout its length.
On! therefore, onward strain!
With might and main
On! onward! on!

On! onward! on!
This stroke, if winning, wins for me the race.
For all are but a this-one to the coast;
And this, if slacked in hope of quicker pace
In strokes to come, will be the whole race lost.
On! therefore, onward! on!
Till all is won.
On! onward! on!

On? onward still?
Yea, onward! for each surf wave is the all
That I must pass.   Unpassed it is the whole
Wide surf before me.   Not one wave is small
If swelling twixt me and the coast my goal.
On! doubly speed the pace!
With each wave race
On, onward still!

On, onward all!
That plank drift past me!   Naught but Christ my
        stay!
That toy too drift!   For all my wealth is He.
I shall by Him be at the goal some day;
And now am there, whilst it alone I see.
On! on! soul, ghost, and mind!
Look none behind!
On, onward all!

On! onward! oh!—
Yet onward!   Bide within me!   Let me drink
Thy life, Lord Jesus, more!   The tide to death
Would sweep me off.   (He will not let me sink.)
On, onward!   More to me of heavenly breath!
More, Lord! of strength, of speed!
These most I need.
On, onward! oh!

THE END.

A BLESSING PRAYED FOR, AND WAFTED AFTER, 'AARBERT' BY THE WRITER OF THE POEM.

Although of Thee unworthy be this liedsong,[1]
Thy blessing I beseech, oh, Lord God, for it!
Whatever worth it has by Thee was given,
Whatever speed it may have, if the speed be
Not sent by Thee, will to its hearer's welfare
Be worthless. Thou be through it light and power!
And till Thy Herald, e'en the Hebrew chosen
By Thee to keep alive that fire from heaven,
The holy Gospel, rise to do his duty,
Bless still the Briton and the Briton's children,
All sprung from Albion's or from Erin's Islands,
Who, whilst that herald sleeps within some cavern,
Sit watching by the fire to breathe beneath it
The blast of prayer, and to be also sending
Thence through the world's black night of sin and
      priest-craft
By faithful erranders[2] lamps lighted from it!
For Thou hast known the Briton. As an Aidan,
A Patrick, Wickliffe, Cranmer, Knox, and Tyndale,
He stood on earth as warden of Thy Gospel;
And such hast Thou acknowledged Him, by giving
To Him as warden might and wealth and glory
And sway as wages, though he but be Gentile.
He keeps his watch; keep Thou, himself! The harlot
Has lured him to her lap; her Eastern daughter
Abetting her in this. Behold him writhing

[1] Poem.   [2] Messenger.

Beneath her deadly spells to stay from slumber!
Let not her shear his strength, nor let her dagon
Have him, with eyes put out, within his temple!
Not, not as man, but as a man protesting
Thy gospel, he has been in might and main
A dwarf gigantic, father of young giants,
All strong as yet in like faith thus protesting
And puritan.   Oh, keep them from the traitors
Midst them, who, whilst those storms are now begin-
      ning,
Wherein earth's night shall end, would make them
      partners
With Babylon in all her lurid glory _
On earth, her lurid flames in deep Gehenna.
Keep them in one with Christ from her far sundered;
And keep them looking out to spy the Hebrew
Who, when he comes, will as the great Outrider
Of Christ, Thy holy Son, bring day.   Come, Herald
Of day!   Come, Hebrew!   Come, Lord Jesus!
      quickly.

www.ingramcontent.com/pod-product-compliance
Lightning Source LLC
Chambersburg PA
CBHW051218120726
47905CB00004B/1171